Wicked
in the
Regency
BALLROOM

Margaret McPhee

MILTON KEYNES
COUNCIL

THIS ITEM HAS BEEN
WITHDRAWN FROM
LIBRARY STOCK
PRICE:

D8676479

This is a work of fiction. References to historical events, real people or real places are used fictitiously. Other names, characters, places and incidents are the product of the author's imagination, and any resemblance to actual persons, living or dead, events or locales is entirely coincidental.

All Rights Reserved including the right of reproduction in whole or in part in any form. This edition is published by arrangement with Harlequin Enterprises II B.V./S.à.r.l. The text of this publication or any part thereof may not be reproduced or transmitted in any form or by any means, electronic or mechanical, including photocopying, recording, storage in an information retrieval system, or otherwise, without the written permission of the publisher.

This book is sold subject to the condition that it shall not, by way of trade or otherwise, be lent, resold, hired out or otherwise circulated without the prior consent of the publisher in any form of binding or cover other than that in which it is published and without a similar condition including this condition being imposed on the subsequent purchaser.

® and ™ are trademarks owned and used by the trademark owner and/or its licensee. Trademarks marked with ® are registered with the United Kingdom Patent Office and/or the Office for Harmonisation in the Internal Market and in other countries.

Mills & Boon, an imprint of Harlequin (UK) Limited,
Eton House, 18-24 Paradise Road, Richmond, Surrey TW9 1SR

WICKED IN THE REGENCY BALLROOM
© Harlequin Enterprises II B.V./S.à.r.l 2013

The Wicked Earl © Margaret McPhee 2007
Untouched Mistress © Margaret McPhee 2008

ISBN: 978 0 263 90616 5

052-0613

Harlequin (UK) policy is to use papers that are natural, renewable and recyclable products and made from wood grown in sustainable forests. The logging and manufacturing processes conform to the legal environmental regulations of the country of origin.

Printed and bound
by CPI Group (UK) Ltd, Croydon, CR0 4YY

Margaret McPhee loves to use her imagination—an essential requirement for a trained scientist. However, when she realised that her imagination was inspired more by the historical romances she loves to read rather than by her experiments, she decided to put the ideas down on paper. She has since left her scientific life behind, retaining only the romance—her husband, whom she met in a laboratory. In summer, Margaret enjoys cycling along the coastline overlooking the Firth of Clyde in Scotland, where she lives. In winter, tea, cakes and a good book suffice.

In The Regency Ballroom Collection

The Wicked Earl

Chapter One

London—February 1814

'Sit up straight, Madeline. And can you not at least attempt to look as if you're enjoying the play?'

'Yes, Mama.' Madeline Langley straightened her back. 'The actors are very good, and the play is indeed interesting. It's just Lord Farquharson...' She dropped her voice to an even lower whisper. 'He keeps leaning too close and—'

'The noise in here is fit to raise the roof. It's little wonder that Lord Farquharson is having trouble hearing what you have to say,' said Mrs Langley.

'But, Mama, it is not his hearing that is at fault.' Madeline looked at her mama. 'He makes me feel uncomfortable.'

Mrs Langley wrinkled her nose. 'Do not be so tiresome, child. Lord Farquharson is expressing an interest in you and we must encourage him as best we can. He will never offer for you if you keep casting him such black looks. Look at Angelina—can you not try to be a little more like her? No scowls mar her face.' Mrs Langley bestowed upon her younger, and by far prettier, daughter, a radiant smile.

Angelina threw her sister a long-suffering expression.

'That is because Angelina does not have to sit beside Lord Farquharson,' muttered Madeline beneath her breath.

Angelina gave a giggle.

Fortunately Mrs Langley did not hear Madeline's comment. 'Shh, girls, he's coming back,' she whispered excitedly. Amelia Langley straightened and smiled most encouragingly at the gentleman who was entering the theatre box with a tray containing three drinks glasses balanced between his hands.

'Oh, Lord Farquharson, how very kind you are to think of my girls.' She fluttered her eyelashes unbecomingly.

'And of you too, of course, my dear Mrs Langley.' He passed her a glass of lemonade. 'I wouldn't want you, or your lovely daughters, becoming thirsty, and it is so very hot in here.'

Mrs Langley tittered. 'La, Lord Farquharson. It could never be too hot in such a superior and well-positioned theatre box. How thoughtful of you to invite us here. My girls do so love the theatre. They have such an appreciation of the arts, you know, just like their mama.'

Lord Farquharson revealed his teeth to Miss Angelina Langley in the vestige of a smile. 'I'm sure that's not the only attribute that they share with their mama.' The smile intensified as he pressed the glass into Angelina's hand.

'So good of you, my lord, to fight your way through the crowd to fetch us our lemonades,' Mrs Langley cooed.

'For such fair damsels I would face much worse,' said Lord Farquharson in a heroic tone.

Mrs Langley simpered at his words.

Madeline and Angelina exchanged a look.

Lord Farquharson's fingers stumbled over Madeline's in the act of transferring the lemonade. The glass was smooth and cool beneath her touch. Lord Farquharson's skin was warm and moist. 'Last, but certainly not least,' he said and gazed meaningfully into Madeline's eyes.

Madeline suppressed a shudder. 'Thank you, my lord,' she said and practically wrenched her hand free from his.

Lord Farquharson smiled at her response and sat down.

Madeline turned to face the stage again and tried to ignore Cyril Farquharson's presence by her side. It was not an easy matter, especially as he leaned in close to enquire, 'Is the lemonade to your taste, Miss Langley?'

'It is delicious, thank you, my lord.' The brandy on his breath vied with the strange, heavy, spicy smell that hung about him. He was so close that she could feel heat emanating from his lithe frame.

'Delicious,' he said, and it seemed to Madeline that a slight hiss hung about the word as he touched her hand again in an overly familiar manner.

Madeline suddenly discovered that drinking lemonade was a rather tricky task and required both of her hands to be engaged in the process.

Thankfully the lights dimmed and the music set up again to announce the resumption of *Coriolanus*. Mr Kemble returned to the stage to uproarious applause and shouts from the pit.

'He's a splendid actor, is he not?' said Lord Farquharson in a silky tone to Mrs Langley. 'They say that Friday is to see his last performance.'

'Oh, indeed, Lord Farquharson. It will be such a loss. I've always been a staunch admirer of Mr Kemble's work.'

Madeline slid a glance in her mother's direction. Only that afternoon Mrs Langley had made her feelings regarding John Philip Kemble known, and admiration was not the underlying sentiment.

The second half of the play had not long started when Lord Farquharson proclaimed he was suffering with a cramp in his left leg and proceeded to manoeuvre his chair. 'It's a souvenir from Salamanca. I took a blade in the leg,' he said to Mrs Langley. 'I'm afraid it plays up a bit from time to time.' He grimaced, and then stretched out his leg so that it brushed against Madeline's skirts.

Quite how her mother failed to notice Lord Farquharson's blatant action, especially given that she was seated on her elder daughter's left-hand side, while his lordship was situated a few feet away on Madeline's right, Madeline did not know. She threw her mother a look of desperation.

Mrs Langley affected not to notice. 'Such bravery, Lord Farquharson.'

Lord Farquharson smiled and touched his foot against Madeline's slipper.

'Mama.' Madeline sought to catch her mother's eye.

'Yes, dear?' said Mrs Langley, never taking her eyes from the stage.

'Mama,' said Madeline a little more forcefully.

Lord Farquharson leered down at her, a knowing look upon his face. 'Is something wrong, Miss Langley?'

'I'm feeling a little unwell. It is, as you have already observed, a trifle hot in here.' She fanned herself with increasing vigour.

'My dear Miss Langley,' said Lord Farquharson, mock-concern dripping from every word as he attempted to squeeze her hand.

Madeline pulled back. 'A little air and I shall be fine.' She rose and made for the back of the box.

Mrs Langley could scarcely keep the look of utter exasperation from her face. 'Can you not wait a little? Angelina and I are enjoying the play. Oh dear, it really is too bad.'

Lord Farquharson saw opportunity loom before his eyes.

'It seems such a shame for all three of you charming ladies to miss the play, and just when Coriolanus is about to deliver his soliloquy.'

Mrs Langley made a show of sighing and shaking her head.

'I do not mind,' said Angelina. But no one heeded her words.

'What if…?' Lord Farquharson looked at Mrs Langley hopefully, and then tapped his fingers across his mouth. 'Perhaps it is an impertinence to even suggest.'

'No, no, my lord. You impertinent? Never. A more trustworthy, considerate gentleman I've yet to meet.'

Madeline's shoulders drooped. She had an awful suspicion of just what Lord Farquharson was about to suggest. 'Mama—'

'Madeline,' said Mrs Langley, 'it is rude to interrupt when his lordship is about to speak.'

'But, Mama—'

'Madeline!' her mother said a trifle too loudly, then had the audacity to peer accusingly at Madeline when a sea of nearby faces turned with curiosity.

So Madeline gave up trying and let Lord Farquharson ask what she knew he would.

'Dear Mrs Langley,' said his lordship, 'if I were to accompany Miss Langley out into the lobby, then both your good self and Miss Angelina could continue to watch the play uninterrupted. I give you my word that I shall guard Miss Langley with my very life.' He placed a hand dramatically over his heart, the diamond rings adorning his fingers glinting even in the little light that reached up from the stage. 'You know, of course, that I hold your daughter in great affection.' A slit of a smile stretched across his face.

'I would be happy to accompany Madeline,' said Angelina, and received a glare from her mother for her pains.

'And miss Mr Kemble's performance when it is unnecessary for you to do so?' said Lord Farquharson. 'For have I not already said that I will take care of Miss Langley?'

Mrs Langley clutched her gloved fingers together in maternal concern. 'I'm not sure… She is very precious to me,' said Mrs Langley.

'And rightly so,' said Lord Farquharson. 'She would make a man a worthy wife.'

Mrs Langley could not disguise the hope that blossomed on her face. 'Oh, indeed she would,' she agreed.

'Then I have your permission?' he coaxed, knowing full well what the answer would be.

'Very well,' said Mrs Langley.

Madeline looked from her mother to Lord Farquharson and back again. 'I would not wish to spoil his lordship's evening. Indeed, it would be most selfish of me to do so. I must insist that he stay to enjoy the rest of the play. I shall visit the retiring room for a little while and then return when I feel better.'

'Miss Langley, I cannot allow a young lady such as yourself to wander about the Theatre Royal unguarded. It is more than my honour will permit.' Lord Farquharson was at Madeline's side in an instant, his fingers pressed firm upon her arm.

She could feel the imprint of his hand through her sleeve. 'There really is no need,' she insisted and made to pull away.

'Madeline!' Her mother turned a steely eye upon her. 'I will *not* have you wandering about this theatre on your own. Whatever would your papa say? You will accept Lord Farquharson's polite offer to accompany you with gratitude.'

Mother and daughter locked gazes. It did not take long for Madeline to capitulate. She knew full well what would await her at home if she did not. She lowered her eyes and said in Lord Farquharson's direction, 'Thank you, my lord. You are most kind.'

'Come along, my dear.' Lord Farquharson steered her out

of the theatre box and across the landing to the staircase, and all the while Madeline could feel his tight possessive grip around her arm.

Earl Tregellas's gaze drifted between Mr Kemble's dramatic delivery upon the stage and the goings-on in Lord Farquharson's box. He watched Farquharson with an attention that belied his relaxed manner and apparent interest in the progression of *Coriolanus,* just as he had watched and waited for the past years. Sooner or later Farquharson would slip, and when he did Lucien Tregellas would be waiting, ready to strike.

It was not the first time that Mrs Langley and her daughters had accompanied Lord Farquharson. He had taken them up in his carriage around Hyde Park, and also to the Frost Fair with its merry-go-rounds, swings, dancing and stalls. On the last occasion, at least Mr Langley had been present. Indeed, Mrs Langley seemed to be positively encouraging the scoundrel's interest in her daughters; more accurately, in one daughter, if Lucien was being honest. And not the pretty little miss with the golden ringlets framing her peaches-and-cream complexion, as might be expected. No. *She* had been seated safely away from Farquharson. It was the elder and plainer of the sisters that seemed to be dangled before him. Lord Tregellas momentarily pondered as to the reason behind Farquharson's interest. Surely the younger Miss Langley was more to his taste?

Tregellas restrained the urge to curl his upper lip with disgust. Who more than he knew exactly what Farquharson's taste stretched to? He saw Farquharson move his chair closer to the Langley chit. Too close. He watched the brief touch of his hand to her arm, her hand, even her shoulder. Miss Langley, the elder, sat rigidly in position, but he could tell by the slight aversion of her face from Farquharson that she did not welcome the man's attention. Mrs Langley's headpiece was a huge feathered concoction, and obviously hid Lord Farquharson's transgressions from the lady's sight, for she raised no comment upon the gentleman's behaviour.

Miss Langley's attention was focused in a most deliberate manner upon the stage. Tregellas's gaze dropped to take in the pale plain shawl wound around her shoulders that all but hid her dress, and the fact that she seemed not to wear the trinkets of jewellery favoured by other young women. She did not have her sister's dancing curls of gold. Indeed, her hair was scraped back harshly and hidden in a tightly pinned bun at the nape of her neck. Her head was naked, unadorned by ribbons or feathers or prettily arranged flowers. It struck Lucien that, unlike most women, Miss Langley preferred the safety of blending with the background in an unnoticeable sort of way.

Lord Tregellas watched as Miss Langley rose suddenly from her seat and edged away towards the back of the box. He was still watching when Lord Farquharson moved to accompany the girl. He saw Mrs Langley's feathers nod their encouragement. Farquharson and the girl disappeared. Silently Lucien Tregellas slipped from his seat and exited his own theatre box.

'Lord Farquharson, I feel so much better now. We should rejoin Mama and Angelina. I wouldn't want you to miss any more of the play.' Madeline could see that he was leading her in a direction far from the auditorium. A tremor of fear rippled down her spine.

Lord Farquharson's grip tightened until she could feel the press of his fingers hard against her forearm. 'How considerate you are of my feelings, Miss Langley,' he said, drawing his face into a smile. 'But there's no need. I know the play well. I'll relay the ending if you would like. Following his exile, Coriolanus offers his services to Aufidius, who then gives him command of half the Volscian army. Together they march against Rome, but Coriolanus is persuaded by his family to spare the city. Aufidius accuses him of treachery and the Volscian general's men murder Coriolanus. Aufidius is overcome with sorrow and determines that Coriolanus shall have a "noble memory". So, Miss Langley, now that you know the ending, there is nothing for which to rush back.'

Madeline felt a glimmer of panic as he steered her around a corner. A narrow corridor stretched ahead. 'Lord Farquharson.' She stopped dead in her tracks, or at least attempted to. 'I thank you for your synopsis, but I would rather see the play for myself. Please return me to my mother immediately, my lord.'

Lord Farquharson's smile stretched. 'Tut, tut, Miss Langley…' he bent his head to her ear '…or may I call you Madeline?'

'No, you may not,' snapped Madeline, pulling away from him with every ounce of her strength.

But for all that Lord Farquharson was a slimly built man, he was surprisingly strong and showed no sign of releasing her. Indeed, there seemed to be an excitement about him that had not been there before. He stretched an arm around her back and, when she was fully within his grasp, marched her along the length of the passageway. Not even his slight limp deterred their progress.

Madeline's heart had kicked to a frenzied thudding. Blood pounded at her temples. Her throat constricted, tight and dry. But still she resisted each dragging step. 'What are you doing? This is madness!'

His fingers bit harder. 'Have a care what you are saying,

Madeline. And stop causing such a fuss. I only wish to speak
to you in some privacy, that is all.'

'Come to Climington Street tomorrow. We can speak pri-
vately then.' If only she could buy some time, some space in
which to evade him. Thoughts rushed through her head.
Surely Mama would notice that they were gone too long and
come to seek her? Wouldn't she? But Madeline knew deep
in the pit of her stomach that her mother would do no such
thing. The chance of marrying her offspring to an aristocrat,
and a rich one at that, had driven the last vestige of common
sense from her mother's head.

'Please, Lord Farquharson, release me, you're hurting me!'
She saw him smile at her words and felt the bump of his hip
against her as he dragged her onwards.

And then suddenly they stopped and he steered her into a
small dimly lit alcove at the side.

'This shall do nicely,' he announced and pulled her round
to face him, his fingers biting hard against her shoulders.

Madeline's breaths were short and fast. She struggled to
control the panic that threatened to erupt. Sweat trickled down
her back, dampening her shift, and her heart skittered fast and
furious. She forced herself to some semblance of calm, and
looked up at him. 'What do you want?'

'Why, you, of course, my dear.' Excitement had caused the
hint of a flush in his cheeks that contrasted starkly with the
smooth pale skin of the rest of his face. The suggestion of
sweat beaded his brow and upper lip. His dark red hair had
been swept dramatically back to best show the bones of his
cheeks. It was a face that some thought handsome. Madeline
did not. The skin around his eyes seemed tight and fragile,
tinged with a shadow of the palest blue. It served only to em-
phasise the hard glitter of his smoky grey eyes. His gaze fixed
firmly on her.

Madeline gritted her teeth hard to stop the tremble in her lips. 'You are a gentleman and a man of honour, Lord Farquharson.' His actions rendered this description far from the truth, but she hoped that the reminder would prompt him to abandon his scheme, whatever it may be. 'Surely you do not mean to compromise me?'

Farquharson's mouth twisted. His hands were rough against her shoulders. Nothing sounded. Not a hint of music or laughter or applause. No footsteps. No voices. Not even the closing of a door. He looked at her a moment longer, and she had the sensation that not only did he know precisely the extent of her fear, but that it pleased him.

Madeline's teeth clenched harder.

'As if I would do such a thing,' he said and lowered his face to scarcely an inch above hers.

Alcoholic breath enveloped her. Icy fingers of fear clawed at her until her limbs felt numb and useless. She looked up into his eyes, his hard, cold, glassy eyes, and saw in them her doom.

'Just one kiss, that's all I ask. One little kiss.' His gaze dropped to caress her lips.

Madeline struggled, thrusting all of her weight against him in an attempt to overbalance him.

'You cannot escape me, Madeline,' he said softly and lowered his lips slowly towards hers...

'Ah, there you are, Miss Langley,' a deep voice drawled.

Lord Farquharson practically catapulted her against the wall in his hurry to remove his hands from her. He spun to face the intruder with fists curled ready by his side. 'You!' he growled.

Madeline's eyes widened at the sight of her timely saviour. He was a tall gentleman with a smart appearance, long of limb and muscular of build. His hair was slightly dishevelled and black as a raven's wing, and he was dressed in black breeches with a neatly fitted and exquisitely cut tail-coat to match. The man was certainly no one of her acquaintance, although he seemed to be of a somewhat different opinion.

'I wondered where you had got to,' he said in the same lazy drawl and stepped closer to where Madeline and Lord Farquharson stood.

Madeline stared at him, unable to believe quite what was happening.

'I trust that Lord Farquharson has been behaving with the utmost decorum?'

His was a harsh face, angular and stark, a bold nose and square-edged jaw, and clear pale blue eyes that brushed over hers.

'He…' Madeline faltered. If she told this stranger the truth, her reputation would be well and truly ruined. No one would believe that he had dragged her down here against her will, in the middle of a performance of one of the season's most successful plays. Lord Farquharson was a rich man, an aristocrat. Madeline Langley was a nobody. Willing or not, she knew what people would say. She bit at her lip and dropped her gaze. 'I must return to my family. They'll be worried about me.' She hoped.

The stranger smiled, but the smile did not touch his eyes. Casually he turned his face to Lord Farquharson. The Baron blanched. 'Lord Farquharson—' a chill entered his voice as he uttered the name '—will escort you back to your mother. Immediately.'

Lord Farquharson stared in sullen resentment, but said not one word.

'And I need not mention that he will, of course, be the perfect gentleman in doing so.'

It seemed to Madeline that there was some kind of unspoken battle of wills between the two men. Lord Farquharson was looking at the stranger as if he would gladly run him through with the sharpest of swords. The stranger, on the other hand, was smiling at Lord Farquharson, but it was a smile that would have cleaved a lesser man in two.

Lord Farquharson grudgingly took her arm. This time he seemed most disinclined to make contact with her sleeve, touching her as if she were a fragile piece of porcelain. 'Miss Langley,' he ground out from between gritted teeth, 'this way, if you please.' He then proceeded to lead her briskly back down the corridor, retracing the path along which he had dragged her not so many minutes before.

Although Madeline could not see him, she knew that the dark-haired stranger stalked their every step. His presence was her only protection from the fiend by her side. She wanted to shout her thanks to him. But she could not. She did not even dare to turn her head back. They moved in silence, their progress accompanied only by the muffled steps of their shoes upon the carpet. It was not until they reached the landing leading to Lord Farquharson's box that the man spoke again.

'I trust you'll enjoy what is left of the play, Miss Langley.' He executed a small bow in her direction before turning his attention once more to Farquharson. 'Lord Farquharson,' he said, 'perhaps you have not noticed quite how clear and un-impeded the view is from these boxes.' He looked meaning-fully at Lord Farquharson and waited for them to step through the curtain that led into the Baron's box.

'There the two of you are,' said her mother. 'I hope that a little turn with Lord Farquharson has you feeling better, my dear.' Mrs Langley did not notice that her daughter failed to answer.

Angelina eyed her sister with concern.

Madeline sat down in the chair, taking care to make herself as narrow as possible lest Lord Farquharson's hands or feet should happen to stray in her direction. But he made no move to speak to her, let alone touch her. The air was still ripe with the spicy smell of him. She stared down at the stage, seeing nothing of Mr Kemble's performance, hearing nothing of that actor's fine and resonant voice. Her mind was filled with the image of a dark-haired man and how he had arrived from nowhere at the very hour of her most desperate need: a tall, dark defender.

She could not allow herself to think of what would have happened had the stranger not appeared. Whatever her mother thought, Lord Farquharson was no gentleman, and Madeline meant to speak the truth of him in full as soon as they were home. But who was he, the dark-haired stranger? Certainly his was a face she would not forget. Classically handsome. Striking. Forged in her mind for ever. A shiver rippled down her spine. Something, she would never know what, made her glance across to the boxes on the opposite side of the theatre. There, in one of the best boxes in the house, was her dark defender, looking right back at her. He inclined his head by the smallest degree in acknowledgement. Madeline's breath caught in her throat and a tingling crept up her neck to spread across her scalp. Before anyone could notice, she averted her gaze. But, try as she might, she could not rid herself of the foolish notion that her life had just changed for ever.

'What on earth did you think you were doing?' said Mrs Langley to her elder daughter. 'Trying your hardest to undo all of my good work!'

'Mama, he is not the man you think,' replied Madeline with asperity.

'Never was a mother so tried and tested by a daughter.'

Madeline controlled her temper and spoke as quietly and as calmly as she could manage. 'I'm trying to tell you that Lord Farquharson came close to compromising me at the theatre tonight. He is no gentleman, no matter what he would have you believe.'

'What on earth do you mean, child?' Mrs Langley clutched dramatically at her chest.

'He tried to kiss me tonight, Mama.'

'Kiss you? Kiss you?' Mrs Langley almost choked. 'Lord Farquharson tried to kiss you?' Her cheeks grew suddenly flushed.

'Yes, indeed, Mama,' replied Madeline with a sense of relief that her mother would at last understand the truth about Lord Farquharson.

'Lord, oh Lord!' exclaimed her mother. 'Are you certain, Madeline?'

'Yes, Mama.'

Mrs Langley stood closer to Madeline. 'Why did you not speak of this before?'

'He frightens me. I tried to tell you that I disliked him.'

Her mother stared at her. 'Dislike? What has "dislike" to do with it? Now, my dear...' she took Madeline's hand in her own '...you must tell me the whole of it.'

Madeline detected excitement in her mother's voice. 'I've told you what happened. He tried to kiss me.'

'Yes, yes, Madeline, so you say,' said Mrs Langley with undisguised impatience. 'But did he do so? Did Lord Farquharson kiss you?'

Madeline bit at her lip. 'Well, not exactly.'

'Not exactly!' echoed her mother. 'Either he kissed you or he did not. Now, what is it to be?'

'He did not.'

Mrs Langley pursed her lips and squeezed Madeline's hand. 'Think very carefully, Madeline. Are you sure?'

'Yes.'

Mrs Langley gave what could almost have been a sigh of disappointment. 'Then, what stopped him?'

Madeline found herself strangely reticent to reveal the dark-haired stranger's part in the affair. It seemed somehow traitorous to speak of him. And her mother was sure to misunderstand the whole episode. Surely there was nothing so very wrong with a little white lie? 'He...he changed his mind.'

'Gentlemen do not just change their minds over such matters, Madeline. If he did not kiss you, it's likely that he never intended to do so.'

'Mama, he most certainly meant to kiss me,' insisted Madeline.

A speculative gleam returned to Mrs Langley's eye. 'Did he, indeed?' she said. 'You do understand, of course, that were his lordship to compromise you in any such way then, as a man of honour, he would be obliged to offer for you.'

'Mama! How could you even think such a thing?'

'Come now, Madeline,' her mother cajoled. 'He is a baron and worth ten thousand a year.'

'I would not care if he were the King himself!' Madeline drew herself up, anger and outrage welling in her breast.

Mrs Langley sucked in her cheeks and affected an expression of mortification. 'Please afford me some little measure of respect. I'm only your mother, after all, trying my best to catch a good husband for a troublesome daughter who refuses the best of her mother's advice.'

Madeline knew what was coming next. She had heard its like a thousand times. It was pointless to interrupt. She allowed her mother to continue her diatribe.

'You care nothing for your poor mama's nerves or the shame of her having a stubborn plain daughter upon her hands for evermore.' Fortunately a sofa was close enough for Mrs Langley to collapse on to. 'Whatever will your papa say when we are left with you as an old spinster?' She dabbed a tiny piece of lacy material to the corner of her eye. 'I've tried so hard, but it seems that my best just is not good enough.' Her voice cracked with heavy emotion.

'Mama...' Madeline moved to kneel at her mother's side. 'You know that isn't true.'

'And now she has taken against Lord Farquharson, with whom I have tried so hard to secure her interest.' Her mother gave a sob.

'Forgive me,' said Madeline almost wearily. 'I do not mean to disappoint you. I know you wish to make a good match for me.'

Mrs Langley sniffed into her handkerchief before stroking a hand over Madeline's head. 'Not only a good match, but the best. Can't you see, Madeline, that I only want what's best for you, so that I can rest easy in my old age, knowing that you're happy.'

'I know, Mama. I'm sorry.'

Her mother's hand moved in soothing reassuring strokes. 'It is not your fault that you have the looks of the Langleys and are not half so handsome as Angelina.' The stroking intensified.

Madeline knew full well what a disappointment she was to her mother. She also knew that it was unlikely she would ever fulfil her mother's ambition of making a favourable marriage match.

'That is why I have sought to encourage Lord Farquharson.'

Madeline stiffened.

Mrs Langley felt the subtle change beneath her fingers.

'Oh, don't be like that, Madeline.' She removed her hand from Madeline's hair. 'He's a baron. He has a fine house here in London and a country seat in Kent. Were you to marry him, you would want for nothing. He would take care of your every need.'

Madeline looked with growing disbelief at her mother.

'My daughter would be Lady Farquharson. *Lady* Farquharson! Imagine the faces of my sewing group's ladies if I could tell them that. No more embarrassment. No more making excuses for you.'

'Mama,' said Madeline, 'it is not marriage that Lord Farquharson has in mind for me.'

Mrs Langley laughed. 'Tush! Don't be so silly, girl. If we but handle him properly, I'm sure that we can catch him for you.'

Madeline placed her hands over her mother's. 'Mama, I do not wish to catch him,' she said as gently as she could.

Amelia Langley's eyes widened in exasperation. She snatched her hands from beneath her daughter's and narrowed her lips. 'But you'll have him all the same. Such stuff and nonsense as I've ever heard. Madeline Langley turning her nose up at a baron! I'll bring Lord Farquharson to make you an offer if it's the last thing I do, so help me God. And you, miss, will do as you are told for once in your life!'

Chapter Two

⸎

The ballroom was ablaze with candlelight from three
massive crystal-dropped chandeliers and innumerable wall
sconces. The wooden floorboards had been scraped and
polished until they gleamed, and the tables and chairs set
around the periphery of the room were in the austere neo-classical style of Mr Sheraton. The hostess, Lady Gilmour, was
holding court in a corner close to the band and its delightful
music. Despite the heat, the French doors and windows that
lined the south side of the room remained closed. It was,
after all, still only February and the year had been uncom-
monly cold. Indeed, frost was thick upon the ground and the
night air held an icy chill. With the Season not yet started,
London was still quiet, but Lady Gilmour had managed to
gather the best of London's present high society into her
townhouse. Everybody who was anybody was there,
squashed into the noisy bustle of the ballroom, and spilling
out into the hallway and up the sweep of the staircase.

Mrs Langley was in her element as Lord Farquharson had
managed to obtain an invitation for her entire family. She was
making the most of the evening and taking every opportunity

to inveigle as many introductions as possible. Mr Langley, having found an old friend, had slipped discreetly away, leaving his wife to her best devices.

'Lady Gilmour,' gushed Mrs Langley, 'how delightful to meet you. May I introduce my younger daughter, Angelina? This is her first Season and we have such high hopes for her. And this is my elder daughter, Madeline. She is such a dear girl,' said Mrs Langley. 'She has engaged the interest of a certain highly regarded gentleman. I cannot say more at the minute other than…' Mrs Langley leaned towards Lady Gilmour in a conspiratorial fashion and lowered her voice to a stage whisper '…we are expectant of receiving an offer in the very near future.'

Madeline, who had been smiling politely at Lady Gilmour, cringed and turned a fiery shade of red. 'Mama—'

'Tush, child. I'm sure that Lady Gilmour can be trusted with our little secret.' Mrs Langley trod indelicately on Madeline's slipper. Her smile could not have grown any larger when Lady Gilmour offered to introduce Angelina to a small group of other débutantes. Looking fresh and pretty in a ribboned white creation that had cost her poor papa a considerable sum he could not afford, Angelina followed in Lady Gilmour's wake.

'Keep up, Madeline,' whispered Mrs Langley as Madeline trailed at the rear. 'What a perfect opportunity for Angelina.'

Less than fifteen minutes later, Angelina's dance card for the evening was filled. A crowd of eager gentlemen stood ready to sweep the divine Miss Angelina off her feet. Mrs Langley's head swam dizzy with excitement, so much so that she clear forgot all about her plans for Madeline and Lord Farquharson. 'Oh, I do wish your father was here to see this. Where is Mr Langley?'

'He's talking to Mr Scott,' answered Madeline, happy that her father had managed to escape.

'Typical!' snorted Mrs Langley. 'Angelina is proving to be a success beyond our wildest dreams and her father's too busy with his own interests to even notice.' Mrs Langley shook her head sadly, but her spirits could not remain depressed for long, especially when Angelina took to the floor with Lord Richardson, who was the second son of an earl. 'La, is she not the most beautiful child on the floor?' demanded Mrs Langley, clutching at Madeline's hand.

'Yes, Mama,' agreed Madeline with a soft smile. 'She is indeed beautiful.'

'And elegant,' added Mrs Langley.

'Elegant, too,' said Madeline.

'And graceful.'

'Yes.'

Mrs Langley looked fit to burst with pride. 'That's my baby out there, my beautiful baby. Oh, how it brings it all back. I was just the same when I was eighteen.'

Mrs Langley and Madeline were so taken up with Angelina's progress around the dance floor that they did not notice the arrival of Lord Farquharson.

'Mrs Langley, Miss Langley,' he said, lingering a little too long over Madeline's hand. 'I hope I'm not too late to claim a few dances from the delightful Miss Langley.'

Madeline's lips tightened. 'I'm afraid I'm not dancing tonight, my lord. I twisted my ankle earlier in the day.'

Mrs Langley drew her a scowl before announcing, 'I'm sure that your ankle is much repaired, Madeline. And a dance with Lord Farquharson shall not tax you too much.'

'But—' started Madeline.

'Madeline.' Her mother threw her the 'wait until I get you home' look.

Grudgingly Madeline held the card out to Lord Farquharson, who smiled and tutted and lingered over the empty spaces beside each dance name.

'Can it be that Miss Langley has kept her dance card free for my sake? Is it too much for my heart to hope?'

Mrs Langley cooed her appreciation of the sugary compliment.

Madeline examined a scuff on the floor and waited until he pressed the card back into her hand. It was now warm and slightly damp to the touch. She held it gingerly by the edge and scanned to see which dances he had selected. A lively Scotch reel and, heaven help her, the waltz!

Lord Farquharson's slim white fingers took hold of one of her hands. 'Just in the nick of time,' he said as the band struck up. 'I believe this is my dance, Miss Langley.' And with that he whisked her out to join the lines of bodies upon the floor.

The dance had a nightmarish quality about it. Not only was Madeline thrust into the limelight, a place in which she was never happy, but she had Lord Farquharson squeezing her hand, whispering in her ear and peering down the bodice of her dress for the entirety of the time. She was perforce obliged to smile politely and skip daintily about, as if she were enjoying the occasion immensely. It seemed to Madeline that a piece of music had never lasted so long. She progressed down the set, birling in the arms of every man in turn, each one granting her but a brief respite from Farquharson's company, for no sooner had she thought it than the dance had led her to meet in the middle of the set with Lord Farquharson once more. At long last the music ceased, and Lord Farquharson returned her to her mother. His eyes glittered with something that Madeline did not understand.

'She has the grace of a swan,' he said to Mrs Langley.

Mrs Langley, who had seen Madeline tread on Lord Farquharson's toes no less than four times, miss several steps, and drop her handkerchief halfway through, marvelled that a gentleman could be so forgiving of her elder daughter's failings. 'Dear Lord Farquharson, you are so kind to Madeline.'

They smiled at one another.

Madeline looked away and counted to ten—slowly.

Mrs Langley raved about Angelina's growing posse of admirers. Was the young man with blond hair merely a baronet? Angelina could do so much better. Let them move here to better see Angelina's progress around the floor. And they simply must gain an introduction to a patroness of Almack's. Mrs Langley could not survive without securing tickets for one of the assembly room's famous balls. It would be quite the best place to catch a husband for Angelina. And so the time passed. Madeline did not mind. She preferred her place in the background, quietly observing what was going on around her. Nodding her head and smiling politely, but never really engaging. At least there was no Lord Farquharson forcing his attention upon her. Even so, he managed to catch her eye across the room on several occasions as if to remind her of what lay ahead: the waltz. Madeline's throat grew dry and tight at the very thought. She could see him watching her through the crowd, licking his lips, smiling that smile that made her blood run cold.

Quite suddenly Madeline knew that she could not do it; she could not let him rest his hands upon her and draw her close, pretending to be the perfect gentleman when all along he was just biding his time, waiting for an opportunity to strike. And strike he would, like the snake in the grass that he was. She shuddered. No matter what Mama thought, Lord Farquharson was not honourable. He would ruin her and there would be no offer of marriage. He did not want her as a wife any more than Madeline wanted him as a husband. What his lordship wanted was something quite different. Madeline drew a deep breath and determined that, come hell or high water, she would keep herself safe from Lord Farquharson's attentions. Mrs Langley scarcely noticed when Madeline whispered that she was going to find her papa.

Mr Langley was not anywhere in the grand ballroom. Nor could he be found in the magnificence of Lady Gilmour's entrance hall. Madeline followed the stairs up, searching through the crowd for a sight of her father. It seemed he was not there either. She spent a little time within the ladies' retiring room, just because she was passing that way, and enquired of several ladies within if they had seen a gentleman by the name of Mr Langley. But the ladies looked at her as if she had just come up from the country and said that they knew no Mr Langley. So that was that.

She left and was about to make her way back downstairs when a hand closed tight around her wrist and pulled her to the side.

'Miss Langley, what a pleasant surprise to find you up here.' Lord Farquharson pressed his mouth to the back of her hand. 'But then perhaps you were looking for me.' He stepped closer and did not release his grip on her wrist.

Madeline knew that the people surrounding them afforded her protection from the worst of Lord Farquharson's intent. But she also knew that she could not risk drawing attention to herself or her situation lest they think the worst. 'No,' she said, and tried surreptitiously to disengage herself.

But Lord Farquharson had a grip like an iron vice, and tightened it accordingly. 'Tut, tut, why don't I believe you?' he laughed.

'I'm looking for my papa. Have you seen him?' Madeline

hoped that Lord Farquharson did not know just how much he frightened her.

The sly grey eyes watched her. 'I do believe that I saw him not two minutes since, Miss Langley. But it was in the strangest of places.' Lord Farquharson's face frowned with perplexity.

In the strangest of places. Yes, that sounded most like where Madeline's papa would be found. Papa hated large social occasions and would frequently wander off to hide in the most obscure of locations. 'Where did you see him, my lord?'

Lord Farquharson's grip loosened a little. 'On the servants' stairwell at the other side of that door.' He gestured to an unobtrusive doorway at the other end of the landing. 'He seemed to be wandering upstairs, although I cannot imagine why he should be heading in such a direction.'

Madeline could. Anywhere away from the hubbub of activity. Papa would not notice more than that. 'Thank you, Lord Farquharson.' She looked pointedly at where he still held her.

'You've not forgotten my waltz?'

How could she? 'No, my lord, I've not forgotten.'

'Good,' he said, and released her.

Lord Farquharson fluttered a few fingers in her direction, then turned and walked briskly down the main staircase.

Madeline waited until she could see that he had gone before heading towards the servants' stairwell.

'Papa?' she called softly as she wound her way up the narrow staircase. The stone stairs felt cold through her slippers. 'Papa?' she said again, but only silence sounded. The walls on either side had not been whitewashed in some time and, as there was no banister, bore the marks of numerous hands throughout the years. A draught wafted around her ankles and the band's music dimmed to a faint lilt in the background.

The stairwell delivered her to the rear of the upper floor. She stepped out, scanning the empty landing. Several portraits of Lord Gilmour's horses peered down at her from the walls. Where could Papa be? A number of doors opened off the landing, to bedchambers, or so Madeline supposed. She stopped outside the first, listening for any noise that might indicate her father's presence. Nothing. Her knuckles raised and knocked softly against the oaken structure.

'Papa,' she whispered, 'are you in there?'

Madeline waited. No reply came. The handle turned easily beneath her fingers. Slowly she pushed the door open and peeked inside. It was a bedchamber, decorated almost exclusively in blue and white. A large four-poster bed stood immediately opposite the door. Mr Langley was clearly not there. Madeline silently retreated, pulling the door to close behind her. Quite suddenly the door was wrenched from her grasp, and Madeline found herself pulled unceremoniously back into the bedchamber. The door clicked shut behind her. Madeline looked up into the eyes of Lord Farquharson.

'My dear Madeline, we meet again,' he said.

Madeline kicked out at him and grabbed for the door handle. But Lord Farquharson was too quick. He embraced her in a bear hug, lifting her clear of the door.

'Now, now, Madeline, why are you always in such a hurry to get away?'

'You tricked me!' she exclaimed. 'You never even saw my father, did you?' How could she have been so stupid?

Lord Farquharson's shoulders shrugged beneath the chocolate brown superfine of his coat. 'You've found me out,' he said and pulled her closer.

She could feel the hardness of his stomach, and something else, too, pressing against her. 'Release me!'

'The Earl won't save you this time, my dear. He's not even here. I checked.'

Madeline refused to be bated. Speaking to him, pleading with him, would be useless. Cyril Farquharson would not listen to reason. She willed herself to stay calm, forced herself to look up into his eyes, to relax into his arms.

Lord Farquharson's eyes widened momentarily, and then he stretched a grin across his face. 'I think we begin to understand one another at last.'

Madeline sincerely doubted that.

Lord Farquharson's grip lessened. 'Madeline,' he breathed, 'you are such a fearful little thing.' The intent in his gaze was so transparent that even Madeline, innocent as she was, could not mistake it. 'I will not hurt you.' His fingers scraped hard down the length of her arm.

Apprehension tightened in her belly. 'But you are doing so already, my lord,' she said, drawing back her leg and delivering her knee to Lord Farquharson's groin with as much force as she could muster. She did not wait to see the effect upon Lord Farquharson, just spun on her foot and ran as fast as she could, banging the door shut behind her. Across the landing, down the stairwell, running and running like she had never run before. The breath tore at her throat and rasped in her ears. Her feet touched only briefly against each stair. And still she ran on, pulling her skirts higher to prevent them catching around her legs. Anything to flee that monster. She rounded the corner, dared a glance back, and then slammed hard into something large and firm. A gasp escaped her. She stumbled forward, her feet teetering on the edge of the stair, arms flailing, reaching for some anchor to save her fall.

A pair of strong arms enveloped her, catching her up,

pulling her to safety. Please God, no. How could Lord Farquharson be here so quickly? She had been so sure that he was behind her; even thought she'd heard the pounding of his feet upon the stairs. But it was only the sound of her own blood pounding in her ears. 'No!' She struggled within his arms, reaching to find some purchase against the smooth surface of the walls.

'Miss Langley?' The deep voice resonated with concern.

Madeline ceased her fight. She recognised that voice. Indeed, she would have known it anywhere. She looked up into a pair of pale blue eyes. It seemed that her heart skidded to a stop, before thundering off again at full tilt. For the arms wrapped around her belonged to none other than her dark defender. She glanced nervously behind, fearful that Lord Farquharson would creep upon them.

Her defender raised one dark eyebrow. 'I take it Farquharson is behind this—again?'

Madeline nodded nervously. 'He…' Her voice was hoarse and low. She cleared her throat and tried again. 'He's upstairs in one of the bedchambers.' Only when she said it did she realise exactly how that must sound.

His eyes narrowed and darkened. She felt the press of his hands against her skin. 'Farquharson.' The word slipped from his throat, guttural and harsh in the silence surrounding them. He set her back upon the stair and brushed past her. Anger radiated from his every pore. He began to climb quickly and quietly up the narrow stairwell.

'No!' shouted Madeline, twisting to follow him. Her feet thudded after his. 'No,' she shouted again. 'It's not what you think. He didn't—' She reached ahead, grabbed for the tails of his coat disappearing round the next bend and tugged. 'Wait!'

The man stopped suddenly and looked back down at her.

She released her grip on his coat and leaned back, panting against the wall.

'What do you mean, Miss Langley?'

'He tried to kiss me,' she said, still catching her breath. 'But I managed to get away before he could succeed.'

She could see the tension in the muscles of his neck and around the stiff set of his jaw. His eyes were sheer ice. 'Did you learn nothing from the last time? What the hell were you doing alone in a bedchamber with Farquharson?'

Madeline's mouth gaped in shock. 'He tricked me. I didn't know he would be there. I was looking for my father.'

'And your father is likely to be hiding in one of Lady Gilmour's guest bedchambers?' He raised a cynical eyebrow.

'It is not unlikely,' she said quietly.

Long fingers raked his hair, ruffling it worse than ever. 'Miss Langley, if you are too foolish to know it already, I will tell you in no uncertain terms. Lord Farquharson is a dangerous man. You would be wise to steer well clear of him.'

'That's what I'm trying to do, but my mother wishes to promote a match between Lord Farquharson and myself. She's determined to encourage his interest.'

'Is your mother insane?'

Madeline's lip began to tremble. She clamped it down with a firm nip of her teeth. It was one thing to know she would be left upon the shelf, and quite another to have so handsome a gentleman imply the same bluntly to her face.

'I mean no insult, but believe me, Miss Langley, when I say that Lord Farquharson has no interest in marriage.'

Lord, he thought she was hopeful of such a thing! 'And I have no interest in Lord Farquharson,' she said curtly. She turned away and started to retrace her steps back down the stairwell, then hesitated and faced him once more. 'Thank you, Mr....'

He made no effort to introduce himself.

'Both for tonight and last week. I'm indebted to you for your intervention.'

Those pale eyes watched her a moment longer before he said, 'Don't thank me, Miss Langley, just stay away from Farquharson.'

She chewed at her bottom lip, wondering whether to tell him. He would think the worst of her if she did not, and somehow the stranger's opinion mattered very much to Madeline. 'Sir,' she said shyly.

'Miss Langley,' he replied and crooked his eyebrow.

The lip received several nasty nips from her teeth. She looked at him, and then looked at him some more.

'Was there something you wished to tell me, Miss Langley?'

Madeline twisted her hands together. 'It's…just that Lord Farquharson has claimed me for the waltz. Perhaps he will not recover in time, but—'

'Recover?' her defender enquired. 'What in Hades did you do to him?'

'My father showed me how to disable a man by using my knee, should the occasion ever arise.'

His mouth gave only the smallest suggestion of a smile. 'And the occasion arose.'

'Yes,' she said simply.

They looked at one another.

'Find whatever excuse you must, Miss Langley, but do not waltz with Farquharson.'

Madeline seriously doubted that the Prince Regent himself could come up with an excuse acceptable to her mother. But there was always the chance, after the incident in the bedchamber, that Lord Farquharson would have changed his mind over dancing with her. 'I'll try,' she said. And she was gone, her feet padding softly down the cold stone stairs that would lead her back to the ballroom.

* * *

'There you are, Madeline. Where is your papa? Did you not tell him of Angelina's success?' Mrs Langley was all of a flutter.

Madeline opened her mouth to reply.

'Never mind that now. You've missed so much. You will not believe what has just happened.' She clapped her hands together in glee. 'Mr Lawrence was taken quite ill, something to do with what he ate at his club earlier in the day.'

'Poor Mr Lawrence,' said Madeline, wondering why Mr Lawrence's malady so pleased her mother.

'Yes, yes,' said Mrs Langley. 'It meant that he could not dance with Angelina as he promised.' Her excitement bubbled over in a giggle.

'Mama, are you feeling quite well?'

Mrs Langley touched a hand to her daughter's arm. 'You'll never guess what happened.'

Madeline waited expectantly.

'The Duke of Devonshire stepped in to take his place and danced with Angelina!' She clasped her hand to her mouth. 'Isn't it just too, too good?'

Madeline glanced across the dance floor to see a rather dashing-looking young man with twinkling blue eyes and warm sand-coloured hair twirl her sister through the steps of a country dance. Angelina was glancing up at the man through long lashes, her golden curls bouncing against the pretty flush of her cheeks. 'Yes, it is wonderful.'

'Wonderful indeed!' Mrs Langley breathed.

Madeline cleared her throat. 'Mama, my head hurts quite dreadfully.'

'Mmm,' mused Mrs Langley, barely taking her eyes from Angelina's dancing form. 'You do look rather pale.'

'I wondered whether Papa might take me home in the carriage. I'm sure that he wouldn't mind.'

'I tell you of Angelina's success and in the next breath you're asking to go home.'

'Mama, it isn't like that. Lord Farquharson—'

'Lord Farquharson!' interrupted her mother. 'I begin to see how this is going. Your papa may not realise what you're up to, but I most certainly do!' Mrs Langley turned on Madeline, her mouth stretched to a false smile in case anyone should think that Mrs Langley and her daughter were having anything but the most pleasant of chats. 'You are so determined to refuse a dance with Lord Farquharson that you will destroy the evening for us all. You think to thumb your nose at a baron and care not a jot if you ruin your sister's chances.'

'No, Mama, you and Angelina will stay here, nothing would be ruined for her.'

'Are you so wrapped up in your own interest that you cannot see Angelina has the chance to catch a duke? That child out there,' said her mother, 'has only kindness in her heart.' Mrs Langley glanced fleetingly at her younger daughter upon the dance floor. 'Not one word has she uttered about Lord Farquharson's preference for you. Not one!'

'Little wonder! She is relieved that she does not have him clutching for her hand.' As soon as the words were out Madeline knew she should not have said them. Oh, Lord. She shut her eyes and readied herself for her mother's response.

Mrs Langley's eyes widened. The false smile could no longer be sustained and slipped from her face. 'Madeline Langley, you go too far. Your papa shall hear of this, indeed he shall. All these years I've slaved to make a lady of you, so that you might make a decent marriage. And now, when I'm on the brink of bringing all my hard work to success, you threaten to ruin all, and not only for yourself.'

Madeline counted to ten.

'Pray do not look at me in that superior way as if I know not of what I speak!' Mrs Langley's small lace handkerchief appeared.

Madeline continued to fifteen.

'You have not the slightest compassion for your poor mama's nerves. And all the while Mr Langley makes your excuses. Well, not any more.'

And twenty.

'You are not going home,' Mrs Langley announced. 'You will sit there and look as if you are having a nice time, headache or not. When the time comes, you will dance with Lord Farquharson and you will smile at him, and answer him politely. Do I make myself clear?'

'Mama, there's something I must tell you of Lord Farquharson,' said Madeline.

Her mother adopted her most stubborn expression. 'I know all I need to know of that gentleman, Madeline. You will waltz with him just the same.'

Madeline looked at her mother in silence.

'Mama. Madeline.' Angelina appeared at her mother's shoulder. As if sensing the atmosphere, she glanced from her mother's flushed face to her sister's pale one. 'Is something wrong?'

'No, nothing is wrong, my angel,' replied Mrs Langley with a forced smile. 'Madeline was just saying how much she was looking forward to dancing this evening.'

Angelina coiled an errant curl around her ear. 'Oh,' she said, 'I came to war— I came to tell Madeline that Lord Farquharson is over there looking for her.'

'How fortuitous,' said Mrs Langley.

Fortuitous was not the word Madeline would have chosen. She turned her head in the direction Angelina had indicated.

Lord Farquharson raised his glass to her in salutation. Even across the distance Madeline could see the promise upon his face.

'What is it, Lucien? First you insist on uprooting me from a very cosy hand of cards at White's, then you trail me here after Farquharson, and now you've got a face like thunder on you.' Guy, Viscount Varington, regarded his brother across a glass of champagne.

'Farquharson's up to his old tricks again.' Lucien rotated the elegant glass stem between his fingers. The champagne inside remained untouched.

'You cannot forever be dogging his steps. Five years is a long time. Perhaps it's time to leave the past behind and move forward.'

Lucien Tregellas's fingers tightened against the delicate stem. 'Move on and forget what he did?' he said bitterly. 'Surely you jest?'

Guy looked into his brother's eyes, eyes that were a mirror image of his own. He smiled a small, rueful smile.

'Farquharson has not changed. He's been a regular visitor to a certain establishment in Berwick Street these years past, slaking his needs, and you know for what manner of taste Madame Fouet's house caters. I could do nothing about that. Even so, I always knew that it would not be enough for him. He wants another woman of gentle breeding, another innocent. And I'll kill Farquharson rather than let that happen.' There was a stillness about Lucien's face, a quietness in his voice, that lent his words a chilling certainty.

'You think he will try again, even with you waiting in the wings?'

'I know he will,' came the grim reply. 'He's planning it even as we speak, and that foolish chit over there is practically falling over herself to be his next victim.'

Guy followed his brother's gaze across the room to the slender figure of the girl seated by the side of an older woman.

'Miss Langley thinks to catch herself a baron. Or, more precisely, her mama does. Miss Langley herself appears to be strangely resistant to any advice to the contrary that I might offer.' A scowl twitched between his brows.

'Then leave her to it,' said Guy with a shrug of his shoulders. 'If the girl refuses to be warned off, then perhaps she deserves Farquharson.'

Lucien's gaze still had not shifted from Miss Langley, his eyes taking in her downcast face, her rigid posture. 'No woman deserves that fate.'

A wry little laugh sounded, and Guy drained the remainder of the champagne from his glass. 'What would London say if they knew that the notorious Earl Tregellas, the man of whom they are all so very afraid, is on a mission to safeguard every virgin in this city from Farquharson's roving eye? There's a certain irony in that, wouldn't you say?'

'There's no comparison between me and Farquharson,' Lucien said. The fragile glass snapped between his fingers. He set the broken pieces down on the tray of a passing footman.

'Calm down, big brother. I loath what Farquharson is as much as you.'

'No. I assure you, you do not.'

'Your feelings are understandable, given what happened,' said Guy quietly.

A muscle twitched in Lucien's jaw.

'What about the girl? Is she really in danger?' Guy glanced again at Miss Langley.

'She's in much more danger than she could ever realise,' replied his brother, looking him directly in the eye.

Earl Tregellas and Viscount Varington, two of society's

most infamous bachelors, albeit for vastly differing reasons, turned their gaze upon the slight and unassuming figure of Miss Madeline Langley.

Chapter Three

Madeline glanced uneasily around. It was almost time. She knew he would come for her; her actions of earlier that evening would not stop him. The stranger had been right to tell her to make her excuses, but he had never dealt with her mother. It was bad enough having to suffer Lord Farquharson's assaults without having her own mother encourage the situation in the hope of forcing him to a wedding. Madeline shuddered at the thought.

She sneaked a glance at her mother. Mrs Langley was engrossed in chattering to Mrs Wilson. Madeline's eyes raked the ballroom. Still no sign of Papa. Over at the far side, partly hidden by some Grecian-styled columns and lounging beside another man, was her dark defender. Their gazes locked. Her heart kicked to a canter. She felt the blush rise in her cheeks and looked hastily away. What would he think of her sitting waiting for Lord Farquharson to come and claim her for the waltz? And he was right! But what else could she do with Mama guarding her so well? A visit to the retiring room had been refused. And at the suggestion that she go home with

Miss Ridgely her mama had warranted a warning glare. Even now Mama's hand rested lightly against her arm. Madeline dared not look at the stranger again, even when she saw Lord Farquharson begin to make his way slowly, steadily, towards her. Every step brought him closer.

Madeline felt the coldness spreading throughout. Her mouth grew suddenly dry and her palms somewhat clammy. She bowed her head, coaxing her courage. *I can do this. I can do this,* she inwardly chanted the mantra again and again. *It is in full view of everyone. What can he do to me here, save dance?* But just the anticipation of being held in his grip, within his power, brought a nausea to her throat. She steeled herself against it. Willed herself to defy him. *Don't let him see that you're afraid.* She steadied her breath, curled her fingers to fists. The spot on the floor disappeared, replaced instead by a pair of large, black-leather buckle slippers. Madeline swallowed once. The shoes were connected to a pair of stockinged shins. The shins led up to a pair of fine black knee breeches. The breeches stretched tight to reveal every detail of well-muscled and long thighs. Madeline's eyes leapt up to his face.

'I believe this is my dance, Miss Langley,' her dark defender said smoothly and, without waiting, plucked Madeline straight from her chair on to the floor.

Lord Farquharson came to an abrupt halt halfway across the ballroom, and stared in disbelief.

Mrs Langley's mouth opened to squawk her protest, and then shut again. She could only sit and stare while her eldest daughter was whisked into the middle of the dance floor.

'Well, really!' exclaimed Mrs Wilson by her side. 'You do know who that is?'

'Indeed,' replied Mrs Langley weakly. 'That is Earl Tregellas.'

'The Wicked Earl,' said her friend with a disapproving frown. 'What an earth is he doing, dancing with Madeline?'

For once in her life Mrs Langley appeared to be lost for words.

The dark-haired stranger held her with a firm gentleness. The light pressure of his hand upon her waist seemed to burn straight through the material of her dress and undergarments, to sear against her skin. The fingers of his other hand enclosed around hers in warm protection. Beneath the superfine material of his coat she could feel the strength of his muscles across the breadth of his shoulders. The square-cut double-breasted tail-coat was of the finest midnight black to match the ruffled feathers of his hair. He looked as if he had just stepped out of the most elegant tailor's establishment in all England. A white-worked waistcoat adorned a pristine white shirt, the collar of which stood high. The white neckcloth looked to be a work of art. Madeline felt suddenly conscious of her cheap dress with its plain cream-coloured material and short puffed sleeves. As usual she had declined to wear the wealth of ribbons and bows set out by Mama. Neither a string of beads nor even a simple ribbon sat around her neck. The square-shaped neckline of her dress was not low; even so, in contrast with the other ladies, she had insisted upon wearing a pale pink fichu lest any skin might be exposed.

'Miss Langley, you seem disinclined to follow my advice.'

The richness of his voice drifted down to her. She kept her focus fixed firmly on the lapel of his coat. What else was he to think? Hadn't she known that it would be so? 'I could not leave,' she said. It sounded pathetic even to her own ears.

'Could not, or would not? Perhaps you are in concordance with your mother's plans to catch yourself a baron after all.'

'No!' Her gaze snapped up to his. His eyes were watching with a dispassion that piqued her. 'No,' she said again. 'It isn't like that at all.'

He raised a dark eyebrow as if in contradiction. 'Perhaps you even welcome Lord Farquharson's attentions.' His gaze meandered down over her body, lingered momentarily upon her well-covered bosom, and dawdled back up to see the blush flood her normally pale cheeks.

She gripped at her lower lip with her teeth, as if to hold back the answer that would have spilled too readily forth. 'If you really think that, then you may as well pass me to him this very moment.' Her body tensed as she waited to see what he would do.

His steps were perfection, smooth and flowing, guiding her first here, then there, progressing with grace around the floor. For such a big man he was certainly light on his feet. As they turned to change direction, the irate face of Lord Farquharson swam into view. He was standing ready to catch her by the edge of the dance floor. Madeline's eyes widened. The stranger swung her closer towards Lord Farquharson. Her heart was thumping fit to leap free from her chest. A tremble set up in her fingers. The stranger was going to abandon her into Lord Farquharson's arms! Madeline's eyelids flickered shut in anticipation. She readied herself for the sound of Lord Farquharson's voice, prepared herself to feel the grasp of his hands.

'You can open your eyes now,' the stranger said. 'I haven't the least intention of releasing you to Farquharson.'

Madeline opened her eyes tentatively to find that they had progressed further around the ballroom, leaving Lord Farquharson well behind. She allowed herself to relax a little.

He felt the tension ease from her body and knew then that she hadn't lied about her feelings for Farquharson. And although it shouldn't have made the blindest bit of a difference, the knowledge pleased him. He wouldn't have abandoned her to Farquharson even if she'd been screaming to get there. She seemed so small and slender in his arms, much smaller than he had realised. He looked into her eyes and saw with a jolt that they were the clear golden hue of amber. Strange that he had not noticed that during either of their previous meetings. He had never met a woman with quite that colouring before. They were beautiful eyes, eyes a man might lose himself in. The sound of Miss Langley's voice dragged him back from his contemplation and he chided himself for staring at the chit.

She was looking at him expectantly, as if waiting for some kind of response.

'I beg your pardon,' he said. 'My attention was elsewhere.' The shadow of something flitted across her face, then was gone.

'Lord Farquharson does not look happy. You have stolen his dance,' she said.

'He has no damn right to dance with any woman,' he said harshly, then, remembering the woman in his arms, said, 'Forgive my language, Miss Langley. I did not mean to offend you.'

She smiled then, and it was a smile that lit up her face. Lucien wondered how he could ever have thought her plain. 'Rest assured, sir, whatever else you have done, you have not offended me.'

Lucien studied her closely.

'Indeed, you have nothing but my gratitude,' she continued. 'I dread to think of my circumstance now had you not intervened on my behalf.' He could feel the warmth of her beneath his fingers; he could see it in her face. No, Madeline Langley had not encouraged Farquharson. There was an honesty about her, a quiet reserve, and a quickness of mind that was so lacking in most of the young women he had encountered.

She smiled again and he barely heard the notes of the band, concentrating as he was on the girl before him. The prim plain clothing could not completely disguise what lay beneath. The narrowness of her waist beneath his palm, the subtle rise of her breasts, those slender arms. Lucien could see very well what had attracted Farquharson. Innocence and fear and something else, something he could not quite define.

'Who are you?' she said, looking up at him. 'I don't even know your name.'

Of course she didn't know. She wouldn't be looking up at him so trustingly if she had known who he was. Some women attempted to court him for his reputation. Madeline Langley would not. He knew that instinctively. She would shun the wicked man Earl Tregellas was reputed to be.

A shy amusement lit the amber eyes. 'Will you not tell me, sir?'

He hesitated a moment longer, enjoying the innocent radiance in her face. No woman looked at him like that any more. Artful coquetry, pouting petulance, flagrant fear, and, of course, downright disapproval—he had known them all. Miss Langley's expression fell into none of those categories.

She smiled.

Lucien traced the outline of it with his eyes. He doubted that he would see her smile again once he told her his name.

The band played on. Their feet moved in time across the floor. Silence stretched between them.

'I am Tregellas.' There was nothing else he could say.

'Tregellas?' she said softly.

He watched while she tried to place the name, the slight puzzlement creasing a tiny line between her brows. Perhaps she did not know of him. And then he saw that she did after all. Shock widened the tawny glow of her eyes. The smile fled her sweet pink lips. Uncertainty stood in its stead.

'Earl Tregellas? The Wick—' She stopped herself just in time.

'At your service, Miss Langley,' he said smoothly, as if he were just any other polite gentleman of the *ton*.

Her gaze fluttered across his face, anxiety clouding her beautiful eyes, before she masked them with long black lashes. He thought he felt her body stiffen beneath his fingers.

'I'm not Farquharson,' he growled. 'You need have no fear of me.' Hell, he was trying to save her, not ravish her himself. And anyway, he had no interest in young ladies of Miss Langley's ilk. Indeed, he had not paid attention to any woman in five long years, or so he reminded himself.

She raised her eyes and looked at him, really looked at him, as if she could see the man beneath, the real Lucien Tregellas.

'No, you're not Farquharson.' Her voice was scarcely more than a whisper.

Lucien found that he could not take his eyes from hers. The censure that he expected was not there. There was nothing except an open, honest appraisal.

The music came to a halt.

'Thank you, Miss Langley,' he said, but whether it was for the dance or for her recognition that he and Farquharson were miles apart, he did not know. Her small hand was still enclosed in his. Swiftly he placed it upon his arm and escorted her back to her mother in silence.

And all the while he was conscious that Miss Madeline Langley had seen behind the façade that was the Wicked Earl.

'Madeline, what on earth do you think you're playing at?' her mother demanded. 'Do you know who that is?' she whispered between clenched teeth.

'Earl Tregellas,' Madeline said slowly, her words slightly stilted.

'Of all the most ill-mannered men. He takes you off without even consulting your mama! Not so much as a by your leave! How could you dance with him when Lord Far-quharson's name is written clearly upon your card against the waltz!' Mrs Langley's hand scrabbled for her handkerchief. 'I declare my nerves are in a terrible state. Oh, Madeline, whatever were you thinking of? He has the blackest reputation of any man in London!'

'I could not refuse him without causing a scene.' She omitted to mention that she would rather have danced with the infamous Wicked Earl a thousand times over than let Lord Farquharson lay one finger upon her. 'I did not wish to embarrass you, Mama.'

'Embarrass me? Embarrass me?' The words seemed to be in danger of choking Mrs Langley. 'Never has a mother been more embarrassed by the actions of such a vexing daughter!' She dabbed at her eyes. 'And what will Lord Farquharson think of this?'

Madeline held her tongue.

'How could you do it, Madeline? It was as good as giving him a cut in front of the world.' Mrs Langley's bosom heaved dramatically.

Madeline tried to ignore the numerous stares that were being sent in her direction. She made no sign of having heard the whispers from the ladies in the seats surrounding them. 'No one knew what was on my dance card. Most likely they would have believed it to be empty as is usual.'

The whispers grew louder.

Angelina tugged at her mother's arm. 'Mama,' she said. 'You must not upset yourself. People are staring.'

Mrs Langley surveyed the attention turned upon her family. It was not the interest she had hoped for. She noticed that even Mrs Wilson had distanced herself somewhat and was now conversing with Mrs Hammond, casting the odd look back at the Langleys. Amelia Langley held her head up high and said in a voice intended to carry, 'Unfortunately, girls, your mama has developed one of her headaches. There is nothing else for it but to retire at once. What a shame, when we were having such a nice time. Come along, girls.' And Mrs Langley swept her daughters from the ballroom. 'I shall have a footman find your papa.'

The journey back to Climington Street was not pleasant. Madeline suffered several sympathetic looks from Angelina, a continuous harangue from her mother, and only the mildest expression of reproof from her father.

The harangue from Mrs Langley paused only while the family made their way into their home, and resumed once more when the front door had been firmly closed. Madeline made to follow Angelina upstairs.

'Where do you think you're going?' her mother screeched. 'We shall discuss this evening's nonsense, miss. Through to the parlour with you. Now!'

Madeline started back down the stairs.

'Think I might just have an early night myself,' mumbled her father and tried to slope away.

But Mrs Langley was having none of it. 'Mr Langley,' she cried. 'Will you not take control of *your* daughter?'

It was strange, or so Madeline thought, that she was always *Papa*'s daughter when she had displeased Mama, which, of course, was most of the time.

The long-suffering Mr Langley gave a weary sigh and led the way through to the parlour.

'She has made a spectacle of us this evening,' ranted Mrs Langley. 'And most certainly destroyed any chance of an alliance with Lord Farquharson!'

'Calm yourself, Mrs Langley, I'm sure it cannot be quite that bad,' said Mr Langley.

Mrs Langley's face turned a mottled puce. Her mouth opened and closed convulsively. Madeline had never seen her look so distressed. 'If you had not been hiding in Lady Gilmour's conservatory all evening, then you would realise that it is worse than bad!' she shouted.

'Perhaps Lord Farquharson can be persuaded otherwise,' said Mr Langley in an attempt to pacify his wife.

'Madeline snubbed him to dance with Earl Tregellas, for pity's sake!'

'Really?' mumbled Mr Langley, 'I'm sure he'll get over it.'

'Get over it! Get over it!' huffed Mrs Langley. 'How can you say such a thing? Lord Farquharson is unlikely to look in her direction, let alone offer her marriage! She has ruined her chances. We will never be invited anywhere ever again!' wailed Mrs Langley. Tears squeezed from her eyes and began to roll down her cheeks.

'Now, Mrs Langley,' Mr Langley cajoled, 'please don't take on so. I will sort it all out. Come along, my dearest.' He pressed a soothing arm around his wife's quivering shoulders.

But Mrs Langley steadfastly refused to budge. 'What are we to do? Lord Farquharson will never have her now.' The trickle of tears was in danger of becoming a deluge.

Madeline watched the unfolding scene, never uttering a word.

'Speak to her, Arthur,' Mrs Langley pleaded.

Mr Langley patted his wife, straightened, and cleared his throat. 'So, Madeline.' He cleared his throat again. 'What's all this about? How came you to dance with Lord Tregellas over Lord Farquharson?'

Madeline found that she could not tell even her dear papa what Lord Tregellas had done for her; how he had saved her from Lord Farquharson on, not one, but two separate occasions. 'He asked me and took my arm. There did not seem any polite manner in which to decline his request.' Indeed, there had been no request. Lord Tregellas had plucked her straight from her seat and on to the dance floor as if he had every right to do so.

'Did you know who he was?'

'No,' she answered. That, at least, was true. She had not known that her dark defender was the notorious Wicked Earl, not then.

Furrows of worry ploughed across her father's forehead. 'But how came you to his attention, my dear?'

Somehow it seemed strangely traitorous to reveal the truth about Lord Tregellas. She didn't understand why, just knew that it would not be what he wanted. It made no sense. Surely to tell them that he had stepped in to save her honour would have done him only good? Common sense affirmed that. Instinct fought against it...and won. 'I do not know,' said Madeline. She was not in the habit of lying, especially to her papa. Guilt sat heavily upon her shoulders.

'I understand he does not normally dance. Why should he then suddenly take it into his head to dance with a quiet, unassuming and gently bred girl like you?' Mr Langley pondered his own question.

Madeline understood exactly why Lord Tregellas had waltzed with her. She was not foolish enough to think that he actually *liked* her. There was nothing to recommend Madeline Langley to him, indeed to any man, when it came to that. It was simply a matter of saving her from enduring the dance within Lord Farquharson's arms. What she did not understand was why Lord Tregellas should care. She kept her thoughts to herself and shook her head at her father's question.

Mrs Langley snorted in the background. 'Quiet and unassuming?' she echoed. 'It is clear you have spent little time of late in your daughter's company!'

Mr Langley chose to ignore this comment. 'Madeline,' he said as carefully as he could, 'Lord Tregellas is a gentleman of some renown. He may be an earl and in receipt of a large fortune, but…' He hesitated, unsure how best to phrase the next words. 'He has a rather dubious reputation, my dear—'

'Everyone knows what he is reputed to have done,' cut in her mother.

'What did he do?' asked Madeline.

Mrs Langley's mouth opened. 'He is a murderer of the very worst kind. Why do you think he's called the Wicked Earl? He killed the—'

'We shall not lower ourselves to become gossip-mongers, Mrs Langley,' said her father reprovingly.

Madeline looked from one parent to the other. Even she, prim and proper Miss Madeline Langley, had heard talk of Lord Tregellas. He was said to have committed some heinous crime in the past. That fact alone made him strangely fascinating to half the women across London, although he was reputed to treat them all with a cold contempt. Madeline knew that, and still it did not matter. The man that had forced Lord Farquharson to leave her safe in the Theatre Royal, who had warned her against that fiend, and had saved her again at this evening's ball, was not someone she could fear. He had, after all, given her every reason to trust him. 'It was only one dance,' she said in defence of Lord Tregellas and herself.

'It was the *waltz!*' sobbed her mother. 'Madeline is quite ruined after this evening's fiasco.'

Mr Langley said patiently, 'Come now, my dear, she's hardly ruined. It was, as she said, only a dance.'

The sobbing burst forth into a wail. 'Oh, you understand nothing, Mr Langley!'

Mr Langley wore the weary air of a man who knew

exactly what the forthcoming weeks would hold if he did nothing to resolve the situation. 'Perhaps I could have a word with Farquharson.'

'He'll have nothing to do with Madeline now. All my plans lie in ruins.'

'He's a stout fellow. He'll listen to reason,' said Mr Langley.

Her mother stopped wailing and dabbed at her eyes. 'Do you really think so?' she hiccupped.

'Of course,' her father replied. 'I'll go round there tomorrow and explain that Madeline had no notion to dance with Tregellas, that she was taken unawares, and, as a young and inexperienced lady, had no say in the matter. Perhaps I could invite him to dinner.'

Madeline could not believe what she was hearing. Her father thought Farquharson a stout fellow? 'Papa,' she said. 'Please do not. If you knew Lord Farquharson's true nature, you would not suggest such a thing. He is not an honourable man.'

'Mr Langley,' said her mother, 'pray do not heed her. She's taken a set against Lord Farquharson and is determined to thwart my plans. He's a wealthy and respected member of the aristocracy, a war hero and more. And he's worth ten thousand a year. Does that sound like a dishonourable man?'

'Papa, if you knew what he had done—'

'Then tell me, child,' encouraged her father.

'Arthur!' her mother whined.

But Mr Langley made no sign of having heard his wife's complaint. 'Madeline, what has happened?'

Madeline sighed. Papa would listen. He would not make excuses for Lord Farquharson or, worse still, encourage the man's attentions. Once Papa knew the truth, she would be free of Lord Farquharson for ever. It did not matter that she would never marry. Rather that, than wedded to Lord Farquharson. No man other than that villain had ever expressed so much as an interest in her. She was four-and-twenty years old, with a string of failed Seasons behind her. She did not blame her mother and father for not sending her out on to the circuit last year. In fact, it was a blessed relief, and they did, after all, have Angelina to think about. Surely Angelina would more than compensate them for Madeline's failings?

'Madeline?' her father prompted.

Madeline shook the fluttering thoughts from her head. The truth must be told—just without any mention of Lord Tregellas. Taking a deep breath, she relayed what Lord Farquharson had been about, both in the Theatre Royal and at Lady Gilmour's ball. There was no embellishment, no dramatics, just plain facts, minus a certain earl's involvement.

By the end of it Mr Langley was no longer looking his usual mild-mannered self. He fixed a stern eye upon his wife. 'You knew of this, Amelia?' Incredulity edged his voice.

'Only about the theatre. But he did *not* kiss her, Arthur.' Mrs Langley cast imploring eyes up to her husband. 'I knew nothing of this evening. She said not one word of being alone in a bedchamber with Lord Farquharson. Had I but known…' Mrs Langley pressed her tiny lace handkerchief to her mouth and fell silent.

A small cynical part of Madeline wondered as to her mother's claim. Would she still have had her daughter dance with Lord Farquharson, knowing all that he had done? Mama had been unwilling to hear Madeline speak against the Baron. And social standing and money were so very important to Mrs Langley. It was a pointless question.

'We shall discuss this further, Mrs Langley, once the matter has been satisfactorily resolved.'

Madeline had never seen her father like this before. There

was a determined glare in his normally kind brown eyes, a tension in his usually relaxed stance. He rang the bell and requested that the carriage be brought back round. 'Papa?' said Madeline. 'Where are you going?'

'To see Lord Farquharson.'

Madeline felt the blood drain from her face. Visions of duelling pistols and her father lying wounded, or worse, swam in her head. She prayed that he would not do anything so foolish as call out Lord Farquharson. Not her papa, not her mild-mannered, gentle papa. 'Please, Papa, do not go.'

'I must, my dear,' he said. 'It's a matter of honour.'

'Arthur?' Mrs Langley raised a trembling voice.

'Do not wait up, I may be some time,' said Mr Langley and walked from the parlour.

The clock on the mantel struck midnight as the front door slammed behind him.

'So you waltzed with Miss Langley just to prevent Farquharson from doing so?' Guy, Viscount Varington, raised a cynical brow.

The library was quiet; only the slow rhythmic ticking of the clock and the occasional spit from the fire punctuated the silence.

'Why else?' Lucien Tregellas didn't even glance round at his brother, just stood by the carved marble fireplace looking into the dancing yellow flames. They glowed golden in the darkness of the library, reminding him of the lights in Madeline Langley's eyes. Such warmth and honesty as he had not seen in any other woman's eyes. Long dark lashes and that straight little nose…and a clean pleasant smell that reminded him of… It came to him then exactly what Miss Langley smelled of—oranges!

'You've done far more damage to her reputation just by dancing with her than Farquharson ever could.' Guy leaned across the small drum table and captured the decanter.

'Hell's teeth, Guy! I only danced with the girl. Farquharson would have done a damned sight worse. It wasn't as if I ravished her.'

'Might as well have, old chap,' said his brother. 'You haven't danced in the last five years. And when you decide to take again to the dance floor, after such a long absence, you don't choose just any old dance, but the waltz.'

'So?'

'So, all of London's eyes will be upon you now to see what Tregellas meant by waltzing with the very proper Miss Langley.' Guy filled two balloon glasses with the rich amber liquid from the decanter.

'Then London will have a long wait.'

Guy pressed a glass into his brother's hand. 'Really?'

Lucien arched an eyebrow and ignored the comment.

Guy continued on, knowing full well his brother's irritation. 'You know, of course, that the chit will now be thrust under your nose at every opportunity. Why should Miss Langley's mama settle for a mere baron when an earl has just *waltzed* right into her sight?'

'Your puns get worse, Guy.' Lucien's fingers rubbed against the Tregellas coat of arms artfully engraved upon the side of his glass. 'Mrs Langley may do her worst. I had no interest in Madeline Langley other than to stop Farquharson getting his hands on her.'

'Had?' queried Guy with an expression that bellied innocence.

'Had, have, what's the difference?'

'You tell me,' came Guy's rejoinder.

Lucien took a large swig of brandy. The liquid burned a

satisfying trail down to his stomach. 'I made my meaning clear enough to Farquharson.'

'And what of Miss Langley? Did you make your meaning clear to her, too? Perhaps she has expectations following her waltz this evening. A girl like that can't have too many men hanging after her.'

Lucien took another gulp of brandy. 'Miss Langley has no expectations of me.' He thought momentarily of Madeline Langley's clear non-judgemental gaze, and a touch of tenderness twitched at his lips. The girl didn't have a conniving bone in her body.

'News of your waltz with Miss Langley will be all over town by tomorrow afternoon, and you know what people will think.' Guy paused to take a delicate sip from his glass. 'Dallying with a respectable girl can only mean one thing in their tawdry little minds—that you have finally decided to take a wife and beget an heir.'

'Let them think what they will,' Lucien shrugged. 'We both know that I have no intention of marrying, and as for the Tregellas heir…' Lucien raised his glass in the direction of his brother '…I'm looking at him. Hell will freeze over before I find myself in parson's trap.'

A peculiar smile hovered around Guy's mouth. 'We'll see,' he said softly. 'Only the devil or a fool tempts fate.'

Not so very far away in Brooks's Club on St James's Street, Cyril Farquharson was also sipping brandy. His attention was not on the small circle of fashionable gentlemen with whom he was sitting. Indeed, Lord Farquharson's thoughts were concerned with someone else entirely; and that someone was Miss Madeline Langley. The whores at Madame Fouet's had been meagre rations to feed his appetite. Five years was a long time to starve. He had grown tired of them. They were too willing, too coarse and worldly wise, and, even though they role-played otherwise, that fact detracted something from the experience for Farquharson. And he was tired too of Tregellas's constant watching, his constant waiting. Damn the man for curtailing the best of his pleasures. But Farquharson would be held in check no longer. He hungered for a gentlewoman, someone young and innocent and fearful, someone with that unique *je ne sais quoi;* in short, someone like Madeline Langley.

She had taken years in the finding, but Farquharson had known that Madeline was the one from the moment he had seen her. She was quiet and reserved and afraid of him, all the things he liked in a woman. He played with her, like a cat played with a mouse. He liked to see her discomfort when he stepped too close or lingered too long over her hand. He liked the way she tried to hide her fear and her futile efforts to avoid him. Dear, sweet, fearful Madeline. He meant to take his pleasure of her…in the worst possible way. If the empty-headed Mrs Langley was determined to dangle her delicious daughter before him in the hope of trapping him in marriage, who was he to refuse the bait? Cyril Farquharson was far too cunning to be caught. So he had enjoyed his game with Madeline Langley until Tregellas had entered the scene.

The interruption in the Theatre Royal during the play had been an irritation. Tregellas's dance with the girl at Lady Gilmour's ball went beyond that. It smacked of more than a desire to thwart Farquharson. Tregellas had not looked at a female in years, and now he had waltzed with the very woman that Farquharson held within his sights. Perhaps Tregellas had an interest in Miss Langley. There was an irony in that thought. Lord Farquharson mulled the matter over. By the time that he finished his brandy and headed for home, he knew just what he was going to do. In one fell swoop, not only would he secure Miss Langley to do with whatsoever he might please, but he would also effectively thwart any move that Tregellas might mean to make. And that idea appealed very much to Cyril Farquharson. He smiled at his own ingenuity and looked forward to Madeline Langley's reaction when she learned what he meant to do.

Chapter Four

Madeline did not see her father again until the next morning. All the night through she had lain awake, unable to find sleep; tossing and turning beneath the bedcovers, until her cheeks burned red with the worry of it all. Papa was well meaning, but he had no real appreciation of the malice contained in a man like Lord Farquharson. It seemed that Madeline could see the cruel grey eyes and the sneer stretched across Lord Farquharson's lips. Dear Lord in heaven, Papa didn't stand a chance! Lord Farquharson would dispense with her gentle father before Mr Langley had so much as taken his second breath. What good did Papa think that complaining would do? None, as far as Madeline could see. And God forbid that he took it into his head to challenge Lord Farquharson! She did not even know if her father owned a pair of duelling pistols. Papa was far too sensible to call Lord Farquharson out. Wasn't he?

The bed linen was very crumpled and Madeline very tired by the time morning came. The foggy dullness of her brain contrasted with the tense agitation of her body. She rose early, washed, dressed, took only the smallest cup of coffee and waited in the quiet little dining room, ignoring the heated salvers of ham and eggs. Her stomach was squeezed so tight by anxiety that even the smell of the food stirred a wave of nausea. It was not until after nine o'clock that her father finally appeared, with her mother in tow.

Mrs Langley was surprisingly calm in the light of what had yesterday been cited as the biggest catastrophe of the century. In fact, Madeline might even have gone so far as to say that her mother was looking rather pleased. At least Papa did not seem to have taken any hurts. His arm was not in a sling nor did he limp. His eyes were bagged with tiredness, but were not blackened from bruising. Indeed, he had not one visible scratch upon him. Madeline breathed a sigh of relief. Tension's hold slackened a little. 'Papa!' she breathed. 'Thank goodness you're safe.' She ran to him and placed her arms around him in a grateful embrace. 'I was so worried.'

Mr Langley did not return Madeline's tremulous smile. Rather, he reached out a tired old hand and pulled her gently to him. 'Madeline,' he said, and there was sadness in his voice.

Something was wrong. Madeline felt it immediately. She started back and stared up into his eyes. 'What is it, Papa? What has happened?' It did not make sense. He was home, returned safely, hurt, it seemed, by nothing more than Farquharson's words. The first hint of apprehension wriggled down Madeline's spine. What had Lord Farquharson said? And then a worse thought made itself known. 'You have not…killed him, have you?' she asked.

'No, child.' Mr Langley shook his grizzled head. 'Although, I begin to think that I would be better placed if I had.'

'Then what…?'

Mrs Langley touched a hand to her husband's arm; she could no longer hide her smile. 'Pray tell Madeline the good news, Mr Langley,' she said.

Madeline looked up into her father's face and waited for the words to fall.

'Lord Farquharson apologised for his lapse of control. He said that his normal behaviour was overcome by the magnitude of his feelings for you.'

The first tentacles of dread enclosed around Madeline's heart. 'And?' Her voice was nothing more than a cracked whisper.

'He has offered to do the decent thing. Lord Farquharson wishes to marry you, Madeline.'

His words clattered harsh against the ensuing silence.

She stared at her father, resisting the enormity of what he had just said.

Mr Langley's palm dabbed against Madeline's back as if to salve the hurt he had just dealt her. 'As a gentleman he should never have tried to compromise you. But the deed is done and he would redeem himself by making you his wife. He said it was ever his wish since first he saw you. I believe he does care for you, my dear. Perhaps in time you will come to be happy together.'

'No.' Madeline shook her head. 'No!' The word reverberated around the room. 'I cannot marry him, Papa. I will not!'

Mrs Langley came forward then. 'Your father has already agreed it. Lord Farquharson is already organising a party at which your betrothal will be announced. The invitations are to be written and sent today.'

'The party can be cancelled.'

The smile wiped from Mrs Langley's face. 'You see how she tortures me, Mr Langley!' she cried. 'She would rather make fools of us before all of London than do as she is bid.'

None of it seemed real. They were but players upon a stage, mouthing lines that would wreck her life for ever. Madeline struggled to shake the thick fleece that clouded her thoughts. 'Papa, please, I cannot do this.'

'Madeline,' he said gently, and it seemed as if his heart were breaking. 'If you really cannot bear to marry Lord Farquharson, then I am obliged to take other steps. He has impugned your honour. As your father, I cannot just sit back and let that happen. If word were to get out of your meeting with Farquharson in Lady Gilmour's bedchamber, then your reputation would be utterly tarnished, and even Angelina would not remain unharmed.' His eyes shuttered in anguish, and prised open again. 'Either he marries you or I must call him out. The guilt is Farquharson's, not yours, never doubt that, my dear, but we both know that society will not view it that way, and I cannot let you suffer their persecution should the matter come to light.' His fingers fluttered against her hair, drawing her face up to look at him. 'I will not force you to this marriage, Madeline. The choice is yours to make. If you truly cannot bear to have Farquharson as your husband, then so be it.'

Mrs Langley gripped at her husband's arm, pulling it away from Madeline. 'Oh, Mr Langley, you cannot seriously mean to challenge his lordship?' Her voice rose in a panic. 'Duelling is illegal...and dangerous. You might be killed!' She clung to him, tears springing to her eyes. 'And what good would it do? Madeline's reputation will be ruined if she does not marry him, regardless of the outcome of any duel. I beg of you, Mr Langley, do not give her the choice. Madeline must wed him and be done with it.'

'It is a matter of honour, Mrs Langley, and I shall not force her to wed against her will,' said Mr Langley.

Madeline's teeth clung to her lower lip. Her throat constricted ready to choke her. She would not cry. She would not.

'You may have some little time to think on your decision, but if you decide against the marriage, Madeline, speed might yet prevent the sending of the invitations.'

Mrs Langley was tugging at her husband's hand. 'No, Arthur, no, please!'

For Madeline there was, of course, no decision to be made. Marry Lord Farquharson, or have her father risk his life. The choice was not a difficult one, and in its making, a cold calm settled upon her. Tears and fear and anger would come later. For now, Madeline moved like an automaton.

Mr Langley turned to go.

'Wait, Papa…' Madeline stayed him with a hand '…I've made my choice.'

Her father's kindly brown eyes looked down into hers.

'I will marry Lord Farquharson.'

Mrs Langley's face uncrinkled.

'Are you certain, my dear?' he asked.

'Yes.' Such a little word to tilt the axis of the world.

An uncertain smile blossomed on Mrs Langley's face. 'It will not be so bad, Madeline. You'll see. His lordship will make up for his mistakes, I'm sure he will.' She patted at her daughter's arm. 'And he *is* a baron.'

Madeline barely felt her touch. Yes, Lord Farquharson would more than make up for his mistakes, just not in the way her mother thought. There had been nothing of care or affection in his eyes. Whatever he meant to do, Madeline knew that it would not be with her welfare or her wishes in mind. Neither would matter once she was his wife. He could do what he pleased with her then, and no one would mind in the slightest. Farquharson's wife. The ball of nausea within her stomach started to grow. 'Please excuse me, Mama, Papa. I feel suddenly rather…tired.'

'Of course, my dearest,' said Mrs Langley.

Her father looked drained, wrung out. 'It's for the best,' he said.

Madeline tried to smile, tried to give him some small

measure of false assurance, but her lips would do nothing but waver. 'Yes,' she said again, and slipped quietly from the room.

'Hell!' Earl Tregellas's curse drew the attention of several of the surrounding gentlemen dotted around the room.

'Lucien?' Guy watched the rigidity grip Lucien's jaw and saw the telltale tightening of his lips. He leaned forward from his chair, all previous lounging forgotten, keen to know exactly what was printed in today's copy of *The Morning Post* that had wrought such a reaction from his brother. Lucien normally preferred to keep his emotions tightly in check in public.

Lucien Tregellas threw an insolent stare at those gentlemen in White's lounge area who were fool enough to be still expressing an interest. The grandfather clock over by the door ticked its languorous pace. A few newspapers rustled. The chink of porcelain and glass sounded. And the normal quiet drone of conversation resumed. 'Come, Guy, I've a mind to get out of here.' He folded the newspaper in half and threw it nonchalantly on to the small occasional table by his elbow.

Both men rose, and, with their coffee still unfinished on the table, left the premises of White's gentlemen's club without so much as a backward glance.

Lucien's curricle was waiting outside, the horses impatiently striking up dust from the street. 'Do you mind if we walk?'

Guy shook his head. Things must be bad.

A brief word to his tiger and Lucien's curricle was gone, leaving the brothers alone in the late winter's pale sunlight.

They walked off down St James's Street. 'Well?' said Guy.

Lucien made no reply, just clenched his jaw tighter to check the unleashing of the rage that threatened to explode. To any that passed it would seem that Earl Tregellas was just out for a casual morning stroll with his brother. There was nothing in his demeanour to suggest that anything might be awry in his usual lifestyle. Lucien might disguise it well, but Guy was not indifferent to the tension simmering below the surface of his brother's relaxed exterior. That Lucien had failed to prevent his outburst in White's was not a good sign.

'Are you going to tell me just what has you biting down on your jaw as if you were having a bullet extracted?'

Lucien's long stride faltered momentarily and then recovered. 'Lord Farquharson entertained a small party last evening in Bloomsbury Square to announce his betrothal to Miss Madeline Langley, elder daughter of Mr Arthur Langley and Mrs Amelia Langley of Climington Street.'

Guy stopped dead on the spot. 'He means to *marry* her?'

'It would appear so.' There was a harshness in Lucien's features, an anger that would not be suppressed for long.

'But why?' Guy turned a baffled expression upon Lucien.

'Keep walking, Guy.' Lucien touched a hand briefly to his brother's arm.

'Why not just turn his attention to another, easier target? By Hades, I would not have thought him to be so desperate for Miss Langley above all others. The girl has nothing particular to recommend her. She doesn't even look like—' Guy caught himself just in time. 'Sorry, Lucien, didn't mean to…'

'I warned him if he ever tried to strike again that I would be waiting. Perhaps he thought that I was bluffing, that I would just sit back and let him take Madeline Langley. I did not think he would resort to marriage to get his hands on her.'

They walked in silence for a few minutes before Guy slowly said, 'Or he may have misinterpreted your defence of Miss Langley.'

'Don't be ridiculous,' snapped Lucien. 'Why on earth would he think that I have any interest in the girl?'

Guy raised a wry eyebrow. 'For the same reason that half of London did only yesterday.'

'What else was I supposed to do? Watch him run his lecherous hands all over her? Let him force her to a dance she did not want…and more?'

'It seems that Miss Langley has changed her opinion of Farquharson. She might not have wanted to dance then, but she wants to marry him now.'

Lucien thought of the fear and revulsion on Miss Langley's face as that brute had tried to force himself upon her; of her terror when she'd quite literally run straight into him on that servants' stairwell; and her loathing at the prospect of waltzing with Farquharson. 'I cannot believe that it is so.'

'There's nothing so fickle as women. You should know that, Lucien. Saying one thing, then changing their minds at the drop of a hat. It's amazing what the odd bauble or two can buy these days.'

'Madeline Langley isn't like that. You've seen her, Guy. She isn't that sort of woman.'

'Plain and puritanical maybe, Lucien, but still as likely to yield to temptation as any other. The Langleys are not wealthy. The pretty golden looks of the younger Langley chit are bound to catch her a husband. Not so with the elder Miss Langley. Perhaps she decided Farquharson was preferable to life as an old maid.'

Lucien shook his head. 'No.' He could not imagine Miss Langley agreeing to touch Farquharson, let alone marry him.

'Let it rest, Lucien,' his brother advised. 'You've done all you can to save the girl. If she's foolish enough to become his wife, then there's nothing more you can do. Your conscience, at least, is clear.'

'My conscience is anything but clear. My actions have brought about this situation.'

'You don't know that,' countered Guy.

'I threw down the gauntlet and Farquharson took it up.'

'Perhaps he planned to marry her all along.'

'Perhaps. Whatever the reasoning, I cannot let Miss Langley become his wife.'

'Oh, and just how do you propose to stop the wedding? Stand up and announce the truth of what Farquharson did? Stirring up the past will release Miss Langley from the betrothal, but at what cost? It's too high a price, Lucien.'

'I'll find another way.'

Guy sighed. 'What is Miss Langley to you? Nothing. She's not worth it.'

'Whatever Madeline Langley may or may not be worth, I'll be damned if I just abandon her to Farquharson. You know what he'll do.'

'He might have changed, learned his lesson over the years.'

Lucien drew his brother a look of withering incredulity. 'Men like Farquharson never change. Why else has he been visiting Madame Fouet's all these years?'

'Face it, Lucien. Short of marrying Miss Langley yourself, there's not a cursed thing you can do to stop him.'

A silence hiccupped between them.

A crooked smile eased the hardness of Lucien's lips. 'You might just have an idea there, little brother.'

Guy laughed at the jest. 'Now that really would be beyond belief, the Wicked Earl and Miss Langley!' Still laughing, he grabbed his brother's arm. 'What you need is a good stiff drink.'

'Amen to that,' said Lucien.

The more that Lucien thought on it, the more sense it seemed to make. He knew what would happen if Farquharson married Miss Langley, knew that he could not stand by and let another woman walk to her death, willing or not. For all that his brother said, Lucien still could not bring himself to believe in Miss Langley's sudden capitulation. Could she really want Farquharson as a husband? Lucien drank deeper and stared unseeing into the dying embers of the fire. Did the answer to that question even make any difference? Farquharson was Farquharson. No woman, knowing the truth about him, would willingly agree to so much as look at the man. Lucien remembered too well that of which Farquharson was capable. Mercifully the brandy anaesthetised the worst of the pain that the memories triggered. He emptied the contents down his throat and reached for the decanter again.

Farquharson. Farquharson. Farquharson. For five long years Lucien had thought of little else. Nothing but that and his own vow to ensure that Farquharson never struck again. Then Miss Madeline Langley had entered the picture and history was suddenly in danger of repeating itself, while all he could do was watch it happen. Lucien's lip curled at the very thought. His eyes closed tight against the spiralling anger. When they opened again, he was perfectly calm, his thinking never clearer. Lucien Tregellas knew exactly what he was going to do. Raising the stakes was a risky move but, if played well, would resolve the situation admirably. Guilt prickled at his conscience. He quashed it. Even if he was using her for revenge, Miss Langley would also benefit from the arrangement. And besides, being with him would be infinitely safer for the girl than being with Farquharson.

Madeline sat demurely on the gilt-legged chair, her mother positioned on one side, Angelina on the other. Since the announcement of her betrothal to Lord Farquharson, Madeline had been elevated in her mother's order of things. There had been trips to cloth warehouses, milliners, drapers and Burlington Arcade. Shopping, shopping and more shopping. Life had taken on a frenzied whirl of dances and parties and balls. The little house in Climington Street looked more like a florist's shop following the daily arrival of Lord Farquharson's bouquets. And now, Mrs Langley had managed to obtain the ultimate in social acceptance—vouchers for Almack's Assembly Rooms. Amelia Langley had finally arrived, and the look on her face told the world that she knew it was so.

Through it all Madeline appeared as the ghost of the person she had been. She moved mechanically, her emotions disengaged by necessity. It was the only way to get through this, the only way to survive Lord Farquharson's little visits to take afternoon tea with the Langley household, to bear his hand upon her arm, the touch of his lips to her fingers. It was the shell of Madeline Langley who allowed Lord Farquharson to lead her out on to dance floor after dance floor, to whisper promises of love into her ear, to take her up in his chaise around Hyde Park at the most fashionable of hours for all the world to see. The real Madeline Langley was curled up tight in a ball somewhere in the deep, dark recesses of that protection. So it was Madeline's shell, and not Madeline herself, who sat that night in Almack's.

It did not matter that they were in the famous assembly rooms. It did not matter that the night was chilled, or that the air within the dance rooms was stuffy and hot. It did not even matter when one of the ladies patronesses gave permission for Madeline to waltz with Lord Farquharson, or when his fingers lingered about her waist, or when he gazed with such promise into her face. Madeline saw nothing, heard nothing, felt nothing. And by being so, Madeline's shell could do what it had to do.

'Madeline, Mrs Barrington has promised me the recipe for a wonderful lotion that clarifies the skin and removes any blemish or shadow. It will do wonders for your complexion, my dear.'

Madeline sat, like she had done on every other occasion since learning of her betrothal to Lord Farquharson, and said nothing.

Colonel Barclay materialised as if from nowhere. 'My dear Mrs Langley, may I introduce a good friend of mine, Viscount Varington. He has been admiring you and your daughters from across the room for some time now. I have taken pity on the poor man and decided to put him out of his misery by bringing him here for a word from your sweet lips.'

The tall, dark and extremely handsome Lord Varington swooped down to press a kiss to Angelina's hand. 'Miss Langley,' he uttered in a sensuously deep voice. 'Such a pleasure to make your acquaintance, at last.' And delivered her a look of dangerous appreciation.

Angelina smiled and glanced up at him through down-cast lashes.

'I can see from where Miss Langley gets her golden beauty.' He touched his lips to Mrs Langley's hand.

Mrs Langley tittered. 'La, you flatter me too much, sir.'

'Not at all,' said Lord Varington, his pale blue eyes bold and appraising. 'Is it possible that Miss Langley is free for this next dance? A most improbable hope, but…'

Angelina scanned down her dance card, knowing full well that Mr Jamison's name was scrawled against the dance in question, and indeed that every successive dance had been claimed. Her eyes flickered up to the hard, handsome face waiting above them.

Lord Varington smiled in just the way that he knew to be most effective, showing his precisely chiselled features to perfection. He cast a smouldering gaze at Angelina.

Angelina opened her mouth to explain that she could not in truth dance with him.

But Mrs Langley was there first. 'How fortuitous your

timing is, my lord. It seems that Mr Jamison is unwell and is
unable to stand up with Angelina as he promised. She, therefore, is free to dance with you, my lord.'

'I can breathe again,' murmured Lord Varington dramatically, and took Angelina's hand into his with exaggerated
tenderness.

'Oh, my!' exclaimed Mrs Langley and fanned herself vig-
orously as Angelina disappeared off on to the floor in Lord
Varington's strong muscular arms.

It was only then that she noticed that Madeline was missing.

Lucien tucked Madeline's hand into the crook of his arm
and continued walking through Almack's marbled vestibule.

'My lord, what is wrong? The note the girl brought said
that you needed to speak with me urgently.' Madeline felt his
pale blue eyes pierce a crack in the shell that she had so carefully constructed.

'And so I do, Miss Langley, but not here.' He scanned the
entrance hall around them, indicating the few bodies passing
in chatter. 'It's too dangerous.'

'Dangerous?' Madeline's voice faltered, the crack growing
exponentially wider. 'I don't understand—'

Lord Tregellas stopped behind one of the large Ionic pillars
and gently pulled her closer. 'Miss Langley,' he interrupted,
'do you trust me?'

'Yes.' The shell shattered to smithereens. 'Of course I do.'
Logic deemed that she should not, instinct ensured that she did.

A strange expression flitted across his face and then was
gone. 'Then come with me.'

For the first time in two weeks Madeline felt her heart leap
free of the ice that encased it. Surely she had misheard him?
She looked into his eyes and what she saw there kicked her
pulse to a canter.

'Miss Langley.' His voice was rich and mellow. 'We do not have much time. If you wish to escape Farquharson, come with me.'

Come with me. It was the dream that she dare not allow herself to dream. Lord Tregellas had saved her before. Perhaps he could save her now. But even in the thinking Madeline knew it was impossible. No one could save her, not even Tregellas. Foolish hope would only lead to more heartache. Slowly she shook her head. 'I cannot.'

His hands rested on her upper arms. 'Do you desire to marry him?' His voice had a harsh edge to it.

'No!' she whispered. Now that her shell was broken she felt every breath of air, suffered the pain from which she had sought to hide. 'You know that I do not.'

His voice lost something of its harshness. 'Then why have you accepted him?'

She could not tell him. Not here, not like this, not when she knew that in three more weeks she would be Lord Farquharson's wife. 'It's a long story.'

'Too long for here?'

'Yes.' She felt the brush of his thumb against her bare skin between the puff of her sleeve and the start of her long gloves. It was warm and reassuring.

'There are other places,' he said.

Temptation beckoned. Lord Tregellas was more of a man than she ever could have dreamt of. She blushed to think that he could show her any interest…and that she actually welcomed it. Were she to be seen leaving Almack's in the company of the Wicked Earl, she would be ruined. Strangely, the prospect of her own ruination in that manner did not seem such a terrible atrocity. Life with Lord Farquharson seemed far worse. But what Lord Tregellas was suggesting would not only ruin her, but also her family and that was something she could not allow. She shook her head again. 'No.'

'I mean only to help you. You should know something of Lord Farquharson's history before you take your wedding vows. You said that you trusted me. Then give me half an hour of your time, nothing more, to let me tell you of Farquharson's past and of a way you may evade him.'

Madeline bit at her lip and remained unconvinced. It would be wrong of her to go with him. She had her family to think about.

It was as if the Earl read her mind. 'He's a danger not only to you, but to your sister and your parents, too. And you need not be concerned that our departure together shall be noticed. I assure you it will not.'

'My family are truly in danger?' His gaze held her transfixed. He was a stranger, a man reputed by all London to be wicked. She should not believe him. But inexplicably Madeline knew that she did.

'Yes.' He released his hold upon her, stepping back to increase the space between them. 'We're running out of time, Miss Langley. Do you come with me, or not?'

A sliver of tension stretched between them. Pale ice blue merged with warm amber. Madeline looked a moment longer. It seemed so right. Reputations could be wrong. There was nothing of Lord Farquharson in the man that faced her. Lord Tregellas would not hurt her. 'Half an hour?' she said.

'Half an hour,' he affirmed and reached his hand for hers.

The interior of the Tregellas closed carriage was dark, only the occasional street light illuminated the dimness.

Lucien could see the stark whiteness of Madeline Langley's face against the black backdrop. Huge eyes, darkly smudged beneath, and cheeks that were too thin. He doubted that the girl had slept or eaten since the announcement of her betrothal. Guilt stuck in his throat. He swallowed it down. He had done what he could to save Miss Langley. He need have no remorse. Or so he told himself. But telling and believing were two different things. 'It's not much further now.'

'We will be back in time, won't we?' She nibbled at her lip.

The knot of guilt expanded to a large tangle. 'Of course.'

She relaxed a little then, leaning back against the dark drapery in the corner. Her implicit trust stirred his heart.

'Miss Langley.' He ensured that his voice was without emotion. He could not tell her all of it, but he would tell her enough. The girl was not stupid. She would realise that he was right. 'Cyril Farquharson is not to be toyed with. He is evil, pure and unadulterated. What you have seen of his behaviour is nothing compared to that of which he is capable.' Lucien paused, tightening the rein on his self-control. 'He is a man that delights in plucking the most tender of blooms to crush beneath his heel.'

'What do you mean?' she whispered.

'Exactly that.'

'I don't understand. What did he do?'

Lucien slid another bolt across the barrier to the memories. 'He took a woman, a young and foolish woman, and...'

Madeline waited.

'...killed her.'

Only the sound of their breathing filled the carriage.

'*Killed* her?' He could hear the horror in Miss Langley's words. 'Who was she? Why did he not stand trial?'

Lucien turned his face to the window. 'It could not be proven.'

'Why not? If he was guilty—'

'He was most definitely guilty, but Farquharson was careful to destroy the evidence.' Lucien's jaw clamped shut.

There was a moment's silence before Madeline asked, 'And you think he means to...to kill me too?'

He looked back across at the fear-filled little face—fear that he had put there with his revelation. He hardened his compassion. She had to know. 'Oh, he will kill you all right, Miss Langley, and anyone who tries to stop him.'

'I cannot believe it,' she said in a small voice.

'Can't you? What do you feel when you stand close to him, when he touches you? What do you feel then, Madeline?'

She barely noticed the use of her given name. 'Fear... loathing... repulsion.'

'Then listen to your instinct, it speaks true.'

'But I am bound to marry him.' She sighed and recounted what had happened that night after Lord Tregellas had waltzed with her. 'I cannot dishonour my papa and there is Angelina to think of.'

'There is another way,' Lucien said softly, and leaned forward. 'Give me your hand, Miss Langley.'

Every sensible nerve in her body was telling her to resist. Madeline warily reached her hand towards him.

His fingers closed around hers. Her hand was small and slender and chilled. 'You're cold. Here, put this travelling rug around you.' Through the darkness he felt for her, moving across to the other side of the carriage, wrapping the woollen rug across her shoulders, running his hands briskly over the sides of her now-blanketed arms. 'The night air is chilled and you have no cloak.'

'Lord Tregellas.' Madeline's plea brought him up short.

He stopped. Dropped his hands from her arms. Stayed seated by her side. Rumble of carriage wheels. Horses' hooves. Bark of dogs. Men's voices cursing coarse and loud. Bang of doors. Lucien let them all pass, breathing in that small space of time, waiting to utter the words he had never thought would pass his lips. 'Miss Langley,' he said, 'there is one way that would most certainly prevent your marriage to Farquharson.'

'Yes?'

There was such hope in that one little word. The subtle scent of oranges drifted up from Madeline Langley's hair. Anticipation squeezed at Lucien's heart. *Fool!* he chastised himself. *Just ask her the damn question and be done with it.* 'Will you marry me?' He felt the start of the slim body beside him, felt more than saw the shock upon her face.

'You want me to be your wife?' Disbelief raised her voice to a mere squeak.

'Yes. It's by far the best solution to our problem.' He tried to convey that it was the logical answer for them both.

'Lord Farquharson is my problem alone, my lord, not yours. You have no need to marry me. Why should you even care what he does to me, let alone wish to sacrifice yourself on my behalf?'

'I have my reasons, Miss Langley. Suffice to say, it is in both our interests to stop him.' Sacrifice was a very strong word, and the wrong word. It did not describe at all what it was that Lucien Tregellas was doing.

'But marriage?'

Why should she find it so unbelievable? 'Think of it as a marriage of convenience, if you prefer,' he said, trying to make her feel easier.

'I cannot just marry you.'

'Why not?'

'My family, the scandal—'

'Would blow over. Your family will not suffer. I'll ensure that. I'm not without influence, Madeline.'

She seemed embarrassed at the sound of her Christian name upon his lips, and glanced down nervously at her lap. He remembered how innocent she was.

'Lord Farquharson would sue for breach of contract.'

'It's only money, a commodity of which I have plenty.'

A short silence, as if she was digesting his words. He heard her hands move against the blanket.

'Such an act would publicly humiliate Lord Farquharson. He would be obliged to demand satisfaction of his honour.'

'We both know that Farquharson has no honour.'

'Society does not. He would call you out.'

'So much the better.'

'But your life would be in danger. He might injure you, or worse!'

He smiled then, a chilling smile, a smile that held in it five years of waiting, five years of hatred. The light from a street lamp glanced across his stark angular features, casting a sinister darkness to his handsome looks. 'Have no fear of that. I promise you most solemnly that when I meet Farquharson across a field again I will kill him.'

Her breath expelled in one rush.

'Have you any more objections, Miss Langley?'

'It…it does not seem right, my lord.'

'I assure you that it would be the best for everyone, involved.'

'I-I'm a little shocked,' she stuttered.

'That is only to be expected,' he said. 'If you marry me, you would be well provided for, have anything you desire. I have no objection to you seeing your family as and when you please. You would be free to live your own life—within reason, of course. And, most importantly, you would be safe from Farquharson.'

'What do you wish from me in return, my lord?'

He blinked at that. What did he want? All his careful thinking had not made it that far. He had not expected her to ask such a thing. And then he understood what it was she was asking, or at least thought he did. 'Discretion,' he replied, trying to be tactful.

When she still did not understand, he elaborated. 'It would be a marriage in name only, Madeline. We would both go on just as before, nothing need change save your name and our living arrangements for a short while.'

She bowed her head. 'You seem to have considered everything, my lord.'

Another silence.

'Then you must choose, Madeline. Will you be my wife or Farquharson's?'

She touched the fingers of her right hand against her forehead, kneading the spot between her eyes.

He could sense her tension. The small body next to his was strung taut as a bow. 'Madeline,' he said softly, and captured her left hand into his. 'Your half-hour is fast expiring. Will you not give me your answer?'

She shivered. 'Yes, my lord,' she whispered, not daring to look round at his face. 'I will marry you.'

His fingers communicated a brief reassurance to hers and were gone. 'Thank you,' he said, then thumped the roof of the carriage with his cane and thrust his face out of the window, 'Home, please, Jackson.'

'But…but aren't we going back to Almack's? What of my mama—?'

'Speed is of the essence. I'll send a note to your mother explaining our decision.'

'I would prefer to tell her myself, my lord.'

The anxiety in her voice scraped at his conscience. 'I'm afraid that's not possible, Madeline. You'll see her soon enough when we're safely married. I'll explain all once we reach Cavendish Square.'

The carriage drove on in silence.

Chapter Five

Tregellas's townhouse in Cavendish Square was not a house at all, not in the sense that Madeline knew. Mansion was the word she would have used in its stead. It was a large imposing building set back in a fine garden. The hallway alone was bigger than the parlour and dining room put together in the Langleys' home. Floors beautifully laid with Italian marble, walls covered with exquisite neo-classical plasterwork—all nymphs and cherubs, wreaths and festoons—expensive oriental rugs, windows elaborately dressed with rich curtains, huge crystal chandeliers that shimmered in the light of a hundred candles. Madeline stared around her in awe.

'This way, Miss Langley.'

Lord Tregellas steered her down a passageway and into the most palatial, enormous drawing room she had ever seen. But it wasn't the luxurious décor or the expensive furniture that drew Madeline's eye. That was accomplished much more readily by the two gentlemen standing before the fireplace, one of whom she had just seen at Almack's Assembly Rooms, dancing with her sister: Viscount Varington and Colonel Barclay. Realisation dawned. She peered round at Lord Tregellas with great wide eyes. 'You used your friends to distract Mama and Angelina!'

'I did not think that Mrs Langley would welcome my direct approach.'

That was putting it mildly. Mama would have run squawking to Lord Farquharson as fast as her legs would carry her. Madeline's brow wrinkled. But what, then, were the gentlemen doing here?

The men stepped forward, the taller of the two electing to speak. 'Miss Langley, honoured to make your acquaintance at last.' When he looked into her face she saw that he had the same pale blue eyes as Lord Tregellas. 'I am Varington, and this is our good friend, Barclay.'

'Your servant, Miss Langley,' said the Colonel.

Then Madeline saw who was sitting quietly in the background. And the sight stilled the breath in her throat and brought a tremble to her legs. The elderly clergyman had dozed off in the comfort of the wing chair. The faint catch of a snore resonated in the silence of the room. 'Lord Tregellas!' Madeline swung round to find the Earl directly at her back. 'You cannot…I did not think…Tonight?'

'I took the liberty of procuring a special licence,' Lord Tregellas said.

A snuffling and then a yawn. 'Lord Tregellas, please do forgive me. Must have nodded off. One of the vices of old age, I'm afraid. And this…' he rummaged in his pocket, produced a pair of small round spectacles, and perched them on the end of his nose '…must be the bride.' He peered short-sightedly in Madeline's direction. 'Lovely girl.'

Madeline blinked back at him, wondering if the clergyman could see at all.

'Now…' the clergyman placed an ancient liver-spotted hand on her shoulder '…I should check that this handsome devil hasn't abducted you from beneath your mother's nose.' The clergyman chortled at the hilarity of his joke.

Viscount Varington smothered a cough and grinned at Tregellas.

Lord Tregellas showed not one sign of having heard anything untoward.

'As if Lucien would have any need to do such a thing! Known him since he was a boy, and his brother there, too.' The clergyman glanced across at the Viscount.

Madeline followed his gaze. So Lord Varington and Lord Tregellas were brothers. That explained the similarity in their looks.

'Knew their father, too, God rest his soul.' The clergyman patted her shoulder. 'Sterling fellows, all three. Why, I remember in the old days—'

Lord Tregellas cleared his throat. 'Reverend Dutton, Miss Langley is rather tired after her journey.'

'Of course. Know the feeling myself.' He peered in Lord Tregellas's direction. 'And you, sir, are no doubt impatient to make this lovely lady your wife. Now, where did I put it…?' The clergyman patted at his pockets and gave Madeline a rather confused look. 'Had it a minute ago.'

She felt Lord Tregellas step close against her back, looking over her head, impatience growing sharper by the minute. Her scalp prickled with the proximity of his large and very male body.

'Ah, here we are!' A battered old book was waved before them and the clergyman cleared his throat. 'Dearly beloved, ye have brought this child here to be baptised… Oops, wrong one,' mumbled Reverend Dutton. 'Getting ahead of myself there somewhat. You won't need that one for a little while yet.'

Madeline's face flamed.

Lord Tregellas stiffened behind her.

'Dearly beloved, we are gathered together here in the sight

of God, and in the face of these witnesses, to join together this man and this woman in holy matrimony.' He stopped and beamed at Madeline. 'Now we're getting somewhere.' Lord Tregellas moved round to stand at her right-hand side and the rest of the old clergyman's words passed as a blur. This was a binding ceremony in the eyes of both God and the law. By the end of it she would be Lord Tregellas's wife; his wife, no less. Not half an hour ago she had been sitting in Almack's, existing minute by minute, doomed by a promise to marry Lord Farquharson, empty save for despair. Now the threat of Cyril Farquharson was gone, removed in one fell swoop by the man standing by her side.

'Madeline.'

His voice invaded her thoughts, pulling her back to the present, to the reality of her situation.

'Madeline,' he said again.

She looked up into those stark eyes. Saw a tiny spark of anxiety in them. Knew he was waiting for her answer. He was a stranger, she had only spoken to him on three evenings, and this was one of them. And he was Earl Tregellas. *Tregellas,* for goodness' sake. The Wicked Earl! How did she even know that what he had told her about Lord Farquharson was true? What she was doing was madness. Absolute insanity. She should have been afraid, but she wasn't. Well, only a little, if truth be told. He had spoken of instincts and trusting them. Every instinct in Madeline's body told her that Lord Tregellas would not hurt her. He had saved her twice from Farquharson. Now he was prepared to give her his name to save her yet again. If she refused him, she knew full well what awaited her—Cyril Farquharson. Just the thought of that man conjured real fear.

His fingers touched to hers as if willing her to speak the words.

And she did.

More voices, more words, warmth of his hand on hers, touch of cold metal upon the third finger of her left hand. Then, with a brush of Lord Tregellas's lips against her cheek, it was done. There would be no going back. She had just become Earl Tregellas's wife, while all the while her mama sat unknowing, waiting for her in Almack's.

'Hell, I thought for a minute that she meant to refuse me in front of Reverend Dutton.' Only Tregellas and his brother remained. Colonel Barclay had volunteered to see the clergyman safely home, and the critical letter had been dispatched to Mrs Langley via Lucien's most trusted footman. Lucien filled two glasses, loosened his neckcloth, and sat down in the buttoned wing chair opposite his brother. Heavy burgundy-coloured curtains hung at the library window, blotting out the night beyond. The room was dark save for a single branch of candles upon the desk by the window and the flames that danced within the fireplace.

Guy helped himself to one of the glasses. 'What would you have done if she had? The best-laid plan would have crumbled beneath a simple refusal.'

Lucien's dark eyebrows angled dangerously. That would have necessitated the introduction of plan B.'

'Plan B?' echoed Guy intrigued.

The firelight exaggerated the clean angles and planes of Lucien's face and darkened his eyes. 'The one in which Miss Langley spends the night unchaperoned in the bachelor residence of Earl Tregellas. Come morning, without so much as touching her, I would have ensured that Miss Langley had no other choice but to marry me.'

'My God, that's wicked. Wicked but effective.'

Lucien shrugged and took a swig of brandy. 'Desperate

times call for desperate measures. It would have been in her best interest. And the Wicked Earl is, after all, expected to execute such things.' But the blunt words did not prevent the stab of guilt at the thought of his betraying Miss Langley's trust.

'Then old Dutton's reference to abducting Miss Langley from beneath her mama's nose was even more applicable than we thought,' laughed Guy.

'I did not abduct her,' said Lucien. 'She came most willingly once I had explained the situation.'

'And why not? I do not think there was much chance of her turning down your offer, Lucien. Half the women in London would give their right arm to become Lady Tregellas, no matter what they might say to the contrary. Little Miss Langley has done rather nicely out of your arrangement. Her mama could not have done half so well. Discarded a baron and came up with an earl.'

'Guy,' Lucien argued, 'it isn't like that.'

'Why did you marry her? Like you said, you could have just kept her here for the night. That alone would have been enough to make Farquharson discard her and call you out. Then Farquharson would have been dead, Miss Langley safe, and you in a position to choose a more suitable bride.'

'Miss Langley's reputation would have been ruined. For what that counts for in this town, she might as well be dead, as be carved up by the tabbies. What kind of man do you take me for?'

Guy rolled his eyes and gave a cynical sigh. 'To hear you speak, one might be pardoned for thinking they were talking to a bloody saint! Have you forgotten what you've spent the last five years doing, big brother? A one-man crusade to deliver vengeance on Farquharson.'

'That's irrelevant. I'm trying to protect her, not ruin her life.'

'Oh, come, Lucien. Face facts. This isn't really about the

girl at all. It's about appeasing your conscience and killing Farquharson.'

Lucien refilled their glasses. 'Have a care that you don't go too far, Guy,' he warned.

'Not far enough and not soon enough,' said Guy. 'Hell knows why I agreed to help you in the first place.'

'Then why did you?'

In one swig Guy downed the remainder of his brandy. 'Because you're my brother, and I'm a fool, and…like you, I would not see Farquharson do to Miss Langley what he did to Sarah.' He sighed. 'It's just that marriage seems rather drastic. If you think there's not going to be any repercussions over this, you're sadly mistaken, Lucien. When it comes to an heir, the Langleys aren't exactly the best of breeding stock.'

'You need not worry, Guy. I've told you already, as far as I'm concerned, you're my heir. This marriage doesn't alter that.'

Guy faced his brother with growing exasperation. 'Unless you mean to leave the marriage unconsummated, then I don't see how you can be so…' His eyes narrowed and focused harder on Lucien. 'That's exactly what you're planning, isn't it?'

Lucien tipped some more brandy down his throat. 'As you said, little brother, although I might not have chosen to put it quite so bluntly, this marriage satisfies my need to protect an innocent woman and lure Farquharson to a duel, nothing else. I'll see that Miss Langley is safe and has everything that she wants. But that's as far as it goes. Our lives will resume as normal.' He raked a hand through his ebony ruffle of hair. 'All aspects of it.'

'I think you may have underestimated the effects of married life.' Guy replaced his empty glass upon the drum table.

'And I think we'd better ready ourselves for a visit from Farquharson and Mr Langley.'

Guy waited until his brother reached the door before saying, 'By the way, if Farquharson finds out that you haven't bedded the girl, he'll push to have the marriage annulled.'

'Then we had better convince him otherwise,' came the reply. But as Lucien closed the library door quietly behind him, unease stroked between his shoulder blades and the faint echo of oranges teased beneath his nose.

He took the stairs two at a time and knocked at the door that led to the Countess's rooms. 'Madeline,' he said through the wooden structure, wondering as to the woman whom he had delivered here to this same door not twenty minutes since. He had warned her that Farquharson would come. It was not a matter of if, rather when. He remembered how pale she had looked and the slight tremor in her small cold hand as it lay in his. His grandmother had been a small woman, but her ring had swamped Madeline's slender finger. He reminded himself for the umpteenth time that he had done what he had to to help the girl, to save her from Farquharson, but that didn't stop him from feeling a brute.

She feared Farquharson…and trusted a man who had practically kidnapped her from an evening's dancing. Why else would she have agreed to marry him? Guilt tapped harder at his heart. She trusted him, little knowing that he had sealed her fate from the moment she had climbed into his carriage. 'Hell,' he cursed through gritted teeth. It wasn't supposed to feel like this. The guilt was supposed to get better, not worse. He wondered what would have happened had he been forced to resort to plan B. Thank God it had not come to that. Madeline need never even know of its existence. At least this way she would feel that the choice had been hers. 'Madeline,' he said a bit louder and slowly opened the door that led to his wife's bedchamber.

The room was empty; well lit, warm, luxurious, but empty. The only signs that Madeline had even been there were the slight crinkling of the bedcover as if she'd sat on top of it, and that faint familiar scent. Something rippled down Lucien's spine. 'Madeline,' he said louder still, moving swiftly to the small dressing room and bathroom that led off from the main bedchamber. But Madeline wasn't there either. 'Madeline!' It was almost a shout. Where the hell was she? Didn't she know that Farquharson was out there, coming for them? He felt the pulse throb in his neck.

It was a long time since Lucien had felt fear, but it was fear for Madeline that was now pulsing the blood through his veins with all the force of Thor's hammer. He reacted instantly, backing out of the room, moving smoothly, steadily towards the staircase. Adrenalin flooded through his muscles, lengthening his stride, tightening his jaw. The candle flames in the wall sconces billowed in the draught created by his progress, casting the long dark shadow of a man against the wall. He had almost reached the top of the stairs when he saw her treading up them.

'Madeline.' Her name snapped from his lips. His stride didn't even falter, just continued right on up to her with the same determined speed. His arms closed around her, pulling her up against him, reassuring himself that it was really her, that she was safe. His lips touched to the sleek smoothness of her hair, his cheek grazing against the top of her head that reached just below his chin. The scent of oranges, so light, so clean, engulfed his nostrils. She was soft and malleable beneath his hands, warm and feminine. 'Madeline.' In that word was anger and relief in dual measure. 'Where have you been?' He knew that his voice was unnecessarily harsh. Her face raised to look up into his. Those amber eyes were dark and soulful, as if she was hurt, as if something had been shattered. All the anger drained away, to be replaced with relief. He made no effort to release his hands from her back. 'Where were you?' His eyes scanned her face, taking in the tension around her mouth and the pallor of her cheeks.

'I was looking for you,' she said in a quiet steady voice. 'I wanted to ask you about when Lord Farquharson comes.' Then she turned her gaze away. 'I went to the drawing room, I thought you would be there.'

Lord, he was a fool. The girl had been through the mill. He supposed that this evening had not exactly been the wedding of which most women dreamed of. And Madeline was as likely to have had her dreams as any. It had been a long night and it wasn't over yet. The worst was still to come. Farquharson would come before the night was over. Of that he could be sure. Without thinking he pulled her against him and dropped a kiss to the top of her head. 'I was in the library with Guy, and I was coming to find you to discuss the same thing.' He found he was strangely reluctant to disengage himself from her. He did so anyway, taking her hand in his. 'Come,' he said, leading her slowly back the way he had walked. 'You should rest while you can. And what I have to say is rather delicate and requires some privacy. Your bedchamber is probably the best place.' The irony of his last sentence struck him. She made no resistance, just followed where he would lead, but something had changed, he could see it in her eyes. He just didn't know what.

Madeline perched at the edge of the pretty green striped armchair, beside the fire.

Lucien leaned against the mantelshelf above the fireplace, his foot resting against the white marble slabs.

She watched the warm glow of firelight illuminate his face. Such classically handsome features that could have come straight from one of the statues of Apollo displayed in the antiquities rooms of the British Museum, except she had always envisaged Apollo as golden and this man's colouring was as stark as a raven's wing against snow. Ebony hair, darkly shaped eyebrows and eyes of a blue so pale as to draw the attention of any woman who breathed. She could see why women still cast desirous looks in his direction despite the blackness of his reputation. Just to look at him caused a flutter in her stomach. Madeline stilled the flutter with a heavy hand. She did not know what the emotion was that caused the ache in her breast, just knew that it was there, raw and sore, since she'd overheard his words through the library door, since she knew that he had been untruthful.

Trust. So foolishly given, against all sense of reason, against all that society whispered him to be. She had deemed her own judgement better. And she had been proven wrong. His voice calling her name had been so filled with alarm and anger that she'd been sure that he knew of her eavesdropping. Not that she'd intended to do any such thing. She *had* been looking for him. That much was true. But it hadn't been the drawing room to which she'd been directed by the young footman. Her knuckles had been poised to knock when she'd heard his voice, and that of Lord Varington. Despite knowing that it was against every shred of decency to listen, that was exactly what she had done. Now she would suffer the hurt of learning the truth. She waited for what he had to say.

'Madeline.' He sighed and raked his fingers through the ruffle of his hair, with the merest hint of agitation. 'Farquharson will come tonight, hoping to forestall the marriage ceremony and…and subsequent events.'

She barely heard his words, rerunning the memory of his hands pulling her to him, the feel of his mouth against her hair, almost as if he cared for her. But Madeline knew otherwise. His voice had held relief. Why? The lie had slipped from her tongue; drawing room was so much easier to say than library. Lucien Tregellas did not need to know what she had heard.

'The marriage certificate will prove him too late.'

'Yes, my lord.'

'There is also the matter of the...' He paused and rephrased what he had been about to say. 'It is important that we do not leave him any loopholes to exploit.' He looked at her expectantly.

Madeline felt his gaze upon her. 'No, my lord.'

'You need not call me that, Madeline. You're my wife now. My name is Lucien.'

'Lucien,' she whispered into the silence of the room. The name sounded too intimate upon her lips.

Lucien rubbed his fingers against the strong angles of his jawline. 'As it stands there is such a loophole for Farquharson to find.'

Whatever was he talking of? She was married to him. He had said that would be enough to save her from the fiend. Had he lied about that too? 'What loophole?'

'There are certain expectations following a wedding.'

'My lord?'

'Lucien,' he corrected.

'Lucien, then,' she said. 'I don't understand. You said that marriage to you would protect me from Lord Farquharson. Now you're saying that it does not.'

He pulled the matching chair out from the side of the fireplace and dragged it so that it sat before her. Then he perched his large frame on its dainty green cushion and leaned forward to take both her hands within his. 'No, Madeline. What I'm saying is...' his thumbs caressed her fingers as if seeking to apply a balm to his words '...if it is discovered that the marriage has not been consummated, then it is possible for an annulment to be sought. It is not an easy process, but Farquharson may use anything that is available to him.'

Madeline stiffened and felt the blood warm in her cheeks. 'But you said that you did not wish to…that it was not necessary.' Her pulse picked up its rate. The butterflies stirred again in her stomach.

'No, no,' he said quickly, his thumbs sliding in fast furious strokes. 'You're quite safe.'

Was she? Beneath that sensuous stroking Madeline was starting to feel quite unlike herself. She became acutely aware of just how close his body was to hers, of the warmth that it generated, much hotter than any fire could ever be. The scent of his cologne surrounded her, causing an unexpected tightening in her breasts.

'We need only pretend.' One hand loosed to touch a finger gently to her chin. 'Don't look so afraid. I did not mean to frighten you.'

'I'm not afraid,' she said, and knew that she lied. But it was not Lucien Tregellas that frightened her, but the strength of the feelings that he ignited in her, feelings that the very righteous Madeline Langley had no right to feel. And then she remembered that she wasn't even Madeline Langley any longer, but someone else altogether.

A loud thumping set up below. Someone was at the front door, someone intent on kicking it in by the sound of things.

'Quickly!' Lucien pulled her over to stand by the bed and peeled off his coat with a speed surprising for such a tight-fitting garment. The coat was thrown to the floor, closely followed by his waistcoat and neckcloth. 'Take out your hairpins and remove your dress.'

'My dress?' Madeline gasped.

'Make haste, Madeline,' he said and began to tug his

shirt out of his breeches. 'We must make it look as if we have lain together.'

'Oh, my!' Madeline's face blushed scarlet as she swiftly averted her eyes and made to follow his instructions. Pins scattered all over the bedchamber rug beneath their feet and soon her hair was long and flowing. Her heart thumped as loud as the banging at the door. She struggled to loosen the tapes at the back of her dress, but her fingers were shaking so badly that they fumbled uselessly. 'Lucien,' she breathed in panic, 'I cannot—'

In one fluid motion her new husband ripped the dress open; the remainder of the tapes dangled torn and useless. His fingers brushed against her petticoats and shift, burning a path across the skin exposed above them. Madeline almost gasped aloud at the ensuing shimmer, but Lucien gave no sign of having been similarly affected. Together they stripped what remained of the dress from her. She stepped out of it, leaving it in a pile upon the floor.

'Your petticoats and stays, too.' His gaze dropped lower, 'Slippers and stockings as well,' he instructed.

Madeline did as she was bid, until she faced him wearing only her shift. As she clutched her arms across her front in embarrassment, she felt his fingers run through her hair, rubbing and raking, until neat tidiness was no more. She thought she heard him stifle a groan. Maybe he was worried that Farquharson wouldn't be convinced. And then quite suddenly he stopped and stood back, scanning her appearance.

'Very good,' he said rather hoarsely, then touched his hand to her shoulders. 'Rumple the bedcovers as if we have lain there. I'll have Sibton bring you my dressing gown. Put it on over your shift and then wait here until I send for you. All you need do is agree with everything that I say and do not offer any other information. I will deal with all else.'

She nodded her agreement. No matter that he had misled her, she would rather marry Beelzebub himself than Cyril Farquharson.

'All will be well, Madeline.' His fingers slid against her face. 'I'll see Farquharson in hell before I let him touch you.'

Then he was gone, leaving only the trace of his cologne and the scald of his fingerprints against Madeline's cheek.

Madeline sat on the edge of the bed, tense and alone, Lucien's dressing gown wrapped around her. She had rolled the sleeves up as best she could, but still the blue-and-red paisley-patterned silk swamped her, making her feel like a little girl dressing up. She touched the sleeve against her nose, breathed in the clean smell of him, and somehow felt reassured. The strains of Lord Farquharson's voice reached even here. Righteous indignation layered over malice and rage. And still he ranted on. The clock marked the pace of time, second by second, minute by minute. Lucien would send for her soon.

Gingerly she touched her fingers to where his had lingered, wondering that she could react to him in such a way. Her blood surged too strong, too fast. She closed her eyes, letting the sensation flood over her, trying to understand the nature of it. Her body was taut, but not through fear, primed as if readied, waiting, wanting. Wanting!

Madeline's eyes flickered open with a start. Guilt washed a rosy hue across her cheeks. She buried the feelings back down where they belonged, deep in place from where they should never find release. Her heart was beating so loud she barely heard the discreet knock at the door. Thud. Thud. Thud. Her heart galloped. Her cheeks burned hotter.

'My lady.' The hushed voice sounded through the wood.

Madeline jerked back to reality. She rose from the bed, painfully aware of just what it was she was being summoned to do. Persuade Lord Farquharson that she had already lain with her husband, while all the while knowing the irony of the truth. Lucien did not want a wife. Most certainly he did not want to consummate his marriage. A mutually convenient agreement, he had said. Lucien would protect her; she did not doubt that for a minute. He would give her his name, let her live in his house, see that she did not want for money or anything that it might buy. She would be his Countess. She would be safe from Farquharson. It should have been everything that Madeline could want. So why did she have this feeling of loss and longing? There was no time to speculate. Drawing deep on her breath and her courage, she opened the bedchamber door and went to face what waited below.

Chapter Six

Anger resonated from Farquharson. His grey eyes darkened and there was a slight snarl about his lips. The waves of his deep red hair had been arranged to perfection. A slight shimmer of perspiration beaded above his lip. 'I tell you, sir, he's lying. Madeline is a gently reared woman. Do you honestly believe that she would abandon her mother and sister midway through an evening at Almack's to elope with this…this scoundrel?'

'I must confess, Lord Farquharson, that such an action seems most out of character for Madeline,' said Mr Langley wringing his hands. He turned to the tall dark-haired man standing by the drawing-room fireplace. 'You have shown us the marriage certificate, my lord, which does indeed appear to prove that you are now legally married to my daughter, but how do we know that Madeline consented to wed you? She is…she was betrothed to Lord Farquharson. To my knowledge she is not even acquainted with you.'

'Then your knowledge is wrong, sir,' said Lucien succinctly. He had no argument with Arthur Langley. The man was only doing what he thought right to protect his daughter.

Lucien wondered that Langley ever could have agreed to marry Madeline to that snake in the first place. But then again, Langley wouldn't have stood a chance against Farquharson.

'He bloody well abducted her!' snarled Farquharson. 'Everyone knows of his reputation. He's downright evil.'

'Lord Farquharson,' said Mr Langley, 'I understand your distress, but rest assured that it does not measure in comparison with the extent of mine. We are all gentlemen here, I hope, and as such we should try to keep our language accordingly.'

'Please excuse my slip, Mr Langley,' said Farquharson from between stiffened lips.

Lucien looked at Arthur Langley. 'The matter is easily enough resolved, sir. Call back tomorrow and speak with Madeline yourself. She will soon set your mind at ease.'

'No!' Farquharson moved to stand between the seated figure of Mr Langley and the tall, broad frame of Tregellas. 'He seeks to buy time in which to consummate the marriage. Let him bring her out to face us now, before he has had time to intimidate her. By tomorrow the poor child will be so distraught she won't know what she's saying.'

'Madeline is resting. It would be unfair to subject her to such scrutiny.' Lucien's teeth gritted with the rage that roared within him. That Farquharson had the audacity to accuse anyone else of the heinous crimes for which he himself was responsible!

Farquharson turned to plead his case with Mr Langley, dropping his voice to a more controlled volume. 'Please, Mr Langley, I beg of you,' he wheedled. 'Do not subject Madeline to rape at this man's hands. Look at his state of undress. He was readying himself for the task.' He stared down into the older man's eyes that were heavy with fatigue and worry.

'We've arrived in the nick of time,' he said convincingly. 'There's still time. Demand that he bring her out now. If she was party to this crime, as he claims, then why is he disinclined to do so?'

'Lord Farquharson has a point,' said Arthur Langley slowly. 'I find myself unwilling to accept your word alone, sir. I cannot rest contented without seeing my daughter. Let me hear the words from her own lips and only then will I believe it.' His skin was washed an unhealthy grey and the skin beneath his eyes hung in heavy pouches.

Lucien rang the bell, whispered a word in the suddenly appeared butler's ear, and straightened. 'As you wish, Mr Langley.'

Farquharson glanced at Mr Langley's profile, then glared across the room at Lucien. 'If you've so much as harmed one hair on my betrothed's head…'

Ice-blue eyes locked with smoky grey. 'Madeline's my wife now, Farquharson.'

The tension in the room magnified one hundredfold. The challenge in Lucien's voice was as blatant as a slap on the face.

Arthur Langley stared from one man to the other.

A soft tapping sounded and the door swung open to reveal Madeline.

Lucien's heart turned over at the sight of her: small and slender, his dressing gown covering from her shoulders to her toes and beyond. Eyes the colour of warm aged honey sparkled in the candlelight and lips parted in expectation. Her dark blonde hair was mussed and beddy, its long tresses sweeping sensuously down to her waist. From the hint of a blush that sat across her cheeks to the little bare toes that peeped from beneath the edge of his robe, Madeline had the look of a woman who had just been loved. Lucien found the words emptied from his head, every last rehearsed phrase fled. He stared at her as if seeing her for the first time, wondering that this woman could be his wife.

'Lucien,' she said softly and moved to stand by his side.

'Good God!' Mr Langley uttered weakly.

Farquharson stared, eyes bulging, panting like an enraged bull.

'You see, Lord Farquharson,' said Lucien, 'Madeline is my wife in every sense of the word, and completely by her own volition.'

The drop of a pin would have shattered against the silence that followed his words.

'Madeline?' Mr Langley staggered to his feet. 'Is what he says true? Did you willingly elope with Lord Tregellas?' The brown eyes widened, scanning every inch of his daughter's face.

'Yes, Papa,' she said in a quiet voice. 'I'm sorry. I did not mean to hurt you, or Mama, or Angelina.'

Farquharson's lips curled to reveal his small white teeth. 'He is forcing her to this. The poor child is scared for her life!'

'I assure you that is not the case. Madeline has nothing to fear from *me.*' The emphasis on Lucien's last word did not go unnoticed.

Mr Langley slowly shook his head, his eyes crinkling into closure, his shoulders rounding as if the burden upon them had suddenly become too much to bear. 'Madeline, how could you? I thought that I knew my own daughter, but it seems that I'm wrong.'

'No, Papa…' Madeline made a brief move towards her father, only to find Lucien's hand upon her arm.

Farquharson saw his chance. 'See how he controls her! He's trying to trick us!'

Mr Langley's eyes slowly opened.

'There has been insufficient time for him to have wedded

and bedded her!' Farquharson said crudely. 'For all of the rumours, Tregellas is only a man, like any other. He would have to be superhuman to have had her in that time!'

'Lord Farquharson, must you be so blunt?' complained Mr Langley, but there was a light of revived hope in his eyes.

'Madeline, my dove, you must tell us the truth,' said Farquharson, edging closer towards Madeline. 'We will not be angry with you.' His eyes opened wide in an encouraging manner.

Lucien stepped forward, forming a barrier between Madeline and the two men. 'Are you calling me a liar?' he asked in a quiet voice that could not hide the threat beneath.

Farquharson's eyes narrowed, exaggerating the fox-like character of his features. His mouth opened to speak—

'Lucien speaks the truth.' Madeline shifted to stand by her husband's side before Lucien knew what she planned. He felt her small hand slip into his. 'I married him because I love him. And for that same reason I lay with him in the bed upstairs. He is my husband in truth; that fact cannot be undone, for all that both of you would wish it.'

Lucien's heart swelled. He felt the faint tremble of her hand and knew what it cost her to say those words. His fingers squeezed gently against hers, his gaze dropping to the courageous stance of her slight frame.

'I'm sorry, Papa. I hope that you may come to forgive me.'

Farquharson's fury would be leashed no longer. 'And what of me, Madeline? Where are your pretty words of apology for me?' His anger exploded across the room. 'Or don't I count? Doesn't it matter that you have just publicly humiliated me?'

'Lord Farquharson, please!' Mr Langley exclaimed.

'I gave you my heart, Madeline, and this is how you repay me. It would have been kinder to decline me at the start.'

'I tried to tell—'

But Farquharson was in full rant. 'But no. You encouraged me, led me to believe that you would welcome my addresses. And now you run to Tregellas because you think to catch yourself an earl rather than an honest humble baron. There's a name for women like you!'

'Farquharson!' The word was little more than a growl from Lucien's mouth. 'Don't dare speak to my wife in—'

Farquharson continued unabated. 'He only wants you because you were mine. He's an evil, jealous, conniving bastard, and believe me when I say that—'

Lucien struck like a viper, his fist contacting Farquharson square on the chin.

Farquharson staggered back, reeling from the shock, his hand clutching at his jaw.

'Now get the hell out of my house,' said Lucien.

Farquharson drew his hand away and looked at the blood that speckled his fingers. 'Don't think you'll get away with this, Tregellas. You've gone too far this time.'

'Impugned your honour?' suggested Lucien. 'What do you mean to do about it?'

Mr Langley inhaled loudly.

Madeline's face paled.

'You'll find out soon enough, Tregellas,' said Cyril Farquharson, making his way towards the door. 'And as for you, my sweet…' his gaze lingered over Madeline '…you had better start praying. He's not named the Wicked Earl for nothing. You'll rue the day you cast me over for him.' Farquharson peered round at Arthur Langley. 'Come along, Mr Langley,' he instructed. 'There is nothing more than can be done this night.'

Mr Langley cast one last glance at his daughter and then followed. The last Madeline saw of her father was his face, pale and haggard and filled with hurt. The door banged and Mr Langley and Lord Farquharson were gone.

* * *

Lucien stood alone at the library window, the heavy burgundy curtains closed around his back. From the room behind came three chimes of the clock. The night sky was a clear inky blue; a waxing moon hung high amidst a smattering of tiny stars. The orangey-yellow glow of the street lamps showed the road to be empty aside from the sparkling coating of frost. Across the square the houses sat serene and dark, not even a chink of light escaping their windows. It seemed that all of London was asleep, all curled in their beds. The hectic humdrum of life had ceased—for now. Somewhere in the distance a dog howled; it was a lonely eerie sound that resonated all the way through to Lucien's bones. It struck a chord. Lucien knew what it was to be lonely.

His thoughts shifted to the woman that lay upstairs: Lady Tregellas, his wife. It had been Madeline who had saved the evening, Madeline who had convinced Farquharson and her father that the marriage was real. He heard again her words, *I married him because I love him.* Such a quiet voice, but so strong in conviction that he had almost believed her himself. God only knew how much he wished it could be true. That any woman could love the man he had become: the man from whom God-fearing women fled, the man whose name was used to frighten naughty children into doing what they were told. It was something he would not ask of Madeline. He had promised her safety and that is exactly what he would give. The bargain they had agreed did not include anything else.

A marriage to ease the terrible guilt that had gnawed day and night at his soul these past five years. A marriage to bring Farquharson to his knees once and for all. That was all he wanted. The memory of Madeline's small soft hand slipping into his, the sweet smell that surrounded her, the feel of that long silky hair beneath his fingers. Lucien shut his eyes against it. Such thoughts were not allowed. He could not. He would not. She deserved better than that. He parted the curtains to move back into the library, refilled his brandy glass, sat down in his favourite wing chair, and waited for the rest of the night to pass.

Madeline lay in the great four-poster bed in the bedchamber of the wife of Earl Tregellas. She had tossed and turned and sighed, and still sleep would not come. Wife. The word refused to enter her brain. Legally she was Lucien's wife. In the eyes of God and the Church she was his wife. But she didn't feel it. She still felt like plain Miss Madeline Langley, the same as she was yesterday and the day before, and the day before that. It was only the world around her that had changed. The threat of Farquharson had vanished. Mama, Papa and Angelina were fast asleep on the other side of town. Her own bed in the little bedchamber in Climington Street was empty while she lay here alone.

Her eyes travelled again to the mahogany door in the wall that separated her bedchamber from Lucien's. Was he asleep? Did the fact that he was now married mean anything to him? Anything other than a means to bait Farquharson, and protect herself? She wondered why her safety and Farquharson's demise meant so much to him, enough to marry a woman far beneath him, who was so plain as to have been unable to engage a single gentleman's attention, save for Cyril Farquharson. But then again, Lucien barely knew her enough to stand up for a dance, let alone care if she suffered under Farquharson's hands. And she barely knew him.

He had called Farquharson a murderer and said that her own life was at risk, so much so that he had been prepared to hold her hostage overnight to ensure her agreement to a marriage he promised would protect her. He had underestimated her loathing of Lord Farquharson if he thought that necessary. Madeline had the feeling that she had stepped inside something very dark where there were no answers to her questions. Maybe the answers lay with the woman that Farquharson had killed, if, indeed, Lucien had been telling the truth.

Madeline shivered. She thought of those ice-blue eyes and the cold handsome perfection of his looks. Thought, too, of the heat of his touch and the warmth in his voice. And of how his relief had washed over her as he wrapped her in his arms out in the hallway, and the gratitude in his eyes when he faced her after Farquharson and her papa had gone. No, Madeline thought, she had not escaped unchanged at all. Lucien Tregellas had awakened something deep within her. And that something was not part of their arrangement. A marriage of convenience, he had called it. A marriage to suit them both. Better this a thousand times over than facing Farquharson. It was the escape of which she could only have dreamt. She should have been basking in cosy contentment. But she wasn't. When she finally found sleep, it was with the thought of the strong dark man who had made himself her husband.

The following morning Madeline and Lucien sat at opposite sides of the round breakfast table in the morning room. Sunshine flooded in through the windows, lighting the room with a clear pale clarity. The smells of eggs and ham, chops and warm bread rolls pervaded the air. Lucien poured a strong brown liquid into her cup, added a dash of cream, and soon the aroma of coffee was all that filled Madeline's nostrils.

'Did you sleep well?' The answer was plain to see in her wan cheeks and the dark circles below her eyes, but he asked the question anyway.

Madeline nodded politely. 'Yes, thank you. And you?'

'Very well, thank you,' he lied.

An awkward little silence followed.

'Would you care for some eggs, or a chop, perhaps?'

'No, thank you. The coffee will suffice.' She gave a small half-smile and looked around the room, unsure of what to say next.

Lucien helped himself to some ham and rolls. 'I was thinking,' he said.

Madeline's eyes wandered back to him.

'Perhaps it would be better if we went away for a short while. It would let the worst of the gossip die down and allow your parents to grow accustomed to the idea of our marriage.'

'Go away where?' she asked.

Steam rose from Lucien's coffee cup. 'I have an estate in Cornwall. The house is close to Bodmin Moor and not so very far from the coast. There is not much shopping, but you could have a mantua maker take your measurements before we leave and have whatever you wish sent down from London.' Lucien paused, trying to think of something else with which to make Cornwall sound enticing to a woman. 'There is also the latest fashion for sea bathing in which you might care to indulge, and a very pretty beach at Whitesand Bay.' He omitted to mention the positively arctic temperature of the sea at this time of year.

Shopping? Sea bathing? Madeline tried to look pleased. 'It sounds very nice.'

Lucien continued, 'There are frequent house parties in the locality and assembly rooms in the town of Bodmin some few miles away.' Fourteen miles to be precise, but he did not want to put Madeline off.

'For how long would we be away?' She sipped at her coffee, cradling the cup between her hands as if it were some small delicate bird.

Lucien gave a casual shrug of his shoulders. 'A few weeks,' he said nonchalantly.

'Very well.' She smiled nervously. 'I have nothing to take with me save the clothes I am wearing.' She smoothed her hand a little self-consciously over the skirt of the evening dress she had been wearing at Almack's last night; the dress in which he had married her.

Then he remembered what had happened to the tapes in his haste to remove that same dress. Something inside him tightened. Surreptitiously his eyes travelled to her neckline and sleeves. Nothing seemed to be amiss. He wondered if he ought to make an excuse to view the back of her, and thought better of it. 'That can soon be remedied. Buy anything that you like, as much as you want, whatever the cost. Two days should suffice to make your purchases. We'll leave the day after.'

'I was not…I didn't mean that you should…' A delicate pink washed her cheeks.

A slight frown marred Lucien's brow. 'Then you do not wish to go?'

'Yes,' she said looking at him a little embarrassed. 'I want to go to Cornwall. It's just that…my requirements are not what you seem to think. I would like—'

'More days to shop?'

'Oh, no.' Heaven forbid.

'Then what?'

She bit at her bottom lip. 'Nothing.'

Nothing? He looked at her expectantly.

'I had better go and get ready. Such a long day ahead.' She flashed a brief smile and escaped out of the morning room in a flurry of steps.

It was only when she had gone that it dawned on Lucien

that Madeline was as ready as she would ever be, for she didn't even have a pelisse or a bonnet in which to dress before facing the world.

Madeline sat across from the maid and the footman in the Tregellas carriage on the way back from a truly horrendous day's shopping. It seemed that either Mama or Lord Farquharson had lost no time in ensuring that all of London had been apprised of the fact that she had eloped with Earl Tregellas. No one else had known and the notice of their marriage would not be published in *The Times* until tomorrow. Not that anyone had actually said anything directly to her face. Indeed, most people did not know who she was. But even so there were several speculative glances, a few hushed whispers and one episode of finger pointing. Mrs Griffiths in Little Ryder Street, studiously polite, gave no hint of knowing that her customer was at the centre of the latest scandal sweeping the city and furnished her with the bulk of her clothing requirements very happily. Brief visits to the perfumery in St James's Street and Mr Fox's in King Street went in much the same way. Only when in Mr Rowtcliff's, the shoemaker, did she actually hear anything that was being said. Two robustly large ladies were deep in conversation as she arrived.

'Abducted a girl clean from beneath her mother's nose,' said the shorter and ruddier of the two.

'And forced her to a wedding,' nodded the other. 'He has a soul as black as Lucifer's, that one.'

The smaller woman screwed up her face. 'Who *is* she? Does anyone know yet?'

'Oh, yes,' replied her friend. 'Plain little thing by the name of Miss Langley. That is, Miss Langley the elder. Got a pretty sister by all accounts. Heaven knows why he didn't take her instead. Not quite the thing, the Langleys. House in Climington Street.'

The women exchanged a knowing look before continuing on their way, none the wiser that Madeline Langley had just witnessed every word that passed their lips.

Mr Rowtcliff and his assistant Mrs Phipps hurried back through, each with an armful of shoes and boots. 'Of course, my lady, once we make your own shoes up they will fit like a glove. These are just some that we have that may pass in the meantime.'

Madeline bit down hard on her lip, pushed the women's cruel words from her mind and chose some footwear as quickly as she could.

The clock struck three and still Cyril Farquharson had not roused himself from his bed. It was not that he was sleeping. Indeed, he had not slept at all since returning home from Tregellas's townhouse last night. Anger had ensured that. The boiling of his blood had diminished to a simmer. At least now he could think beyond the desire to grind Tregellas's face into the dirt. The Earl had outwitted him, snatching the girl to an elopement before Farquharson had realised his intent. And Farquharson's best-laid plans lay in ruins. Madeline Langley would not be his. Her tender innocent flesh belonged to Tregellas now.

He had dismissed his initial instinct to call Tregellas out and kill him. Farquharson was no fool. Tregellas was bigger, stronger, his aim truer, his shot straighter. In a one-on-one confrontation, Tregellas would always win, just as he had won their duel five years ago. Farquharson's leg still carried the scars to prove it. But one victory did not win the war. There were better means to that, underhand means that involved stealth and bribery and corruption. Farquharson had ever relied on others' stupidity and greed.

Stealing Farquharson's betrothed from beneath her mama's nose at Almack's was a stroke of genius. Even through his anger, Farquharson had to admire Tregellas's move. It was an action worthy of Farquharson himself. And it sent a message loud and clear. Farquharson knew what this was about. Hadn't he always known? A mirror of past events. Farquharson smiled. No, he would not call Tregellas out. There were easier ways to catch the Earl. He thought of Madeline Langley and the way that her hand trembled beneath his. He thought too of the fear in her pretty amber eyes and how she struggled within his grip. He wanted her and he would have her, and the fact she was Tregellas's wife would serve to make the experience all the sweeter. After five long years, the game had begun in earnest once more.

The journey to Earl Tregellas's country seat in Cornwall was long and tiresome. It did not matter that Lucien's travelling coach was of the most modern design, sprung for comfort and speed. Or that the man himself had filled it with travelling rugs and hot stone footwarmers to keep her warm. Madeline's bones ached with a deep-set weariness, not helped by the fact she had not slept properly for the past few nights. Every night was the same. Nightmares in which Cyril Farquharson's face leered down at her, whispering that he was coming to catch her, promising that there would be no escape. She woke in a cold sweat, terror gnawing at her gut, afraid to let her eyes close lest Farquharson really did make true on those nightmarish oaths.

Lucien sat opposite her, long legs stretched out before him, looking every inch as if he was sitting back in the comfort of an armchair. The bright daylight shining in through the window showed him in clarity. The stark blue eyes were hooded with long black lashes, the harshness of his handsome features relaxed in sleep. Gentle even breaths sounded from his slightly parted lips. Madeline's gaze lingered on that finely sculpted mouth. All signs of tension around it had vanished. No tightly reined control remained. Just hard chiselled lips. She wondered what it would be like to place a kiss upon them. Madeline licked her own suddenly dry lips, gulped back such profoundly unsuitable thoughts and concentrated on looking out of the window. The countryside surrounding the Andover Road swept by in a haze of green and brown. The daylight was white and cold. Madeline found her eyes wandering back to Lucien once more.

His skin was a pale contrast to the darkness of his angular-shaped eyebrows and the black dishevelment of his hair. Sleep stole the severity from Lucien's face, imposing on it a calm serenity, as if it was only in sleep that he found peace. The fine lines around his eyes and mouth seemed to disappear. Indeed, the more that Madeline looked, the more she found she could not drag her eyes away. Her fingers itched to touch against that blue-stubbled jawline, that bold strong nose, those lips. Although the air within the carriage was cool, Madeline began to feel rather warm. She stared and stared some more. She was just considering the length of his legs and how muscular his thighs were through those rather tight pantaloons when she noticed that Lucien's eyes were no longer closed. Indeed, he was regarding her with something akin to amusement.

Her eyes raised to meet that lazy stare.

He smiled, and it seemed that something of sleep must still be upon him for his face still held a peaceful look. 'Warm enough?' he asked.

Madeline's cheeks grew hotter still. 'Yes, thank you.' Had he seen her staring?

The smile deepened.

Oh, Lord! Madeline hastily found something that necessitated all of her attention out of the window.

'We'll reach Whitchurch by nightfall and put up in an inn there. The White Hart usually serves me well.'

Madeline didn't trust herself to speak, just nodded.

'Are you hungry? There's still some cold pie left in the lunch basket.'

'No, thank you. I'll wait until we reach Whitchurch.'

'Well, in that case…' said Lucien and closed his eyes once more.

Madeline was careful to keep her gaze well averted.

The White Hart was quite the busiest coaching inn that Madeline had ever seen. Not that she was in the habit of frequenting such places, but there had been that time that Mama had taken her and Angelina to visit Cousin Mary in Oxford. The inn seemed to consist of a maze of dimly lit, winding corridors leading from one room to another. This said, the private parlour that Lucien had arranged for them was clean and tidy, as was the place as a whole. The food that the landlord and his wife brought was simple, but wholesome. A stew of beef with carrots, a baked ham, potatoes and a seed cake. They called her my lady and were polite. No whispers followed her here. No gossip. Madeline breathed a sigh of relief and ate her stew.

'Some ham?' suggested her husband.

'No, thank you.'

'A slice of cake, then?'

'No.' Madeline shook her head.

Lucien's brows twitched together. He seemed to be finding Madeline's dinner plate worthy of a stare. 'You don't eat very much,' he finally said.

'I eat enough,' she replied defensively. In truth, her appetite had shrunk since meeting Cyril Farquharson. She picked at her food, nothing more. Three days as Lucien's wife had not changed that.

He said nothing more, just looked at her with those pale eyes.

Madeline knew she should not have snapped at him. It was not his fault that her bones ached and her head was so tired she could scarcely think. 'Forgive me, Lucien. I'm just a little tired.'

'It's been a long day and we have an early start in the morning. We should go to bed. Finish your wine and I'll take you up.'

His words caused Madeline's heart to stumble. She sipped a little more of the claret, then pushed her chair back.

He looked at the half-full glass but forbore to comment on it.

'We are to share a room?' Madeline glanced up at her husband, surprise clear upon her face as he followed her into the room and closed the door.

'It is not safe to sleep alone,' he said.

'But—'

'No buts, Madeline. It is for a short while only and you'll be safe. I'm not quite the monster society would paint me.' There was a hard cynical catch to his voice. 'I'll go back downstairs that you might undress. Lock the door and do not open it for anyone except me.'

She nodded her head.

And he was gone.

The key turned easily within the lock as if it was kept well oiled. She turned to survey the bedchamber. The bed was situated on the right-hand side, facing out into the room and towards the warmth of the fireplace where a small fire burned. At the right-hand side of the bed and behind the door was a sturdy chest of drawers on top of which sat a pitcher and basin and a towel. A plain spindle chair and a small rug had been placed beside the fireplace.

Madeline walked over to the bed, running her hands over the bed linen, feeling the firmness of the mattress. Everything was clean and fresh, if a little worn. Such humble simplicity seemed a surprising choice for a man who held an earldom. She'd imagined him demanding something more luxurious, more ostentatious. And the landlord and his wife hadn't cowered from Lucien. In fact, when she thought about it, their attitude hadn't been dutiful at all. Friendly was definitely a more accurate description. Strange. Especially for a man with Lucien's reputation.

She sat down heavily on the bed, fatigue pulling at her shoulders and clouding her mind. Her new brown pelisse slipped off easily enough, folding neatly beneath her fingers. Next came her bonnet, shoes and stockings. The dark green travelling dress proved more difficult to remove without assistance, but with perseverance and a few elaborate body contortions Madeline soon managed. She made her ablutions, resumed the protection of her shift, removed the warming pan from the bed, and climbed in. The sheets were warm against her skin, thanks to the thoughtfulness of whoever had placed the warming pan within. She stretched out her legs, wriggled her toes and, breathing in the smell of freshly laundered linen, relaxed into the comfort of the mattress. Bliss. For the first time in weeks Madeline was asleep as soon as her head hit the pillow.

A soft tapping sounded from the door. Madeline opened one drowsy eye and peered suspiciously at the oaken structure.

The knocking grew louder.

The pillow was so soft and downy against her head, the covers so enticingly warm.

'Madeline,' a male voice whispered.

Madeline forced the other eye open, levered herself from beneath the sheets and padded through the darkness of the room towards the sound. Her hand touched to the key and stilled.

'Madeline, it's Lucien.'

Her fingers hesitated no longer. The key turned. The door cracked open by the smallest angle, letting in the candlelight of the well-lit landing. Lucien was looking right back at her. The piercing gaze of his eyes blasted away any remnants of sleep from Madeline's mind. She said nothing, just opened the door wider and watched with a beady eye while he entered. There was only one bed: Madeline waited to see what her husband intended.

He locked the door before moving to the chair by the glowing hearth. First his coat was discarded, followed closely by his neckcloth and waistcoat. The bottom drawer in the chest opened to reveal a blanket. Lucien extracted it, kicked off his boots, sat himself down in the chair, and pulled the blanket over his body. All in less than two minutes.

Madeline's toes were cold upon the floor. She still lingered beside the door.

'Goodnight, Madeline,' he said and, leaning back in the chair, closed his eyes.

Her mouth opened, then closed. 'Goodnight.' She climbed back beneath the covers, looked again at the figure of her husband slumped awkwardly in the small chair. The bed was spacious and warm. Madeline bit at her lip. Offering to share the bed might be misconstrued. And he could have taken two rooms for the night instead of only one. Madeline stifled the guilt and closed her eyes against the discomfort of the chair, only to open them several times to check upon Lucien's immobile figure. Sleep crept unobtrusively upon her and Madeline's eyes opened no more.

Chapter Seven

'Madeline.' His voice was honeyed, but beneath the sweetness she knew there was venom. 'My love,' he whispered against her ear. His lips, hard and demanding, trailed over her jaw. 'Did you think that you could escape me, my sweet?' Bony fingers clawed at her arms, raking her flesh, tearing at her dress. 'There's a name for women like you.'

'No,' she whispered.

'I know the truth,' he said, his mouth curving to reveal those small sharp teeth. She looked up into the eyes of Cyril Farquharson. 'And I'm coming to get you. Tregellas cannot stop me from taking what is mine.'

'No.' Madeline shook her head, denying the words she dreaded so much. Nausea churned in her stomach. Fear prickled at her scalp and crept up her spine.

The blow hit hard against her cheek. Breath shuddered in her throat. She staggered back, searching for an escape, running towards the door. Her skirts wound themselves around her legs, contriving to trip her, pulling her back to him. She fought against them, reaching out towards the doorknob. Her fingers grasped at the smooth round wood. Turned.

Pulled. The door held fast. The handle rattled uselessly within her clasp. Panic rose. She wrenched at it, scrabbled at it, kicked at the barrier. And then she felt the hot humid breath against the back of her neck and the gouge of his nails as he tore her round to face him.

'No, please, Lord Farquharson, I beg of you. Please do not!'

Cyril Farquharson only laughed and the sound of it was evil to the core. He was laughing as he ripped open her bodice to expose her breast, and still laughing as he raised the dagger ready to plunge it into her heart.

'No!' Madeline screamed. 'No! No!'

'Madeline.'

Madeline's eyes flew open with a start to find herself sitting up in the bed with a man's strong arms around her. Fear surged strong and real. Farquharson? She struggled against him.

'It's all right.' The voice was calm and soothing. 'You've had a nightmare.' Cool fingers stroked at her head and then ran over her cheeks to gently tilt her face round to look at his. 'Farquharson isn't here. It's just a bad dream.'

'Lucien?' The word trembled, as did the rest of her. Her heart still kicked in her chest and her throat felt like its sides had stuck together. Slowly she remembered the room in the White Hart and saw the dying embers of the fire across on the hearth.

Firm lips touched to her forehead, murmuring words of comfort. 'Go back to sleep, Madeline. I'm here, nothing can harm you.'

The darkness was so thick as to mask him. Just the hint of the angle of a jaw and the suggestion of a nose. She moved her hands up to his face, lightly caressing his features. 'Lucien?' she said again, touching her fingers against the stubble on his chin.

'Yes,' came the deep reassuring voice that she had come to recognise. He eased her back down against the bed, pulling the covers up and tucking them around her. 'You should go back to sleep. You're safe. I'll be watching over you.' His fingers trailed a tender caress against her cheek as he moved away.

His skin had felt cold against hers. Madeline sat back up, peering towards the fireplace. 'Lucien?'

'Mmm?' There was the sound of a woollen blanket being arranged and the creak of the wooden chair beneath his weight.

The air within the room was not warm. Madeline shivered against its chill. No wonder he was freezing, sitting in that uncomfortable little chair all night with just one thin blanket against the plummeting temperature. 'You…you could come and sleep over here.'

Silence. As if he hadn't heard what she'd just suggested.

But Madeline had felt his weariness and the chill in his limbs. 'There's plenty of room for us both and it's nice and warm. Much better, I'd guess, than that chair.'

A moment's hesitation and then from the other side of the room, 'Thank you, Madeline, but my honour does not allow me.'

Madeline stifled a snort. Lord, but he had the pride of the devil. She dozed for what was left of the night, stealing looks into the darkness, guarding against the return of Farquharson, even if it was in her dreams.

The next day both Lucien and Madeline were tired and wan-faced. A hasty breakfast and then their journey resumed, moving slowly, increasingly closer to Cornwall and the Tregellas country estate. They travelled along the Dorchester Road, making good progress despite the chill wind. A brief stop at the Three Swans in Salisbury for lunch and then they pushed on, travelling further south as the daylight dimmed and the dark clouds gathered. The rain, when it started at first, was a collection of a few slow drops. But each drop was heavy and ripe, bursting to release a mini deluge. One drop, then another, and another, faster and faster, until the road was a muddied mess of puddles, and the rain battered its din against the coach's feeble body. They put up for the night at The Crown in Blandford, a coaching inn that had none of the welcome of the White Hart, and was filled with travellers wishing to escape the worst of the downpour. Only the production of several guineas served to procure them a room for the night and the shared use of a small parlour. They ate hurriedly, exchanging little conversation, listening to the hubbub of noise that drifted in from the public room, and the batter of wind and rain against the windows.

Lucien downed the remainder of the brandy and scanned the faces around the room. Old men, young men, peasants, servants, farmers and gentlemen. The weather was an effective leveller of class. Even the odd woman, hag-faced, sucking on a pipe, or young with an obvious display of buxom charm. But thankfully the face that Lucien sought was not present. He wondered how long it would be before Farquharson would come after them, for he had not one doubt that he would. Now he knew that Farquharson would never call him out. The weasel wasn't man enough to face him again across an open field. Farquharson would use different methods altogether. The lure had worked, just not in the way that Lucien might have imagined. Farquharson would be part of the gossip: an object of ridicule, someone to be pitied. That was not something that Cyril Farquharson was likely to suffer for long. With cold and deliberate calculation Lucien had unleashed the demon. Farquharson would come for him now, at long last. Finally, after all these years. The satisfaction was tempered by the knowledge that he would not be Farquharson's only target.

He remembered the expression on Farquharson's face the last time he had looked at Madeline, when he had spoken so cruelly to the woman who was now Lucien's wife. She was a softer, easier target for revenge and one that would enable Farquharson to score Lucien's old wounds afresh. And in that memory he realised that it was Madeline that Farquharson would target. Lucien's mouth compressed to a hard line. He had promised her safety. And, by God, she would have it. When Farquharson came, Lucien would be ready. He blinked the fatigue from his eyes, wondering if Madeline would be beneath the covers yet. Then he sat the glass upon the wooden counter and slowly took himself up the stairs that led to their chamber.

He shifted restlessly in the small hard chair, feeling the ache in his shoulders and back growing stronger by the minute. His head was foggy with exhaustion, his eyes gritty and sore. Yet still merciful sleep eluded him. The memory of Farquharson jabbed at him like a sharp stick, taunting him with the terrible deeds from their shared past. Deeds that had stolen Lucien's peace, destroyed the man he used to be, and made him the cold hard cynic he was now. The mean fire had long since burned out; grey raked ashes lay in a cold pile. Lucien huddled beneath the layers of his coat and the blanket, and tried to breathe warmth into his fingers. He pushed the thoughts far from his mind, struggled to escape from their oppression. Another sleepless night stretched ahead. He should be used to it by now. Then he heard it: the small movement from the bed; the change from her soft even breaths to staccato gasps; a mumbled cry; the twisting of her body beneath the sheets.

He trod quietly across the wooden flooring and leaned towards the bed.

'No, Lord Farquharson…' A whisper of torment that wrenched at his heart.

Lucien's teeth clenched tighter. Last night had not been in isolation then. Madeline too knew what it was to suffer the terror of the night demons. There was an irony in the fact that the same man lay at the root of both their nightmares. He reached a hand out towards her, touched it gently against her face. The skin was wet beneath his fingers. Sobs racked her body. He could feel her fear, understand her terror. 'Madeline,' he whispered, trying to pull her from its grasp.

'No!' she sobbed louder.

His mouth tickled against her ear. 'Madeline, wake up. It's a nightmare. You're safe.'

'Lucien?'

He stroked her hair and wiped the dampness from her cheek. 'You're safe,' he whispered again and again, lying his length on top of the covers, pulling her into his arms.

Gradually he felt the tautness of her body relax as she snuggled into him. Her breathing slowed, the frenzied beat of her heart steadied against his chest. He inhaled the scent of her, revelled in the feel of her softness, of her trust, and knew that he didn't deserve it. He swallowed down temptation and with steadfast resolve gently began to ease a space between them. He had just managed to roll away when he felt the sudden grip of her hand around the flat of his stomach.

'Please stay,' she whispered into the darkness.

And Lucien knew that he was lost. He could no sooner ignore the plea in her voice than he could cut off his own arm. She was afraid. She needed him, he told himself, and ignored the stubborn little voice deep down inside that told him that he needed her, too.

'Come beneath the covers.'

'Madeline.' There was an agony of denial in his whisper as he gently shook his head.

'I'm so cold.'

'Oh, God,' Lucien ground out and promptly climbed beneath the covers of the bed.

She didn't feel cold. In fact, Lucien would have sworn that she was positively warm. He lay motionless by her side, trying not to feel the slight body that rose and fell against him. She snuggled in closer and wrapped her arm around him. Lucien closed his eyes and enjoyed the soft gentleness of his wife, basking in her smell and her warmth. Slowly, he floated on a feather cushion of bliss into the black comfort of sleep.

Madeline felt the chill in her husband's body and opened herself against him, sharing her warmth. Her hand slid over the soft lawn of his shirt, resting against the strong muscle beneath. She noticed how strange a man's body felt in comparison with her own—all taut hardness, large, long and lean, with such a suppressed strength that her eyes flickered open, straining through the darkness to see him. He lay rigid as a flagpole, completely immobile, as if he exerted some kind of tense control over his muscles and limbs, almost fighting sleep. It appeared that Lucien Tregellas was not a man who allowed his guard to slip. He might feign an easiness of style, as if he did not care what happened around him, but it seemed to Madeline that there was something dark and watchful about her husband. What was it that he guarded so carefully against? The only time she had seen the guard drop was yesterday in the travelling coach when he had fallen asleep. Peace had touched his face then. There was nothing of peace in the large body now lying beside her own.

She lay her palm flat against his ribs and snuggled in close so as to feel the beating of his heart. She breathed in the scent of him—a heady mix of bergamot and the underlying smell that was uniquely Lucien. Cyril Farquharson and the stuff of Madeline's nightmare drifted far away. All she knew, all she felt, was the presence of the man lying next to her, filling her nostrils, beneath the tips of her fingers, against her breast and waist and thighs. Warming. Strong. Sure. No matter that theirs was a marriage of convenience, a marriage in name only—nothing had ever felt so right as the man that she called husband. She closed her eyes against him, felt the tight muscles beneath her fingers relax. His breathing eased, letting go, the guard slipping slowly and steadily, until she knew that he slept. She smiled a little smile of contentment into his chest, placed a kiss through the lawn of his shirt, and gave herself up to follow the same path.

Lucien awoke with an unusual sense of calm contentment. He lay quite still, trying to capture the essence of the fragile moment, reticent to lose it. The first strains of daylight filtered through the thin curtains stretched across the window. Lucien opened one bleary eye and reality jolted back into place. As the warm body beside him nestled in closer, he realised the exact nature of his predicament. A woman's soft body was curved into his, like a small spoon lying atop another. Her feet touched against his leg, her back fitted snug all the way up from his abdomen to his chest. Not only did he find that his arm was wrapped possessively around her, but his hand was resting against the small mound of her breast. As if that were not bad enough, her buttocks were pressed directly against his groin. Worst of all, Lucien was in a state of blatant arousal. The breath froze in his throat.

Madeline gave a little sigh and wriggled her hips closer into him.

Lucien captured the groan before it left his mouth, and gently removed his hand from the place it most certainly should not have been. Sweat beaded upon his brow. No woman had ever felt this good, like she belonged in his arms.

He could have lain an eternity with Madeline thus and never wished to resume his life. Except that he must not. Never had he wanted to love a woman as much as he wanted to love Madeline right at that moment. Every inch of his body proclaimed its need. Lucien gritted his teeth. A fine protector he would be if he took advantage of her. Little better than Farquharson. *Not like Farquharson,* a little voice whispered. *She's your wife. You care for her.* Lucien slammed the barrier down upon those thoughts. What he cared about was justice and retribution. He eased a distance between their bodies, but he had reckoned without Madeline.

From the depths of her dream Madeline felt him slipping away and sought to recapture the warm contentment that he had offered. She rolled over and thrust an arm over his retreating body.

Lucien stifled the gasp. Hell, but was a man ever so tempted? For a brief moment he allowed himself to relax back into her, feeling the steady beat of her heart against his, inhaling her scent, sweeping his hand lightly over her back to rest upon the rounded swell of her hips. 'Madeline.' Her name was a gentle sigh upon his lips. In the greyness of the dawn he studied her features: the long black lashes sweeping low over her eyes, the straightness of her little nose, the softness of her lips parted slightly in the relaxation of slumber. Lucien swallowed hard as his gaze lingered over her mouth. He experienced the urge to cover her lips with his; to kiss her long and deep and hard; to show her what a husband and his wife should be about. But he had promised both her and himself that he would not.

He heard again her question of that night that now seemed so long ago, although it was scarcely four nights since: *What do you wish from me in return, my lord?* And he remembered the proud, foolish answer he had given: *Discretion...a marriage in name only...nothing need change.* But as he lay there beside her, he knew that he had lied. Everything had changed. He knew very well what he wanted: his wife. Lucien's jaw clenched harder. That wasn't supposed to be part of the deal. He looked at her for a moment longer, then allowed himself one chaste kiss against her hair, her long glorious hair, all tousled from sleep. Quietly he slipped from the bed.

Madeline reached for the warm reassurance of her husband's body and found only bare sheets. Her fingers pressed to the coolness of the empty linen. Gone. She sat up with a start, eyes squinting against the sunlight filtering through and around the limp square of material that passed for a curtain. His name shaped upon her lips, worry wrinkled at her nose.

'Good morning, Madeline.' He was lounging back as best he could in the small chair, watching her.

Surely she must still be dreaming? Madeline watched while his mouth stretched to a smile. A tingling warmth responded within her belly. Most definitely this could only be a dream. Part of the same nocturnal imaginings in which she had lain safe within Lucien's strong arms all the night through, shared his warmth, and felt his hand upon her breast. Madeline blushed at the visions swimming through her mind, rubbed at her eyes and cast a rather suspicious look in his direction. 'Lucien?'

'I thought I might have to carry you sleeping out into the coach. You seemed most resistant to my efforts to wake you.' He was fully dressed, his hair teased to some semblance of order; even the blue shadow of growth upon his chin had disappeared. Her gaze lingered over the strong lines of his jaw and the chiselled fullness of his lips.

Madeline's blush deepened as she remembered exactly what she had been dreaming about. 'I must have been very tired to sleep so long. I'm normally awake with the lark. I don't usually lie abed.'

'You appear to be mastering the art well,' said her husband with a wry smile. 'Did you sleep well?'

Madeline's heart skipped a beat. Had last night been real? Or a wonderful dream that followed hard on the heels of a hellish nightmare? The touch of him, the smell of him, the chill in those long powerful limbs. No, she couldn't have imagined that, could she? 'Yes. After you…after the nightmare passed, I slept very well, thank you.'

The smile dropped and his voice gentled. 'Do you dream of Farquharson every night?'

'How did you know?'

'You uttered his name aloud.'

They looked at one another. Warm honey brown and pale blue ice.

'I did not mean to wake you,' she said.

'I was awake anyway. As you correctly observed, the chair does not make the most comfortable of sleeping places.' He paused. 'You have not answered my question.'

There was a difference about his face this morning. Nothing that she could define exactly, just something that wasn't the same as yesterday. 'Yes. He has haunted my dreams since I first met him. Even before…before he tried to…' She let the sentence trail off unfinished. 'Every night without fail, he's there waiting in the darkness. I know it sounds foolish, but sometimes I'm afraid to fall asleep.'

Understanding flickered in Lucien's eyes. 'He would have to come through me to reach you, Madeline, and that will only happen over my dead body.'

It seemed that in the moment that he said it a cloud obliterated the sun, and a cold hand squeezed upon her heart. 'Pray God that it never happens,' she said.

'It won't,' he said with absolute certainty. 'I'll have stopped him long before.'

'We'll be safe in Cornwall, though. He won't follow us there, will he?'

Lucien did not answer her question, just deflected it and changed the subject. 'Put Farquharson from your thoughts. The fresh water was delivered only a few minutes ago; it should still be warm.' He gestured towards the pitcher. 'I'll go and order us breakfast. Will fifteen minutes suffice to have yourself ready?'

Madeline nodded, and watched the tall figure of her husband disappear through the doorway. So, even down in Cornwall, so far away from London, the threat of Cyril Farquharson would continue.

The hours passed in a blur. At least the weather held fine until the light began to drain from the day. Then a fine smirr of rain set up as the darkness closed, and they sought the sanctuary of the New London Inn in Exeter. It was the same pattern as the previous two nights. He had promised that they would reach Trethevyn by tomorrow. This would be their last night on the road, his last excuse to share her bedchamber. Lucien thrust the thought away and denied its truth. His presence was just a measure of protection. Or so he persuaded himself. If Lucien had learned anything in the years he'd spent waiting, it was to leave nothing to chance. The busy throng within a coaching inn provided opportunity for Farquharson, not safety from him.

Sharing a bed with Madeline had been an unforeseen complication. Lucien's loins tightened with the memory. He tried to turn his mind to other matters, but memory persisted. No matter how damnably uncomfortable the chair, or the sweet allure of her voice, or, worse still, her soft welcoming arms…

Lucien's teeth ground firm. He'd be damned to the devil if he was stupid enough to make the same mistake twice. Take the chair, not the bed, he thought, and made his way up the scuffed wooden staircase of the New London Inn.

Surprisingly the room was not in darkness. The fire still blazed and a candle flickered by the side of the bed. The small room welcomed and warmed him. Still hanging grimly on to his determination, he made his way over to the chair and slipped out of his coat. Not once did he permit his gaze to wander in the direction of the bed and the woman that lay within it. He just kept his focus on the chair, that damned wooden chair, and started to undress.

'Lucien,' she said in a quiet voice.

He stilled, his boot dangling in his hand. Temptation beckoned. His eyes slid across to hers…and found that she was sitting up, watching him, her hands encircling the covers around her bent legs, her chin resting atop her blanketed knees. 'Is something wrong?' he asked, hoping that she would not notice the huskiness in his voice.

'I wondered if you might…if you would…' The candle-light showed the rosy stain that scalded her cheeks.

Oh, Lord! Lucien knew what it was that his wife was about to ask.

'I thought perhaps if you were here that…that Farquhar-son…that the nightmares might not come.' She glanced away, her face aflame, her manner stilted.

Lucien felt her awkwardness as keenly as if it were his own. How much had it cost her to make such a request? Hell, but she had no idea of the effect that she had upon him. She was an innocent. The boot slipped from Lucien's fingers. He raked a hand roughly through his hair, oblivious to the wild ruffle of dark feathers that fanned in its wake. 'Madeline,' he said gruffly, 'you don't know what it is that you ask.'

She gestured towards the empty half of the bed. 'It seems silly that you should be cold and uncomfortable on a hard rickety chair when there is plenty room for both of us in this bed.'

Better that than risk the temptation that lay in what she was so innocently offering. Lucien opened his mouth to deny it.

'I do trust you, Lucien.'

She trusted him, but the question was—did he trust himself? The warmth of her sweet gaze razed his refusal before it had formed.

'Madeline,' he tried again, raking his hair worse than ever.

She smiled, and pulled the bedcovers open on the empty side of the bed, *his* side of the bed. 'And it's not as if my reputation can be ruined by our sleeping in the same bed. We are at least married.' She snuggled down under the covers and waited expectantly.

Lucien knew that he was lost. Could not refuse her. Swore to himself that he would not touch her. Still wearing his shirt and pantaloons, he climbed in beside her.

Madeline felt the mattress dip beneath his weight. Safety and excitement in equal dose danced their way through her veins. She knew that she should not have asked. Perhaps he thought her wanton to have done so. But the need for him to be close was greater than the shame in asking. And so she had spoken the words that Madeline Langley had never thought to utter and asked a man to come into her bed. They lay stiffly side by side. Each on their backs, careful not to look at the other, determined that no part of them should actually touch. His warmth traversed the space between them, so that the full stretch of the left-hand side of her body tingled from his heat. She wondered that he could have brought himself to marry a woman that he found so…lacking. For all that she was neither his social nor financial equal, he did not despise her, for surely something of that would have communicated itself in his manner? When he touched her she felt warm, happy, breathless with anticipation. Clearly Lucien did not feel the same. He did not want to touch her. The gap between them widened. That was when a glimmer of understanding dawned upon Madeline.

'Lucien.'

'Mmm?' Still he did not turn his head towards her.

It probably was the very question that she should not ask of her new husband, especially when he was lying in bed beside her. Indeed, any sensible woman would not have dreamed of so foolish a folly. But as the prospect of monumental guilt began to blossom, Madeline had to know. Whatever the cost. 'May I ask you something of…of a personal nature?' She felt him edge infinitesimally away from her.

'You can ask, Madeline. It does not mean that I will answer.'

A pause, while she searched for the right words. Eloquence of speech had never been Madeline's strong point. She sneaked a glance across at her husband. 'Before you married me…before Lord Farquharson…' She stopped, unsure of how best to frame her question. And started again. 'I know that you did not wish to marry me, that you only did so to prevent Lord Farquharson from…to keep me safe from him.'

It seemed that the large body next to hers tightened with tension.

'Was there another lady that you…' she took a deep breath '…that you had hoped to marry?' An ache tightened across her chest as she waited for him to answer.

Lucien looked at her then, a look of icy incredulity in those blue eyes.

She swallowed. 'I beg your pardon, I should not have asked, but…' Why had she asked? *To find if he has given his heart to someone else,* came back the little whisper.

'Then why did you?' he said curtly.

She shook her head. 'I-I thought that…' *It might explain why you seem so determined to keep this distance between us,* the silent voice came again. She stoppered her ears to its treachery.

'Don't think. The details of my past life do not figure in our arrangement, Madeline.' Then he rolled away on to his side, turning his back on her, and blew out the candle.

The sting of his rejection wounded her. She knew that she was not pretty, not like Angelina. The message was loud and clear. He might have taken her for his wife. He was prepared to share her bed…under duress. But he did not want her as a woman. Could not bring himself to touch her. But last night… Dreams, only silly foolish dreams, from a silly foolish girl. A marriage of convenience. A contract of protection. Safety from Farquharson. That was what he had offered. Clearly. In terms that could not be uncertain. That was what she had accepted. She had no right to expect anything else.

The bed was warm and blissfully comfortable. The first hint of grey light crept around the curtains. She wriggled her toes and sighed a sigh of utter contentment. Lucien's arm was draped around her, holding her against him as if to protect her from the world. Her cheek rested on the hardness of his chest, the material of his rumpled shirt soft against her skin, rising and falling in slow even breaths beneath her face. The scent of him surrounded her, assailing her senses: cologne and something else that was undoubtedly masculine. Where her breasts crushed against him she could feel the beat of his heart, strong and steady like the man himself. Madeline revelled in the feel of him. Everything about him filled her senses and triggered some current of underlying excitement that she did not understand. Their legs were entwined together so that she could not have freed herself even had she wanted to. His arm was heavy and possessive. She resisted the urge to open her eyes, wanting to hold the dream for a little longer before she awoke to find that the bed was empty.

Inquisitive fingers explored across his body, sneaking beneath the loose linen of his shirt. Even in sleep his muscles were hard, with nothing of softness. A light sprinkling of hair dusted across the breadth of his chest. Her fingertips lightly swept through it, dancing in small circles against his skin. Madeline obeyed her instinct and followed her fingers with her mouth, touching her lips against his chest. A sleepy sigh escaped him as she pressed a small kiss against his skin. Lucien groaned, the rumble of the sound vibrating against her lips. So real, too real. Madeline's eyes flickered open. Warm contentment vanished in a second, to be replaced with utter shock.

Lucien's shirt was pushed up to expose his naked skin, and she was kissing him! Lucien groaned again and swept a hand down to caress her buttocks. Madeline froze, desperate to escape the situation she had created, yet afraid to waken Lucien. Slowly she tried to ease herself away from him. Lucien murmured something and slid his fingers against her hip. The material of her shift was no protection against him. His touch branded her with its heat. Another attempt to extract herself, gently easing her legs from his. 'Sweetheart,' he murmured and in one smooth motion rolled over to press her beneath him.

She felt him probe against her, something that willed her thighs to open. Madeline wanted nothing more than to comply, to give herself to him. The strange compelling need that burned in her, that made her crave his touch, his kiss, stoked higher, chasing reason and sensible thought from her head. Madeline fought back. She wanted him, but not like this. Not when he was sleep-drugged and did not know what he was doing. One magical hand stroked across her thigh. She gasped, knowing that this was all wrong, part of her wanting it just the same. 'Lucien!' His name was thick upon her lips. His hand moved to capture her breast, fingers teasing across the soft mound of skin, hardening its tip, until she thought she would faint for the need of him. Need. Her thighs burned with it. Her pulse throbbed with it. 'Lucien!' she cried out with the one last strand of sanity that lingered where all others had fled. 'Lucien!' a cry of desperation and of longing.

Lucien came to with a start to find that the glorious dream in which he was making love to his wife was a horrendous nightmare. He stared down aghast at the sight of Madeline lying half-naked beneath him. 'Madeline?' The word was raw and disbelieving. Her hair splayed across the pillows, long and straight, framing her face. Huge wide eyes that stared back at him in shock and disbelief, lips parted, panting small breaths of fear. And he, like a great beast, swooping over her, with his arousal pressed against her softness. 'Hell!' he swore and rolled off her as quickly as he could. Disgust tore at him, sickening him to the pit of his stomach. He was every bit as bad as Farquharson. He had become the devil that everyone thought him. A man about to rape his own wife— had it not been for his breeches. A thrust of the covers and he was out of the bed, standing staring at her. She looked as shocked as he felt.

'Madeline—' his voice was harsh and gritty '—forgive me. I was sleep-addled. I did not know what I was doing.' It was a feeble excuse, even to his own ears. As if that could justify what he had been about to do, what he would have done if her pleading shouts had not woken him to the villain he was. He wiped a hand across his mouth.

'It was not your fault,' she said.

God in heaven! What had he done to her? 'It won't happen again. I give you my word, Madeline.'

'No.' She shook her head as if to clear the daze from her mind.

How could he expect her to believe him when he had so glibly given his word before and broken it just as easily? 'It was a mistake to share the bed. I shall not do so again and you shall be perfectly safe.' His throat tightened. His jaw clenched.

'But—' Desolation struck at her beautiful eyes.

'Forgive me,' he said again, and gathering up the rest of his clothes in his arms, walked out of the room. It was the best he could offer her. His absence. He could only hope that through time Madeline would come to forgive and to forget.

Chapter Eight

⟨ornament⟩

The rest of the journey, from Exeter to Liskeard and then on past Tregellas village, was made in sullen silence. Lucien attended to her every need: ensured she was warm enough, that she was not hungry, that she was not too tired. But there was a formality between them, a distance that could not be breached. He did not touch her, or smile or even lounge back in his seat as he had done during the journey so far. Instead, he sat rigid and stern-faced, as if an anger bristled beneath the surface. His words, the few that he actually spoke to her, were not unkind. But his eyes sparked with something that she could not name. Loathing? Disgust? She did not blame him. He had made it very clear that he did not want her and she had behaved like nothing short of a trollop, tempting his kisses, craving his touch. Her face flamed just at the memory. Little wonder that he could hardly bear to look at her. Shame flooded her soul. She bit down hard on her lip, and averted her face.

Clearly he was a man to whom honour was everything. Why else throw himself away on a marriage to the likes of her? He had sacrificed himself to save her and all because of something in the past with Lord Farquharson. This was how she repaid him. Wanton. The word taunted her, playing again and again in her head, until she thought she would scream from it. Her teeth bit harder, puncturing the soft skin. She didn't even realise she was doing it until the metallic taste of blood settled upon her tongue. The road passed in a blur of mud and field and hedgerow. Madeline was blind to it all, concentrating as she was on holding herself together. His voice echoed through her mind, disgust lacing his every word. *It won't happen again... It was a mistake to share the bed.* She wanted to weep tears of shame and loss. Instead she took a deep breath, and sat calmly, steadfast and enduring, as if her heart wasn't bruised and aching. Strength rallied. She had survived a betrothal to Farquharson with his wandering hands and cruel promises. She could survive Lucien's disgust.

A shameful situation and each believing themselves to be to blame, neither Madeline nor Lucien noticed that both their dreams had been free from the presence of Cyril Farquharson.

Trethevyn was a large manor house that stood on the edge of a great, barren stretch of moorland. Madeline's heart sank as she caught sight of it through the cloud and rain. A huge imposing structure of grey stone, as dismal as the bleak countryside that surrounded it.

She supposed that Lucien must have sent word that he would be arriving, for the staff were assembled in the black-and-white chequered hallway to welcome the master of the house. An austere elderly butler and a large-boned elderly woman who answered to the name of Mrs Babcock seemed to be in charge. Mrs Babcock, who Madeline soon learned was the housekeeper, had a huge bun of wispy grey hair clearly displayed without the pretence of a cap of any kind.

Her cheeks were rosy and her eyes were as dark as two plump blackcurrants. As far as Lord Tregellas was concerned, she showed not one iota of the respect that one might have expected. Indeed, she was of a rather no-nonsense approach. She eyed the new mistress with obvious curiosity.

Lucien kept his distance. If the servants thought there anything strange in the fact that his lordship barely looked in the direction of his new wife, they made no hint of it. What would be said below-stairs was quite a different matter all together.

'No doubt you will wish to rest after such a long journey. Mrs Babcock will show you to your rooms.' Madeline was dismissed into the care of the housekeeper without a further word. Lucien disappeared into a doorway on his immediate right, closing the door firmly behind him.

Madeline looked at the large woman.

Mrs Babcock stared right back, and then a huge smile beamed across her face. 'Come along then, m'lady. Best get you settled upstairs and warmed up before anythin' else.' The housekeeper hobbled up towards the staircase that veered off to the right.

Madeline hesitated for a moment longer.

'This way, if you please, Lady Tregellas,' came Mrs Babcock's voice. The kindly blackcurrant eyes peered round at Madeline. Mrs Babcock's ample girth set off at a dawdle up the stairs. She turned her head with frequent regularity to check if the lady of the house was following in her wake, and struggled up stair by stair with her uneven stomping gate. 'Oh, my word, these stairs get steeper all the time,' complained Mrs Babcock, her breath coming in wheezes.

Madeline followed with mounting concern. The housekeeper certainly seemed to be labouring. 'Mrs Babcock, perhaps you should take a short rest.'

'Nonsense!' exclaimed Mrs Babcock cheerfully. 'Up and

down these stairs all the day long, I am. Not too old to be showin' the new mistress to her rooms.'

'No. I didn't mean to suggest—'

Mrs Babcock cut her off. 'Trethevyn is a lovely house. I'm sure you'll come to love it as much as his lordship does. Not the best of weather to be arrivin' in, but old George reckons as the weather will turn cold and fine again in the mornin', and then you'll see the place in all its glory. Expect you don't want to be bothered thinkin' about nothin' 'cept gettin' some nice warm food down you. But don't you fret, m'lady, Cook has got a special treat prepared, a lovely selection, and his lordship's favourite apple puddin' an' all.'

Madeline absorbed all this in silence. Her stomach felt small and tight and not a bit hungry. She forced a smile to her face and tried to sound enthusiastic. 'That sounds lovely.'

The wheeze of Mrs Babcock's breath grew louder. From down below there was the bustle of footmen unloading the baggage from the coach. Voices shouted and the fast flurry of footsteps on marble and wooden floors sounded. Madeline followed the housekeeper as the stairs swept back on themselves to reach a landing. From there Mrs Babcock turned to her right and followed down a dimly lit passageway.

'It seems a pleasant house,' said Madeline.

'Once you're settled, m'lady, you won't want to leave. I can promise you that,' replied the housekeeper.

Madeline sincerely doubted the truth of that remark, but said nothing.

Eventually they stopped outside a door, a door that looked to be the same as every other dark mahogany door along the passageway. Mrs Babcock reached forward, turned the handle, and swung the door open.

'The bedchamber of the mistress of the house. In you go, m'lady.' She waited for Madeline to move.

Madeline hesitated, peering in through the heavy mahogany doorway with a feeling of awe.

'Just as her ladyship left it,' said Mrs Babcock.

Madeline looked round with a start. 'Her ladyship?'

The housekeeper chuckled. 'The dowager Lady Tregellas. His lordship's mum, 'fore she passed on, that was. God rest her soul.'

'Oh.'

'And now the bedchamber is yours,' beamed Mrs Babcock, linking her arm through Madeline's and walking her into the room. 'I'm sure you'll be very happy here, m'lady.'

Madeline bit at her lip. 'Yes,' she murmured, unable to meet Mrs Babcock's eye.

The room was large in the extreme, bigger even than the one in Lucien's London house. Even the four-poster bed seemed small in comparison.

Mrs Babcock nodded towards the full-length window in the middle of the opposite wall. 'Have a care if you go out on the balcony until them there railings are mended. There was a right bad thunderstorm a few nights past and lightnin' hit the ironwork. All of a crumpled mess it is.' An ancient finger pointed to the side. 'Dressing room and bath's through there. His lordship even has one of them new water closets installed. Newfangled falderal, if you ask me. A chamberpot was good enough for his father and his grandfather before, but Master Lucien always was rather headstrong. Wouldn't listen as a boy. Still won't listen.' Mrs Babcock sniffed loudly to show what she thought of Lucien's wilful ways. 'Sit yourself down, m'lady. I'll have Betsy bring you a nice strong cup of tea with plenty of sugar. You're lookin' a bit pasty, if you don't mind me sayin'.'

Madeline found herself being steered towards the sofa, an elderly hand patting at her shoulder.

'I'll stop my chatterin' and let you catch your breath then. Anythin' you want, just ring. Betsy'll be right up.' Mrs Babcock got as far as the door before turning her face back towards Madeline. 'Took his lordship long enough to find himself a bride. But I reckon he's made the right choice with you, m'lady. Welcome to Trethevyn.' Then she was off and lumbering back along the length of the corridor.

Madeline stood where she was, listening to the scuffling of Mrs Babcock's shoes against the wooden flooring, eyes scanning what lay before her. A rose-coloured bedchamber, warm from a fire that had clearly been burning for some time within the centre of the carved white marble fireplace. Rain battered against the large full-length window in the centre of the room, and would have lent a greyness to the light had it not been for the warming yellow glow from a multitude of lighted candles. The room did indeed have a peaceful air to it, just as Mrs Babcock had said.

Madeline surveyed the furniture. There was a matching desk and chair, a small bookcase, a large wooden box on top of a stand, and an easel. There was even a vase of snowdrops, bowing their shy white little heads low towards their green stems. She pushed the door shut and walked quietly across the pink patterned rug. A pale brocade-covered sofa with matching cushions was positioned before the fireplace, a corresponding armchair by its side. A tallboy and a wardrobe in the left-hand corner. Two bedside tables. Symmetrically placed in the walls of both the left- and right-hand sides of the bedchamber were two identical doors, painted the same pale rose colour to merge with the walls. Madeline moved first to the right, the side that Mrs Babcock had indicated. The door led into a dressing room complete with dressing table and mirrors, and from there into a bathroom. She looked across the length of the bedchamber towards the matching door on the other side. Madeline suspected what lay behind that. She walked steadily towards it, placed her hand on the smooth wooden handle and turned. The door was locked. She backed away from it. Only in her retreat did she notice the walls.

Every inch of space upon the walls had been hung with framed paintings: paintings of woodland scenes, paintings of dogs, paintings of wild sweeping moorland, and colourful bright studies of flowers. Two children playing in the sunlight, a man walking through the snow. A rainbow lighting a dark sky, and a rugged ruined castle on a cliff edge so sheer as to plunge into a white-foamed sea. They drew Madeline like a magnet. Chilled fingers soon warmed, tension and unease melted away. Madeline forgot all else as she studied the works. Delicate translucence of watercolour, and bold rich oils. Absorbing her into the scenes, drawing her in with the artist's eye. At the bottom of every paper, every canvas, were the same entwined initials: A and T. The same artist had rendered all these paintings, and with such love and passion and clarity. Everyday scenes immortalised for ever by the careful strokes of a brush.

A quiet knock sounded, timid knuckles tapping on wood.

'Come in.' Madeline looked up to find a young woman carrying a tray hovering by the doorway.

'Beggin' your pardon, m'lady, but Mrs Babcock sent me with your tea.' The girl hunched her lanky frame and smiled a nervous little smile.

Madeline returned the smile. 'Thank you. You must be Betsy.'

'Yes, m'lady. Betsy Porter.' Another nervous smile. 'Shall I set it down here on the table by the fire?'

'Yes, please.' The girl's hair was fair, not unlike Madeline's own, but the eyes that looked back were blue washed with grey. 'Betsy, I was just admiring the pictures on the walls. Who painted them?'

'Oh, that was old Lady Tregellas. Mrs Babcock says that her ladyship painted all her life. 'Cept at the end. Wasn't well enough to paint 'fore she died.'

'When was that?' asked Madeline, intrigued to learn something more of Lucien's family.

'Long time 'fore I started work here,' answered Betsy. 'Perhaps five years, or so, ago.' A little silence before she said, 'I hope you like the flowers, m'lady. Mrs Babcock had me pick them specially for you.'

Madeline glanced towards the vase holding the snowdrops. 'They're beautiful, Betsy. I like them very much, thank you.'

Betsy pleated her apron and smiled. 'Mrs Babcock says to tell you that dinner will be served at five o'clock, so there's time for a short nap if you're tired. I'm to come back to help you dress at half past four. There ain't no lady's maid here. Mrs Babcock thought you would be bringin' your own.' Betsy ground to an awkward halt.

'No,' said Madeline, and then, making a spur-of-the-moment decision, 'Perhaps you might like to be my maid?'

Betsy looked as if she'd been struck by lightning. Then the blood rushed with a fury to heat her pale cheeks. 'But I ain't trained, m'lady. I don't know how to do hair stylin' or...' The words trailed off.

'I don't know how to be a countess,' confided Madeline. 'Perhaps we could learn together.'

'Oh, m'lady!' burst out Betsy. 'I won't let you down, that I won't, m'lady.'

Madeline was left with reassurances from Betsy that she only needed to ring and the maid would be straight there. If Betsy and Mrs Babcock were anything to judge by, it seemed that perhaps Trethevyn's staff were a great deal more welcoming than its master. 'Betsy, please can you send up some—'

But Betsy had gone.

Madeline jumped up and half-ran out the door to catch the maid, but of Betsy there was no sign. She'd drink her tea and then ring for warm water to wash in, giving poor Betsy time to catch her breath. She left the door ajar and went to pour the tea. A hot cup of tea and she would feel much better... perhaps.

'Max, come back here at once,' Lucien bellowed. 'Confound that blasted dog!' Lucien strode out of the library, dressed casually in only his shirt and waistcoat. The superfine black coat lay disregarded upon the library chair. 'Back five minutes and the hound deserts me,' he told an amused-looking Mrs Babcock, who just happened to be hobbling past the library at the time.

'Dear, oh, dear,' she said, casting a beady eye over the dark circles beneath his lordship's eyes and the stubborn tilt to his chin. 'Whyever that might be I just wouldn't know.' She surveyed the new leanness to his face and the tiny worry line that always appeared between his brows when he was at his most aggrieved...and wondered. 'Savin' that you look like you've been suckin' lemons. Bad journey down from London, was it?'

Lucien's glare would have had most other women beating a hasty and apologetic retreat.

Mrs Babcock was made of sterner stuff. 'Surprised you haven't frightened that poor girl to death if you've been glarin' at her like that.'

'Mrs Babcock...' began Lucien with indignant pomposity.

Obviously a raw nerve had been touched if his lordship had abandoned the use of her pet name in favour of full formality. Mrs Babcock placed her hands on her ample hips and sniffed. 'Now, don't you Mrs Babcock me, m'lord. That dog's not daft. Knows a sourpuss when he sees one and seeks out better company up them stairs.' Mrs Babcock shook her head.

'Cook's down there makin' you your favourite apple puddin' an' all and you're up here with a face like thunder.'

'Did you say Max ran upstairs?'

'Disappearin' up there like he'd caught the scent of a rabbit, he was.'

Lucien raked a hand through his hair. 'But Madeline's up there and you know how Max hates strangers.'

Mrs Babcock chuckled, 'Nearly took Lady Radford's hand off the last time she called.' She delivered Lucien a hefty pat on the arm. 'Now don't you worry, her ladyship's door will be shut. He won't get into her room. And besides, don't you think we would have heard by now if it wasn't?'

Earl Tregellas's face was still creased into a frown. 'True. But the dog's too quiet. No doubt up to something he shouldn't be. I'd best find him.'

'Dinner at five, m'lord,' said Mrs Babcock, and limped off in the direction of the kitchen.

Blasted dog. Probably chewing on his favourite top boots. Ten years hadn't diminished Max's taste for good-quality leather. Lucien took the stairs two at a time, reaching the upper landing in a matter of seconds. He scanned the corridor running in both directions. Thankfully the door to his own room appeared to be closed. Indeed, every other door along both passageways seemed to be in the same position, save for one. And that was the door that led into the bedchamber of the Countess Tregellas. A sudden trepidation gripped Lucien. 'Max!' he shouted and hurried down the length of the hallway to reach the room. He thrust the door open and barged in, fully expecting to find his wife backed into a corner by a snarling Max. Really, the dog could be a bad-tempered brute at times.

The sight that greeted his eyes could not have been more different. His jaw dropped. For there on the sofa was Madeline

The Wicked Earl

with the great black dog lying docilely across her lap, angling himself so that she could scratch his head in just the right spot. Lucien's entry brought only the most casual of glances from Max. Madeline looked up with a start.

'Lucien? Is something wrong?' She tried to stand, but Max showed no inclination to move from the warm comfort of her lap.

Lucien cleared his throat, feeling a turnip for dashing in to solve a crisis that did not exist. He fixed Max with an accusatory stare. 'I thought that Max might have found his way in here, and he can be somewhat…aggressive with those he doesn't know.'

Max turned his best sad expression towards Madeline and gave a pathetic little whimper.

'Oh, poor old boy,' said Madeline, tickling the dog's ears. 'Do you hear what he's saying about you? Look at those eyes.' The innocence in Max's liquid brown eyes intensified. 'As if he could even know what aggression was.' Max's tail set up a thumping wag against the pink brocade of the sofa and he laid his head on Madeline's thigh, looking up at Lucien with as smug an expression as is possible for an old dog to give.

'I assure you, he can be a brute at times,' said Lucien.

'Really?' said Madeline, raising her clear brown eyes to his.

Lucien had the feeling that they were talking about something else altogether. A small silence stretched between them. He made an abrupt change of subject. 'Is the room to your liking? If not, you have free rein to change it as you see fit. The same goes for the rest of the house, excepting the library, which is my…which I would prefer to remain as it is.'

First he ignores her for the whole day's coach travel, then he tells her she might redecorate his entire house if she wants!

'I love this room,' she said. 'I will not change it.' Her fingers scratched a massage against Max's head.

Lucien found his eyes drawn to the slender white fingers moving rhythmically against the dog's sleek black coat. He felt mesmerised, a strange relaxation creeping across his scalp.

'Your mother's paintings are beautiful.'

Lucien dragged his gaze away. 'Yes, they are. I'm glad you like them.' Her face was raised to his. Not angry. Not afraid. Just peaceful.

'Madeline…'

'There you are, you naughty boy!' Mrs Babcock heaved herself into the room.

Both Lucien and Madeline's heads shot round, unsure whether the housekeeper was referring to the master of the house or his dog.

'Ah, would you look at that,' cooed Mrs Babcock. 'I believe he's fallen in love.'

Lucien felt the tips of his ears begin to burn. 'Mrs Babcock,' he said coolly, 'was there something that you wanted?'

'Oh, don't mind me,' the housekeeper said. 'I just popped up to tell her ladyship that Betsy will bring her up some warm water to freshen herself in, shortly. I'll be off then.' And she promptly disappeared.

The moment was lost. 'I'll leave you to enjoy your tea in peace,' said Lucien. 'Come on, Max.' Then, to Madeline, 'I don't know what's got into him. He's normally so obedient.'

Max yawned and snuggled closer into Madeline.

'Max,' Lucien persevered. 'Come on, boy!'

Max shot him a speaking look. It said, loud and clear, *Are you mad?*

'Can't he stay?' asked Madeline.

One last-ditch attempt from Lucien. 'He'll cast hairs all over your dress.'

'I don't mind a few hairs,' said Madeline.

'Well, in that case…'

Max gave a little grunt of triumph.

Traitor! Lucien turned and walked alone from the room.

Lucien dozed fitfully, his dreams interspersed with Farquharson and the ever-present past. The muted sound of a woman's voice pulled him free of the torture. He knew the words beneath that hushed mumble, had heard them every night over the past weeks since the journey down from London. Correction, every night save for when he had… That was something Lucien could not bring himself to think about. Guilt was not assuaged by the desire that burned low and steady for the woman who was his wife. He had not thought that he, Lucien Tregellas, could have lowered himself to the base level of Farquharson. It seemed that he was wrong. He had taken Madeline to save her from a fate that had befallen another young woman not so very different from herself. That, and as part of his scheme to deliver retribution to Farquharson.

He'd thought he could control that carnal part of himself. He had not slept with a woman in five long years. Since meeting Madeline, Lucien had found himself suddenly obsessed with the longing. Try as he might to deny it, he wanted his wife in his bed. He pushed the thought away, just as he had on every other occasion, and lay listening to her muffled cries.

God, but it rent at his soul! He found himself standing by the door that connected his room with hers. Hand resting on the doorknob, cheek pressed against the smoothness of the wood, listening and listening, fighting his every instinct to stride right in there and take her into his arms. He wanted to kiss away the worry and the fear, to tell her it was only a nightmare and that he would protect her. But who then would protect her from him? *I do trust you, Lucien,* she had said. He had taken that trust and destroyed it, like everything else in his life. So he stood and listened until there was silence once more and he knew that the nightmare had passed.

Every night was a torture. Every day, too. They dined together. Nothing else. The strain of keeping such a rigid formality between them wore at him. To make matters worse, Guy had written to say that Farquharson was still in London, feeding the *ton* a story that the Wicked Earl had abducted Farquharson's bride-to-be and forced a marriage upon her. Little wonder that sleep evaded him. Lucien pulled on his dressing gown and quietly made his way down to his library, and the bottle of brandy that would deaden the sting of his thoughts.

'Gravy soup, skate with caper sauce, kidney pudding, boiled potatoes, leeks, and apple pie on Wednesday. Onion soup, jugged hare, baked ham, turnips in white sauce, and sago pudding on Thursday. And on Friday, lentil soup, roast beef, pork pie, roast potatoes, carrots and stewed prunes. Good. Well, now that we've sorted them menus there's the linen mendin' to think about.' Mrs Babcock swept on regardless. 'But I shall fetch us a nice cup of tea and some scones to sustain us.' Mrs Babcock never missed an opportunity to attempt to fatten up her mistress.

'Thank you, Mrs Babcock, I don't know what I would do without you.'

'Get away with you, doe!' cried Mrs Babcock, beaming a face full of pleasure. 'I've been meanin' to ask you,' she said. 'Are you plannin' anythin' for his lordship's birthday?'

'His birthday?' echoed Madeline in surprise.

'Didn't he tell you? What a man he is! Would try the patience of a saint, he would.'

Madeline shook her head. 'It must have slipped his mind. He is very busy with the estate work.'

Mrs Babcock snorted at that. 'Never too busy for birthdays,' she said. ' Always loved 'em when he was a boy. Apple puddin' and spice biscuits, lemonade an' presents. We used to set a treasure hunt for him and young Guy to follow. Like two little scamps they were. Babbie this, Babbie that, tryin' to get me to help them solve the clues. Little rascals!' The housekeeper chuckled. 'You just let me know if you want a special dinner or the like, m'lady.' Mrs Babcock beamed a smile of reassurance at Madeline. 'I'll be off, then.'

'Mrs Babcock,' Madeline said before she could think better of it.

'Yes, m'lady.'

Madeline nipped at her lip with her teeth and then asked, 'Would you be able to organise one of those treasure hunts again?'

'Me? Heavens, no!' said Mrs Babcock. 'I was a fine children's nurse, and I'm a fine housekeeper, but I could never set them there clues. Was her ladyship that saw to all that. I wouldn't know where to start, doe.'

'I could help you.'

Mrs Babcock didn't look too convinced. 'It's a lot of work.'

'I'm sure that we would manage if we worked together,' said Madeline.

'Very well, then, m'lady.'

'Thank you.' Madeline smiled.

Mrs Babcock gave Madeline an affectionate pat on the arm and then she was off and exiting the parlour at a speed surprising for a lady quite so plagued by infirmities.

Madeline was left alone in the small drawing room, wondering what on earth she had just got herself into.

* * *

The days passed and Madeline found herself busy planning the treasure hunt for Lucien. He ate breakfast and dinner with her every day like clockwork, enquired about her welfare, and gave her copious amounts of pin money. But that was the extent of their relationship. Lucien kept a distance even when he was only seated at the other end of the table. Farquharson's name was never mentioned, and neither was a return to London. Madeline had to confess that she was happy in Trethevyn—well, as happy as a woman could be whose husband did not love her. She missed Angelina and her parents. She wondered how they were managing amidst the scandal she had left behind, and wrote to them each week. No replies were ever forthcoming. Madeline had to accept that her family had yet to forgive her. But with spring in the air, and the secret excitement surrounding Lucien's treasure hunt, Madeline could not be blue-devilled for long.

'Oh, m'lady, you are clever!' Betsy said with a giggle. 'Won't his lordship be surprised when he finds what you've done.'

Mrs Babcock hunched her broad shoulders with all the excitement of a small child. 'Such a way with words, doe!'

A surprised smile slipped across Madeline's face. No one had ever uttered such a compliment.

Mrs Babcock wrapped her arms around Madeline's shoulders and pressed a kiss to her cheek.

Madeline blushed with pleasure.

'It reminds me of the old days when her ladyship planned the treasure hunts, and the master was just a youngster wanderin' about the place with jam all round his mouth, his shirt tails hanging out and hair sticking up like a bird's nest. Always was a mucky pup. Her ladyship used to say he was like a little ruffled raven. How we laughed.'

Madeline was having difficulty imaging her austere, most serious husband as a small, sticky, messy boy. The picture conjured up was quite unlike a child that could have grown to become a man feared by half of England.

'It would be good to have little 'uns about the place again,' said Mrs Babcock, unaware of the more intimate arrangements within Madeline and Lucien's marriage.

Madeline stilled.

'What little 'uns?' asked Betsy in all innocence.

'Master and mistress's, of course,' said Mrs Babcock as if it were the most obvious assumption in the world.

Madeline's face flamed. She rose hastily, and cleared her throat. 'I've just remembered that we said we would visit the parson's wife over by the village. I had best be away if I'm to be back before dark.'

'Right you are, then, m'lady,' said Mrs Babcock and trundled off to let Betsy fetch Madeline's pelisse, cloak and bonnet, and, of course, her stout walking shoes.

If Madeline thought to escape embarrassing talk of babies she was to be disappointed, for Mrs Woodford, the parson's wife, was only too keen to reveal the good news that she was increasing and another addition to the Woodford brood could be expected late in the summer.

Madeline sipped her tea and hoped that Mrs Woodford would restrict the conversation to her own breeding. Her hopes were in vain. For it soon transpired that the entirety of the village of Tregellas had an avid interest in the prospect of a Tregellas heir. Indeed, Mrs Woodford's euphoria at her own joyous anticipation led her to divulge that Mr Turner in the King's Arms inn was running a sweepstake on when precisely Lady Tregellas would produce a son and heir for the estate. Madeline paled and heard the cup rattle against her saucer.

Reverend Woodford chose this precise moment to wander in from the garden with Lucien. The two men were still deep in conversation about the parson's plans for Lady Day as they strolled into the small drawing room.

'Ah, Lady Tregellas, I trust that Mrs Woodford has informed you of our expected happy event?' Reverend Woodford's eyes twinkled.

Madeline found her throat suddenly very dry. 'Yes, indeed. It's wonderful news.'

Lucien looked from his wife's pink cheeks to Mrs Woodford's bubbling happiness, and finally to the proud swell of the parson's chest. Comprehension dawned. 'Let me extend my wife's sentiment and offer my congratulations to you both.'

Reverend and Mrs Woodford beamed their pleasure.

Madeline could bear it no longer. 'Please do excuse us, Mrs Woodford. We must be back at Trethevyn before darkness.' She bit at her lip and threw Lucien a pleading look. 'Thank you so much for the lovely tea. S-such wonderful news,' she managed to stutter. 'If there's anything I can do to help, please just ask.'

Mrs Woodford's two-year-old daughter scampered in to the room at that very minute, running full pelt towards her mother before the sight of Madeline brought her up short. She stopped and pointed a small chubby finger at Lady Tregellas, her tiny pink lips forming an expression of surprise.

'Sally!' chided Mrs Woodford, looking anything but displeased. 'Naughty child.' With one scoop of the arms the small girl was resting on her mother's lap. 'No pointing,' said Mrs Woodford, and kissed the miniature extended finger. 'This is Lord and Lady Tregellas, come to visit your mama. Say how do you do, very pleased to meet you, my lord and my lady.' Sally giggled at the absurdity of this, her big blue baby eyes staring first at Lucien and then at Madeline.

Madeline found that the lump in her throat had become a

veritable boulder in danger of choking her, and something gritty was nipping at her eyes, so that she had to blink and blink to stop them watering. 'Goodbye, then.'

But escape was not so easy. For little Sally had taken quite a shine to the nice Lady Tregellas and insisted upon placing a kiss on the lady's soft cheek.

Madeline practically ran out to the waiting coach.

'What's wrong? Why did you wish to leave?' Lucien enquired as the door slammed shut.

Madeline swallowed hard, but the lump refused to be dislodged. 'I have a headache,' was all she managed to say, and hoped that Lucien would not press the matter.

He nodded, and, aware of the moist glisten in her eyes and the quiver of her lips, lent her the space and the silence that she needed to fight whatever it was that was distressing her. Somehow he did not believe her story of the headache.

She stared blindly from the window, willing herself not to cry, and all the way back on the narrow winding road to Trethevyn Madeline began to realise just how much she wanted what she could never have.

Chapter Nine

Fortunately the next day was taken up in hiding the clues that Madeline had written, and Mrs Babcock organising the kitchen for the preparation of the secret birthday lunch, so much so that there was little time to dwell upon such things. Madeline slumped exhausted into bed, wondering what Lucien would think of his birthday surprise.

The day of the birthday was fine and dry with a cold weak sun to brighten the morning room. She rose especially early so that she would be seated at the breakfast table before Lucien even entered the room. She sat quite still at the table, basking in the sunlight that flooded in through the large window. Tiny particles floated on the sunbeam, suspended like small specks of silver within the air. Everything was quiet, so quiet that Madeline could hear the sound of her own breath. She waited with a calm easiness, surprised at her own hunger. A whole plate of eggs, ham and mushrooms had been devoured before she heard the tread of her husband's footsteps. She was sipping her coffee, with Max lounging at her feet, when he entered.

'Madeline?'

She heard the question in his voice.

He glanced towards the clock as if to check that he had not mistaken the time. 'You're up early this morning.'

'Yes,' she said, trying not to look at the neatly folded note that lay beside his place setting. She smiled, a warm anticipation surging through her veins. 'Happy birthday, Lucien.'

Surprise widened his eyes, and then he recovered himself to thank her most politely, and went to help himself to breakfast from the warming plates. It was only when he sat down that he noticed her scraped-clean plate. 'You've already eaten?'

'I couldn't wait for a certain slug-a-bed or I might have starved.'

That drew the vestige of a laugh and eased the tension between them. He found the note beside his plate and scanned the contents. The severity in his face fled, replaced instead with something of the boyish delight she imagined he must have had all those years ago as a child. 'A treasure hunt.'

'I thought you might like it.'

Lucien laughed again, and she couldn't help but notice how it transformed his face. It was like looking at two different men. One cold, handsome and remote, the other, warm and lovable. 'And you were right.'

For the first time since arriving at Trethevyn Madeline saw a glimpse of the man who had swept her off her feet from a dance room and married her before a clergyman that same night.

Lucien held the piece of paper between his fingers. The sun dazzled his eyes, forcing him to squint to make out the words.

First follow beneath me where strong winds blow. I am a cock that cannot crow.

He raised a quizzical eyebrow and looked at Madeline.

Madeline returned a look that belied innocence.

'Do you mean to give me an extra clue?'

'Certainly not,' retorted his wife. 'Mrs Babcock warned me of your lazy ways. You are to solve the clues by yourself.'

Lucien smiled.

They were standing out in the patchwork garden at the rear of the house, with Max in between them. Lucien scanned the surroundings, his eye alighting on the small summer-house built on the top of a grassy knoll in the distance. 'I think perhaps a stroll to the summer-house is in order.' He held out his arm to Madeline and the two wandered off towards the small buff-coloured structure. The weathervane in the shape of a cockerel atop its peaked roof glinted in the sunshine. Max ran off in search of rabbits.

The second does not live and cannot be found above the ground.

Lucien puzzled over that, watching the happiness light his wife's face. He had not seen her looking so relaxed or happy, since before… He pushed that thought away, and continued to look at the warmth radiating out from those sherry-gold eyes. 'Cannot be found above the ground,' he repeated softly as if mulling the clue.

Madeline laughed and clapped her hands together.

He looked directly at his wife. 'I hope you are wearing stout walking shoes, for the Trethevyn mausoleum is on the other side of that woodland.'

Madeline lifted her skirt and dangled a foot encased in a most sensible shoe. 'I think perhaps that my clues are too easy for you.'

'Quite the contrary,' he said, averting his gaze from the slim, shapely ankle that had just presented itself before his eyes.

* * *

By the tenth and final clue, it was time for lunch, and Lord and Lady Tregellas had traced a path that intertwined every feature of the Tregellas estate, even if it did require a two-mile walk there and back. They were standing in the wine cellar beneath Trethevyn, straining to read the clue beneath the light of a solitary flickering candle.

The tenth, and last, can be found where love and peace abound. In golden swathes and purple hues, the answer simply lies in 'you'.

Lucien's brow knitted and something of the old tension returned to his face.

'Have I beaten you at last?' Madeline asked softly.

Their eyes met, and lingered. Hearts beat loud in the silence.

'It would seem so,' Lucien replied. But it was not the treasure hunt to which he was referring. He stepped towards her.

A scrabbling sounded at the cellar door, followed by an inquisitive woof.

'Max!' laughed Madeline. 'He's worried that he's missing something.' She moved to open the door.

Lucien watched his wife stoop to pat the snuffling dog. *He very nearly did,* said the little voice in his head.

'Come on, I'll give you another clue. You should look more closely in the gardens.'

Lucien cocked an eyebrow and followed his wife back up the narrow stairs into the daylight.

Cool spring sunshine bathed the couple as they meandered through the gardens, Madeline's hand tucked within Lucien's arm. There did not seem to be the need to talk. A peaceful companionship had settled upon them. They were happy just to feel the warmth of the sun upon their faces and the nip of fresh air within their noses. A blackbird scuttled beneath the box hedge, a spindle-legged fat-bodied robin whistled its cheeky challenge from the safety of the handle of Old George's gardening fork over by the herb garden. The sky was a clear pale blue, revealing a new clarity of colour to the countryside surrounding them: cold brown earth that crumbled beneath their feet; lawns of green grass; bare branches on ancient old trees; the first hint of buds upon the bushes. They walked towards a battered old wooden seat, and sat down, together.

Madeline breathed in the cool spring air, feeling it cleanse the last of the cobwebs from her lungs. Over the past few weeks tension had just melted away, starting from that very first day when she entered Lady Anne's bedchamber and admired her paintings. There had been a sense of coming home, with the house and all its occupants making her welcome. Max and Babbie and Betsy, Old George and Mr Norton, whose beady butler eye missed nothing. Even Lucien seemed to have allowed his guard to slip a little.

She felt the warm strength in his arm beneath hers and rubbed her fingers against the wool of his coat. Beneath that cold exterior lurked a kind and loving heart. With every passing day she'd watched as her husband saw to his tenants with a fair hand. He was interested in his people, cared enough to know their names, and what happened in their lives, from the birth of the first lamb to Bob Miller's wife's dropsy. No one in Tregellas was afraid of him; no one called him the Wicked Earl here. Was it her imagination, or, since coming home, had something of that cold handsome austerity thawed? Madeline glanced up at her husband's face. He was looking at her and smiling.

'Love and peace,' he said. His smile deepened as his gaze moved to linger on the statue that stood behind the small colourful patch of spring flowers. A stone Cupid looked back at him, complete with stone dove perched upon his bow. 'Golden swathes, and purple hues.' The blue eyes twinkled as he saw what she had done. Daffodils and crocuses had been planted to spell out his name—LUCIEN. He chuckled, shaking his head as if he couldn't believe what was before him. In the middle of the letter U, lying on the damp brown soil, was a battered old box. He moved towards it, pulling Madeline up with him. The simple hook latch opened easily, the lid swung open. Inside, a lady's lavender silk scarf had been wrapped around something. His fingers eased under it, lifting it carefully out. Slowly he unwrapped the scarf, to find a small embroidered portrait of a young boy. It had been fitted into a simple wooden frame.

Madeline held her breath while her husband stared down at the needlework that she had laboured at secretly for the past weeks.

His fingers touched the small neat stitches that had been worked with such care.

'Do you know who it is?' she asked.

'I should do. You have captured the likeness very well.' He regarded her quizzically. 'But how on earth did you…?'

Specks of gold glittered in her amber eyes. 'One of your mother's paintings on my bedchamber wall shows two small boys playing together. It was not difficult to work out which one was you. Babbie was happy to confirm my suspicions.'

Lucien grinned.

'George made the frame. We…we hoped that you would like it,' she said shyly.

'I like it very much.' Then he snaked an arm around her waist and dropped a kiss to the top of her head. 'Thank you, Madeline. It's a fine and thoughtful gift.' Clear blue eyes met lucid brown and smiled until little lines creased their sides, and the warmth of his smile engulfed her so that her heart swelled and her head felt light and dizzy. And when his hand covered hers she thought that life had never been so good.

Hand in hand they strolled back into Trethevyn and the birthday lunch that awaited.

The fire blazed upon the hearth, every candle in the massive crystal chandelier had been lit, and the small drawing room was cosy and warm. Madeline and Lucien sat together on the sofa. Lucien's birthday gift had pride of place on top of the mantelpiece, the stitched boy looking with a cheeky grin over proceedings. Max lay at their feet, beating the edge of the sofa with his tail, and chewing on what had been one of Madeline's dancing slippers.

'I see that his appetite is not limited to my footwear.' Lucien decanted the sherry into two small glasses and handed one to his wife.

Madeline laughed and tickled a black silky ear. 'I made the mistake of leaving my slippers on the floor and he sneaked off with one before I noticed. I salvaged the other before he came back for it, although quite what good one slipper is, I do not know.'

They chuckled together and sipped at their sherry.

Lucien dropped his hand on to his wife's. 'Thank you, Madeline.'

She looked up in surprise. 'What for?'

'For today. For understanding.' His thumb stroked small circle over the back of her hand. 'For...forgiving.'

'Lucien...' her fingers closed around his thumb, trapping it, stilling its motion '...there is nothing to forgive. You saved me from Farquharson.' Her fingers slid from his thumb up to stroke against the inside of his wrist. 'You are my husband,' she said softly.

His eyes closed at her words, struggling against the sensation that her fingers conjured up. Would that he were her husband in every sense of the word. 'That does not mean that I have the right… We had an agreement. I promised you protection, Madeline, not—'

'Not what, Lucien?'

'Not what happened that night in the inn.' He thought he saw wounded anger flash in her eyes and then it was gone. God, he was a fool to have hurt her.

Her teeth nipped at her lower lip, as she entwined her fingers between his. 'I'm sorry that I—'

Lucien felt the constriction in his chest. 'Married me,' he finished for her.

'No!' she gasped. 'Never that.'

Relief loosed the breath from his throat.

Their fingers clung together with a gentle desperation.

'You've nothing to be sorry for, Madeline. You've done nothing wrong.'

The teeth bit harder against the small pink lip. 'I'm sorry that I made you angry that night. I know that you do not want…that you don't want to—'

Lucien could stand it no longer. He pulled her into his arms, tilting her face up to his. 'It was my fault,' he said harshly. 'I should have known better, but found to my shame that I was wrong. Let's put it behind us, Madeline. I wish only for you to be happy.' He touched his lips to her temple in a chaste kiss and put her away from him. Temptation was a terrible thing. And he was determined not to spoil this most precious of days.

Three weeks had passed since Lucien's birthday and signs of new life sprouted everywhere from small green shoots in the soil to tiny buds upon bare brown branches. Lucien was consideration itself. He smiled more. Laughed more. Held her hand, took her arm. He told her stories of his and Guy's boyhood, carried her with him on most of his estate calls, even walked with her to visit the nearby Neolithic stone burial tomb and the mysterious stone circles called the Hurlers. He bought her a beautiful docile bay mare and rode out with her most days. He accompanied her on visits to the local gentry and took her dancing in Bodmin and shopping in Truro. With each passing day Madeline grew to love the man who was her husband.

What had been naïve pleasure at his touch in London had grown to a burning need. She craved him. Didn't understand why his merest glance caused a flutter in her stomach. Just knew that she needed more of him. The memories of that one night when she'd kissed him in the bed of the New London Inn tortured her. She wanted him. Every last bit of him. To touch his naked skin. Trace a pathway through the hairs upon his chest. To feel the strength of his body moving over hers. Wanted him, despite knowing that the desire was not reciprocated. Madeline blushed at her wantonness.

The exact nature of the marriage bed remained a mystery but Mama had hinted often enough that a wife's duty lay in it. Henrietta Brown, from the ladies' sewing group, had delighted in telling them all that she had heard it from her sister that a woman must do her duty and submit to her husband. Duty and submission did not beckon. Memories of what she had shared with Lucien, however, did. Maybe she had done something wrong to disgust him. Maybe women weren't supposed to kiss their husbands. She lay in the great four-poster bed and pondered the problem. As if sensing her mood, Max crawled up from the bottom of the bed to lie next to her, licking her face with a warm pink tongue, and whining.

'Go to sleep, Max.' Madeline patted his head and took

comfort from the old dog's presence. But as she drifted off to sleep she couldn't help but wish that it was Lucien by her side.

'Oh, m'lady, I'm so sorry, the ribbon just slipped an'…I'm not usually so butter-fingered!' Betsy burst into tears and ran from the room.

Madeline started after her in alarm. 'Betsy!'

But Betsy had disappeared down the servant stairwell at the far end of the landing. Madeline quickly plaited her hair back from her face in a queue, securing it with the ribbon that had fallen to the floor, and set off in pursuit. She almost ran straight into Mrs Babcock at the bottom of the stairs. 'Mrs Babcock, have you seen Betsy?'

'What's all this Mrs Babcock?' demanded the large woman, elbows akimbo. 'I thought we'd agreed I'm Babbie.'

'And so you are,' Madeline consoled. 'It's just that Betsy seems rather upset this morning. She only dropped a ribbon and that prompted a flood of tears. She hasn't seemed herself for a week or so now. I'm worried about her, Babbie.'

Mrs Babcock sucked at her bottom teeth, a sure sign of stress. 'It's Mrs Porter,' she said in a loud whisper. 'Betsy's mother. She's not been keepin' well. Right poorly she is. In her bed for nigh on a fortnight and not lookin' any better for it. There's only the two of them. Mr Porter was a real scoundrel, ran off and left the pair of 'em high and dry when Betsy was still a little 'un. Betsy's been lookin' after her mum. An' she's real worried.'

'Why didn't she say something? She should be at home with her poor mother, not here combing my hair!'

'Needs the money,' confided Mrs Babcock. 'Poor as church mice. Mrs Porter normally takes in mendin', but with her illness that's stopped. Betsy's wage is their only income.'

Madeline stared at the housekeeper. 'Then we must do something about that.'

'Now, m'lady, there's no need for you to go worrying yourself about them.'

But Madeline was worried. 'Has Mrs Porter seen a doctor?'

'Old Dr Moffat's been out. He's a real gent. Don't take no money from them that can't afford to pay. A consumption of the lungs, he said, accordin' to Betsy.'

A determined look came over Madeline's face. 'Has Lord Tregellas returned from the Granger farm yet?'

Mrs Babcock shook her head. 'Not as I know of.'

'Then have Cook pack up a basket of food: bread, eggs, pie and the like, and if she's made any soup so much the better. Ask Boyle to harness the gig and tell Betsy to wait ready by it.' Madeline whirled and ran back up the stairs.

'M'lady!' shouted Mrs Babcock at the receding figure. 'Don't you be getting any ideas like. His lordship wouldn't want you doin' nothin' silly, m'lady!'

But Madeline was gone.

When the housekeeper saw Madeline again she was heading for the front door, wearing a warm pelisse and cloak, and carrying two large folded blankets on top of which her reticule was balanced.

'M'lady!' Mrs Babcock hobbled across the marbled floor of the hallway at a surprising speed.

Madeline halted in her tracks. 'Oh, Mrs Babcock, there you are. I'm going to take Betsy home, and visit her mother. Has the gig been brought round yet?'

Mrs Babcock ignored the question. 'You might catch that dreadful disease. Best to stay here, m'lady.'

Madeline pressed a hand to her arm. 'Babbie, it's the very least I can do for them. Poor Betsy has been worrying herself sick all week and saying not a word about it. They're probably not eating properly and the weather has been so very cold.'

The housekeeper's brow furrowed. 'His lordship won't like it. He gave strict instructions that you weren't to be out alone.'

'I won't be alone. Betsy and Mr Boyle will be with me,' Madeline said. 'Besides, Lucien will understand.'

Mrs Babcock looked very much like she knew exactly what Lucien's understanding would be. The furrow across her brow deepened. 'Well, at least let me come with you.'

Madeline shook her head and smiled. 'Dear Babbie, I know how very busy you are today, and the weather's enough to smite the ears from your head. You know what the cold does to your knees. Stay here and keep warm. Somebody needs to check if Cook is making those delicious scones.'

The housekeeper mumbled.

'My stomach's rumbling at the very thought. I swear I'll be ready to eat a horse when I get back.'

Mrs Babcock nodded. 'Off with you then, but mind you don't stay too long. Scones won't take long in the makin' and you'll be wantin' them nice and warm from the oven.'

Madeline laughed and disappeared out of the door, running down to meet Betsy, who was waiting patiently by the gig.

'What do you mean, she's gone out?' Earl Tregellas did not look to be in the best of moods.

Mrs Babcock faced him with a defiant calm. 'Gone to visit Mrs Porter, who is poorly in her bed. Taken Betsy with her, a hamper of food, blankets and a purse of money.'

'And when did she go?'

'Ten o'clock, m'lord,'

'That was two hours ago,' said a poker-faced Lucien.

'She's only out the other side of the village. It's safe enough there.'

'Babbie,' he said with barely concealed exasperation,

'there is a very specific reason that I have tried to ensure that Madeline is always accompanied on her every outing. I would not have her safety compromised.'

'Lord Tregellas,' said Mrs Babcock a little more gently, 'there ain't nothin' goin' to happen to her at Mrs Porter's. Time's moved on; her ladyship's in no danger.'

Lucien turned the full strength of his gaze upon the old woman. 'Madeline is not unknown to Cyril Farquharson. Indeed, he has what might be termed a special interest in her. Only here in Trethevyn is she truly safe.'

Mrs Babcock tightened her lips and sucked hard on her bottom teeth. 'Oh, Lord! You should have told me.'

'I'll take Nelson and ride out to find her.'

Mrs Babcock clutched a veined hand to Lucien's arm. 'Forgive me, I'd never have let her go had I but known.'

A nod of his head, and Lucien stepped away.

Carriage wheels crunched against the gravel of the driveway outside.

Lucien and Mrs Babcock looked at one other. Lucien was out the door before the gig had even come to a halt.

Madeline clambered down from the gig and looked at the two tense faces regarding her. 'Lucien, you're back.'

Lucien said nothing.

The housekeeper eyed the empty gig behind Madeline.

'I thought it best that Betsy stayed with her mother until the poor woman felt better. I'll manage without her for a few weeks.'

A welcoming bark sounded and Max trotted down the stairs to greet her, jumping up at her skirts until she scratched at his head.

Two pairs of eyes continued to stare at her with blatant accusation.

'Is something wrong?'

'You mean something apart from you sneaking off unaccompanied in the gig?' said Lucien.

Madeline blinked in surprise and continued to stroke the dog's head. Her husband's mood had been fine at breakfast. Evidently matters had altered that. 'I didn't sneak. Betsy's mother is ill. I merely went to visit her, that's all.' Puzzlement was clear upon her face as she glanced at Mrs Babcock.

The housekeeper looked every bit as cross as Lucien.

'We'll discuss this inside, Madeline.' Lucien stalked back inside the front door.

She followed him to the large drawing room, Max dogging her every step.

Not one word was said until he had closed the door carefully behind him. Then he turned and raked her with a blast from those piercing eyes. 'Do you mean to explain yourself?'

'I beg your pardon?' Madeline stared at him as if he had run mad. 'I have not the least notion of what you mean.'

'Then let me remind you of a certain man who displayed an unhealthy interest in you. Can it be you have forgotten him so easily?'

'What has Cyril Farquharson to do with my visit to Mrs Porter?' She perched herself on the edge of the chair, while Lucien loomed before her.

'You gave me your word that you would not go out alone.'

'And I didn't. Betsy and Mr Boyle were with me.'

'A lady's maid and Boyle hardly count as adequate defence against someone like Farquharson. Boyle's seventy if he's a day. And even at that you came back without Betsy.'

'You're exaggerating the danger,' said Madeline.

Lucien arched one dark eyebrow. 'Really?'

Max looked from master to mistress in confusion and gave a loud booming bark.

'Yes, you are!' Madeline stood up and glared at him. 'Farquharson is far away in London. He's hardly likely to just pop up in Mrs Porter's house. I don't see what the problem is.'

'Then let me enlighten you.'

'There's no need. I think I begin to understand.' Madeline turned on her heel and walked towards the door.

'Madeline,' he said in a soft, deadly voice.

Madeline walked on regardless, not even showing that she'd heard. Her fingers had reached the handle when she felt herself gripped in a pair of strong hands and spun round to face him.

'Cyril Farquharson hasn't been in London for two weeks. It's likely that he's here in Cornwall.' His hands held her firmly, but without hurt.

Her eyes widened at that. Her heart skipped a beat.

A high-pitched whine sounded in the room. Madeline and Lucien looked down to find their normally docile pet in a state of distressed confusion.

'Max?' Lucien said.

Max whined louder and then set up a raucous barking.

'Good God!' exclaimed Lucien and, letting his hands drop, backed away.

The barking stopped and Max trotted quickly in to fill Lucien's place, taking great delight in sniffing around the hem of Madeline's skirt.

Madeline gave a quick raise of her eyebrows and a little sheepish smile. 'Perhaps I should take Max with me the next time I go visiting. He's really a rather good guard dog.'

Lucien did not return the smile. His pale eyes bored into hers. 'Let me make it crystal clear, Madeline. You are not to leave Trethevyn unless it is in my company. You may underestimate Farquharson. I do not.'

In the weeks that followed, spring blossomed in all its glory, warming the earth and setting everything in growth.

Lambs gambled in the fields and what had been bare and barren and brown when Madeline arrived in Cornwall turned green. Since the day of their argument Lucien had shown no signs of changing his mind. As the days wore on with no sign of Farquharson, her husband grew increasingly wary rather than more relaxed. Madeline began to question what lay behind her husband's zealous guarding. She stood at her bedchamber window, watching the stark outline of his dark figure riding out down the sweep of the driveway. Betsy sat noiselessly in the chair close by, trying her best to repair the damage inflicted upon a shawl by Max.

'Naughty dog,' said Betsy. 'You've nigh on ruined her ladyship's good shawl.'

Max raised innocent eyes as if to say, *Who, me? Impossible.*

Madeline chewed on her lip and followed the dark figure until it disappeared from sight. 'Betsy…' she began.

'M'lady?' Betsy concentrated on making her stitches small and neat.

It was probably not an appropriate subject to discuss with the maid, but other than Babbie, Madeline had no one else to ask, and Babbie was desperately loyal to Lucien. Much as the housekeeper bossed and harangued Lucien in a way that no one else dared, Madeline couldn't imagine the old woman standing to hear a word spoken against him. 'Do you not wonder on his lordship's preoccupation with danger, Betsy?'

'Ain't my place to wonder, m'lady.'

'We've been here over two months, yet still he rides out every day to check across the length and breadth of the estate. It's as if he expects the imminent arrival of Lord Farquharson.'

'Who's this Lord Farquharson, then, m'lady?'

Madeline plucked out a hairpin that was pressing uncomfortably against her scalp. 'A villain of a man who has a disagreement with Lord Tregellas,' replied Madeline. There was no need for Betsy to know the full details of what had happened in London. 'I cannot help but wonder over Lord Tregellas's response. What happened with Farquharson is far behind us. He cannot harm us now. Yet Lucien would keep me a practical prisoner in this house for fear that Farquharson means to exact some revenge upon my person.'

'If he's an evil man, then perhaps his lordship has a right to be worried,' reasoned Betsy.

'But the passage of time should diminish the threat, not make it worse. If Farquharson were here, we would have known of it by now. No one can arrive in the village, or leave for that matter, without one of Lord Tregellas's men reporting it back to him. I'm worried about him, Betsy,' confessed Madeline. 'He thinks of nothing but Farquharson. I believe it's an unhealthy obsession, something that has grown out of all proportion. Perhaps the threat from Farquharson is not what he would have me believe. Perhaps it never was,' she said quietly.

'Stands to reason, though,' said the maid, 'that he's likely to be a bit overreacting about such things, given what happened.'

'What do you mean?' Did Betsy know that she had jilted Farquharson to elope with Lucien? And if Farquharson was of a mind to call Lucien out, he would have done so before they left London. He had told her Farquharson had killed a woman, but it wasn't Farquharson that London whispered was a murderer. For the first time Madeline began to doubt the truth of what Lucien had told her. She had married him on the basis of his assertion that she was at risk from Farquharson, that and her own instinct that there was something intrinsically rotten about the Baron. Looking back, she began to see that she had been blindly trusting of a man that she had not known at all. And now that she knew him, had come to care for him… His behaviour towards Farquharson smacked of something more, something dark and obsessive. Madeline shivered, and waited for the maid's answer.

'What happened with his betrothed, all them years ago.'

Foreboding prickled across Madeline's scalp. 'His betrothed?' she whispered.

Betsy looked up and blushed beetroot. ''Cept we're not supposed to talk about that, m'lady.'

'Betsy?'

But Betsy had suddenly remembered an urgent appointment with Mrs Babcock and was off and away before Madeline could say another word.

Madeline rubbed her arms against the sudden cold that chilled her. She thought she had come to know her husband, to learn something of his childhood, of his life before he had met her. Now she realised that she knew nothing at all, save for a queer, hollow dread that had opened within her heart.

Chapter Ten

The letter arrived at midday while Lucien was still out on the estate. The writing comprised spiky narrow letters that were vaguely familiar. Something tickled in her memory, lurking just beyond recall. Faint unease shimmied down Madeline's spine.

'Somethin' the matter, doe?' enquired Mrs Babcock, topping up Madeline's cup with tea.

Madeline shook her head. 'No, nothing at all. What kind of soup did you say?'

'Mock turtle, and as well as that George brought in a lovely brace of partridges fresh this morning.'

'That sounds fine, Babbie.' The seal broke easily beneath her fingers and she opened the letter. A glance over the first line, then her eyes leapt down to the signature and she quickly closed the piece of paper back over and tucked it beneath her leg.

'You sure you ain't sickenin'? You're lookin' a touch pale, m'lady.' Mrs Babcock stared with concern as the blood drained from Madeline's cheeks, leaving her ghost white.

'No, no,' gasped Madeline. 'Just a little light-headed, that's all. It will pass. I'm fine.'

'Light-headed?' Babbie said, her blackcurrant eyes growing rounder by the minute. 'Can't be due to lack of food. You've developed a right healthy appetite since you come here. I remember when you first arrived, picked at your food like a little sparrow, you did. Not good for a body, that is. Got a bit more meat on you now, I'm glad to say.' Babbie's brain weighed up the evidence, feeling faint, increased appetite, weight gain, and a new closeness between the master and mistress...and reached quite the wrong conclusion.

'Yes,' said Madeline rather weakly. 'I think I might just go and lie down for a little. Will you manage the rest of the dinner arrangements?'

'Course I will, doe,' replied Mrs Babcock, beaming. 'You got to get your rest, m'lady. Don't want you takin' too much out of yourself. I'll leave the scones and tea here in case you want to finish them later. Got to keep your strength up.'

Madeline waited for the housekeeper to leave and wondered why Mrs Babcock seemed so pleased. She didn't ponder the problem for long. As soon as the door shut the letter was hauled from its hiding place and, with a dry mouth, she began to read each and every one of the words penned upon it, hearing once again that cruel voice that Trethevyn had made her forget. For the sender of the letter was none other than Cyril Farquharson.

London
April 1814
My dearest Madeline
I hope that this letter finds you in good health, and that Tregellas has not yet subjected you to the worst of his nature. I write to tell you that I bear you no malice for marrying that scoundrel—indeed, the blame lies entirely upon his head. For what choice had you in the matter, my love?

I strike my breast and deliver myself a thrashing when I think how you misinterpreted my eagerness for our union. Forgive my cruel words that I last threw at you, I was overwrought. I love you, Madeline. I have loved you from the first minute that I saw you. But I should have realised that my very great consideration for you would overwhelm such a fragile flower as your-self. I beg your forgiveness, most humbly, if I ever acted as anything but a gentleman. You should know that I have ever held you in the highest regard, and I truly re-gret if I let my passion frighten you. It was my dream to make you my wife and care for you in the manner you deserve. Alas, Tregellas has destroyed all of my hopes.

I wish you well, Madeline, but my conscience could not sit easy if I did not at least try to warn you of Tregel-las's true nature. I am afraid that there is, indeed, sub-stance behind his reputation as the Wicked Earl. Although I do not wish to increase your hurt any more than it is already, as a Christian gentleman it is my duty to tell you the truth of what lies behind your forced ab-duction and marriage.

Many years ago, as a young and impetuous man, I met a young lady who captured my heart. She was sweet and good in much the same way as you, my dear Madeline. We fell in love and wished for nothing other than to be married. But the lady was betrothed to Tregellas and he would not release her from their contract. For the sake of our love we had no other choice than to elope. Per-haps it was wrong of me to return her love when she was promised to another, but I cannot be ashamed of some-thing so pure. Tregellas was like the devil with rage. He came after my sweet wife, and...pen and ink tremble at the words I know I must write...killed her.

Forgive me, Madeline, for breaking such a harsh and horrible truth to you. I can do nothing else but warn you of his terrible evil. From that day until this, he has stalked me, desiring nothing more than my death. He hates me with the haunting compulsion of the insane. You must realise by now that he cares nothing for you, and, indeed, that he wed you in an act of selfish revenge. I do not know the extent of the lies he has told you, but I truly fear for your safety, Madeline. Should you need my help at any time, you have but to send me a message and I will come. I did not think to love again in this life, but God blessed me with you. I could not stand to live if Tregellas were to kill you, too, my darling. I pray with all my heart that you will be safe from danger.
Ever your servant,
Cyril Farquharson

Madeline read the letter, and reread it, until the words blurred upon the page. His love, his darling? Never. She remembered the biting grip of his fingers bruising against her skin, the hardness of his mouth as it sought hers. One close of her eyes and she could see the cruel promise in his face. She shuddered and set the letter down upon her desk. Yet time and again as she sat there her eyes drifted back to catch at the page. He wrote of a woman who had been betrothed to Lucien. Betsy had let slip those same words. Lucien's betrothed. Her stomach knotted at the very thought. *He came after my sweet wife, and...killed her.* The words stood out boldly on the paper before her. It was not possible. Not Lucien. Not when he had only ever treated her with kindness and care. That, at least, could not be denied. He might not desire her, he most definitely did not love her, but Madeline knew in her heart of hearts that Lucien would never hurt her. From the first time she had looked into those intriguing pale eyes, she had trusted him and felt safe. Surely her instinct could not be so wrong?

But Farquharson was right in certain aspects: Lucien's increasingly obsessive behaviour; Lucien's hatred of Farquharson, so intense as to be almost palpable. Could Farquharson be right about the others? Her teeth gripped hard at her lip, contemplating what she had learned. She wondered what truth lay behind Cyril Farquharson's letter. Had Lucien wed her solely for revenge? Was he guilty of Farquharson's accusation? Or was it Farquharson who had murdered the woman, as Lucien had claimed that night so long ago in London? Madeline's head whirled dizzy with the thoughts. Cold fingers touched again and again to the letter before, at last, she folded it up and placed it carefully in the bottom drawer of her bureau, beneath a pile of fresh writing sheets. She rose to stand before the window in her bedchamber.

Farquharson made her flesh crawl. Lucien engendered different emotions altogether in her breast. For all the dark mystery that had surrounded Earl Tregellas, that still surrounded the man she called her husband, she trusted him over Cyril Farquharson. From what she knew of Farquharson, it was likely that he had fabricated the entirety of the story. Lucien might have been betrothed once upon a time, in the past. It was hardly a fitting subject to raise with his new wife. Little wonder he had not spoken of it. There would be no link between Farquharson and the woman promised to marry Lucien. And as for Lucien killing anyone...well, the whole idea was just preposterous.

Madeline lifted her face to the sun, letting the brightness of its rays through the pane glass warm her and banish the dark suspicions from her mind. Cyril Farquharson might

think to fool her, but Madeline refused to be so easily hood-
winked. She would not let her worries over Lucien's behaviour add substance to Farquharson's lies. She thought once
more on how increasingly bedevilled her husband was
becoming with Farquharson. The letter would only make
things worse.

A wood pigeon soared high in the sky, heading for the trees
at the far end of the drive. Madeline watched the hurried beat
of its wings and felt the freedom that surrounded its flight. In
the clarity of the moment she knew what she should do.
Lucien had tried to protect her. Now it was her turn to protect
him. Whatever reason lay behind Cyril Farquharson's torment
of her husband, Madeline meant to see that it would go no
further. She lifted the pen and opened the lid of the inkpot.
By the time she was finished, Lord Farquharson would be
under no illusion as to where her allegiance lay.

It was early the next morning when Madeline received
the news that Mary Woodford was unwell. She ceased her
rummaging amidst the linen cupboard and scanned the hurriedly scrawled note pleading that she attend Mrs Woodford
at the parsonage.

Madeline nipped at her lip and pondered the problem. It
was clear that she should visit Mrs Woodford to offer what
help she might. But Lucien had left at dawn to travel to Ta-
vistock and would not return to Trethevyn until late. And
since her visit to Mrs Porter, Lucien had ensured that she did
not leave the house unless he accompanied her. What to do?
Madeline worried some more at her lip, concern about the
kindly parson's wife snagging at her conscience. Mary
Woodford was a friend. The woman would not plead for help
without good reason. Surely Lucien would understand why
she could not just sit here uselessly while heaven only knew

what Mary Woodford was going through. If she were to be accompanied by one of the grooms, as well as Betsy, and have Mr Boyce to drive the carriage, and they were to carry a cudgel with them… He could not be angry that she had taken no precautions against danger. Besides, he need never know that she had gone. She would be back well before him.

'The linen can wait. Mrs Woodford is unwell and has asked that I visit her. We must make ready.' Madeline replaced the bedsheet back upon the neatly folded pile on the shelf closest to her within the press. 'And, Betsy—' she delivered her maid a worried look '—ask John Hayley to accompany us and to bring a large cudgel with him.'

'J-John Hayley?' stuttered a suddenly rather pink-cheeked Betsy.

'Yes, the groom with the blond, curly hair, arms like a cooper, looks like he's made of solid muscle, bright blue eyes.'

Betsy's face flushed a deeper hue. 'Why ever should he accompany us, m'lady?' Her hands plucked at her apron in a decidedly flustered manner.

'As our guard,' answered Madeline, gaining an inkling as to the reason for her maid's rosy complexion. 'Do you know him at all?' she asked rather wickedly.

'A little,' admitted Betsy with an averted gaze.

Madeline tried hard to keep a straight face. Only the hint of a smile tugged at the corners of her mouth. 'Then this will be a good opportunity for you to get to know him better. He looks very strong, does he not?'

'Yes, m'lady, quite strong indeed.'

'And I suppose that some ladies might even describe him as handsome.'

'Very handsome,' agreed Betsy.

'Well, then, it's settled. You run down and ask Mr Boyce

and John Hayley to make ready in, say, half an hour. I will speak to Babbie. That sounds like a good plan, does it not?'

Betsy grinned. 'Yes, m'lady, a fine plan.'

The two women laughed together before setting off downstairs to make the necessary preparations for their journey.

Four hours later neither Madeline nor Betsy were laughing. They stood by the side of a muddy road, a fine drizzle soaking through their clothes and ruining their bonnets. Mr Boyce and John Hayley were hunkered down examining the axle of the carriage, scratching at their heads. One large wheel lay forlornly in the middle of the road. A sea of mist had gathered on the horizon and was creeping closer towards the little group.

'Well, at least Mrs Woodford is feeling better. Dr Moffat said that the baby is fine. She's to rest for the remainder of the week. Poor little Sally does not know what to make of her mama tucked up in bed.'

But Betsy had other things than the parson's wife on her mind. She gave a shiver. 'They say the ghost of Harry Staunton haunts this moor, puttin' the fear of death into any wayfarin' travellers who he happens to chance upon.'

'Who was Harry Staunton?'

'A ruffian and a highwayman. Hundred years ago they hanged him, they did, and when they cut him down and placed him in his grave he was still breathin'. But they buried him anyway...alive, and he's haunted the moor ever since. A wanderin' soul, robbin' and terrorisin' them he meets on the moor, him and his great black stallion, appearin' out of the mist and disappearin' just as easily again.' Betsy wiped a hand across her runny nose, then rubbed at her eyes. 'Oh, m'lady, what are we to do? Harry Staunton's out there, I knows it.'

'There's no such thing as ghosts, Betsy. It's just a story told to frighten people. Even if this Harry Staunton was ever a real person, he's dead and buried, not haunting Bodmin Moor.' Madeline placed a comforting arm around the maid's shoulder. 'You're just tired and cold and wet. Things will seem much better when we get back to Trethevyn.' She pulled a clean pressed square of white linen from her reticule and placed it into Betsy's hand. 'Here, take my spare handkerchief.'

Betsy sniffed. 'Oh no, m'lady, I shouldn't.'

'Of course you must,' insisted Madeline before turning to Mr Boyle. 'How fares the repair, Mr Boyle? Will it take much longer?'

The elderly retainer scratched at his head. 'Not lookin' too good, m'lady. Need some tools to sort this. Young Hayley could run back to fetch 'em and bring the coach back out to collect you. But that'll take some time, and I don't like the look of that mist. Ain't too much shelter on the moor neither. Master won't be best pleased when he finds out 'bout this.'

Guilt twinged at Madeline. It was her fault, not the servants. She didn't want them getting into trouble. Especially when Lucien had forbidden her to leave the house without him. 'Lord Tregellas need not know of our trip. Could not the wheel be repaired this afternoon before he returns?'

With a great deal of effort, and some help from John Hayley, Mr Boyle clambered to his feet. He wiped the dirt from his hands down his breeches and gave her a look that was enough to make Madeline shrink with shame. 'Are you askin' me to lie to his lordship?'

She felt her face colour with embarrassment. 'No. I just thought…I was thinking that, perhaps—' The muffled drum of horses' hooves in the distance stopped her.

The fine bays still attached to the carriage pricked up their ears and whinnied.

Betsy gave a shriek. 'It's him, m'lady. Harry Staunton and his black devil horse. God help us all!'

Mr Boyle armed himself with an ancient blunderbuss and John Hayley grabbed the cudgel from the interior of the carriage. 'Stand behind us, quickly, m'lady, Betsy,' ordered Mr Boyle, his gnarled old hands aiming the gun at the bank of thick white mist into which the road disappeared.

Betsy started to sob.

'Come along, Betsy,' Madeline urged. 'There's no need to cry. It's just another traveller. Perhaps they will be able to help us.' She did not miss the look that passed between the two men.

Betsy whimpered even louder.

Madeline tried again. 'Mr Boyle and John will protect us.'

Betsy's whimper turned to a wail.

Madeline patted at the tearful maid's shoulder, then wrapped an arm around her, to no effect. 'Hush now, Betsy.'

But Betsy would not be hushed.

'He's comin', I knows it!' she wailed again and began to tremble from head to toe.

John Hayley stepped back briefly. 'It'll be all right, Betsy,' soothed the young groom. 'We won't let nothin' happen to neither of you.' A large hand touched against the maid's arm, a bright smile flashed, and Betsy's crying miraculously ceased.

'Promise?' she hiccupped through breaths still small and panting from her sobbing.

'I promise,' said the young man.

The mist closed in around them. The hooves grew louder. John Hayley stepped forward to be level with Mr Boyle. They waited in silence, tension crackling all around them, eyes trained upon that spot where the road had been. Waiting. Poised. Afraid. Knowing that the encroaching mist distorted sound, aware that the horseman could be closer. They strained their attention towards that one single point. Both wishing and dreading his appearance.

Suddenly, from out of the mist, the horseman appeared. A large dark shape astride a huge black horse.

Betsy screamed. 'It's Harry Staunton!'

An almighty flash and a loud explosive crack burst forth from the blunderbuss, the recoil of which knocked Mr Boyle to the ground. The air was heavy with blue smoke and the stench of gunpowder. It seemed that the shattering noise echoed amidst Betsy's incessant screaming. Raising the cudgel John Hayley prepared to protect them all from the attack of the ghostly highwayman.

'What the blazes…?' Lucien saw the flash of gunpowder ignite and threw himself flat against his horse's back, bracing himself to control the petrified beast. From behind he heard the shout of alarm from his man Sibton, and reined the gelding in hard. Nelson reared on to his hindlegs, eyes rolling back in terror. Lucien clung on for dear life, whispering calming reassurances in the horse's flattened-back ears, using every ounce of strength to stop the beast bolting directly into the small huddled group before him. Nelson skittered forward and reared again, sending deadly hooves crashing down dangerously close to the fair-haired man standing to their fore. The bodies scuttled backwards, the woman's piercing screams unnerving both Nelson and his master. With a firm press of the knees Lucien managed to quiet the great black horse enough to draw the pistol from the pocket of his greatcoat. He jumped down from Nelson's back, throwing the reins to Sibton, and pointed the muzzle at the shape before him. 'Unhand that woman or I'll fire.'

The screaming intensified.

'What the hell are you doing to her?' He prowled

forward, the mist thinning as he did so. The pistol cocked beneath his finger.

'Lord Tregellas?' a familiar elderly voice sounded. 'Can it be you?'

'Boyle?' One more step and he saw them clearly. Young Hayley with cudgel raised, standing before Boyle, who lay upon the ground. Two women, one trying to help the old man up, the other huddled in a frightened ball, screaming and sobbing in terror.

The stick dropped from the young groom's hand and the defensive stance relaxed. 'M'lord, thank God it's you. We thought…'

Lucien surveyed the scene before him closer, his eyes moving quickly from one face to another, until it came to rest on that of his wife. 'Madeline.' Her eyes were huge and dark in the pallor of her face. He stepped past Hayley. 'What happened?' He saw the blunderbuss down by Boyle's side.

'Forgive me, m'lord. I didn't know 'twas you. Thought you were a villain comin' out of the mist. Couldn't take no chances on account of her ladyship bein' present,' Boyle murmured, clutching at his shoulder.

Comprehension dropped into place. 'You mean it was you that shot at me?'

Boyle nodded weakly. 'Praise the lord that the shot went high. I could have killed you.'

'Never mind that now. Let me have a look at that shoulder.'

'Just a bruise,' gasped Boyle from between gritted teeth. 'See to her ladyship, I'll be fine,' he whispered, cheeks turning chalkier by the minute. Lucien had to bend an ear close to the old man's mouth to catch the faint words amidst Betsy's hysteria. Lucien turned an irritated eye towards the maid. 'By Hades, will someone quieten that girl before I do it myself?'

'Lucien!' exclaimed his wife. 'Don't be so unkind. Betsy is distraught. She thought you were a ghost coming out of the mist.'

Lucien's gaze swivelled to Madeline. He raised one dark eyebrow. 'If that bullet had been an inch lower, I damn well would have been.' He looked into her eyes and saw fear mixed with relief. He caught back the words from the tip of his tongue. 'See to your maid,' he said and turned to Hayley. 'Help me get Boyle up to a sitting position. I think he may have dislocated his shoulder.' Between them, Lucien and the young groom manoeuvred Boyle until Lucien had a gentle grip upon the coachman's shoulder. 'Hold him tight, this is going to hurt like hell.'

The one short grunt that issued from Archie Boyle's lips were more distressing than all of Betsy's screaming put together.

Madeline averted her face, holding her arms around Betsy, until the sobbing was nothing more than a series of shudders through the maid's body.

Lucien spoke to Hayley. 'That should have done the trick, but I want Dr Moffat to look him over when we get back. Stay here with Boyle and Betsy.' He rose and, walking over to Sibton who was still holding the horses, pressed a pistol into his servant's hand. 'Just make sure you know who's coming out of the mist before you fire it. I'll take Lady Tregellas back to Trethevyn with me, and send the coach out for Boyle and the others. Tether the bays and bring them back in at the same time. We'll come back for the carriage once everyone is safe.'

Sibton nodded his compliance.

Lucien returned to stand before his wife. Not trusting himself to speak, he just reached a hand down towards her and pulled her up into his arms. He felt the subtle resistance, saw the flicker of her eyes towards the maid.

'I cannot leave Betsy,' she murmured.

'Hayley will look after her,' he said, and steered Madeline towards his horse. 'We're going home.'

Home. Madeline realised that she had indeed come to think upon Trethevyn as her home. It offered safety and comfort, and a whole lot more. Despite the threat of Farquharson, and the mystery surrounding Lucien, Madeline acknowledged that she was happier in the large country house than she had been at any other time in her life. The strength of Lucien's arm curled around her waist, securing her firmly to both the saddle and himself. She felt the warmth of his chest press against her, chasing away the worst of the damp chill. One hand clung tight to him, the other gripped the edge of the saddle. He was angry. She could see it in the tense muscles around his mouth, feel it in his body's rigidity. Yet every so often his arm squeezed a little tighter around her, as if to reassure himself that she was still there, still safe. Nelson's steady canter enabled her to keep her seat easily enough. But the mist was thickening so that they could barely see the road before them.

'Nelson knows his way home, Madeline. We can trust that he will keep to the road easily enough.'

'Lucien…' she looked up at his face '…I'm sorry. Mrs Woodford is unwell and I was so worried… I did not anticipate that the visit would turn out in this way.'

'We'll discuss the matter when we get home.' His voice was firm, but the fingers that caressed her waist were gentle and reassuring.

The smirr of rain grew stronger. She nestled in closer, trying to shield herself from its seeping dampness. Lucien stopped the horse, unbuttoned his greatcoat, and, unmindful of her wet clothing, pulled her against his body, inside the shelter of the coat. And that was how she stayed all the way back to Trethevyn, her cheek pressed against the hard muscle of his chest, listening to the beat of his heart.

It was an hour later and all of Lucien's staff were safely back at Trethevyn. Lucien made his way upstairs. A curt knock and, without waiting for a reply, he swung the door open. He entered the bedchamber silently, dismissed Betsy, ensuring that she took a grudging Max with her and closed the door quietly behind them. His wife had at least changed from her wet clothes into something warm and dry. She knelt on the rug before the marble fireplace, head bowed, drying her hair by the heat of the flames. Her hair tumbled in a tousled waterfall, pooling around her shoulders in a sensual reminder of what he was missing. Lucien banished such thoughts, forcing himself to remember exactly why he had come here and what he meant to say.

'Lucien.' She looked up and smiled. Her cheeks were pink with warmth and her eyes sparkled a clear golden brown. A thick cotton nightdress showed above her dressing gown. Lucien's eyes flicked down to take in the bare feet that peeped out from under the cotton, and rose to take in a very shapely pair of hips. Stirrings of a highly inappropriate nature made themselves known. Lucien cleared his throat and strolled over to survey the view from the window until he could regain control over his body. Lord, but she looked so adorable he longed to just pull her up into his arms and kiss her. He swallowed hard. If he was entirely honest, that's not all he wanted to do. It would be so easy to scoop her up into his bed and keep her there the whole night through. Such thoughts were not helping his problem. He glanced down. Indeed they seemed only to be making it worse. He strove to think of Farquharson and the danger that he presented. And from that to

Madeline's blatant disregard of his request that she did not travel from Trethevyn unless in his company. That seemed to do the trick.

'Is something wrong?' The soft pad of bare feet sounded behind him.

'Nothing apart from the fact you seem determined to place yourself in the worst of situations.'

The clear honey eyes blinked back at him. 'I've said my apologies. Mary Woodford is my friend. She might have lost the baby, Lucien, so I went in response to her note, to offer my help. Thankfully, matters were not so bad as she had thought. The doctor has said that the baby is safe.' A tenderness came into her eyes.

He swallowed back the reciprocal feeling that it engendered. 'I asked you not to leave Trethevyn without me.'

'Would you have had me ignore her plea and just sit here while she was enduring such agonies?' Madeline looked up at him. 'They are your people, Lucien. Do you not care for their welfare?'

'That's an unfair question. You know that I do. Besides…' he raked a hand through his hair '…I have no issue with you visiting the parsonage, or anywhere else for that matter, as long as I'm with you. And you understand the reason that I've asked such a thing.'

She sighed, and moved to stand beside him.

'You should have waited until I got back. We could have gone together, tomorrow.'

'It might have been too late by then. I was worried and she asked me to go as soon as possible.'

'I know you were, Madeline, but not half as worried as I was when I heard that blunderbuss and saw you stooped over Boyle's body.'

'I'm sorry.'

But 'sorry' would not save her from Farquharson. 'You play a dangerous game, Madeline. Farquharson could have plucked you as easy as a berry from a bush.'

A little line of pique appeared between her brows. 'I took John Hayley and a cudgel. My Boyle took his blunderbuss. I thought we would be safe.'

'Indeed?' he said. The memory of the pounding of his heart and the dread when he saw her through the drifting mist and gunpowder plume spurred him on. 'Had I been Farquharson, or any other villain, do you think that Boyle would have stopped me? I could have put a bullet through Hayley before the cudgel was even raised in his hand. Then where would you have been, Madeline? Completely at my mercy.'

Madeline's chin tilted in defiance. 'You are obsessed with Farquharson. Of all the places he is likely to be, Bodmin Moor late on a damp misty afternoon is not one of them.'

'And you know that beyond all reasonable doubt, do you? You are willing to take the risk? Believe me, Madeline, I know, better than most, the evil of which that man is capable. I will not have you expose yourself to such danger.'

'We weren't going far. I did not know that the wheel would come off.' She turned from the window so that they were facing one another.

'That does not matter.' He pushed her excuses aside. 'You disregarded my request not to travel alone.'

'I wasn't alone,' she protested.

'You understand my meaning well.' Exasperation lent an edge to his voice. 'You seem intent on trying to throw yourself into Farquharson's path.'

'Oh, don't be so silly!' she replied, anger lending her a foolhardy courage. 'I'm just getting on with living. I cannot forever be looking over my shoulder. Would you lock me behind these doors, never to venture out again for fear of him?'

'That's not what I'm saying, Madeline.'

'Then what are you saying?'

'It's not too much to ask that I accompany you.'

Madeline's breast rose and fell beneath the dressing gown in a flurry. 'I'm beginning to feel like a prisoner, Lucien. I love Trethevyn, but I should be able to at least visit a friend when she is ill without waiting for you!'

'Under normal circumstances I would agree entirely. But the circumstances are far from normal. Until I have dealt with Farquharson, we must both live by certain constraints.'

She hesitated. Dealt with Farquharson. The claims of Farquharson's letter came back to her. *He has stalked me, desiring nothing more than my death.* 'What do you mean to do to him?' she asked.

'Whatever it takes to stop him.'

Madeline shivered.

He reached across and pulled her into his arms. She was so small, so vulnerable. 'Farquharson's more dangerous than you realise.' He stroked a hand over the damp tumble of hair, smelling the sweetness of her and her orange fragrance. 'He will come after you in the most unexpected of places.'

'But if he meant to hurt us, would he not have done so by now?'

Lucien shook his head. 'He's biding his time. But our waiting is nearly at an end. Farquharson will strike soon. And when he does, I want us both to be ready.'

It should have been her husband that she asked, but it wasn't. Madeline was desperate and so she asked Babbie about the woman Lucien was to have married.

'Terrible affair it was,' said Mrs Babcock. 'Almost drove Master Lucien insane. It's not my story to tell, but what I will say to you, m'lady, is please don't judge him too harshly. He was a young man and he made a mistake like all young men do. 'Cept his mistake cost him dearly. Can't forgive or forget. Blames himself even yet, though it weren't his fault.' Mrs Babcock's eyes dampened with a terrible sadness. Her eyelids flickered shut as if gathering the strength to carry on.

Madeline touched cold fingers to Mrs Babcock's hand. 'What happened?' she asked carefully. 'Will you not at least tell me that? Please, Babbie.'

'She was a young lady. I won't divulge her name. Wealthy, titled, only daughter of a viscount. Quiet and shy. Beautiful she was, tall and slender with long black hair and big blue eyes. The most beautiful girl in all of Cornwall.'

Beautiful, tall, black hair, big blue eyes—in short, everything that Madeline was not. A little ball of nausea rotated in Madeline's stomach. She didn't want to hear the words. She knew that she had to.

'And the most foolish. She was just eighteen when they were betrothed.'

Madeline pressed a hand to her stomach and swallowed hard.

'Even so, she went up to London for her first Season. Met a gentleman there. Next thing she ran off and married him, even though she were under age and had not so much as a word of consideration for Master Lucien. Whisked off with the gent in the middle of a dance. Most out of character for her, by all accounts. Needless to say, it was a right scandal.'

In the middle of a dance! 'Oh, God!' Madeline could stop the expletive no longer. For she had a horrible premonition of where this story was heading.

Mrs Babcock's hand balled to a fist tight against her own lips. 'I've said too much. You should hear the whole of it from his lordship. He'll tell you when he's ready, m'lady. Please, give him some more time. He don't mean to be high-handed. He's just worried and wants to keep you safe.'

Madeline bit down hard upon her lip. 'Who was the gentleman that the girl ran off with?'

'That's for his lordship to tell,' said Mrs Babcock.

'It was Cyril Farquharson, wasn't it?' Madeline stared at the housekeeper.

Mrs Babcock's mouth stayed firmly shut.

'Wasn't it?' said Madeline, and there followed a deadly hush.

'Yes,' said Mrs Babcock miserably, 'Lord Farquharson was his name.'

Madeline gazed in anguish for a moment longer. 'Please can you go now? I'm tired and would like to rest.'

'But, m'lady, you don't know the full of it. It weren't just that. There's more. Much more. And—'

Madeline shook her head. 'I've heard enough, Babbie. Please just go.'

Mrs Babcock rose and hobbled out of the room, closing the door quietly behind her.

Chapter Eleven

It seemed to Madeline that her heart had ceased to beat. She sat stunned, unable to move, barely able to breathe for the tightness that constricted her throat. Everything suddenly made sense. Cyril Farquharson had told the truth. The pieces of the puzzle had fallen into place to reveal the picture in full. She knew now why Lucien had been so determined to save her from Farquharson, why the wealthy Earl Tregellas had plucked a plain little nobody from beneath that fiend's nose to make her his wife. For in truth it was not Lord Farquharson who was the fiend at all—that title belonged to her husband. He had married her for nothing more than to exact revenge upon Farquharson, to do unto Farquharson precisely what the Baron had done unto him. Madeline Langley was just the silly little fool who had lent herself as the weapon of his vengeance. And that vengeance had not been for her. It had never been for her. It was for another woman from across the years who had betrayed him.

All talk of saving her from Farquharson, of protection, was just a lie. With the harsh brutality of realisation she knew that everything he had said had been a lie. Lies and more lies.

Madeline blinked back the tears, determined not to cry. The tip of her nose grew numb and cold. A lump balled in her throat. London had called him the Wicked Earl and with good reason. Madeline had thought she knew better, had refused to believe the rumours. And Madeline had been proved wrong. Now she knew why he would not share her bed. Lucien Tregellas would never love her, for he loved another woman, a tall woman with big blue eyes and long dark hair…the most beautiful woman in all of Cornwall.

Blood trickled down from Madeline's lip and still she did not realise the pain or the pressure of her bite. 'Damn him,' she whispered. 'Damn him for the devil he is.' She had thrown common sense to the wind, risked all to avoid a marriage with Cyril Farquharson. Now that she had made her bed, as Mama would say, she would have to lie in it. Madeline screwed her eyes tight against the tears that threatened to fall. She'd be damned if she'd let him see just how much he'd hurt her.

Then a little thought made itself known. If Farquharson had told the truth about Lucien's betrothed, was it also true that Lucien had killed the woman? That he meant to kill Madeline too? No matter how angry she was, no matter how hurt, she could not bring herself to believe either. If Lucien wanted a wife in name, then that's exactly what he would get. That meant no more allowing him to dictate what she could and couldn't do. What had he said the night that he asked her to marry him, or at least when she believed she had a choice in the matter? *You would be free to live your own life.* That was his bargain. A cold-hearted bargain. And, by God, she would hold him to it!

Guy, Lord Varington, was concentrating on the two piles of cards on the table when the sensation of someone having walked across his grave shivered across his shoulders. He glanced up to find Cyril Farquharson watching him from across the room. Guy delivered him an arrogant sneer and switched his attention back to the game. Ace. He won the last turn and bowed out with a sense of unease still upon him. It was quite out of character for a man whose lazy arrogant confidence was renowned the length and breadth of London. He meandered towards the fireplace, ignoring the call of several voices for him to rejoin the game of faro. The night was still young, but curiously White's seemed to have lost its atmosphere of indulgent relaxation. He ordered a brandy, sat himself down in a comfortable armchair, and started to browse through a copy of *The Times*.

'Varington...' a familiar voice feigned pleasance '...the very man I was hoping to see.'

Guy looked up into the face of Cyril Farquharson. Without showing the slightest hint of surprise he answered, 'Back in London so soon, Farquharson? But then again, I had forgotten your need to trawl the marriage mart.'

The barb hit home as Farquharson's cheeks ruddied, but he controlled his temper well. 'What ever made you think that I had departed the metropolis? Gossip can be so misleading.' He sat himself down in the chair opposite Guy's. 'Don't mind if I join you, do you?'

Guy became aware of the murmur of interest in the room around them. He smiled a smile that did not warm the ice of his eyes. 'You have five minutes to say what it is you that you've come to say, and then...' Guy's smile deepened '...if you're still here I feel I must warn you that I'm not endowed with my brother's restraint.'

'Five minutes shall more than suffice,' said Farquharson. The grey of his snugly fitted coat mirrored the smokiness of his eyes.

They looked at one another, dislike bristling beneath a veneer of civility.

'How fares Lady Tregellas in Cornwall?'

A dark eyebrow arched in sardonic surprise. 'All the better for choosing my brother over you as her bridegroom.'

Farquharson's lips narrowed. 'That's not what I've heard, sir.'

'Then you ought to have a care to whom you listen.'

The closed face opened with mock-innocence and he leaned forward in a confidential manner. 'Even if it comes straight from the horse's mouth, so to speak?'

Guy smiled his deadly smile again. 'Your time is running out, Farquharson. Waste the remaining minutes in riddles if you wish.' But the chill of anticipation was upon him and Guy knew that Farquharson would not be sitting there attracting the attention of White's patrons if he did not have something worth revealing.

'Perhaps it would be better if you saw the evidence yourself.' Farquharson reached into his pocket and produced a letter, ensuring that no one in the room missed him pass the paper into Varington's hand. 'I should tell you that I've had my lawyer make a copy signed as a true representation of the original…should anything untoward happen to the letter while it's in the possession of another.' A row of teeth was revealed.

Even before he touched it Guy could see that the broken wax seal was that of Tregellas. The note opened to reveal a tidy flow of ink script upon his brother's headed writing paper. Guy's eyes followed each and every word down to the flourish of the neat signature. He balked at the letter's contents, but the face he raised to the red-haired man seated opposite showed nothing but a bland disinterest. 'Another one of your efforts at amusement.' Guy let the paper fall to his lap and proceeded to examine his fingernails. 'And another failure. May I remind you, sir, that forgery is a crime.'

'Indeed it is. That's why I've had the authenticity of the paper and seal checked. I wouldn't want anyone to believe any misrepresentations that may have been circulated about me. The letter verifies what I've said all along about Tregellas. That's why I plan to publish it in a certain London newspaper, so that all may see it.'

Pale blue eyes locked a focus on smoky grey.

'But as you are aware, Varington, I'm a just and fair man, and even though Tregellas has wronged me I'm prepared to give him the chance to do the right thing.' A slim white finger stroked his upper lip. 'Take the letter and show it to him. If I hear nothing from him within the next fortnight, then I'll go ahead and publish.'

'Go to hell, Farquharson. I'll not be your messenger.'

Farquharson's mouth stretched to a semblance of a smile. 'Then you forfeit your brother's chance to prevent publication. Thank you for your time, sir.' Farquharson reached to retrieve the letter, but Guy's fingers were there first, removing the letter, tucking it safely inside his coat, knowing that he had no other option.

Farquharson stood and made to leave. 'Just one more thing, Varington. When you see Tregellas, ask him if he has come to appreciate Madeline's acting skills. She is really rather good, but then again I did train her myself. Tregellas is so very predictable. I couldn't have "guided" his actions nearly so well without her.'

Guy rose quickly, but Farquharson was halfway across the room, making his escape, smiling his gratitude at the captive audience that allowed it. There was nothing that Guy could do without causing a scene, and that was the last thing that Lucien needed right now. Guy forced himself to sit back down, to finish his brandy and read a few more news articles in *The Times* before strolling out of the gentlemen's club as if he had not a care in the world. It was only when he reached the haven of his townhouse that the affected air of boredom was cast aside.

At first light next morning, Viscount Varington was seen leaving his house, travelling light on the fastest horse in his stables, with only his trusty valet for company.

When Farquharson heard the news that Varington had left town he could scarcely contain his glee. The bait had been swallowed. He knew there was only one place that Varington would have gone, and that was exactly where Farquharson wanted him to be: Trethevyn. Farquharson smiled. The first aim of the letter had been achieved. The second would follow soon, when Tregellas read the words penned upon that paper. Farquharson's smile deepened. Contrary to his threats, he was not ready to publish, not until matters in Cornwall were completed. Publication of the letter would meet its third and final aim: a fitting end to Tregellas. Farquharson sniggered. The five years of waiting would almost be worth it. His plan was coming together nicely…beginning with Varington. The last of Farquharson's valises was carried from his bedchamber. He made his way down the stairs and out to his waiting carriage to begin the journey to Cornwall. And the thought of just what he planned to do there excited Cyril Farquharson almost to a frenzy.

The woman who faced Lucien over dinner that night was not the woman he had come to know in the months since he'd married her. It seemed that the light in Madeline's eyes had dimmed and a new coolness had crept into her manner.

'I met Mr Bancroft while I was out today. He invited us

for dinner tomorrow evening. Mr and Mrs Cox will be there, along with Mrs Muirfield, Reverend and Mrs Woodford, and Dr Moffat.'

'Unfortunately I shall be unable to attend,' said Madeline in the voice of a stranger.

He couldn't help but notice that her cheeks looked pale tonight. Indeed, something of the bloom that had settled upon her in the past weeks seemed to have faded. She was once more picking at the food set upon her plate. 'Why might that be?'

'I'm planning to return to London tomorrow morning. It's a while since I have seen my family, and I would like to visit them.'

The sudden silence within the dining room grated. Only the clock upon the mantel sounded.

Lucien dismissed Mr Norton and the footmen. Only when the door had been closed behind their departing bodies did he speak. 'I'm sorry to disappoint you, but it does not suit me to leave Trethevyn so soon. Perhaps in a week or two we shall make the journey. I'm sure that your parents will understand.' Lucien waited for his wife's reaction.

Madeline did not look up from her dinner plate. 'I'm perfectly content to travel alone. You may stay here.'

Another silence.

Was she so keen to be rid of his company as to risk exposing herself to Farquharson? A sliver of hurt stabbed at Lucien's heart. Even as he closed his mind to the pain, he wondered how she had managed to pierce the protective numbness that the years of torment had forged. 'I'm afraid I cannot allow that, Madeline,' he said.

Her knife and fork were set down upon her plate, the pretence of eating the food forgotten. Gone was the warm biddable woman, replaced instead by someone that he did not know. 'Cannot allow?' For the first time he saw a spark of anger in her eyes. 'Did we not have an agreement, sir?' Without waiting for a reply she rushed on. 'I have fulfilled my side of the bargain—do you seek to renege on yours?'

Lucien found himself frowning across at her. 'I'm doing exactly what I said I would.'

'You said that I may visit my family whenever I wished. Well, I wish to do so now.' A hint of a pink stain stole into her previously pale cheeks.

Lucien gritted his teeth. 'You may also recall that I promised to protect you. And I cannot do that if you are insistent upon exposing yourself to danger. It's not that I do not wish you to see your family, but I won't have you put your life at risk to do so. Patience is a virtue, Madeline. The visit will be all the sweeter for waiting a few weeks more.'

'You would know all about patience, wouldn't you? Please do not presume to lecture me on it, for I would rather act on one foolish impulse after another than have your cold, calculated patience!' A deeper blush flooded her cheeks and her chair scraped back hard against the polished wooden floor. 'And as for protection and safety…please spare me any more of your untruths. I know full well what this is about, sir. You may cease your game.' She rose swiftly, threw her napkin down upon the table and started to walk towards the door.

In one seamless motion he was out of his chair and across the floor, his hand grasping her arm, pulling her back to face him. He was aware of the tension that resonated through them both, of the pulse that throbbed at her neck. 'I think you had better explain your words, Madeline.' The softness of his voice belied the turmoil of emotion that roared beneath that calm façade.

She looked up into his cold pale eyes and felt a tremor flutter deep within, but it was too late to pull back. She had fired the first shot and now she would have to finish the fight. 'You know of what I speak. There is no need for me to spell it out.'

'Humour me,' he said in a flat tone. 'Every word, every letter.'

His fingers burned against the flesh of her upper arm. He was so close she could feel the brush of his breeches against her skirt, smell the scent of soap and cologne upon his skin, see the detail of the dark shadow of stubble upon his chin. Her heart hammered in her chest. 'I know the truth,' she whispered.

His eyes bored into hers. 'Pray enlighten me with it.'

'I know why you married me.' She saw a muscle twitch in the tightness around his jaw. 'I was never in any danger from Cyril Farquharson, was I?' she said in a low voice. 'Only from you.' She thought she saw shock and something else in the depths of those ice-blue pools, a reflection, there, then gone.

'You really have no idea of the lengths to which Farquharson will go, the depths to which he will plummet, to have you. He means to kill you, and he will, unless I stop him.'

'No, Lucien! I won't listen to any more of your lies.' She tried to pull back from him but he made no effort to release his grip. 'Why did you not just call him out and have done with it?' she shouted at him. 'It would have saved us both a lot of trouble.'

'I did, albeit too damned late. Have you not noticed his limp? My aim was flawed. A leg is a poor substitute for a heart. I shall not make the same mistake again.' His face was white and bloodless against the stark black of his hair.

'Your fight with him has nothing to do with me. Just let me go. You may seek a divorce at the Consistory Courts. I will not stop you. I'll return to my family until I'm able to think of what to do with my future. You need not fear I will speak of the matter—I give you my word that I will not.'

Lucien's hands tightened around her arms. 'Divorce? By heaven and hell, Madeline, if that's what you're hoping, then

I tell you now that I will never divorce you. You knew when you agreed to marry me that there was no going back. I haven't gone through all of this to hand you to Farquharson on a plate. If he has his way, you won't have a future.'

'Cease this pretence, Lucien. Can you not forget what he did, carry on with your own life?'

A gasp of incredulity escaped Lucien's lips. His eyes burned with cold blue fire. Anger coiled tight. 'I will never forget, and I will never rest until Cyril Farquharson is dead.'

'He was right,' she whispered. 'Jealousy has driven you mad.' She struggled to release herself from him.

He hauled her closer. 'Jealousy?' The straight white teeth practically bared. 'And of what is it that you think I would be jealous? Rape? Torture? Murder?'

Disbelief blasted at her from every pore of his body. The breath grew ragged in her throat. They stared at one another with the frenzied ticking of the clock in the background goading the squall of emotion higher. The mask slipped. Raw and bleeding hurt showed clear upon his face. All her beliefs of what lay between him and Farquharson, of his callousness in using her for revenge, turned on their head. 'Lucien…' she reached a hand towards him, but it was too late.

Letting his hands fall loosely by his sides, he stepped back from her. 'Good God, you really don't believe me, do you? You think I'm lying about protecting you? About what he means to do to you?'

She shook her head. 'I…I don't know.' She watched the harsh shutter drop back across his face, shielding whatever he was really thinking from her view. 'He stole your betrothed. So you stole his. *Quid pro quo.*'

His eyes held hers. There was about him an agony of tension that reached across the small distance between them. 'Never think that,' he said. 'I will not let him hurt you in the way that he hurt Sarah.' He reached across and with a feather-light touch caressed her cheek. 'I failed before and two women died because of it. I will not fail again. Hate me if you will, but I'm the only thing that stands between you and Farquharson, and I have no intention of giving up an innocent to him again. You're my wife, Madeline, and while Farquharson still breathes that's the way it's going to stay.'

The gentleness of his fingers stilled against her cheek, transfixing her, wooing her against her will. But beneath it all she heard the steely determination of his tone.

'Lucien, I cannot…I will not…' She was determined to finish what had to be said. 'You loved her.' Madeline ploughed on through the weight of crushing pain that had settled upon her chest. It pricked at her eyes and tightened around her throat as if to choke her. 'I didn't know it, that night in the inn…in the bed. I would never have…I wouldn't have done what I did, had I known.' *And I wouldn't have married you had I known that your heart had already been given, and I would lose my own to you,* the little voice inside her head whispered. She would not hear it, could not allow herself to. Tonight she would say everything she must, for tomorrow she would be gone—whatever Lucien said to the contrary.

'You did nothing. I was the one who forgot myself, not—'

'No, Lucien. That's not true.' She looked at him a moment longer. The blush scalded her cheeks. 'I understand why I disgusted you.'

She thought she disgusted him? Lucien reeled at the frank admission. 'What ever gave you such a ridiculous idea?' But as the question formed upon his lips, he remembered his reaction on waking to find himself in the throes of making love to his wife. He'd been disgusted all right, but with himself, not Madeline.

The amber eyes looked up to his.

'I can assure that you do not disgust me, Madeline. Quite the reverse, in fact.'

'Then why—?'

Lucien's fingers slid round to cradle the nape of her neck. In one step he closed the space between them, his other hand sweeping down to press against the small of her back. She felt the superfine of his coat brush against her breasts. His head lowered towards hers until his breath tickled against her neck, licked against her cheek, her chin, her nose, igniting a trail of passion. Ice-blue eyes locked with warm amber. The words died in her mouth. Madeline found she could not move, could not breathe for drowning in the cool blue water that was his eyes. 'Lucien…' The word was nothing more than a hoarse breath between them. She watched his gaze drop to her mouth and linger. Felt hers do the same, cleaving to that finely sculpted mouth. 'Lucien…' Need grew stronger.

The sweet allure of her lips beckoned. Moist. Pink. His lips moved to capture her protestation, claiming hers. Sliding together in possession as his fingers stroked against the skin of her neck. Her mouth opened beneath his, responding to his call, answering with a passion of her own. His tongue teased against her lips, then probed further, seeking within, until it touched against her own small hesitant tongue. Urgency exploded between them.

Madeline arched her back, instinctively driving her breasts against the hardness of his chest, gasping with the sensations taking over her body. She moaned a protest as his mouth left hers. Her hands entwined themselves around his neck to pull him back down to her. But Lucien had other ideas. He pressed a trail of hot kisses to her nose, eyebrow, temple and ear, tracing the delicate line of her jaw with his tongue.

'Lucien!' She gasped his name aloud, dizzy with desire,

blind to everything save the man that pressed against her, deafened by the thud of their hearts.

His fingers moved to close around her breast. His palm scorched the mound, his finger and thumb teasing against her nipple until it hardened and peaked between them, as if the silk of her dress was not there. And still the madness continued. It was not enough. She wanted more. Needed more. Her breasts ached with need. And it seemed that her thighs were on fire, burning her, scalding her with desire. His hands slid down across her stomach, following over the curve of her hips round to cup her bottom. She nestled in closer, feeling her own desperation echoed in his body. His mouth raided hers once more, hard, demanding, needful, but the hands that stroked against her were gentle and giving.

His breath was ragged against her ear. 'Madeline!' The ravaged whisper sounded against the hollow of her throat, against her lips.

Her legs trembled as she gave herself up to him, lost in the ecstasy of the moment. Strong arms supported her, would never let her fall.

He pulled back enough to look into her face and she wondered that she ever could have thought his eyes cold, for they held in them such a look of warm tenderness.

'Madeline,' he said again, more gently this time, 'you make me forget myself and all of my promises. Disgust, indeed!' A wry eyebrow arched and a wicked smile curved his mouth. His fingers caught a tendril of hair that had escaped its pins to feather across her cheek, and tucked it back behind her ear. 'If you are set upon returning to London tomorrow, then I will take you. But as long as Farquharson lives then I will never let you go. And, Madeline, if you really did know the truth of what happened here five years ago, then you would understand why. Idle gossip weaves lies with truth in equal measure.

I thought you knew that. You would have done better to ask me.'

He still held her, close and intimate. Her body burned for want of his touch. 'Would you have told me?' she whispered the words against his chest.

Lucien's chin rested lightly on the top of her head. He hesitated. 'In truth, I do not know. It's a difficult matter for me to speak of.' She deserved the truth about that at least.

'Will you tell me now?' She looked up and shyly touched a small kiss to his throat. Palms laid flat against the muscle of his chest, feeling the strong steady beat of his heart.

His gaze held hers as he moved his thumb against the soft cushion of her lips. 'It does not make for a pleasant story,' he said. 'Are you sure that you want to know?'

She nodded once. 'I need to know, Lucien. All of it.'

She felt the slight tightening of his muscles beneath her hands, saw him swallow hard.

'Very well, then,' he said. 'But not here. Let's go to the library.'

The library. His special place into which she had never before been invited. She knew then that he meant to tell her everything.

His hand closed over hers and together they walked towards the dining-room door.

They had almost reached it when a stiff little knock sounded against the wood. Lucien swung the door open to reveal the portly figure of Mr Norton. The butler recovered well, hiding his shock. In all the forty-seven years Mr Norton had served the Tregellases, he had never had the Earl open the door in person. 'M'lord,' he said with only a shade less than his usual aplomb. A slightly horrified expression flitted across his face as he caught sight of the barely touched serving dishes and food-laden dinner plates upon the dining table. 'Perhaps the meal was to not to your liking?'

'It was very good, thank you, Norton.'

Mr Norton showed not the slightest intention of moving. He stared with barely disguised confusion first at Lord Tregellas, and then at his wife.

'The meal was lovely, thank you, Mr Norton.' Madeline smiled at the butler.

'We are retiring to the library and are not to be disturbed,' said Lucien, and, taking her hand in his, swept Madeline off in the direction of the library.

Madeline sat in one of the battered old wing chairs positioned close to the hearth. The library was not a large room. Down the full length of the wall opposite the fireplace were shelves of books. All were bound in a burgundy-leather cover, with gilt lettering upon the front cover and spine. There was a desk that was bare save for a writing slope, some cut paper, and a pen-and-ink set. A small drum table between the two wing chairs held a decanter and two balloon glasses. Madeline's fingers rested against the worn and cracked leather of the chair arm and she watched her husband push the small table back towards the book shelves, then pull the other chair closer to hers.

He reached across, lifted her hand from the chair leather and held it gently within his own. 'I didn't mean for you to discover the history of what lies between Farquharson and me. It is, as I said before, hardly a pleasant subject…especially so for you, Madeline.' He lifted each of her fingers in turn, rubbing them, playing with them as he sought to find the words to tell her what needed to be said. 'But half-truths are a dangerous opponent, and so I find I've no choice but the one to which I'm pushed. I ask only that you hear what I would say in full and that you promise never to reveal what passes between us this evening.' He paused, watching her, waiting for the oath that would bind her to secrecy, afraid of what the truth might do to her.

'I promise.' Madeline felt the warmth of his hand around hers, saw the hesitation in his eyes. 'Lucien, you may trust that I will spill your words to no one. I give you my word on all that is holy.'

His gaze held hers a moment longer, then shifted to the golden glow of the fireplace. 'As you must know, it happened five years ago, although sometimes it seems that time has stood still since that night.' His profile was austerely handsome. 'I was betrothed to Lady Sarah Wyatt, daughter of Lord Praze. My father and Lord Praze were friends. It seemed a good alliance for the families to make.' He paused. 'I did not love Sarah, but through time perhaps I would have come to care for her.'

Madeline bowed her head and tried not to be glad.

'She was a very quiet and reserved young girl. Even though it was agreed that we would marry, Sarah had always longed to go to London and be presented for the Season. I saw no reason why she shouldn't do so. The winter had been hard that year and none of the family knew that my father's heart had weakened. I'd been in London only a fortnight when I received the news of his death.'

Madeline squeezed his hand. 'I'm so sorry.'

Lucien gave a barely perceptible nod of the head and continued in the same controlled tone as before. 'My parents didn't care for the town, preferring to spend their time here at Trethevyn. Naturally Guy and I returned with haste. My mother was distraught.' He glanced at her then. 'Theirs had been a love match, you see.'

Madeline briefly touched her cheek to the back of the hand that was still wrapped around hers.

'Sarah didn't return to Cornwall. She sent a letter expressing her condolences and carried on as before.'

'Did you not mind?'

'Not really. She was young and enjoying all that London had to offer.'

Sarah Wyatt also sounded to be a rather selfish young lady to Madeline's mind, but she held her tongue and did not offer her opinion.

'It was two weeks after the funeral when the first rumours reached us. Cyril Farquharson had been seen too frequently in Sarah's company. Their behaviour was giving London something to gossip over. My mother insisted that she would manage and bade me return to London to speak to Sarah.'

'So you went back.'

'Yes, I went back to find that Sarah had been beguiled by Farquharson and was set upon marrying him.'

Madeline shivered. 'She would willingly have wed him?' Her voice rang high with incredulity.

'Indeed, yes,' replied Lucien with surprising calm. 'She told me that I might sue her all I wished, but it would not convince her to marry me or stop her loving Farquharson.'

Madeline's jaw dropped open, her eyes opening wide. 'Love? How could anyone love such a man?'

Lucien shrugged. 'She barely knew him. It was not Farquharson that she loved, but the false image that he played her.'

'What happened?' she whispered the question, wondering what was to follow. Sarah Wyatt was dead, of that she was sure. But by what means and had Lucien played any role in that terrible event?

The stark blue eyes moved to hers. 'The time comes when I must confess my guilt, Madeline, for had I acted differently that night, things would not have unfolded in the same manner. Both Sarah and my mother would still be alive.'

Cold dread crept up Madeline's spine. Her teeth nipped at her bottom lip. She waited for what he would say.

The firelight flickered upon Lucien's face, casting sinister shadows across its hard angular planes. And still he said nothing. A log crackled, sending a cascade of sparks out on to the marble slabs.

'What did you do?' Her throat was hoarse with aridity. It was the question she most feared to ask, and the one question she knew that she must.

'I killed her,' he said softly.

Madeline's heart stopped. Breath trapped in her throat. Time shattered. Her eyes slid to him, gaped in horror at the stillness of his profile.

'Or as good as,' he said, still staring into the flames as if he were locked into some nightmare of the past.

As good as? A sigh of relief. *Then he hadn't, he didn't...* 'Tell me, Lucien,' and she pulled him round to face her. 'Tell me,' she said again.

His eyes held hers. 'I cast her out. Sent her to him, willingly. Told her that I would not sue her because I did not want her.' And still he faced her with defiance. 'I didn't even call Farquharson out over it.'

'But you shot him. I thought—'

He shook his head in denial. 'That was later, after I knew what he had done to her.' The pain was clear upon his face. 'I sent her to her death, Madeline. The guilt is mine.'

'No! She loved him. She wanted to marry him. You did nothing wrong.'

'She was a foolish, innocent young girl. What chance did she have against Farquharson? She couldn't have known what manner of man he was.'

'Did you?'

'There was always something unsavoury about him. But I did not know the extent of it. Not then.'

'Lucien, what else could you have done? You couldn't

have pushed her to a wedding she did not desire.' Clear honey eyes stared into pale blue. Both knowing that the conversation was overlapping on to more recent events.

'Not even to protect her?' he said with a harsh cynical tone. 'To save her life?'

The heavy beat of Madeline's heart thudded in her chest. 'Like you did me,' she whispered.

'Yes.' He raked a hand wearily through his hair. 'Exactly like I did you.'

Only the slow ticks of the clock punctuated the silence.

'How did she die?'

'Horribly.'

The single word hung between them.

'I don't understand.'

'It's better that you don't.'

'Lucien...' a wrinkle crept across her brow '...I should know it all, however bad it is.'

He sighed, and opened his palm beneath her hand. 'Madeline, once you know there's no going back.'

'Tell me,' she said again and laid her hand over his. 'I'm your wife, Lucien, and nothing is going to change that.'

He gave a slight nod. 'Very well. Cyril Farquharson—'

A knock sounded.

Madeline jumped. Lucien glanced round at the library door.

Another knock, slightly louder than the last.

'Come in.'

The door opened to reveal Norton. 'My apologies, m'lord. I know you didn't wish to be disturbed, but Lord Varington has just arrived. I've taken the liberty of placing him in the drawing room.' The butler gave a mild clearing-of-the-throat noise. 'If I may be so bold as to observe that Lord Varington has come only with his man, and that his horses have been ridden long and hard.'

A prickle of foreboding traversed Lucien's scalp. 'I'll come immediately,' was all that he said before turning to Madeline. 'It appears that we must postpone our…conversation until another time.' He waited until the butler's footsteps receded into the distance. 'Guy wouldn't have arrived unannounced, on horseback and at this time of night, if something wasn't wrong. Perhaps it would be better if you waited upstairs.'

He could see the look of hurt in her eyes. 'My brother will not speak bluntly in front of you and I need to discover what's happened to bring him down here at such speed.' His fingers squeezed hers in a gesture of reassurance. 'Guy hates the country. I can't remember the last time he left London.' He stood.

Madeline got to her feet. 'Then matters must be serious.'

'That's what I'm afraid of. Go up to your room…' he spoke gently, his hand still intertwined with hers '…I'll come to you later. We should finish what we've started this evening.' He stared into her eyes. 'There will be time later to speak of it in full.'

'Lucien.' She raised her face to his. 'You will come… tonight, won't you?'

He traced the outline of her cheek with his thumb, regarding her with something akin to wonder.

'Are you sure that you want me to? Perhaps it would be better kept until another time.'

She shook her head and, standing on the tips of her toes, reached up to place a shy kiss upon his mouth. 'No. What happened with Farquharson wasn't your fault.' The thrum of her heart pulsed in her chest. 'Tonight.' She pulled back to look into the cool blue pools of his eyes. 'Please.'

'I'll come to you tonight.'

Their lips touched, lingered together, parted reluctantly.

Both knowing that it was not only the end of the story for which she was asking.

He followed her out, watched while the slender figure mounted the stairs. Subtle sway of her hips and rustle of silk. He breathed in the subtle scent of oranges that surrounded him, felt his heart swell with a long-forgotten tenderness, acknowledged that he wanted her, every last inch of her, from the heavy dark gold of her hair to the tips of her toes. Not only her body, but also her respect, her affection, her love. She did not blame him for the terror from across the years. Would she, once she knew it all? Lucien did not think so. Her belief in him eased the heavy burden of guilt. Her warmth thawed the ice in which he had been frozen. And the realisation that she wanted him was a salve to his soul. After tonight, the possibility of a divorce *a vinculo matrimonii* would be no more. A consummated marriage could not be nullified. But first there was the small matter of his brother.

Chapter Twelve

'What were you doing speaking to him?' Lucien raked a hand through his hair, oblivious to the mayhem he was wreaking upon his valet's hard work.

Guy lounged back in the wing chair, swinging a muddy booted leg over the arm. 'Your concentration seems to be elsewhere, Lucien,' he said. 'I already told you, he approached me in White's. I couldn't very well break the bastard's jaw without drawing a smidgen of attention to the fact. Believe me when I say that I was tempted in the extreme. But I didn't want to give that snake any further fuel to burn upon the fire he's stoking.' Guy looked at his brother's face and took a swig of brandy. 'You'd best prepare yourself, Lucien. The matter's not over.'

'I never believed it was. I've been waiting for him to strike, watching closer with each passing day.'

'Farquharson was ever the coward, Lucien. He's coming after you, all right, but not in the way that you think. He means to convince all of London that Madeline was an unwilling party in your marriage. He's been working on it since you left.'

Lucien paced the length of the small library. 'Let him.

Arthur Langley will vouch for his daughter's story. Madeline spoke before Farquharson and her father. She assured them of her willingness in the matter and confirmed the validity of the marriage.' A vision of a tousled-haired Madeline wrapped in his dressing-gown, asserting before both her father and Farquharson that she had married and bedded him because she loved him, swam into his mind. His heart swelled with tenderness. He'd be damned if he would let either man take her from him by whatever means.

Guy's leg ceased its lazy swing. 'That may have been what she *said*. It's what she has *written* that is the problem.'

A sinking feeling started in Lucien's chest. 'Go on.'

A short silence. Brother looked at brother. And Lucien knew that what Guy was about to say would change everything.

'How certain are you of your wife, Lucien?'

'What do you mean?' A dark frown drew his brows close. 'She's the innocent in all of this mess.'

'Is she really?' asked Guy softly.

'What the hell are you getting at? Farquharson had her in his sights. I married her to protect her.'

'And lure Farquharson to a confrontation.'

'Yes, I admit it, that as well. None of us are safe until he's dead.'

'And Farquharson isn't safe until you're out of the way either. You've never left him alone in all of these years. Everywhere he's gone you've dogged his steps, waiting for your chance.'

'Ensuring that there would never be a repetition of what happened to us five years ago.'

'You knew what you'd do if he found another woman, a woman like Sarah.'

'You know that I did.'

'While you were watching and waiting all those years, did

it never occur to you that Farquharson might be hatching his own plan, to rid himself of you?'

Lucien looked into the eyes that were so like his own.

'That he might use an "innocent little victim" to lure *you?*'

'Are you saying that Farquharson never had any intention of marrying Madeline? That he deliberately set matters up to make it appear that he meant to?'

Guy's lip curled. 'Knowing full well that you would rush to her rescue, even if it meant marrying her yourself.'

The coldness started in his toes and spread up through the core of his body. 'Even if it was all a ploy, I still won't yield her to him. She's my wife now. He may have used her. I have no intention of doing the same.'

'Even if she accuses you of abduction and begs him to rescue her.'

'Don't be absurd! Madeline would never do such a thing.'

Guy set the empty glass down carefully on the table before standing to face his brother. 'She already has,' he said quietly; retrieving the letter from his pocket, he handed it to his brother. 'Farquharson has a copy and means to publish it unless you come to some kind of agreement with him within the next two weeks.' He placed a hand on Lucien's shoulder. 'I'm sorry, but, with Madeline's assistance, Farquharson cannot fail to make you the villain of the piece while he comes out as the unfairly wronged victim of the whole affair, just as he did before.'

'It's not possible.'

'Oh, I assure you that not only is it possible, but that Farquharson and Madeline have their little plan well under way.'

'Are you suggesting that Madeline is somehow complicit in this absurdity?' Lucien's eyes narrowed and everything about him stilled: the calm before the storm.

Guy squeezed Lucien's shoulder, his fingers conveying

the sympathies that he knew his brother would never let him voice. 'Farquharson bade me ask you if you appreciate her acting skills. Said he trained her himself. She's tricked you, Lucien. She's in league with that devil.'

'You would believe *his* word?' Aggression snarled as Lucien batted Guy's hand away.

Guy dropped his hand loosely to his side. 'Look at the letter, Lucien. It bears the Tregellas name and crest at the top of the paper. Even though the seal is broken, it is clear that it is yours. Unless you are in the habit of allowing Farquharson to use your writing desk, I fail to see how he could have faked such things.'

Guy refilled two glasses; the brandy spilled down the decanter, splashing unnoticed against the cherrywood of the table and over the base of the branched candlestick that sat behind it on the table. 'Is the writing from Madeline's hand? Have you nothing against which you can compare it?'

'No.' Then he remembered the letter lying on his desk to be sent; the letter she had written to her mother. Woodenly he moved towards the desk, taking the neatly folded paper up in his hands, dread and disbelief eating at him in equal measure. 'A letter she would have me dispatch to Mrs Langley.'

Guy brought the branched candlestick close.

The two men looked from the incriminating letter to the neatly penned address on the letter to be franked. A short silence. The words did not need to be said—it was quite clear to see that the writing was identical in both cases.

Guy looked with saddened eyes towards his brother and nodded. 'You had best check that the letter within is indeed to her mother.'

Lucien broke the seal, unfolded the paper, scanned the lines of small neat words that stacked tidily, one row upon another. 'It's to Amelia Langley all right. Nothing in it that I would not expect her to say.'

A log crackled upon the fire.

'She must have sneaked her letters to Farquharson through the village post. Your servants are loyal. It should be easy enough to find if anyone carried such a letter in recent weeks.' Guy emptied the contents of the glass down his throat. 'I'm sorry, Lucien.'

'Not as damned sorry as I am,' came the reply, as he settled down to read exactly what his wife had written to Cyril Farquharson.

He sat by the fire for an hour after Guy had gone to bed, trying to make sense of the words, following every avenue of hope, exploring alternative explanations for a letter written in his wife's hand, on his crested paper, and bearing his own seal. A letter that spoke of mistakes and distrust; that accused him of obsessive hate, verging on insanity. A letter that begged Farquharson's forgiveness and pleaded with him to rescue her from the clutches of a madman who held her prisoner. Had she not voiced the very same doubts on his honesty and his sanity earlier that evening? Lucien felt like his ribcage had been levered open and his heart ripped out. Surely Madeline's response to him, her passion, her warmth, could not have been feigned? Could it?

The brandy burned at his throat, searing a path down to his stomach, but did nothing to numb the pain. It was a raw pulsating hurt beyond anything that he ever thought to allow himself to feel again. This had to be Farquharson stirring trouble, seeking some way to blacken Madeline's name. What better way to damage both her and the man who had been his nemesis for so long? Had he not seen it with his own eyes, he would never have believed it. The writing was that of

Madeline's hand. But writing could be copied, words faked. The seal and paper were that of Tregellas. There were only two Tregellas seals: one adorned the ring fitted firmly on the third finger on Lucien's right hand, the other lay within the top drawer of his desk by the window. Damn Farquharson's eyes! Damn his soul! Guy was right. Quizzing of his staff would soon determine if a letter to Farquharson had left the house. With a heavy heart he pulled the bell and waited for Norton to appear.

Madeline curled her legs beneath her on the sofa and stared into the flickering flames in the centre of the fireplace. He would tell her the truth, she knew it instinctively. The story of how Sarah Wyatt had died. Madeline shuddered at the thought. But then again, Sarah had chosen Farquharson over Lucien. Quite how any woman could have come to make that choice was beyond her.

Lord Farquharson and Lord Tregellas. Two men at opposing ends of the spectrum. One gifted with pretty polished words that tripped too readily from his tongue. Red hair, creamy pale skin peppered with freckles, sharp grey eyes and a slim face that some considered handsome. Madeline could not agree. He reminded her of a fox, all slyness and cunning. The other man, a contrast of dark and light. White skin and pale blue eyes that could not fail to pierce the reserve of that upon which he fixed his focus. Classically sculpted features as handsome and as cold as those of the marble Greek god that represented the ideal of manly beauty. Scant of words. Austere. Hair as black as midnight and, if London was to be believed, a soul to match.

But therein lay the problem. Madeline could not believe it, indeed, had never believed the whispered rumours that fanned in his wake. The Wicked Earl, they called him, but when she looked into his eyes it was not wickedness that she saw, but pain and passion, kindness and consideration. Hidden deep behind his cold façade, but there all the same. Whatever Lucien Tregellas would have the world believe, he was a man who felt things deeply. Hadn't she seen the evidence with her own eyes? Felt the warmth of his arms around her, the strength of his determination, the tenderness in his eyes and the burning heat of his lips? It seemed that for all he said, her husband was not indifferent to her, that he didn't just want the unemotional bargain that he had set out that night in his coach in London, any more than she did. She remembered his words, *I'll come to you tonight.*

Excitement tingled through her. He would tell her the truth and then he would kiss her. Without disgust. Without guilt. Only with gentle possession. He would kiss her until she felt hot and all of a tremble. Madeline smiled, knowing that there was a truth of her own to be told. She loved him. No matter what lies Farquharson sought to spread about him, no matter the chill of his veneer, she knew the warm tenderness of the man beneath it. She loved him. Tonight she would tell him. With a smile she picked up the discarded novel by her side and was soon immersed in the description of Mr Darcy proposing to Miss Elizabeth Bennett at the parsonage in Kent.

'Are you certain, Norton? Might the boy not be mistaken as to the addressee? Can he even read?' Lucien thought he saw the hint of a flush touch the old butler's cheeks.

Mr Norton folded his hands behind his back and regarded his employer with his usual servile superiority. 'Hayley is illiterate, m'lord. Lady Tregellas asked him to take the letter to the post office in the village right away. Hayley is sweet on her ladyship's maid, Betsy Porter, and he spent a few minutes in saying his farewells to her before attending to his errand.' Two silver-grey eyebrows raised marginally. 'I noticed the letter lying upon the kitchen table on account of the person to whom it was addressed. Farquharson is a name I'm not likely ever to forget for the rest of my days, m'lord.'

Lucien touched a solitary finger to the hard square line of his jaw. 'Did my wife ask anything else of Hayley with regard to the letter? Not to speak of it before me, for example?'

'No, m'lord.' The old butler shook his head. 'Nothing like that, but she did give him half a crown for his trouble.'

'I see.'

'Will that be all, m'lord?' Mr Norton did not like the dark brooding look that had settled upon his master's face.

'Yes, thank you, Norton. You may retire for the night.'

Only when the butler had gone and the library door was firmly closed did Lucien allow himself to fully contemplate the impact of Madeline's dishonesty.

Madeline closed the last page of the book, well contented with the happy ending. Stretching out her back, she snuggled lower beneath the covers and watched the low flickering flame of her bedside candle. The clock struck midnight and a little furrow of worry creased between her brows. Guy's news must be bad indeed to keep Lucien so late. Momentarily she wondered what had brought Lord Varington to Trethevyn with such speed. Lucien would tell her soon enough, when he came to her as he had promised. Madeline smiled at the thought. Soon he would lie beside her in the bed and tell her the rest of his story. She would kiss him and tell him that he was not to blame, that she loved him, that she would love him for ever.

Guilt was a heavy burden to bear and Lucien had carried it for five long years. In truth, he had done nothing wrong. Sarah Wyatt had chosen Farquharson and she had paid the price with her life. Poor, foolish Sarah. Eighteen was too young to die. Madeline could only be glad that Lucien had intervened to save herself from Farquharson.

A pang of conscience tweaked at her. To think that only this evening she had doubted her husband and had questioned the motives behind their marriage. All along he had blamed himself for Sarah's death and determined to save her from the same fate. An image of Lord Farquharson's face stole into her mind. Hard grey eyes, narrow lips that formed such pretty words, and beneath it all a soul as black as the devil's. Even the memory of his moist breath against her cheek and the pungency of his spicy scent made her feel quite sick. How could she have even contemplated the words of such a man?

Instinct had warned her against him from the start. Lucien had described him as unsavoury. Madeline would have used a much stronger and unladylike word. Yet despite it all she had questioned her husband with ungrateful suspicion. He had gone to such lengths to save her from Farquharson. And she had practically cast it all back in his face. It was a wonder that he had not just sent her packing back to London. But Lucien had not done that. He had told her the truth, and kissed her. Tonight he would come to her bed and everything would be all right.

Madeline awoke with a start and as much a feeling of panic as from her nightmares of Farquharson that had long since ceased. The clock on the mantel chimed two. The room was in darkness, the candle long since expired, and the fire nothing more than a pile of warm ashes. She sat up, stared around her, aware of a feeling that something was wrong. Then she remembered that Lucien was supposed to have come. On the covers beside her lay the warm, heavy weight of Max, giving the occasional whimper while he chased rabbits in his dreams. The small seed of dread deep within her began to grow. An unease. What news was so bad as to have kept Lucien from his promise? All around her was the hiss of nocturnal silence, broken only by the ticking of the clock. The night was black with the occasional glimmer of a cold pale moonlight that crept from behind cloud cover to illuminate her bedchamber. It seemed that a hand wrung at her stomach and she could not rid herself of a bleak, unnatural sensation. Something was badly awry. Had Farquharson harmed another woman? Her mother? Angelina? Madeline could not dispel the notion of dread, even when Max opened a sleepy eye and licked her face.

The floor was cold beneath her feet on the edge of the rug. She peered from her window across the darkened gardens, seeking any sign of movement. There was none. An owl hooted in the distance. She moved silently towards the connecting door that led to Lucien's rooms, Max padding by her side. Her fingers closed around the smooth roundness of the handle, hesitated for a minute and then turned. It was not locked. The door opened noiselessly. Madeline waited where she was, heart racing twenty to the dozen, eyes straining to see through the darkness of the room. Lucien's bedchamber was shrouded in a thick black, by virtue of the heavy curtains closed across his windows. No fire. No lit candles. That did not deter Max. The dog disappeared into his master's room, the black hair of his coat merging with the darkness. 'Max! Come here!' Madeline whispered. A snuffling and the click of canine nails against wooden flooring sounded from the other side of the room. 'Max!' she whispered again.

She stepped across the threshold. Gradually her eyes adjusted to make out the shapes of large pieces of furniture, blacker shapes within the darkness, there, but only just. Without some hint of guiding light, she did not dare proceed lest she knocked something over or tripped over some hidden object. 'Max,' she said softly. No reply. Her hands extended, reaching out before her, probing cautiously into the darkness.

One foot edged forward, then the other, arms waving before her. But Max was not forthcoming. And it seemed that her husband must be in the depths of a sound sleep, for no stirring came from anywhere in the room. Madeline sighed and knew that she would have to leave Max to snuggle his warmth against Lucien. She retreated as silently as she had arrived, the handle scraping slightly as the door closed. The barrier between the two bedchambers was intact once more.

Her fingers fumbled with the tinderbox as she struggled to strike a light. Eventually the small remnants of her candle by the bedside took, casting soft yellow flickers of light to dance around the paintings upon the walls. Madeline had never felt more disinclined to sleep. Her fingers fanned through *Pride and Prejudice,* but the story had been read. Then she remembered Lucien's library with its complete wall lined with books. She looked at the small lump of candle left within her holder. There would be candles down there, too. A good novel would drag her mind from such melancholic contemplation. Madeline lifted the small spluttering candle and headed towards the bedchamber door.

Lucien stared blindly out of the library window. The fire had long since died and the draught infiltrating the window frames caused a flutter of the curtains he had pulled back two hours since. Lucien noticed neither, nor did he feel the chill that had steadily descended upon the room. He lounged back in the chair and threw some more brandy down his throat. Anything to deaden the pain of betrayal.

Every time his eyes closed it was to see Madeline. Sherry-gold eyes and pink parted lips that curved in the sweetness of her smile. *What happened with Farquharson wasn't your fault,* she said, and reached her lips to his. Warm. Willing. So beguiling, yet traitorous. Farquharson would never get beneath the guard he had so carefully erected in the years that had passed. Madeline had managed it without even trying.

He rubbed long fingers against his temples, replaying the scenes for the umpteenth time. She was good. He had to give her that. Feigning such innocence. Responding to his kisses. Asking him to come to her bed. How far would she have gone to be sure of him? Would she actually have given herself to him for Farquharson's sake?

Another swig of brandy, but the pain hung on grimly, refusing to go. Especially in view of what he knew he must do. A faint noise sounded from the hallway. He thought he heard a woman's voice. A pause, then the library door slowly creaked open. There was a moment of faint illumination and then darkness.

'Wretched candle,' the voice muttered.

Lucien froze in his seat, the smell of candle smoke tickling at his nose.

One small hesitant step sounded and then another. Whoever had decided to visit his library in the middle of the night was coming closer. His muscles tensed for action.

Madeline edged towards the window, thankful that her husband had left the curtains open. Now that she thought of it the curtains had been closed earlier that evening when he had brought her here to tell her of his past. He must have opened them before retiring for the night. And he must have retired, for she had seen no glimmer of light escaping the drawing-room door along the corridor. Fleetingly a break in the clouds revealed a shaft of moonlight. It lit enough of the library to show her the desk by the window and the high-backed chair behind it. Maybe Lucien would keep a candle and a tinderbox on his desk. Her father had always done so.

She moved warily forward, hands outstretched in the darkness. If only the clouds would not keep covering the moon, then she would see readily enough. Progress was slow, but Madeline persevered. She reached the desk, and skimmed her fingers lightly across its surface, seeking the means to make light. Writing slope, paper, pens, ink pots, a small knife, more paper. Nothing of any use to Madeline. She tried the drawers, but they were locked. She withdrew her hand and hesitated where she was, unsure of what to do next. Back to the bedchamber and the thoughts that had forced her down here in the first place. She sighed and looked again at the inky cloud-streaked sky beyond the window. Blues and blacks and deep charcoal grey. And every now and again the peep of the bright white lunar disc. The scene beckoned her. Madeline answered its call. Unmindful of the cold, ignoring the darkness, she moved to stand before the window.

Lucien smelled her before he saw her. The faint resonance of oranges, and then she appeared. A small figure in a flowing white nightdress that stretched down to the floor. Her hair was unbound, sweeping long and straight across her shoulders and down to meet her waist. He knew her feet would be bare. She moved forward until she was right up at the window, staring out at the view beyond, seemingly unaware of his presence. He heard the softness of her sigh, saw the relaxed slump of her shoulders, as if something of night had taken a burden of tension away from her.

The empty glass nestled within the palm of his hand. Three-quarters of a decanter of brandy and nothing of the horror of Guy or Norton's words had faded. And now he had caught her searching around his desk in the dead of night. Hell! The pain bit deep. Farquharson had played him for a fool, thanks to the woman he had tried to save. However hard he tried to deny it, he knew that Madeline had found a route directly to his heart. He reined in his emotions and watched the slight figure before him.

The clouds drifted, ever changing, forming patterns against the night-time sky. Madeline watched in fascination, feeling some sense of relief from the foreboding that had gripped her in the bedchamber. She was being fanciful and foolish. She was just overtired and thinking too much on Lucien's story of Farquharson. Everything would seem better in the morning, in the sunlight, with Lucien by her side. As she turned to go, the moon escaped the cover of the cloud and lit Madeline's route across the library with a soft silver brilliance. She smiled a small smile at her good fortune and glanced down at the floor. Still smiling she stepped forward, raising her eyes…to look directly into the face of her husband.

Madeline gave a small yelp of fright and jumped back. 'Oh, Lucien, you startled me. I didn't know that you were there.' Her hand touched against the embroidered neckline of her nightdress.

'Evidently not.' His face appeared unnaturally pale beneath the moonlight, as if he were a carved effigy in white marble. It contrasted starkly with the darkness of his hair. His coat, waistcoat and neckcloth had been cast aside. His shirt was hanging open at the neck. At least his pantaloons and top boots still appeared to be in good order. An empty glass was cradled within his hand and the look upon his face did not bode well.

'Is something wrong?' She bent and touched a hand to his arm.

Lucien pulled his arm back as if scalded. 'He was right, Madeline. You play the game well. I admit that you had me convinced. Not once did I think to question the innocent Miss Madeline Langley.'

Madeline stared at him as if he was speaking double Dutch. Her eyes dropped to the empty glass in his hand. 'You're foxed!' she exclaimed in surprise. Something of the dangerous glitter in his eyes sent a warning. She knew better than to pursue the conversation. 'I'll see you in the morning,' she said and made to leave.

But Lucien had other ideas. He moved with alarming speed, his hand gripping her shoulder before she had even completed one step.

'Lucien!' Madeline gasped.

He hauled her back so that they stood face to face before the window. 'Did you find what you were looking for?' His voice was hard, with nothing of the tenderness that had softened his words earlier in the night.

Madeline's brow creased in puzzlement. 'No. My candle expired too soon. I had hoped to find a new one before it extinguished.'

One harsh breath of laughter grated. 'What a shame you couldn't see to rummage through my desk.'

'I was not rummaging! I couldn't sleep and had finished my book. I came to borrow one of yours. I didn't think that you'd mind.'

'Looking for anything in particular, or just something that might be of use to you both?'

'Lucien, I was looking for a candle and tinderbox.'

Madeline tried to shake him off, but Lucien held her arms in a firm grip.

'Sorry to disappoint you, Madeline, but you'll only find cut sheets of writing paper there. My documents are thankfully locked away.'

'I don't know what you're talking about.'

He lowered his face towards hers. The first thing she noticed was the strong smell of brandy. The second was the coldness of his eyes. 'Oh, but I think that you do, Madeline,' he said silkily. 'You're in league with Farquharson, aren't you?'

'Lucien?' She lifted her hands to rest against the muscles in his arms. 'You're drunk. You don't know what you're saying.'

'I know all right,' came his reply. 'All along I thought I was saving you from him. I would have forced you to become my wife. That's how determined I was to stop him from harming you. And all along you and Farquharson were playing me for the fool.'

'No!' she gasped. 'How could you think it?'

'That night in the Theatre Royal with your mama, and then again at Lady Gilmour's ball, you were very good at feigning fear. I believed you.'

Madeline just stared up at him, aghast at the words spilling from his mouth. Gone was the man she had come to love, in his place, a cold stranger.

'You married me to please him, didn't you? How much further were you willing to go for him? Would you have let me bed you? Make love to you? What then, Madeline? Would you have borne my child?'

She flinched at his cruelty. 'Stop it, Lucien.'

'Or perhaps I never would have survived that long.' His eyes darkened to something she had never seen before. 'Are you his mistress?' His fingers tightened against the skin of her arms.

'You've run mad!' Fear snaked up her spine. All the old doubts flooded back.

His face lowered to hers so that their lips were all but touching. 'How could you do it, Madeline?' he whispered before his mouth swooped over hers, lips sliding in hard possession. She felt the light insistent nip of his teeth and held herself rigid against the onslaught. There was nothing of giving and everything of taking. His hands slid from her arms, moving to claim her breasts, thumbing at her nipples, pulling her close, hard against him. Her lips parted in a gasp, allowing his tongue to raid within, possessing her mouth with what started as a fervour, but soon gentled. The taste of brandy lapped against her tongue with his. She felt his fingers cup

her buttocks, lifting her against the hard bulge in his pantaloons.

'No, Lucien! It's not what you think.'

He seemed to hear her. Ceased his actions. Pulled back to
look into her face. Stared for what seemed to be an eternity.
His grip slackened. But she could still feel the tension
throughout his body pressed against hers. His voice when it
came was quiet and harsh and ragged. 'Damn you, Madeline.'
With that he released her.

She staggered back, unable to comprehend what was happening.

'Pack your bags. You wished to travel to London to visit
your mother. I have arranged for you to leave at the end of
the week. Guy will accompany you on your journey to the
city.'

'And what of you?

'I'll stay here as you suggested.' He heard the soft intake of
breath and saw the confusion upon her face. The brandy lent
him courage to continue. 'But before you go, Madeline, tell
me just one thing. Did Farquharson tell you what he did to
Sarah?'

A little gasp escaped her.

Lucien ignored it. 'Somehow, I doubt very much that he did.
If you knew the truth, you wouldn't be standing here right now,
you would never have danced to his tune. Ask him one day,
when you're feeling brave. I warrant you'll not like what he
has to say.' His gaze held hers directly. 'Goodbye, Madeline.'

Her face glowed white beneath the moon, and her eyes
were huge dark pools of wounded disbelief. If she did not go
soon, he knew he would weaken, give in to the urge to gather
her back into her arms and lavish gentle kisses upon her
mouth. She waited only a moment more, long enough for him
to see the tremble of her lip before her teeth gripped it in a

fury, long enough to see the glisten of moisture in her eyes. Then a flurry of white and she was gone, leaving him alone to remind himself that what he had just witnessed was a piece of consummate acting.

Chapter Thirteen

Madeline fled through the darkness, unseeing, uncaring, until she reached the safe haven of her bedchamber. The door shut forcibly behind her and, for the first time since arriving at Trethevyn, she turned the key within the lock. His words still echoed in her mind. Cruel words, words that never should have spilled from Lucien's tongue, and yet they had, all too readily. It was a nightmare from which there was no waking. Tension gripped her muscles so that they contracted hard and tight. Her heart was thudding too fast, too loud in her chest following her hurried flight from the library. Her mouth was dry, and what had started as a faint hint of nausea was rapidly expanding.

Such was her agitation that she paced the floor of the bedchamber, a small white ghost lit only by the transient light of the cloud cast moon. A scratching came from the connecting door. She moved to the spot, heard Max's muted whimpers, and let the dog back into her own room before locking the door. As if sensing something was wrong, Max looked up at her with a saddened expression. His tongue licked his reassurance over her fingers.

'Oh, Max!' Madeline crouched and clutched the warm black body of fur to her. 'What has happened to make him so angry and suspicious? He must truly have run mad.' She stroked the dog's head, lingering over the silky softness of his ears.

Max looked up at her, eyes dark within the muted nocturnal light, and whined.

Madeline could not bring herself to climb back into the bed she had left with such hopes. Lucien's gentle kisses and whispered promise seemed a lifetime ago. What could have wrought such a change in her husband? Then she remembered that he had gone to meet with his brother and that Lord Varington's sudden appearance probably meant that he conveyed news of great importance, news that had turned her husband against her. Madeline curled herself up on the sofa. Max clambered up next to her and laid his head across her legs. And there they stayed for what remained of the night, until the darkness paled to grey and a new dawn had broken. Never asleep. Just thinking, of a love so newly found and now lost.

By the time Betsy tried the door the next morning the faint outline of a plan had formed in Madeline's mind. If Lucien had no mind to discuss his brother's news rationally with her, then she would seek out the Viscount and ask him herself. She might as well know what had happened to bring about such a change in Lucien. If matters had not changed by the end of the week, she had no other choice than to travel to London with Lord Varington, as directed, and deal with the matter as best she could from there. As gently as she could she dislodged Max's heavy weight, finding that the cost of the great beast's warming presence was a numbing sensation in her left leg.

Betsy's knocking became louder. She whispered hesitantly

through the thick oaken door. 'M'lady? It's Betsy. I have your water here.'

Madeline hobbled faster towards the door, the key turning easily beneath her fingers. 'Forgive me, Betsy, I had forgotten that it was locked.'

The maid stared wide-eyed at her mistress, taking in the dark shadows beneath her eyes, the ashen hue of her complexion, and the fact that she appeared to be having difficulty in walking. 'M'lady!' she whispered in shock. Betsy set the basin down on the nearest table and rushed to Madeline's side. 'What has happened?'

'I slept poorly, that's all,' Madeline sought to reassure the girl.

'But your leg?'

Madeline attempted a smile. 'Max was lying on it and has given me pins and needles. He's rather heavy, must be eating too much.'

Betsy did not look convinced.

'I think I might just take a little breakfast here this morning, Betsy. Please could you bring up some coffee and a bread roll.'

Betsy stared some more. Madeline's next words confirmed in the maid's mind that something strange was going on.

'Oh, and can you find out if Lord Varington is up yet.'

'Yes, m'lady.' Betsy beat a hasty retreat to inform Mrs Babcock that Lady Tregellas was not at all herself this morning.

It was Mrs Babcock herself who returned with Madeline's breakfast on a tray. Red-cheeked and panting with quite an alarming volume, the housekeeper hobbled into the room.

'Babbie! I wasn't expecting you to carry that tray all the way up here. I would have come down to the morning room to save you the trouble.'

'It's no trouble, m'lady,' puffed Mrs Babcock. She peered at Madeline's face. 'Feelin' a bit under the weather, are you, doe?'

'No. I'm quite well, thank you,' lied Madeline.

Mrs Babcock sniffed suspiciously. 'Lord Varington is still abed. Always was a slug in the mornings. Won't see him until this afternoon. Used to keepin' London hours, he is. At least, that's a polite way of puttin' it.' Her lips pursed in disapproval. 'Wayward young puppy!'

Madeline sipped at her coffee. The prospect of waiting for several hours until Lord Varington managed to extract himself from bed was sure only to set Madeline's nerves even more on edge. 'In that case, I think I might spend the morning visiting Tintagel Castle. I've been hoping to see it for some time and I shouldn't like to leave Cornwall without visiting it.'

'Bit of mornin' mist out there, m'lady. It'll be worse on the coast. Best wait until later in the day.

Madeline poked at her bread roll, but found that her appetite had deserted her. 'Perhaps I could wait a little, but I'd like to be back by this afternoon.' She looked up into the housekeeper's blackcurrant eyes. 'It's likely that I'm to leave Trethevyn at the end of the week.'

'His lordship didn't mention nothin' 'bout leavin' so soon.' Mrs Babcock crossed her arms over her ample bosom.

'No,' said Madeline with the colour rising in her cheeks. 'Lucien shall stay here. I'm to travel with…with Lord Varington.'

Mrs Babcock's beady eyes missed nothing, from the bleakness in Madeline's eyes to the embarrassment warming her otherwise pale cheeks. 'I'll ask the master to make ready for your trip to Tintagel, then?'

'No!' Madeline almost shouted the word. 'I mean, no, thank you. I would rather that you didn't disturb Lucien.'

'He won't be best pleased. Told me in no uncertain terms that you weren't to leave this place without him.'

'I think you'll find that he's changed his mind,' said Madeline softly.

The older woman looked at her strangely. 'As you wish. Betsy will be up shortly.' Mrs Babcock had almost reached the door when she faltered and looked back at the slim figure standing by the newly lit fire. 'It's not my place to speak out, but I'm going to anyway. I've loved Master Lucien since he was a baby and I don't want to see any more unhappiness for him. I don't know what the two of you have had words about, and I won't ask. All I do ask is that you don't just leave him, m'lady. I know he's been a bit, well, high-handed, of late, but then I reckon he's got good reason with Lord Farquharson likely to appear at any minute.'

Madeline saw the opportunity rise before her eyes. 'Farquharson stole Sarah Wyatt from Lucien. Did he...? What happened to her?'

'He killed her.'

A heartbeat, then Madeline asked, 'Who killed her?'

Mrs Babcock looked her straight in the eye, knowing the traitorous thought that lurked beneath the question. 'Why, Lord Farquharson, m'lady. Who else did you think it might have been?'

Their gazes locked, golden on black.

'I had to be sure,' said Madeline. 'Farquharson told me that Lucien was responsible for her death.'

Mrs Babcock's upper lip curled in disgust. 'And you believed him?'

'No.' The word was like a sigh in the room.

'But you asked all the same.' Mrs Babcock turned and limped from the room. The quiet click of the bedchamber door closing behind her was louder than any slam could have been.

Madeline calmly pushed the uneaten bread roll away and drained the cooled dregs of her coffee. Time sounded with the steady strokes of the clock's pendulum. A small shaft of sunlight flooded the room, shining a golden spotlight upon the painting of two small boys from which Madeline had worked her embroidery. Outside in the garden, a blackbird whistled. And inside, Madeline knew she had just lost a friend.

Lucien awoke some time the wrong side of noon. His head ached like it had been cleaved with a wood axe and his mouth tasted as if he had been licking the soles of filth-encrusted boots. Sunlight streamed in through the library window, burning at his eyeballs. He moved the discomfort of his back and the pounding in his head intensified. The reek of stale brandy assailed his nostrils and he noticed the empty decanter and broken glass on the floor by his feet. Tentative fingers probed at his scalp and he winced.

God in heaven, it had been a long time since he'd felt this bad as a result of drink. He pushed himself up out of the wing chair in which he'd spent the night and walked gingerly forward, gripping the edge of the desk as his head thumped worse than ever. He had just focused himself enough to make it to the bell pull, when his eye alighted on two objects that should not have been on his desk. The memory of the night's dealings returned with a cruel and battering clarity. Madeline. Her words played loudly through his poor aching head, *I finished my book and came to borrow one of yours...I was looking for a candle and tinderbox.* And there before his very eyes was the evidence of what she had said. A rather battered copy of *Pride and Prejudice* and a single candleholder, complete with the stubby remains of a long-expired candle.

A knock sounded against the door and Guy walked into the library. 'Thought I might find you here, old chap.'

Lucien peered round, his head suffering from the speed of his movement. 'What the hell are you doing up so early?'

'Good afternoon to you, too. From the state that you're in, I would hazard a guess that you drank the rest of the brandy and spent a cold and miserable night in that chair.'

No reply was forthcoming from Lucien.

'I'm sorry to have been the bearer of bad tidings, but I thought it best that you knew.' He looked at his brother's red-lined eyes and the haggard expression upon his face, knowing that the news had affected Lucien far worse than even he had expected. He tried to salve the hurt as best he could. 'Perhaps there's some other explanation lying beneath all of this. Perhaps Madeline didn't send the letter to Farquharson at all. Have you enquired of your staff yet?'

Lucien turned a jaundiced eye in his direction. 'I've spoken to them all right, and it seems that my wife has been writing to him.'

'Oh.' Guy shut the door firmly behind him. 'Then the matter is proven.'

'No, Guy, it is not.' Lucien ran a hand through the dishevelment of his hair. 'She came here last night. Had the chair turned out to face the window, she couldn't see me, didn't know that I was here. Heard her searching around on the desk.'

'Good God! It's worse than I thought.'

'Said she'd finished her book and came down in search of another.'

'In the middle of the night?' Guy raised a cynical eyebrow.

'Couldn't sleep, apparently.'

'A likely story.'

'I believe she was telling the truth.' Lucien raised blood-shot eyes towards his brother.

A silence stretched between them.

Guy shook his head.

'Look.' Lucien gestured towards the well-thumbed book and the candleholder resting not so far from where his hands leant against the mahogany desk top. 'Madeline isn't stupid. Had she come here with the intent of searching my papers, she would have had a decent candle, one that could at least stay alight long enough for her to see what she was doing. She said that the candle had expired and she was looking for a tinderbox on the desk.'

'It's a lame excuse and you know it. The book could have been a cover in the eventuality that she was discovered rifling through your desk in the middle of the night.'

'If you could have seen the expression on her face…shock, horror, disbelief all rolled into one.'

'Farquharson himself told me that she's an actress. She's playing you, Lucien.'

Lucien looked at his brother. 'But we know Farquharson to be a liar.'

'That doesn't mean that Madeline is innocent.'

'I didn't even give her a chance to defend herself against the accusations. Just judged her as guilty.' The hand raked his hair again. 'I shouldn't have been so harsh, but the brandy clouded my judgement. Hell, I haven't felt so angry since I discovered what Farquharson did to Sarah.' He levelled his brother a direct look. 'I was a brute, Guy. Madeline didn't deserve that.'

'Oh, come on, Lucien. Farquharson is brandishing a particularly loathsome letter, written by her own hand, around all of London. You have proof that she dispatched a letter to him from this very house, and to cap it all you catch her rifling through your desk in the middle of the night! What do you think you should have done? Clapped her on the back? Congratulated her? The evidence is stacked against her.'

'I still cannot believe it.'

'You mean you don't want to believe it.'

'I know her, Guy. It's not in her character to be devious or dishonest.'

Guy gave an incredulous snort. 'She has you fooled, big brother, and no mistake.'

'That's just it. She's done nothing to try to fool me. The first time we met in the Theatre Royal she said not one thing against Farquharson, and at Lady Gilmour's ball she was desperately afraid. Such fear and loathing couldn't be faked.'

'You only have her word for it, Lucien. You don't even know if Farquharson was up in that bedchamber.'

'The terror and panic on her face were real enough. Never once has she used tears or pleading or dramatics. Do you not think she would have resorted to such ploys had she been acting?'

'She's too good an actress for that.'

'I cannot help but feel that we have this all wrong, Guy. In these past months I've come to know Madeline. She's not the woman you would paint her. She's more trusting than you could imagine. The evidence might condemn her as guilty, but instinct tells me otherwise.'

'She has bewitched you. Don't let your attraction for the woman blind you to the truth.'

'Oh, don't be absurd, Guy! That has nothing to do with it.'

'Then you admit that you are attracted to her?' Guy waited for the answer.

'Damn it, yes! I want her, all of her, in my arms, in my bed, and more. Is that what you want to hear? I may desire her, Guy, but I haven't touched her. I'm not that much of a fool.' He thought fleetingly of the tenderness of their shared kisses. Even last night, what had started as a kiss of punishment had ended as something else.

There was a pause as something of the situation communicated itself to Guy. 'It's not just desire that you feel, is it, Lucien?' he asked quietly.

'No,' said Lucien, touching his fingers against the misshapen lump of wax at the base of Madeline's candleholder. 'I'm afraid that matters are a little more complicated than that,' and realised, perhaps for the first time, exactly what it was that he was saying.

Guy gave a sigh and twitched a smile. 'Well, in that case, you had best pour some strong coffee down your throat, eat some breakfast, and set about discovering the truth.'

'I owe her an apology for my behaviour last night…and I would hear what she has to say regarding the letter.' A shameful look washed over Lucien's face. 'I told her that I was sending her back to London with you at the end of the week.'

'Ah. Many a lady might relish the prospect of a few days travelling in my company. Somehow, I don't think Madeline is one of them. I'd best ring for that coffee right away.'

It was some little time later when a clean-shaven and rather fresher-looking Lucien, finally sought out the company of his wife.

'She's gone where?'

Mrs Babcock sniffed. 'Tintagel Castle. Tried to put her off, but she weren't havin' any of it. Assured me that your opinion on her travellin' without you had changed. I came to tell you anyhow, but you seemed to be in the sleep of the dead. Couldn't wake you.' The housekeeper folded her arms. 'She left this morning. Asked after Lord Varington. Said she would be back this afternoon. Reckon she had somethin' she wanted to be speakin' to him about.'

Lucien opened his mouth to speak.

'And before you ask, she took Betsy and John Hayley with her. Mr Boyle's back is painin' him today, but he's still drivin' the coach.'

'Thank you, Babbie.' A spur of unease pricked at Lucien. Madeline had gone to Tintagel, little knowing it was there that Sarah Wyatt met her death.

The morning had been particularly fine, all clear pale sunshine and dry cold, apart from the mist that had hovered around their route past Bodmin Moor. Nothing of that remained in Tintagel. She breathed in the fresh sea air, smelling the salt and the seaweed and revelling in the dramatic sight before her eyes. Tintagel Castle was a sprawling medieval ruin balanced precariously close to a cliff whose edge dropped dramatically through a sheer pathway of jagged rocks into the sea. The water was a wash of pale greens and blues, and hissing heads of white froth where it battered against the riot of rocks. She had spent some time exploring throughout the ruins, knowing that the castle was reputed to be the site of the birthplace of King Arthur.

A story of intrigue and deception surrounded the place. King Uther Pendragon had fallen in love with Ygraine, the beautiful wife of his nobleman, Gorlois, Duke of Cornwall. Uther could think of nothing else save that he must have Ygraine and when Gorlois would not yield his lady, declared war upon Cornwall and its Duke. Gorlois hid Ygraine in the impregnable fort at Tintagel while he came under siege at another of his castles. Knowing that the fate of all Britain rested upon it, the druid wizard Merlin cast a spell over Uther so that, for a single night alone, Uther would take on the appearance of Gorlois. Thus, out of the darkness the castle guard saw their lord approach, drew up the gate and welcomed him home. Ygraine, too, went gladly to her husband. Before dawn of the next morning, the man she had lain with all the night through had gone. An hour later a messenger arrived to tell them that Ygraine was a widow, for Gorlois had been slain in battle the previous night. Ygraine knew then what had happened. Nine months later she bore a son. His name was Arthur and he was to clear the invading darkness from Britain's shores and become the best and greatest of kings.

From the seeds of such treachery, goodness and salvation had grown. Madeline mulled over Merlin's part in the plot. She sat alone on the simple wooden bench and looked out across the white flecked roll of water, amazed at the ragged chasms in the cliff face and the scatter of sharp stone below. It was a scene she could have looked at for ever, drinking in the rugged beauty, the wildness of sea and wind and the dark dangerous rocks. The rush of the wind filled her ears, chasing the sadness from her soul and the fatigue from her bones. She was glad that she had asked Mr Boyle to stay by the coach. The poor man's back ached more than he was willing to admit. Madeline had not missed the grimaces of pain when he thought that no one was looking. She was glad, too, that she had sent Betsy and John Hayley off to wander the ruins by themselves. If Madeline was right, she suspected that romance was brewing, and even if she had been staying in Cornwall she might soon be in need of a new personal maid. She turned her head and watched the young couple wander hand in hand through the remains. She swallowed down her own sadness and was glad for them. Her gaze fixed upon where the distant roll of waves met clear blue sky and she wondered what it was that Guy had brought with him to Trethevyn, besides an end to all of Madeline's dreams.

As if from nowhere, the wind whipped up one strong gust that pulled the bonnet from her head, tumbling it along the grassy pathway. Madeline leapt up, trying to catch the bonnet before it dropped over the cliff edge, but to no avail. She peered over, watching it swoop down the sheer rock face to meet the white swirl of waves below, tossed on the violent ebb and flow of water. Her feet stood close to the edge of the precipice. Too close, with the wind gusting as it was. She made to retreat. Someone grabbed at her arm. Madeline gave a small yelp of surprise, her feet stumbled and the firm grasp tightened, lifting her up, hauling her back.

'Madeline!' Lucien's voice strained against her ear. 'What the...?' He clasped her against him and dragged her further inland.

Madeline's heart hammered hard against her breast, first from the fright she had just sustained in almost pitching down to join her bonnet, and now from the man whose arms were wrapped around her. Slowly the thudding subsided enough for her to hear the words he was saying.

'Madeline,' he whispered against the top of her head, then moved her back to drop kisses against her cheek, the tip of her nose, her chin. One hand cradled the nape of her neck, the other pressed against her back. 'I thought I'd lost you,' he murmured against her eyebrow. 'Thank God...' And then he found her lips and kissed her with a passion beyond anything that Madeline had ever known. Gentle, possessive, loving. As if he would never let her go. As if her nightmare of last night had never been. And in the meeting of their lips were all the words that they had not spoken. 'Madeline,' he said again and moved back to look into her eyes.

Even through the dazzlement of surprise Madeline noticed the pallor of his face. 'Lucien?' Her fingers fluttered against his cheek in mounting concern, unsure of the response that they would meet.

'I didn't think…I wouldn't have you lose your life over my foolish words, Madeline.'

Madeline blinked up at him in confusion.

'Forgive my shoddy treatment. I fear that I'd made too freely with the brandy.' He reached and captured her fingers from his face, imprisoning them with great tenderness within his own, his voice suddenly gruff. 'It's not worth killing yourself over, Madeline.'

Madeline suddenly realised what he thought. Her eyes widened and a rather embarrassed expression crossed her face. 'It was just that the wind…my bonnet… I was only looking to see where the wind had taken it.' She waited for his response.

The bold pale eyes held hers. 'Then you weren't planning to leap from the cliff top?'

She shook her head, inadvertently loosening more of the hairpins. The wind instantly took advantage and pulled what had started as a plain and tidy style into a mass of long blowing locks.

'My pins!' Madeline cried and bent to retrieve what she could.

Lucien pulled her back up to face him. 'Leave them.' He ran his fingers through her hair, mussing it worse than ever. 'I prefer it this way.'

Madeline felt two spots of warmth grow on her cheeks.

'I should place you across my knee and give you a thorough thrashing for giving me such a fright.'

Madeline saw the twitch of his smile before it was lost.

'But I've been too much of a brute of late. I shouldn't have treated you as I did last night.'

'What happened? Why were you so angry? You thought that I was searching for papers on your desk…for Farquharson.' Her brow crinkled. 'Why? What did Guy tell you?'

'The news is not good, Madeline.' The pale gaze held hers, watching, measuring. 'Farquharson has a letter from you, pleading that he save you from your madman of a husband. It claims that our marriage was the result of forced abduction and rape.'

'No!' The word slipped loudly from Madeline's tongue. 'No,' she said again, a little more quietly. 'It's a lie. I wrote no such letter.'

'I've seen it with my own eyes. It's written in your own hand, on paper printed with my crest and sealed with the Tregellas seal.'

The accusation hung between them.

'How can that be? It's impossible!'

'So you deny sending a letter to Farquharson?' His eyes did not waver from hers.

She paused. 'No. I don't deny that,' she said slowly.

Lucien felt the tension wrap around his heart and start to squeeze.

'He wrote to me, you see, some weeks ago.' Colour flooded her cheeks. 'You were so worried about him, I thought it would only make matters worse to tell you.'

Lucien said nothing, just waited, and all the while the ache in his chest continued to grow.

'The letter is within the drawer of my bureau, if you wish to see it. Farquharson asked my forgiveness and said that he loved me.' She saw something flit across Lucien's eyes. Pain, hurt, anger? Madeline did not know. 'And then he warned me of you. Told me the story of Sarah Wyatt, much as you did. Except that in his version, he accuses you of killing her. He offered to help me escape you, said I need only ask and he would help.'

Lucien's eyes were as pale a blue as ever she'd seen, the black outline of the iris and the darkness of the pupil lending them an unnaturally brilliant appearance. The thump of her heart sounded slow and steady in her chest. 'So I wrote to him and told him that I knew his words for the lies they were and that the man I knew to be a murderer was not my husband. I asked him to leave us in peace.' She did not mention what else she had said in those carefully penned words: that she loved Lucien, that she would never be sorry that she had agreed to marry him, that they were very happy together. 'I gave the letter to John Hayley to take to the post office in the village.'

'And you have never written anything else to him?'

'No, of course not.'

They looked at one another for a moment longer.

'I believe you. I don't know how he did it, but Farquharson wrote that letter, not you.'

He saw relief colour her eyes, felt the tension slacken from her body.

She slumped forward, resting her forehead against his chest and he knew that no actress could have feigned what he had seen in her face.

'Let's go home, Madeline,' he said, and, placing his arm around her, led her towards the coach in the distance.

Chapter Fourteen

All was quiet at Trethevyn.

Mrs Babcock saw the entwined hands of the Earl and his Countess as they entered the hallway and drew her own conclusion.

Madeline blushed and tried to disengage her hand at the sight of the housekeeper, but Lucien was having none of it. He cast Madeline an intensely intimate look and retained her fingers firmly within his own.

'Lord Varington has gone out for a ride,' said Mrs Babcock, 'I'll be in the kitchen if I'm needed,' and promptly left.

'Then we're all alone with the remainder of an afternoon to fill before my brother returns.' His gaze dropped to her lips before returning to meet her eyes. 'There are unfinished matters between us, Madeline, matters that should be resolved.'

Madeline knew from the hunger of his gaze that it was not letters, or Farquharson, or even Guy of which her husband spoke. She felt the heat intensify as Lucien bent closer and touched his lips gently against hers. 'Lucien,' she murmured as he pulled back enough to look into her eyes.

'I know what I promised you, but I can no longer limit myself to our bargain. My life would be the poorer if you were not in it, Madeline.' He moved his mouth until it hovered just above hers. 'I want you as my wife in every way that it's possible: a full marriage, not some half-witted contract of convenience.'

'Oh, Lucien,' she sighed and met his lips with all the passion that had been burgeoning within her for the past months.

'I've been a fool.' His words were breathy and hot against her skin, trailing a path along the delicate line of her jaw and down on to her neck.

Madeline made one last grip at reality before it would slide away for ever. 'No,' she whispered. 'You saved me from Farquharson; for that I'll always be grateful.'

'It's not your gratitude that I want,' he growled against the soft white skin of her throat.

She moved to look him directly in the eye. 'If not my gratitude, then will you accept my love instead?'

He stilled beneath her fingers, his eyes dilating wide and darkening. 'You love me?' His brows arched in surprise. 'After all that I've done?'

Madeline felt the smile creep to her lips. The tall, handsome man before her was not as arrogantly confident as he would have the world believe. 'Yes,' she said simply. 'What you did was save my life, Lucien, nothing less. I love you. And…' she hesitated, feeling the warmth rise in her cheeks '…and I want you, Lucien.'

His lips twitched with amusement. 'In that case, lady wife, I must insist that you accompany me to my bedchamber this very moment.'

'Lucien!' she exclaimed. 'It's the middle of the afternoon, and broad daylight! Retiring at this time of day would be positively scandalous.'

'Indeed, it would.' His mouth swooped down, halting only a whisper away from hers. 'But not quite so scandalous as being discovered making love upon the stairs.' His fingers teased across the bodice of her dress to rest fleetingly upon her breast. 'The choice is yours, Madeline. What is it to be?'

Madeline shivered at the delicious sensations threatening to overwhelm her. 'Well, if you put it like that, sir, I think I'll choose the bedchamber.'

Lucien delivered her a wicked smile and, without a further word, scooped her up into his arms and advanced up the stairs with some considerable speed. He did not pause until he had deposited Madeline upon the great sprawling four-poster that was his bed.

Sunlight flooded in through the bedchamber windows to bask Madeline in its warm golden glow. She watched in awe while Lucien stripped off his coat, dispensing with it in a heap upon the floor. Next came his waistcoat and a pair of still mud-splattered riding boots. The neckcloth followed, with the same haphazard abandonment. Only when he had discarded his shirt did Madeline protest. 'Lucien, surely you cannot mean to remove all of your clothes!'

Her husband gave her a mischievous look and his grin deepened.

'The sun is still high in the sky!'

Lucien glanced nonchalantly in the direction of the window. 'So it is.' And then he climbed upon the bed.

'But—'

Any further protestations from Madeline were effectively silenced when Lucien claimed her mouth with his own, massaging in a rhythmic slide until her lips parted. His tongue welcomed the invitation and slipped into that intimate cavern, seeking what he knew would be within. Madeline's head danced, dizzy in a haze of floating sensation. Their tongues met. Connected. Moist. Warm. Needful. Danced and twisted and lapped until all vestige of rational thought fled. And when Lucien's hands slipped down across her body, a path of tingling fire followed in their wake. She trembled beneath his touch, both revelling in it and all the while conscious of a growing need for more.

'Madeline, my love,' he murmured against her cheek, her throat, her collarbone and lower, until he touched the neckline where her dress began. His breath moved up, scorched hot upon her shoulder and his fingers moved to deftly undo the row of small jet buttons that fastened the dress to Madeline's body.

Contrary to all her expectations, Madeline was neither shy nor embarrassed. Indeed, it was with a degree of impatience that she assisted her husband to shed not only her dress but her petticoats, stays and shift as well. She lay naked on the bed, his bed, exposed in her entirety by the clarity of the sunshine licking warm against her pale skin.

Lucien sat back, gaze sweeping over her, drinking in every inch of her sweetness. When she made to cover her nudity with her hand he captured those slender fingers within his own, met those amber eyes that were smouldering with passion. 'You're beautiful.' Beneath the heat of his gaze she felt truly beautiful: beautiful and desirable and loved. Then their lips writhed together until all thoughts were forgotten. Her fingers threaded through his hair, pulling the dark silken locks as she had so longed to do. His cologne mixed with his own masculine scent, teasing and tantalising her. She breathed in the intoxicating mix. Awareness narrowed, until there was just the two of them. Lucien and Madeline. Husband and wife. Together in a union of love.

His hands stroked gently around the mounds of her breasts, tracing an inward spiral that stopped just short of their rosy peaks. Madeline shifted beneath him, pressing herself up, nipples tingling with need. And still his fingers teased upon the slopes.

'Lucien!' The whisper was urgent, pleading.

He could withhold no longer. Her nipples stood erect beneath the brush of his thumbs. He rolled the hardened buds between his fingers, hearing her gasps of pleasure. His mouth trailed kisses down her neck and on to her breast. She cried out as he replaced his fingers with the hot moisture of his tongue, lapping against the tender pink skin, suckling first at one and then the other. Her hands clutching the dark ruffle of his head closer, harder. The heat grew between her legs, pulsing down to encompass her thighs. There was a wetness there that she did not understand. Instinctively she pressed herself to him, not knowing what it was that she sought, just conscious of an escalating urgency and her overwhelming love for the man who was stoking such powerful sensations within her body. Lucien. Lucien. It seemed she cried his name a thousand times within her mind. Needing him. Wanting him. 'Lucien.' The cry of desperation burst aloud from her lips, but Madeline no longer knew what was real and what was not, caught as she was in an escalating vortex of sensual force.

Lucien could not fail to answer such a plea. He rolled off her long enough to divest himself of his pantaloons, then, in response to the small murmur of complaint, covered her body with his own, taking his weight upon his elbows lest he crush her. Satin-smooth skin flushed rosy where the roughness of his stubbled chin had lingered and caressed. His fingers moved to her breast, teased fleetingly at their peaks then slid down across her stomach and lower still. The soft white skin of her thighs was hot beneath his touch, as he massaged and stroked and kneaded a pattern of pleasure. She jerked against him as his fingers gently probed the silken secret between her legs, her breathing quickening to short greedy gasps.

Nothing else mattered. Everything was here and now. In this moment. Here with the man that she loved. She wanted him. She burned for him. Felt the start of a deep welling pleasure at the intimate caress of his fingers, the heat of his lips on hers, his tongue tantalising her own. Some part of him pressed against her thigh. She moved her hips against him and reached her fingers to feel him. He groaned, his eyes fluttering shut at her touch. His hand captured her wrist. 'Madeline,' he gasped. 'Any more of that and I'll be unable to finish what we've started.' He kissed her tenderly, stroking her hair back from her face, and drawing back to look into her eyes. 'I love you,' he whispered and deliberately moved himself between her thighs.

'As I love you,' Madeline replied.

Blue and amber, ice and fire, locked as he thrust gently into her, accepting the precious gift that she offered.

Madeline felt the pain sear through her, momentarily blighting the pleasure. But then his mouth was upon hers and his whispers of reassurance were in her ear. Pain diminished. Pleasure grew. And as he began to move within her she gave herself up to the ecstasy that bound them, until his seed spilled within her and they lay entwined and sated in the heady glow of loving. There seemed no need for words. Madeline relaxed, feeling the steady beat of Lucien's heart against her back, the protective curl of his palm against her stomach. What had happened between them had changed her for ever. She had given her heart and shared her body. They were as one, each bound to the other through love. Madeline knew in those blissful moments that nothing could ever change that.

The hours ticked by and Guy still did not return.

'Ask Cook to delay dinner for a further half an hour. He should be back by then.'

'Right you are, m'lord. I'm worried about the youngster. Not like him to be out so long, least not in the country.' Mrs Babcock sniffed, and sucked hard on her bottom teeth with mounting anxiety and disapproval.

Quite how Babbie could describe Guy as a youngster amazed Lucien, but he had to concede that he shared the old housekeeper's concern. His brother was not known for his enjoyment of country pursuits. Indeed, it might even be said that Guy found the countryside abhorrent, describing the peace and clean open air as downright ghastly. But then again, Guy had his own reasons for preferring the town. Not for the first time did Lucien worry over the hedonistic path his brother's life seemed to be taking. Nothing of these thoughts showed upon his face as he sought to reassure the old woman. 'No doubt Guy has forgone the pleasures of cross-country riding for the hospitality of the King's Arms in the village. He might even have ridden into Liskeard or Bodmin. Don't worry, Babbie. He'll be back soon enough.'

Only when the door closed behind the housekeeper did he massage his temples in the action that he knew would reveal his true anxiety to the old woman who had practically raised him as a child.

Madeline rose from the chair and moved silently across the room to stand beside him. 'You're worried, too, aren't you?'

Lucien looked down at the slender figure by his side. The shadowy light from the window spilled across her face, contrasting with the warm glow from the candles. Her cheeks were still pink from their earlier lovemaking and her eyes held a special sparkle. It seemed that she could read him better than he realised. 'Guy is reckless and prone to distraction by…how shall I put it…certain pleasurable activities. But I would have expected him to be back before darkness, especially in light of this morning.'

Madeline gave him a puzzled look. 'What do you mean?'

'He knew I was intent on speaking to you about Farquharson's letter and will be interested to learn your response. Believe me when I say there's no love lost between Farquharson and my brother.'

'He thinks me guilty.' It was not a question, just a plainly stated fact.

Lucien would no longer lie to the woman he loved. 'He doesn't know you as I do. He saw the evidence and drew his conclusion.'

A flicker of pain flitted across her face.

'Together we'll convince him of the truth.' He took her hand in his and gave a little squeeze.

She smiled and the two turned to look out down the length of the driveway.

Only half an hour later and their happiness was destroyed.

Raised voices, alarmed, alert, coming from the hallway, growing louder. Lucien jerked open the door of the small drawing room and strode down the stairs towards the noise. Not far from the front door a group of servants were huddled around something.

'Lord above!' Babbie shouted.

A housemaid began to cry.

'Is he still alive?' Mr Boyle said.

Betsy Porter fainted in a heap upon the floor.

And then Mr Norton's gruff words, 'Fetch his lordship—now!'

Cold dread clasped at Lucien. He thrust it away. Strode to the small throng, afraid of what he would see. Clearing the path anyway. 'What's going on here?' His tone was cold, clinical, the tone of a man in control.

The crowd parted. He heard Boyle by his elbow. 'Was tied

to his horse to make it back here. Couldn't do nothin' other than ride it right up to the front door. Bleedin' badly he is, m'lord. We got him in here as quick as we could. Young Hayley's taken the beast round to the stables.'

A broad smear of blood across the marbled floor of the hallway showed clearly where the body had been dragged. Something squirmed in Lucien's gut. One hand steered the sniffling housemaid to the side until at last he could see the figure that lay there. The man's clothing was darkened and wet. Great slashes in the material showed skin that had been white, now mottled dark. Lucien's eyes travelled up the tortured body, past the wounds, past the blood, until they came to rest upon the face. A breath escaped him. A rush of air so silent that none around would have noticed. A sound both of horror…and relief. For the blood-daubed face was not that of Guy, but his valet, Collins.

Lucien knelt by the poor battered body, touching his fingers to the neck in search of a pulse. Then he stripped off his coat and balling it as a pillow, carefully inserted it behind the man's head.

The gritty eyelids fluttered open. 'Lord Tregellas.'

The man's whisper was so low that Lucien had to press an ear close to the bruised mouth to hear the words. 'It's all right, Collins, I'm here.'

The valet struggled to speak.

'Take your time,' said Lucien, kneeling by the man's side.

'Was a trap. Walked right into it before we knew.' Collins reached a bloody hand to catch at Lucien's. 'There were too many of them. Ruffians. Brawn hired by the gent. Didn't stand a chance.'

The coldness was spreading throughout Lucien's body. He held Collins's hand and waited for him to continue.

The man's swallow was painful to watch. 'We put up a

fight, but they had us in the end. Took us somewhere deep under the ground. No light, just torches. Damp. Horrible. Asked us questions about this place, and you and Lady Tregellas.'

Lucien's lips tightened to a grim line.

'Released me to bring you a message.' Collins paused to gather his strength. 'The gent says if you want to see your brother alive again then you're to meet him tonight at ten o'clock by Tintagel Castle—and take your wife with you. If the both of you don't show, he'll kill Lord Varington.'

'Is Guy…?' Lucien could not bring himself to say the words.

'He's hurt bad.' Collins's eyes filled with moisture. 'Nothing I could do. I'm sorry.'

Lucien patted the man's hand. 'You did your best. Guy will be proud.' He leaned in closer as Collins's eyes began to close. It was a question he did not need to ask, but he wanted to be sure. 'Just one more thing before you rest, Collins. His name—did the one you call a gentleman tell you his name?'

Collins slowly shook his head. 'Said you would know who he was. Hair as red as a fox's pelt. Slim, medium height. Lord Varington called him Farleyson or some such name.'

'Farquharson,' said a woman's voice behind Lucien.

'Yes, m'lord, that was it.' The valet drifted out of consciousness once more.

Lucien slowly turned his head to look over his shoulder, and when the ice-blue eyes raised, they met with the clear amber gaze of his wife.

'Don't be absurd, Madeline! You are not accompanying me and that is final.' Lucien's jaw tightened into what Madeline had come to learn was his stubborn expression.

'And when you turn up to meet Farquharson without me, what then? You'll effectively condemn Guy to death.'

'It's a trap, Madeline. He means to catch us all. If I go alone, at least I have a chance of killing him. To take you along would be to hand you to him on a platter. It's bad enough that he has Guy without giving him you as well.'

'But you mean to walk straight into his trap yourself, and you think that I'll just sit here and let you?'

'We've little choice, Madeline.'

'What about the High Constable. If we inform him, perhaps he could—'

'We're running out of time and, besides, the Constable will be of little use against Farquharson and his cronies. The only chance that Guy has is if I go alone.'

'No.' Madeline shook her head. 'He'll kill Guy anyway, and then he'll kill you.'

'No, Madeline, not if I kill him first. I cannot just leave my brother to die without trying to help him. Farquharson's methods will not result in a quick and painless death. The villain thrives on pain. It gives him pleasure to watch others suffer.'

'Sarah Wyatt…' It was not fair to ask the question with Lord Varington as Farquharson's prisoner.

Lucien's face was a mask of grim severity. 'An endless orgy of torture and rape. He killed her at Tintagel, then brought her here, left her body in the old chapel in the grounds of the house. He thought if her body was found at Trethevyn, then I would be suspected of her murder. My mother found it the next morning. She had been unwell since my father's death. The shock of what she saw that day sickened her more than I can say. She never recovered. Two months later she was dead.'

'Oh, Lucien,' Madeline placed her arm around him. 'I'm so sorry. I shouldn't have stirred such painful memories.'

'It's better that you know the truth,' he said.

'Why did he never stand trial?'

'Farquharson has the cunning of a fox. There was nothing that could link him with the crime. His cronies swore that Farquharson had spent the night of the murder drinking and carousing with them. The High Constable could not proceed. Besides, Farquharson was busy planting the seeds of rumours that I was responsible for Sarah's death. I was, after all, the spurned betrothed, and her body had been found on my property.'

'Was there nothing that could be done to bring him to justice?'

'I employed a Bow Street Runner to investigate the matter, in an attempt to come up with something against him, but there was nothing to be found.'

'How can you be so sure it was Farquharson?'

Lucien sighed. 'At first I wasn't. I suspected him, nothing more. There was always an undercurrent about him, something unwholesome. And then when he knew he was safe, when he knew that there was nothing that could link the grieving husband to Sarah's murder, he approached me in my club one day and told me what he had done.'

'He admitted it?'

'Every detail.'

'But surely you could act as a witness against him?'

'Farquharson had been busy establishing my reputation as the Wicked Earl. The gossip in London said that I had killed Sarah. He would not have been found guilty.'

Madeline said nothing, just shook her head.

'I called him out, thought that I would kill him. But I allowed my hatred for him to affect my aim. My bullet landed in his leg. His shot landed wide. The matter was closed. There was nothing more I could do...but wait and watch, and ensure that he never struck again.'

'Oh, Lucien...' Madeline pressed her cheek to her husband's hand '...you've had a terrible time.' She raised her head and looked at him. 'If Farquharson killed Sarah at

Tintagel, then it explains why he has chosen that same place for an assignation.'

Lucien nodded. 'A repeat of history except that instead of Sarah, this time he wants you. Farquharson's perversion will never diminish. I have to stop him, Madeline. You do understand why I must do this?'

'To avenge Sarah's death.'

He shook his head. 'Once upon a time that's what I lived for, the thought of making him suffer as he did to both Sarah and my mother. Not any more. Vengeance is not mine. Farquharson will reap that in plenty when he meets his Maker.' He took her face between his hands, his fingers resting lightly against the softness of her cheeks. 'I love you, Madeline. For all my denials I think I've loved you since first I held you in my arms and waltzed with you at Lady Gilmour's ball. I will not let him have you. That's why it must stop here, this night. You were right, Madeline, you cannot live your life forever looking over your shoulder.'

She clung to him, pressed her lips to his. 'No, Lucien! I didn't mean that. I love you. Please don't go alone.'

'It's the best way, Madeline.' He looked down into her eyes, seeing tears falling freely from them for the first time. 'Don't cry, my love. One shot is all I need and this time the bullet shall land within his heart.'

'I cannot let you do this, Lucien. I won't.' Her face was wet beneath his touch.

'Madeline,' he said gently. 'Do this one thing that I ask.'

She sobbed aloud. 'Please…'

'No more tears, my love.' And slowly, tenderly, he lowered his lips to hers and in that kiss was everything he wanted to give her: gratitude and joy and celebration for all that she had brought to his life, peace, and faith and eternal love. 'Promise me that you'll stay here.' Her eyes were a clear light sienna flecked with gold. Eyes to lose yourself in, he'd once thought, and he'd been right. 'Give me your word that you won't seek to follow me.'

Her teeth bit desperately at her lower lip. A minute passed in silence, then stretched to two. When she finally spoke her voice was cracked and broken. 'You ask the impossible.'

'Promise me, Madeline,' he said again and took one last chance to inhale the warm orange scent of her. Her hair tickled against his nose as he awaited her reply.

A small sob sounded. The teeth bit harder against her lip. 'Very well,' she croaked, 'I promise.'

One last kiss from her sweet mouth, then Lucien turned and walked towards the door.

'My love,' she whispered as the door clicked shut. 'Oh, my love,' and pressed her fingers hard against her mouth to capture the sobs that threatened to burst forth. Nothing could still the shudders that wracked her body.

Madeline did not know how long she stood motionless, watching the door of the small drawing room. Perhaps she waited in case Lucien changed his mind. Or to see if the whole nightmare was real or just some awful joke that Lucien and his brother had contrived between them. She stood statue still, breath so light as to scarcely be there. Her eyes were red and gritty, her cheeks damp with saline. She stood until there were no more tears to fall. Alone in the small drawing room, while her husband rode out to meet his death, to save both her and his brother. What chance did he stand against Farquharson and his men? The clock marked the passing of the seconds. Each frantic tick taking Lucien further from safety, closer to his doom. Tick, tick, tick, tick. Faster and faster. Madeline walked towards the mantel, lifted the pretty clock into her hands, and threw it hard across the room. It landed with a loud thud. Silence hissed. And the spell that had frozen Madeline shattered.

There was a thud of footsteps, uneven, growing louder. The door burst open. Madeline's head jerked up in expectation, his name soft upon her lips. 'Lucien?'

Mrs Babcock's ruddy face appeared. 'M'lady! Such a terrible noise. I thought you might have tripped and fallen your length…' The small black eyes rested upon the remains of the clock close by the window. 'Ah,' she said. 'No harm done.'

No harm? Madeline felt the urge to laugh hysterically. 'No harm?' she said aloud.

'Come along, doe.' The housekeeper steered Madeline out of the drawing room and along to her bedchamber. 'Master Lucien said you was a bit upset, like. Don't you worry, Babbie's here. I'll make you a nice posset and tuck you up in bed, all safe and sound, until his lordship gets back.'

Madeline allowed herself to be guided by the older woman. Until his lordship gets back, Babbie had said. What would she say if she knew the truth? Lucien wasn't coming back, not tonight, not ever. Madeline looked up into the kindly old face…and could not inflict the hurt the truth would give. 'There's no need for a posset, Babbie, I'll sleep directly. I'm just a little worried for Lucien, that's all.'

'Aren't we all, m'lady, aren't we all? If you change your mind about the posset, just ring and I'll be here.' The housekeeper stroked Madeline's cheek. 'I know you love him, doe. Never thought to see him smile again, not after what happened, what with the dowager Countess and Lady Sarah and all them terrible things. But you've made him happy, real happy. I'm sorry I was snappy with you when you asked me them questions.'

'I should never have doubted him.' Madeline sat down upon the bed.

'You weren't to know, and he can be a bit of a surly old bear when he's got a mind to be.' Mrs Babcock gave Madeline a brief hug, then hurried away with a face flaming like a beacon. She paused briefly by the door. 'I'll send Betsy up to help you change.'

'No, thank you, I'd rather manage by myself tonight.' Madeline raised a small smile. 'Goodnight, Babbie.'

'Goodnight, m'lady, and may the good Lord bring Master Lucien back to us safe and sound.'

'Amen to that, Babbie.'

The door closed, leaving Madeline alone.

Lucien's eyes raked through the darkness. A full moon hung high in the sky, glimmering silver upon the expanse of rippling dark sea, casting the castle ruins up ahead as a sinister silhouette. Nelson trotted closer until Lucien reined him in and dismounted, preferring to lead the horse the rest of the distance. Salt and seaweed and dampness hung heavy in the air, undisturbed by the wind blowing in from the sea. His hand touched briefly against the solid form of the pistol hidden deep within his pocket. He walked the horse up as close as he dared, tethering the reins on a scrubby bush by the final entrance to the site. He paused, instincts alert, face harsh beneath the pale moonlight, eyes scouring the castle walls that lay ahead of him, or at least what remained of them. No sign of Farquharson. The ground was solid beneath his feet as he slipped out from behind the cover of his horse, exposing himself to any shot that Farquharson might care to take. One step, and then another, keeping close to the shadow of the rising crag to his left, he edged round and climbed the steps to the upper ward. His gaze swept every ancient stone. The high place was empty. And that meant that Farquharson had to be in the island part of the castle. Lucien turned and headed towards the narrow winding pathway that would lead him there.

Lap and swirl of waves sounded against the rocks far below, crashing and frothing with a ferocity that contrasted with the tranquillity of the ocean beyond. The men that had built Tintagel Castle had chosen their site well. The castle straddled an unstable neck linking Tintagel Island with the mainland. The remains of the upper and lower wards lay on the landward side, the inner ward and chapel remnants on the island. A pathway connecting the two dropped away to sheer jagged rock. Frothy white water swirled below. A defence designed to thwart the best of attackers. Lucien knew that it was here on the pathway that he was at his most vulnerable. His heart thudded fast yet steady, waiting each moment for the hidden shot to ring from the castle ruins. The longest walk of his life. The slowest. And still the shot did not come. Every step taking him closer. Every breath buoying his confidence that he would make it. He was so close that he could see the individual-hewn stones that made up the thick walls, the ruined apertures of windows and doorways. So close. The path led him directly into what had been one of the castle baileys. He scanned ahead. Wind howled. Emptiness echoed. The hairs on the back of Lucien's neck prickled. Eyes searching, ears straining for the slightest hint of Farquharson's location. Nothing. No one. Lucien's fingers slipped into his pocket, closed around the pistol handle, extracted the weapon. He held it down low, brushing beside his thigh, all the harder for Farquharson to see it. He backed against the rear wall, poised, ready.

'Farquharson!' The wind snatched the shout, to carry it away unanswered. Sweat beaded upon Lucien's upper lip. 'Farquharson!'

A small scrunch of a sound from the other side of the wall.

Keeping his body close to the protection of the ancient stone structure, Lucien moved with stealth to the end of the wall. Readied the pistol, finger on the trigger. One swift lunge and he peered round the other side, pistol aimed with precision at the spot from whence the noise had issued. Bare soil and rock, a trickle of pebbles...a cat disappearing in the distance. Lucien's gaze drifted down from the wall, down to the abrupt fall of the cliff. A shiver tingled down his spine. Close by the solitary cry of a gull sounded. Distorted. Ghostly. A portent of doom. Icy foreboding gripped him.

He retraced his steps, covering the ground as fast as he dared, slipping from the cover of one wall to another, scanning each and every part of the ruin in turn, ever ready for the surprise assault that did not come. Empty. Back across the precarious pathway. Still no one. Still nothing. Chill grew greater. Alone. Blood ran cold. The seed of doubt germinated, grew, and blossomed to reveal the truth. The pistol uncocked, stuffed within his pocket. He ran back through the inner ward to where the great black horse stood, still tethered where he had left it. Didn't even break stride to swing himself up into the saddle.

Lucien rode like he had never ridden before, coat flying, throwing up mud and water in his wake. Through the streets of Tintagel village to Bossmey, then Davidstow, following the road down towards Camelford. Riding as if the hounds of Lucifer snapped at his heels, riding until his lungs were fit to burst and his muscles shook from the strain. Past the gloom of the great moor. Hoping. Praying. Knowing even as he did, that he would be too late.

The knowledge that Farquharson had tricked him was a bitter pill to swallow. For if Cyril Farquharson was not at Tintagel, there was as like only one other place he could be. What was it that Collins had said as he lay bleeding upon the entrance hall floor? *He asked us questions about this place...* The place that now lay unprotected. The place that held the one thing that Farquharson wanted above all else. The place in which Lucien had left his wife, thinking her to be safe. And that place was Trethevyn.

Chapter Fifteen

For all that Madeline had said to Mrs Babcock, she knew that she would not sleep that night. How could she, knowing what her husband was riding out to meet, knowing that Farquharson would kill both Lucien and his brother? She had seen what the scoundrel had done to Collins. She did not doubt how much worse he would inflict upon the man who had thwarted him. The knowledge caused her heart to freeze lest it shatter into a thousand pieces. The fire burned low within the grate, a few small flames licking around a glowing mass. Gooseflesh raised upon Madeline's arms. She had no awareness of the dropping temperature within the bedchamber, nor of the draught that flitted through the great window to ruffle the curtains that hung still drawn back to frame the paned glass. She blew out the candles and watched the wispy smoke, from their quenching, curl in the air.

The sky was an inky dark velvet decorated with a pearly white button moon and a scatter of stars that glittered like diamond pinheads. She stood in the darkness, a small solitary figure garbed in the plain white cotton of her nightdress, and stared out across the lawns that lay before Trethevyn. Lucien would be at Tintagel by now, walking straight into Farquharson's hands like a lamb to the slaughter. She did not allow her thoughts to stray to what that slaughter would entail. And through it all Madeline could not really believe that it was happening. Was it true what they said, that when a man's life ebbed away his soul leapt out and appeared to those he loved? Surely she would know if he were dead, wouldn't she? But Madeline felt nothing of that; indeed, she could feel very little at all due to the numbness that had spread throughout her body.

She turned Lucien's words over in her mind a thousand times, hearing the story of what Farquharson had done again and again. A devious man. A fox. A villain. A man that would always play dirty, for there was no other way of winning. She thought about Cyril Farquharson. She thought about Guy as his hostage. She thought about Collins's tortured body and the words that had strained from his lips. And amidst all of her thinking the truth made itself known to Madeline. It didn't strike like a bolt from the blue. It wasn't a blinding enlightenment. Instead, it just slipped into her head quietly and without any fuss. And she accepted the realisation without question.

A curious torpor settled upon Madeline, a sense of inevitability that stretched almost to relief. She should have been paralysed with fear and dread and terror. But she wasn't. Certainty filled her. Knowledge, even. Worry vanished. Madeline knew what was coming and she was glad, for it could mean only one thing: that Lucien was safe.

She fetched Lucien's knife from the drawer of his desk in the library and slid it, still sheathed, into the pocket of her dressing gown. Then she returned to her bedchamber and sat down in the small armchair in the corner. The knife lay heavy and reassuring against her thigh. Her fingers, hidden within her pocket, rested comfortably around the handle. The monster was coming to get her, yet Madeline was not afraid. It was her nightmare become reality, but Madeline was calm. For once in her life she would not flee. She refused to hide. She had done with running. As she had told Lucien, she could not live her life for ever looking over her shoulder; *they* could not live life forever looking over *their* shoulders.

She knew now that Farquharson would never leave them alone. He would pursue them for eternity. He had already taken Guy. It was just a matter of time before he caught her and Lucien. Madeline could not let that happen, for she loved Lucien above life itself. And all the while Farquharson breathed, Lucien would not be safe. She understood now why Lucien had been so vigilant. She could see now that what she had dismissed as an obsessive hatred had been a frank appreciation of the danger that Farquharson posed. Lucien had been right. He had not underestimated Farquharson. He alone had known of what the fiend was capable. And now Madeline knew. And she knew too that she had a chance to stop this madness. The time had come to face Cyril Farquharson.

The house was quiet with waiting, the servants about their chores or in their beds. There was no point in endangering their lives. It was Madeline that he wanted, and Madeline he would get, alone save for her husband's knife. Max made no sound in the small dressing room that lay beyond. And so Madeline sat and waited for the fox to come to her door.

Cyril Farquharson slipped into Trethevyn like a shadow, silent and unnoticed. The latch on the windowed doors that led from the front garden into the library was easily coaxed into submission. The door swung open beneath his touch. His red hair was paled by the moonlight. He moved without a sound across the floor, thankful that Varington's valet had been persuaded to share the details of the inner layout of the house. The clock on the mantel struck eleven. Anticipation coursed through him.

Of course Tregellas would have long since realised that he had been duped. How long had the Earl spent searching the ruins before he had known that he was there alone? All alone. Searching for a man that was not there. Three hours from home. A smile cracked Farquharson's face. It was not hard to imagine how Tregellas had felt in that moment of realisation. Rage, dread, fear. Excitement tingled deep within Farquharson's gut. Even now, Tregellas would be spurring his horse hard over the roads that led from Tintagel. Pushing himself to the limit, fighting against the inevitable. Three hours was a long journey to make, knowing all the while what was happening to your wife, and being helpless to stop it. In your own bed, with your own servants none the wiser as to what was happening so very close at hand. Farquharson almost sniggered aloud. Tregellas would arrive home just in time to play his part in the final stages of Farquharson's plan. And what a plan it was. Superbly crafted by a master. Executed stage by stage. Using Varington to lure Tregellas to Tintagel, Varington, with whom Farquharson would deal later. And the whole of it built on knowing Tregellas's character, knowing that the Earl would never take Madeline there, knowing that he would leave her here all nicely tucked up ready for Farquharson. Farquharson's thoughts flitted to the woman above, the woman who was no doubt sobbing herself to sleep at this very moment: Madeline.

She had defied him from the start, humiliated him in front of all London. And for that she would reap the punishment that he had promised. How many nights had he lain awake with its planning? For how many months had he waited and watched? Sowing his seeds, biding his time until the right opportunity arose. How very tempting it had been to have her taken that day upon the moor with the maid screaming that Harry Staunton was coming. Or the time she had gone alone to visit the sick old woman on the other side of the village. Not much had escaped Cyril Farquharson's notice, thanks to money and his paid spies.

He knew when Madeline walked in the gardens and when she sat with her needlework by her bedchamber window. Even her midnight sojourn to the library and the drunken harsh response of her husband had not escaped his attention. The faked letter had done its work well, driving a wedge of suspicion between Tregellas and the woman he had stolen. Farquharson remembered those light golden brown eyes, the dark blonde hair swept so primly back. Madeline Langley was no beauty, but she had everything that he wanted in a woman: innocence, modesty and, more importantly fear…and that was what Farquharson craved above all. She had a shy reserve that held her apart from the crowd. She did not chatter the inane nonsense of most of the young ladies of the *ton*. She did not pout or stamp her foot or dab at a tearful eye. Not Madeline Langley. She just melted into the background, and watched what was around her with those magnificent eyes of hers. A little wallflower that hid something beneath. Unless Farquharson was very much mistaken, what flowed in those frightened little veins of hers was a passion that had not yet been brought to life. He hardened at the very thought and moved with impatience steadily closer to Madeline's bedchamber.

Lucien gritted his teeth and rode harder. How the hell could he have been so stupid as not to realise that Farquharson would have double-crossed him? Didn't he know the man for the sly malevolent villain that he was? Now, because of his mistake, because he had allowed Farquharson to outwit him, Madeline would suffer. Lucien had been fully prepared to face his own death, not Madeline's. He pushed aside the thoughts of exactly what Farquharson would be subjecting her to, just harnessed the rage and focused it to carry him with speed in the direction of Trethevyn.

The moon, so clear and high above, lit his path, helping him push Nelson faster than he normally would have dared along the muddy road close by Bodmin Moor. But no matter how much he or his beloved gelding gave, nothing could diminish the distance that separated them from Madeline. Even illuminated as well as it was, the rutted road was too long, too slow. He was approaching Camelford when he found himself plunged headlong into a shroud of thick mist. No warning, just a blanket of low cloud that hid the road ahead. 'Hell, no!' Lucien shouted aloud and pulled Nelson up hard. Breath came in heavy pants and sweat dripped from his face. Every muscle fired with adrenalin. All around was the eerie silence of the moor.

Just a pocket of mist, he told himself. He need only pass through it. It would lift as suddenly as it had descended. 'Come on, Nelson.' He tried to coax the horse to walk on, steering with his knees, making the little clicks of reassurance that the gelding liked to hear. Nelson obstinately held his ground, apparently impervious to all means of persuasion. The gelding's ears flattened and his black eyes rolled to become edged with white. Hind legs stumbled back. Snorting breath muffled in the unnatural quiet that surrounded them. Lucien tried to calm the frightened horse, but to no avail. From somewhere in the distance came a whinny. Nelson's ears pricked up. Lucien backed him out of the mist, scanning the undulating moorland. There, up on the hill to the left, not so far away, outlined black and stark against the brightness of the moon, was a solitary rider on his horse.

Lucien's fingers touched to the heavy weight of the pistol hidden within his pocket. The figure beckoned. Another trap? Farquharson or one of his cronies? Across the distance the man looked to be wearing an old-fashioned cocked hat. The stranger's voice filled the space between them. It was a deep voice, thickly accented with the familiar Cornish lilt. 'If you've a mind to get anywhere fast then you'd best go over the moor, past Brown Willy, cross the main coaching road at Jamaica Inn, then on between the Downs. Could cross it in an hour…if you can ride well and know the land. Goin' that way myself, if you care to follow.' The great black horse reared up on its back legs and both man and beast disappeared over the brow of the hill.

For all his suspicion, Lucien knew the man to be right. He didn't trust him. The stranger might be a cut-throat or a high-wayman. It was a risk Lucien was prepared to take. If he didn't reach Madeline in time, none of it mattered anyway. A brief touch of a booted foot to Nelson's flank and they were off, following in the man's wake, galloping across the clear moonlit hills, crossing hedges and streams, kicking up great clods of mud and grass, pressing onwards at breakneck speed, struggling to maintain the distant figure in sight, breath straining hard in a cloud of condensation. Rider and horse merged.

Urgent. Intent. Madeline. Madeline. Madeline. Her name sounded silently again and again amidst the pounding rhythm of hooves and hearts. Faster and faster, until the first faint sight of Trethevyn's lights appeared in the distance and the stranger was gone.

When at last Madeline saw the doorknob turn and heard the quiet click, she felt a peculiar sense of relief. The waiting was over. The door opened in towards her, sweeping silently across the floor to admit the shadowy figure that followed in its wake. She watched the man creep towards the bed. He seemed smaller than she remembered. A dark shape moving stealthily forward into the room. Even bleached and muted by the silver moonlight, his hair was still discernible as red. The skin on his face was illuminated an unearthly white. He hesitated by the bed, caught unawares by its empty state. Then, like a fox scenting its prey, he raised his head and looked directly at her.

Through the darkness she met his gaze.

He was wary, the situation not quite as he had anticipated. A furtive glance all around, trying to ascertain if she was alone or if he himself had just walked into a trap.

'You came at last,' she said. And her voice sounded strangely calm.

'Madeline,' he breathed, and she heard the promise in the word.

'I did not know if I could wait much longer.'

His steps paused. She could almost see the puzzlement upon his face. 'You knew I was coming?'

'You promised.' She unfolded herself from the chair and stood up.

His perplexity was so palpable as to reach across the distance between them.

'In your letter,' she said as if by way of explanation.

Farquharson made no move towards her, his body poised as if to take flight at any moment.

Her gaze sought his across the room. 'You said that you loved me.'

A sharp frown appeared. His eyes shot right, then left. His hand touched to the shape of a pistol hidden beneath his coat.

'Did you speak true?' The game she played was a dangerous one, but it seemed to be working. She had never seen him so discomposed.

Narrow eyes scanned the darkness. He twitched and glanced around him as if he did not entirely trust the situation into which he had just walked. 'Tregellas is at Tintagel.' It was not a question. Farquharson knew very well that the Earl was exactly where he wanted him to be. He had watched Tregellas ride out alone four hours ago, long enough to ensure that the Earl had not changed his mind *en route*.

'Yes, where you sent him. It was very clever of you. He really had no idea, you know.'

Farquharson could not suppress the smirk.

'Almost as clever as the letter that you showed to Lord Varington.' She tilted her head to the side, almost as if in quizzical admiration. 'How did you manage that, with the Tregellas paper and seal, and, of course, my own writing clear upon it?'

He opened his mouth to tell her, just as she had known that he would. 'The paper was easy enough. It did not take much to discover that Tregellas has always used Hambledon printers and suppliers of fine paper. A small bribe ensured a few sheets went missing from his last order. You, my dear, gave me the means to replicate the seal yourself, with the cold-hearted reply that you sent me. Before I broke the seal on your letter I had a friend of mine impress it in glazier's putty and use the relief to cast a new seal. Something of the detail is lost in the process, but not enough to be noticed when it is pressed roughly into molten wax.' His gaze broke from hers to scan around the room.

But there was more still to know and Madeline meant to learn it all. 'You then had someone forge my handwriting.'

'No.' He could not resist the invitation to brag. 'I have in my possession a copying machine, a so-called polygraph. A most ingenious invention by Mr John Isaac Hawkins. Not designed for forgery, but useful for that purpose all the same. A pen is inserted into one side of it. A second pen positioned on the other side of the mechanism mirrors the movement of the first, to reproduce the identical letters on a fresh sheet of paper. I merely rearranged the words written by your own hand to make them read quite differently, then traced the first pen across them. The result was a letter saying what I wanted, written in the exact style of your hand.'

'I see.' She sighed softly, knowing what it was she had to do.

He stepped back, his expression hardening. 'Enough of this chatter. Come here, Madeline.'

There was only one way she could hope to deter the man before her. He was so sure of her aversion, wanted her to cower and tremble before him, needed her fear. Madeline would satisfy neither his expectations nor his desires, but in order to act she needed him close. 'Will you not come to me?' She stood where she was.

He hesitated and glanced over his shoulder, as if he could not be sure that Lucien had not returned to Trethevyn by some secret route. He took first one step towards her, and then another, before stopping. 'What trickery is this?'

'No trickery, my lord.' She opened her palms, held them out for him to see. 'Are you afraid?' she said.

A moue of displeasure marked his mouth. 'It's not supposed to be like this.' His top lip curled. 'Come here!' And his voice was rough with menace.

A soft laugh escaped Madeline and she stepped back to lean against the wall, slipping her hands into the pockets of her dressing gown as she did so.

'No more of your games!' he snapped and made to catch her.

It seemed to Madeline that he moved in slow motion. She waited until he had almost reached her before withdrawing her right hand from its silky hiding place. She drove the unsheathed knife as fast and as hard as she could towards Farquharson's chest. She saw the blade glint as it arced through the moonlight. She heard his grunt of surprise as the tip of the knife found its mark. And just when she thought that she had him, Farquharson twisted away, grabbing her arm in the process, almost wrenching it from its socket. There was a sharp pain in her wrist where his fingers gripped, and the knife clattered to the floor. Farquharson retrieved it and then held her arms in a tight grip, pinning her against the wall while he stared down into her face. There was a snarl on his mouth, a feral darkness in his eyes. 'Little bitch!' he cursed. 'You would kill me!' He seemed genuinely shocked.

She said nothing. The breath was soft in her throat. She had failed. There was nothing more she could do. She knew her time had come. Farquharson would do to her what he had done to Sarah Wyatt. And curiously, now that she faced that which she most feared, she was not afraid. The fear had all been in the anticipation and the imaginings. The reality of the horror brought only a calm acceptance.

What was it that Lucien had said? *The villain thrives on pain. It gives him pleasure to watch others suffer.* Madeline understood in that moment exactly what Lucien had meant. Farquharson's hands curled tighter, biting into her skin as he dragged her across the room and threw her on to the bed. Still she felt neither pain nor fear. She looked up at the cruel contorted features. 'There's no more pleasure to be had for you, Lord Farquharson.'

He struck her hard across the cheek as she lay there. 'What do you know of pleasure and pain, Madeline?'

She didn't even flinch.

A bark sounded from the dressing room.

Farquharson glanced round to the closed door that separated the two rooms. 'The dog won't bother us from in there,' he said, 'and there's so much I have to teach you, my dear.'

His hand wrapped around her throat and squeezed. The press of his arousal against her leg grew stronger.

It seemed that Madeline was not in the shell that she called her body, but had floated clear of it to rest somewhere up high beside the plasterwork of the ceiling. Was she really looking down at Farquharson throttling her? Even as she watched, he released his grip to straddle her. 'It's too late.' The words croaked hoarse and she saw that it was her own lips that moved. 'Your power is gone, my lord. I am not afraid.'

'Then let me rectify matters, Madeline.' He tore the dressing gown from her. His hands moved to grasp the neckline of her nightdress, ripping down through the stark white cotton to expose the pale flesh beneath. His mouth pounced like a savage upon her breasts.

Still Madeline did not cry out. 'All you are worthy of is pity, sir,' she said. 'You are a man incapable of receiving or giving love.'

Max gave a whine and scratched at the dressing-room door.

From above she felt Farquharson cease his movement upon her. Watched while he raised his face to look into her own. Saw the saliva moist upon his lips and the wetness that dripped to his chin. Looked deep into that dismal grey gaze. *'I do not fear you.'* Each word was dropped with clear enunciation into the space between them. She felt his interest shrivel.

He swallowed hard. 'Whore!' he said and drew Lucien's knife from his pocket. 'So thoughtful of you to provide me with your husband's knife. He won't wriggle out of prosecution so easily this time. Murder is a wicked crime, committed by a wicked man. First against his betrothed, and now against his wife. I named him well, did I not?'

Another bark, followed by some more scratching at the door.

'You can kill me, Lord Farquharson, but no one shall believe Lucien guilty of the crime. Why, all of London knows that we eloped out of love,' she taunted.

'Indeed?' His face was cold and hard. There was nothing of humanity in his eyes. A smile played across his mouth. 'I think you'll find that they believe Tregellas abducted you and forced a wedding. And as for motive, I shall feel it my civic duty to publish the letter that you sent me; the letter in which you beg for rescue from a madman, and speak of your love for me.'

'Lucien shall prove it for the fake that it is.'

'I don't think so, Madeline,' said Farquharson. He paused and watched her. 'They'll hang him, you know. And I shall be there to watch while he slowly expires.' He smiled and licked his lips. 'What better fun than killing you, then watching your husband die for the crime.'

'No!' Rage welled within her. 'No!' she cried again. 'Ever the coward's way, Farquharson. Ever cloak and dagger, and behind his back. You are not man enough to face him. You know he would best you a thousand times over!'

Max barked again, and from outside came the distant thud of horse's hooves.

Farquharson glanced nervously towards the windows.

Someone was riding hard and fast.

'It's three hours from Tintagel to here,' said Farquharson as if to himself.

He touched the blade to her throat, and then in one move gently stroked its cold sharp edge against her skin.

Madeline felt its shallow bite and a wetness trickled down the sides of her neck.

The horseman was coming closer.

'I've waited so long for this,' he said and, bending forward, licked the dribble of blood from her skin and then covered her mouth with his own. The metallic taste of blood touched upon her tongue, and then his mouth was suffocating her.

They heard the sudden crunch of gravel on the driveway and knew the horseman had reached Trethevyn. Max began to bark in earnest.

Madeline's heart leapt. It could not be, could it?

Farquharson scowled and clambered off her. Still clutching the knife, he stalked to the window that led out on to the balcony. Up the gravel driveway came a solitary horseman, riding as if his very life was at stake. The horse's eyes showed white and his great black muzzle was flecked pale with saliva. The man was leaping down from the saddle as the Baron watched. And even through the darkness Farquharson knew that it was Tregellas that had come. 'How the hell…?' But there was no time for questions. He knew he would have to act quickly.

Madeline sat up and slowly, so as not to attract Farquharson's attention, slid towards the edge of the bed.

Farquharson was still peering out of the window. 'He arrives in time to spoil our fun but, Madeline, not in time to prevent your death, for which he will take the blame. A crime of passion. All of London knows what has gone on between us three.' He turned then and looked at her. 'And this time he shall not escape justice, earl or not. I shall toast you, my dear, as I watch his neck being stretched by a rope upon a gibbet.' The blade within his hand glinted in the moonlight. 'And now, my sweet Madeline…' He began to walk towards her.

Madeline sprang from the bed and, unmindful of her nakedness, ran towards the dressing-room door. She heard Farquharson's movement behind her, felt the sudden grasp of his fingers biting hard against her shoulder. She snatched at the handle and the door to the dressing-room opened. Max's frenzied barking grew suddenly loud. She felt the rush of something against her legs, but then Farquharson was wrenching her back, throwing her towards the bed. It all happened so fast that she did not know what was happening. Her head struck against the bedstead. Waves of dizzy nausea washed over her. She lay sprawled upon the floor, struggling to get back up on to her feet, but unable to stop the world tilting enough to do so. 'Lucien!' she cried, but her voice was weak and thick with confusion and no matter how hard she tried she could not see through the darkness that had descended upon her.

There was the thud of feet and the scamper of paws. Something moist snuffled against her face and she knew that it was Max. Madeline ceased the struggle to open her eyes and let her head rest back upon the rug.

The raucous barking had turned to a low-pitched growling.

Farquharson cursed and his boots scuffed away. She heard the opening of the window, and then the rapid sliding of its close.

And Madeline knew that she had failed, for Farquharson would escape. He could swing down from the balcony across to the roof of the front porch. And from there it was not so very far to the ground.

She pushed herself up until she was sitting. Spots danced before her eyes. Her stomach jiggled like a ship on a choppy sea. She looked up to see Farquharson out on the balcony and Max growling with his nose pressed against the glass. A black paw scraped against the pane.

'Max,' she called. And Max ceased his noise and came to stand by her. He whined and licked her face. Her fingers caught in his smooth black fur. She eased herself back to rest against the bedstead, and shut her eyes.

There was the sudden loud crashing sound. A man cried out, followed by a bone-jarring thud. Then there was only silence.

Lucien was taking the stairs two at a time, leaving a trail of muddy footsteps behind, when he heard the cry and the sickening thud of a body landing hard upon the ground. His stomach turned over and the breath tore ragged in his throat as he ran full tilt towards Madeline's chamber. 'Madeline!' he bellowed, fearing what he would find, but charging onward regardless. The door reverberated from his onslaught, swinging back open and wide. Only then did Lucien pause. Madeline was sitting on the floor, leaning against the bed. Her eyes were closed and her face was so white as to appear lifeless. Blood trickled from a gash on her forehead, and blood was dripping down her throat. And she was naked. Max sat by her side. He looked up at his master and gave a whimper. Lucien thought that he was too late.

'Madeline,' he whispered and moved quickly to her side. Down below there were the sounds of feet running and doors banging and servants' voices. 'Madeline!' he said again and it seemed that his heart had stopped.

Her eyes flickered open, and she was looking at him, and he knew that God had heard his prayer. She was alive. His beloved Madeline was alive.

'Lucien, is it really you?' she whispered and reached for him.

He took off his coat and wrapped it around her and lifted her into his arms.

'Lucien!' She clung to him, her fingers touching gently to his mud-splattered cheeks. 'My love.'

He felt the slow trickle of blood back into his face. The crushing burden of dread crumbled and dispersed. 'You're alive. You're safe.' He stared at her, unable to comprehend how that could be. 'Farquharson…' And then he remembered the cry and the thud and looked towards the window that led out on to the balcony.

Madeline saw his gaze. 'He went out there, trying to escape,' she said. 'The railings…I think he fell.'

Lucien laid her gently on the bed, and then with Max at his heels he moved to the window, slid the sash up and stepped out on to the balcony. At the right-hand side the railings had given way completely. Lucien glanced down and over to the right to the roof of the porch. It was empty. He stepped closer to the edge of the balcony where there were no longer any railings. The drop was sheer. Below on the hard stone of the steps lay a man's broken body: Cyril Farquharson. It was over.

Madeline heard him come back into the room, felt him sit down on the bed beside her. 'He's dead,' he said.

'Then we're safe.'

He nodded. 'I thought...' She heard the crack in his voice and his eyes squeezed shut. When they opened again he seemed to have regained some measure of control.

'No,' she said, 'You came in time, you and Max.' And she told her husband what had passed between her and Farquharson.

He stared as if he could not quite believe it. 'I must fetch the doctor for you.'

But she stayed him with a touch of her hand. 'No. There's nothing that shall not mend. The blood makes it appear worse than it is. Stay. Please.' She wrapped her arms around him.

'Madeline!' Her name was a harsh expiration of breath and in that sound was everything of relief and disbelief and love. He cradled her against him.

She kissed his chest, his arms, tilted her face up to press a myriad of butterfly kisses against his jaw. 'I thought I'd lost you,' she whispered.

'My love.' He stroked her cheek. 'I feared I was too late. I couldn't bear to lose you. You are my very life.'

'As you are mine,' she breathed.

'Madeline,' he said again and their lips met in joyous salvation. And Lucien held her as if he would never let her go.

* * *

It was half an hour later when Farquharson's body was being removed that Lucien undertook to search the villain's pockets. A handkerchief, a pocket watch, some calling cards, two dice, a purse full of money…and a sheet of neatly folded paper. It rustled between Lucien's fingers as he splayed it flat to reveal the drawing traced upon it.

'What is it?' Madeline peered over his shoulder.

'A map…' He moved the branch of candles closer, straining to read the small scribbled words amidst the sketch. 'Showing the mine shaft close by the Hurlers stone circles.'

Two heads raised. Blue eyes met brown.

'Collins said Farquharson took them somewhere deep under ground,' said Madeline.

'I think we may just have discovered where he's holding my brother.'

They looked at one another a moment longer, each knowing the other's thoughts…and fears.

'Pray God he's still alive.' Lucien dropped a hasty kiss to her lips and went to ready the men of Trethevyn.

'And pray God that you come back safely to me,' replied his wife softly as he closed the door behind him.

The night was well advanced when Lucien and his party crept silently through the shadows towards the tin mine. The moonlight revealed a large group of men loitering by the entrance to the engine house. There looked to be about ten of them, perhaps as many as twelve. Vicious-looking villains. The hired muscle of which Collins had spoken. Some were armed with wooden clubs. And on some the moonlight glinted against long knife blades. Tobacco smoke drifted in the air; the small orange glowing spots of clay pipes were visible through the darkness. Lucien gestured the advance sign to the men behind him and slowly they began to spread out and edge forward.

The men had clearly been there some time. Some were leaning their backs against the wall of the engine house, others were sitting on what looked to be boxes. A bottle was being passed around. The quiet burr of their voices carried in the night. Someone sighed his boredom and another sniffed the contents of his nose down his throat. One of them gave a soft throaty laugh. None of them suspected what was closing around them.

Lucien and the men of Trethevyn attacked without warning, running in fast, catching the ruffians unawares. Lucien felled one man with a well-aimed blow from the handle of his pistol. The villains fought back, shouting, swearing. All around was mayhem. A fist cracked hard against Lucien's jaw and he tasted blood against his tongue. He lashed out and the man punched no more. The Trethevyn men were well armed, and they were angry. The night resounded with the clash of cudgels and yelling and screaming. A man ran at young Hayley's back with a knife raised ready to strike. Lucien aimed his pistol and pulled the trigger. There was a roar of gunpowder and the man collapsed with a grunt and a wet darkness seeping from his shoulder. The ruffians were falling, and those that didn't, ran away. The rest were easily overpowered. One by one the ruffians were bound and gagged and left where they lay.

Lucien checked inside the building that housed the great steam engine. It lay silent; the pumps that drained the mines of water idle for once. The place was deserted: no more of Farquharson's ruffians hiding. Back out into the darkness, past the tall chimney stalk, he made straight for the mouth of the mine. The tinderbox was struck, the lantern held low. He poured some powder into the pistol's pan and also down its barrel, fitted a patch over the muzzle and rammed a lead ball down into place. He slipped the pistol into his pocket. Those in the mine would have heard his shot. They were warned. Lucien had to be ready.

He peered down the shaft. It was narrow and vertical, and far deeper than the lantern light illuminated. A pit of hell. And down there somewhere Guy was waiting. Lucien could only pray that his brother was still alive. A ladder leaned against the shaft's inner rim. He swung his legs over and, gripping the ladder, began to descend, as fast as he dared. In a matter of seconds he was swallowed down into the narrow well of darkness, to meet what waited below. Sweat dripped down his back, soaking his shirt.

Never once did Lucien falter, just climbed and climbed further, down into the bowels of the earth, while up above his men waited and the moon shone down on a silent landscape.

Madeline paced the library. The woman who had faced Farquharson without fear now found her body chilled with apprehension. She chided herself, reasoning that Farquharson was dead and that Lucien knew what he was doing. *But it is a mine shaft,* the fear whispered, *and you do not know what awaits him.* The thought made her feel queasy. She bit down hard on her lip and tried to calm her fluttering nerves. What of Lord Varington? She dared not dwell too much on that thought, only hoped and prayed that he would be safe. She forced herself down into the large wing chair so favoured by her husband and watched the hands of the clock creep slowly forward. Night had never seemed so long, waiting never so difficult. At last the crunch of hooves sounded upon the driveway gravel. A low murmur of voices filled the night air. Madeline shook off the sleep that hovered so beguilingly close, and ran. She did not stop running until she saw her husband across the hallway.

Lucien was on one side. John Hayley on the other. Between them they supported the weight of a man who was pale and blood-smeared, a man that looked back at her with eyes so like her husband's.

'It was about time you sent him to collect me,' he drawled. 'I was growing bored with the wait.' Something of the familiar arrogance sparkled in his eyes, but his voice was strained and weak.

'Lord Varington,' she said.

'Guy,' he corrected her. 'I owe you an apology, Madeline.'

She saw how swollen and split the lips were that formed those words. Bruising darkened bloodshot eyes. 'There's no need.'

'On the contrary, I must insist that there's every need.' He coughed and fresh blood speckled his lips. A ragged hand wiped them away.

'We'll discuss the matter later when you've rested.'

'No.' The word forced out guttural and loud, echoing in the hallway.

'Come on, Guy,' Lucien coaxed his brother. 'Let's get you cleaned up and attended to by a physician first.'

'Madeline didn't write that letter, the one Farquharson showed to me. He had a copy made of your seal, bribed your printer to obtain the paper, and forged her writing by means of a polygraph.'

'I know. Madeline learned of it from Farquharson himself this evening. He could not refrain from boasting of his sly scheme.'

Guy stopped, an indefinable expression frozen upon his face. 'He's here?'

'Oh, he's here all right.' Lucien regarded his brother. 'But I didn't lie when I said that he was dead. The High Constable will arrange for the body to be removed in the morning.' He tried to pull his brother forward, but, despite the fact that Guy was bone-weary and swaying from the blood loss, the younger man showed not the slightest sign of moving.

Guy held Madeline's eye. 'I shouldn't have doubted you. Should have realised that Farquharson was as devious as the devil and sought only to use me to get to you and Lucien…and I damn well let him, fool that I am. I can only plead your forgiveness, Madeline.'

Madeline gently touched a hand against Guy's sleeve. 'There's nothing to forgive, my lord…Guy. Farquharson tricked us all.'

Guy gave a nod of his head.

'And now, little brother, if you're quite finished setting yourself right with my wife, I must insist that you retire to the blue bedchamber.'

Between them Lucien and his footman helped the wounded man up the main staircase.

Two weeks later, and Madeline and Lucien stood on the steps of Trethevyn, waving goodbye to Guy.

'He's not recovered enough to travel yet and London is so very far. I wish he would have heeded you.' Madeline sighed. 'I mean, what if—'

Lucien touched a finger to her lips. 'No more "what ifs". Guy is as stubborn as a mule when it comes to getting his way in these things.'

'Is the country really so abhorrent to him?' A dove cooed from a nearby bush. The sky above was a clear bright blue. And the air was fresh and rich with the fragrance of spring. 'I cannot imagine anyone preferring the foul-smelling streets of London to this.'

'I think, perhaps—' his eyes held Madeline's '—that there are certain other matters to which Guy is keen to attend.' A dark eyebrow raised suggestively. 'My brother does have a certain reputation to maintain.'

A flush of delicate pink suffused Madeline's cheeks. 'Reputations can be misleading—why, sir, all of London is convinced that you're the Wicked Earl. I must rectify that rumour when we return there next.'

'Beginning with your parents.'

'Did I not tell you?' Madeline raised her eyebrows and drew him a small smile. 'My parents have suffered a change of heart. Angelina writes that Mama has discovered the merits of having an earl in the family and has become quite high in the instep about it. And Papa worries only for my happiness. He is happy as long as I am.'

'And are you happy, my love?'

'Never more so,' she laughed.

His hands slid seductively around her back. 'Am I not wicked? To have forced you to a marriage that you didn't want? To have exposed you to the worst of an evil villain who would have taken your life?'

'Extremely wicked,' she agreed and raised her lips so that they almost touched his.

'Did you believe the whispers that I was a wicked man?'

'Never.'

'How could you be so certain? You didn't know me, after all.'

'Instinct. Trust. I don't really understand it myself, but when I looked into your eyes the night you danced with me at Lady Gilmour's ball...' She shrugged her shoulders. 'I just knew. Besides...' she smiled and stole a kiss from his mouth '...anyone who saved me from Farquharson could not be at all wicked.'

With uncanny timing a black bobbing head appeared in the distance, scampering paws against gravel and barking fit to raise a riot. Max bounded up to where they stood.

'This old boy can chew as much of my footwear as he likes.' Lucien stooped to rub the dog's ears. 'Good dog!'

Madeline smiled. 'I did see him with one of your boots this morning.'

'Mmm.' Her husband's hands were busy plucking the pins from her hair, releasing it to tumble free down her back.

She held up her face to his and traced her tongue against his lips.

A low rumble sounded in Lucien's throat. The pins dropped to scatter upon the steps.

'Will you not tell me again how the ghost of Harry Staunton guided you back across the moor to Trethevyn that night?'

'Madeline…' he briefly covered her mouth with his own. One light kiss. 'There are no such things as ghosts.' A second kiss, harder, more thorough than the first. 'The man was likely someone from a neighbouring village.' When his lips claimed hers for a third time it was with a mounting passion that would brook no more talk of the ghostly highwayman. 'Did I tell you how much I love you?' He swept her up into his arms, his ice-pale eyes thawing to a blue smoulder. 'Or show you?'

'You know very well that you did only this morning, you wicked man!'

'Wicked by name, wicked by nature! Alas, my love, I find I've a need to show you again. And there's the small matter of the village sweepstake on our producing an heir…'

Together they laughed, and Earl Tregellas turned and carried his Countess over the threshold of Trethevyn.

Out on the moor, the figure of a masked man doffed his cocked hat and faded into the sunlight.

* * * * *

Untouched Mistress

Dear Reader,

I've always enjoyed reading Mills & Boon's historical novels and I still do. I love to lose myself in a good romantic story, preferably set in Regency times, with a dangerous, dashing hero, a heroine I'm rooting for and a happy ending. With Mills & Boon I know that's what I will get. I'm so pleased and honoured to be a part of that famous romantic tradition with my own few books.

Knowing how much Guy hated the countryside in his brother's story, *The Wicked Earl*, made me mischievously place him on the rugged coastline of Western Scotland for his own story—*Untouched Mistress*. It was during a cycle along the shore on a cold grey day, with a stiff breeze blowing and a smir of rain in the air, that I thought of the idea of Guy stumbling upon a beautiful, half-drowned woman washed up with the seaweed on the sands. And so came about Guy and Helena's story. I hope that you enjoy reading it.

With very best wishes,

Margaret

Chapter One

1 November 1815—Ayrshire, Scotland

A white froth of waves crashed against the rocks as the solitary figure picked its way along the shore. The morning sky was a cold grey and the fine drizzle of rain had penetrated the woollen cloth of his coat and was beginning to seep through his waistcoat to the cotton of his shirt below. Beneath his boots the sand was firm, each step cutting a clear impression of his progress. A gull cried its presence overhead, and the wind that had howled the whole night through stung a ruddy rawness to his cheeks and swept a ruffle through the darkness of his hair. Guy Tregellas, Viscount Varington, ignored the damp chill of the air and, not for the first time, thought longingly of London: London that had no gales to part a man's coat from his back. No incessant rain. No empty landscape that ran as far as the eye could see, with only the hardiest sheep and cattle for company. Guy suppressed a shudder and continued on, avoiding as best he could the mounds of seaweed and driftwood that the sea had cast upon the sand during the night's storm. The pain in his head was dulling and the nausea in his stomach had almost disappeared; the memory of just how much whisky he had drunk had not. And so he continued, walking off his hangover in this godforsaken place. He crossed the stream that ran down to meet the sea, taking care not to lose his balance on the stepping stones, and followed the curve of the shore round. It was then that he saw the body.

A dark shape amidst the seaweed. At first he thought it was a seal that had been unfortunate enough to suffer the worst of the storm in open water. But as the distance between him and the shape lessened, he knew that what lay washed upon the shore was no seal. The woman was curled on her side, as if in sleep. The dark sodden skirt of her dress was twisted around her body to expose the white of her lower legs. Her feet were bare and the one arm he could see was bloody and bruised beneath the torn sleeve of her dress. Guy rolled her over on to her back and cleared away the long strands of hair plastered across her face. She was not old, in her middle twenties perhaps, and even in her bedraggled state he could see that she was beautiful. He bent closer, touching his fingers to her neck, feeling the faint flutter of her pulse. Guy had seen too many dead bodies in his life. He breathed a sigh of relief that this was not one of them, and as he did so her eyelids flickered open and a pair of smoky green eyes stared up at him.

'An angel,' she whispered with something akin to awe. 'A glorious dark angel come to fetch me.' Her mouth curved to a small peaceful smile before her eyelids closed once more.

'Wait!' Guy gripped at the soft flesh of the woman's

upper arms. He shook her, fearing that she was giving up her fight for life. Her body seemed limp and lifeless beneath his hands. He shook her harder, spoke louder, more urgently, all trace of his hangover gone, leaving in its place a twist of dread. 'Come on, damn it! Do not dare die on me, girl.' And then, just when he thought that it was too late, she came to.

She lay still and silent for a few seconds, as if trying to remember where she was, what had happened. And then her eyes focused upon him.

'Agnes.' It was little more than a whisper, slipped from lips that scarcely moved. He could see the anxiety in her gaze.

'Thank God!' Guy sighed his relief before stripping off the coat from his body and draping it over her. 'I need to get you back to Weir's.'

'Agnes?' she said again, this time with a note of despair in her voice. 'My maid…with me in the boat…and Old Tam.'

He scanned the shoreline, knowing that there was nothing else there save sand and sea and rocks, seaweed and shells and driftwood; no more bodies, definitely no Agnes, and no Tam, old or otherwise.

'They are not here,' he said gently. 'Can you tell me your name?'

'Helena.' The reply was uttered so weakly as to almost be carried off completely by the wind. Nothing else. Just that one name. Her lungs laboured to pull in another breath of air; such a small noise against the howl of the wind and the distant roar of the sea. A few yards away the water rushed in a steady rhythm against the sand.

Guy could see that she was fighting the darkness that threatened to claim her. Her eyelids dipped and her eyeballs rolled up as she fought to remain conscious. Her lips moved again.

He bent his ear to her mouth to catch the faint words.

'Please…' What she would have said he would never know. The woman's eyes fluttered shut, and he sensed that she was slipping away from him.

'Helena.' Guy touched her cheek; the touch became a light slap.

No response.

'Helena,' he said more loudly, pressing his fingers to her neck.

There was only the faintest pulse of an ebbing life.

Guy muttered an expletive and in one motion gathered her up against him.

She was heavy with the weight of seawater soaked through her clothing, and cold; colder than any other living person he had felt, almost as cold as a corpse. Her body was limp and fluid, her head lolling against his shoulder. He wasted no more time. With the woman secure in his arms Guy headed back across the expanse of rocks and sand towards Seamill Hall.

Helena opened her eyes and blinked at the sight of what she thought was her own plasterwork ceiling above her. Mercifully she seemed to be alone. No dip in the other side of the mattress; no possessive hands pawing at her; nothing of his male stench. Just the thought of it caused her bile to rise and a shudder to ripple through her. Her fingers scrabbled to find the top of the blanket. And then she noticed that there was something different about the ceiling. She stilled her movement, and became aware that the daylight seemed much brighter than normal. Forcing herself up on to her elbows, she ignored the pounding in her head and stared at the room in which she found herself.

It was a small bedchamber, decorated predominantly in a cosy shade of yellow, shabby but genteel. The bed was smaller than her own and higher, too, with yellow-and-green striped curtains that had been fastened back. A fire roared on the hearth. Everything was clean and homely. Close by the fireplace was a comfortable-looking armchair. A large painting depicting a panoramic view of the Firth of Clyde and its islands was fixed to the wall above the mantelpiece. Near the door was an oak-coloured wardrobe, and over by the window, a matching tallboy set beside a small ornate dressing table in the French style. Next to the bed sat a table with a blue-and-white patterned pitcher and basin and various other small items. Helena recognised none of it.

Where am I? But even as she thought the question, a sinking sensation was dipping in her stomach. The mist began to clear from her mind. Helena swallowed hard. It was coming back to her now. All of it. Agnes had been with her. Old Tam, too, rowing the boat out into the darkness of the night. There had been no wind, no rain, when they had first started out, just a heavy stillness in the air. They would be there before the rain started, or so Old Tam had assured her. It was as if she heard his voice again within the quietness of the room. *Didnae be feart, Miss Helena. I'll ha'e the pair o' you across to the mainland afore the rain comes on.* But Old Tam had been wrong.

Helena remembered the sudden pelt of heavy rain-drops, and the waves that rose higher in response to the strengthening wind. The sea had seemed to boil with fury, leaping and roaring until their small rowing boat had been swamped and the water had claimed the boat's occupants. She had not seen Agnes or Tam through the darkness, but she had heard the maid's screams and the old man's shouts amidst the furore of the storm.

The water had been cold at first, but after a while she had ceased to notice the icy temperature, pitched as she was in her battle to fight the heavy fatigue that coaxed her to close her eyes and yield to the comfort of black nothingness. She supposed that she must have done just that, for she could remember nothing else until she lay senseless and battered upon the shore with the angel staring down at her.

It was impossible, of course; even if angels existed, they did not come to save the likes of her. And yet the angel's face was so clear in her memory that she wondered how she could have imagined him. She struggled to recall what had happened on the beach, her head pounding with the effort. But she could remember nothing save the angel's face: dark sodden hair from which water dripped down on to his cheeks; pale skin and the most piercing eyes that she had ever seen—an ice blue filled with strength and concern. With him she had known she would be safe. Aside from that image, there was nothing.

She knew neither this place in which she now lay nor how she had come to be here. Knew only that she must leave before Stephen found her. Run as fast as she could. And keep on running. This was reality and there was no handsome angel to save her here. She had best get on with the task of saving herself. She pushed back the covers, swung her legs over the side of the bed, took a deep breath and, rather unsteadily, got to her feet.

The entirety of her body ached and she felt unreal and dizzy. But Helena moved across the room all the same. Determination and fear spurred her on. She washed in the cold water from the pitcher and hastily dressed herself in her own clothes that had been cleaned, dried and mended and placed within the bed-chamber. Unfortunately there was no sign of her shoes and stockings, nor of her hat or travelling bag.

The reflection in the looking-glass upon the dressing table showed a dark bruise on her temple. Her fingers trembled as she touched the tender spot, wondering as to how it had happened, for she had no recollection of having hit her head. Her face was paler than normal and there were shadows of fatigue beneath her eyes. She did not dally for long, but twisted her hair into a rope and tucked the ends back up on themselves, hoping that the make-do style would hold.

Quickly she smoothed the bedcovers over the bed to give some semblance of tidiness. Then she moved to the large wooden box positioned at the bottom of the bed and removed a single neatly folded blanket. Her eyes scanned the room, alighting on the silver brush-and-comb set sitting upon the chest of drawers, knowing they would fetch a good price. But, for all of her desperation, Helena could not do that to whoever in this house had helped her. It was bad enough that she was stealing the blanket. She hurried to the door, then turned and glanced once more around the room. The fire burned within the fireplace. The room was warm and cheery in its yellow hues. For a moment she was almost tempted to stay; almost. But then she turned and, still clutching the blanket to her chest, opened the door to pass silently through.

* * *

'It's a fine piece.' Lord Varington admired the rifle before him. 'Well balanced.' He weighed the weapon between his hands, set the butt of the handle against his shoulder and took aim.

John Weir laughed and looked pleased with his friend's admiration. 'It turns hunting into something else altogether. I can hit a rabbit at fifty paces and a grouse when the bird thinks it's got clean away. Thought you might like to try out the Bakers. I've two of them; this one here and the other kept oil-skinned in my boat.' He looked sheepish. 'Seagulls make for good target practice, you see.' Then his enthusiasm returned. 'I can have it fetched for you. We could go up onto the moor. You could give me some pointers on improving my shooting, if you've no objection, that is.' Then, remembering Guy's dislike of the outdoors, Weir added, 'Brown says the weather will clear tomorrow, that it might even be sunny.'

Guy's eyes narrowed in mock suspicion. 'You wouldn't be trying to tempt me, would you? I've been here a week and there's been no sight of the sun. Indeed, if memory serves me correctly, we've not yet had a day without rain.'

'Mark my words, tomorrow will be different.' Weir nodded his head sagely. 'And I wouldn't want to miss a few hours of rifle practice on a glorious sunny day. Besides, the views from the moor are magnificent. If the cloud clears, you'll see all of the surrounding islands.'

'I've not the least interest in "magnificent views", as well you know. But, fill my hip flask with whisky and I'll willingly accept your invitation.'

'Done.' Weir laughed. 'I do have a rather fine Islay

malt in the cellar, nice and peaty in flavour. I think you'll like it.'

'I'm sure I will,' said Guy.

'Does it take you back to your years in the Rifles?' Weir jerked his head in the direction of the rifle. 'The Baker, that is.'

Guy ran a finger along the barrel of the rifle. 'Naturally.'

'Do you miss it?'

Guy smiled in a devil-may-care fashion. 'Sometimes, but it's been years and there are…' he threw his friend a raffish look '…other interests that fill my time now, and if I've time to waste, then I'd rather waste it on them. Even if you are a married man, I'm sure you'll remember the fun that's to be had in that.'

'If you say so, Varington.'

Guy smiled a lazy arrogant smile. 'Oh, but I do.'

Weir reached down and lifted the Baker rifle. 'We'd best get back to preparing the guns.'

A comfortable silence ensued while the two men set about their task. Then Weir asked, 'What are we going to do about that woman upstairs? She still shows no sign of wakening, despite Dr Milligan's insistence that there's nothing wrong with her.'

'Save exhaustion and bruising.'

Weir nodded in agreement. 'Even so, it has been three days…'

'She'll waken when she's ready.'

'But we don't even know who she is yet.'

'A lady of mystery.' Guy crooked an eyebrow suggestively, making light of the matter. He did not want to think about what had happened on the shore, when the woman's life had literally expired before him, and his stomach had clenched with the dread of it. It reminded him too much of the darkness from a past that he wished to forget.

Weir rolled his eyes. 'You must admit that it is rather curious that a woman is washed up on a beach the morning after a storm and no one reports her missing?'

Guy shrugged. 'Maybe she has no family to notice her absence, or they, too, perished in the storm. What did the constable say?'

'That he would make his own enquiries into the matter.'

'Then you have nothing to worry about.'

'Save a strange woman lying upstairs in one of my bedchambers.'

Guy gave a roguish smile. 'If she was lying in one of my bedchambers, I wouldn't be complaining.'

Weir snorted. 'I doubt you would, but that's not the point. We know nothing about her. She could be anyone. Annabel says that the maidservant who laundered the woman's dress found a key sewn into a secret section in its hem.' Weir dug in his pocket. 'Here, take a look at it.' He extended a hand towards Varington, a silver key upon the outstretched palm.

The key was of a medium size and had been roughly fashioned. Beneath Guy's fingers the metal was cold and hard. 'Looks like the key to an internal door.'

Weir gave a shake of his head. 'Why on earth would she have a key in the hem of her dress? It doesn't make any sense.'

'Maybe she was hiding it from someone.' Guy shrugged his shoulders. 'How should I know?' Closing his fingers around the key, he placed it within his own pocket, patted the pocket and said, 'I'll see that it's returned to the lady at a more appropriate time.'

Weir said nothing, just gave a sigh.

'Has she spoken yet?'

'Nothing of sense. Apparently she cries out in her sleep as if in fear, but that is little wonder given that she seems to have survived some kind of boating accident.'

'To have survived the sea on a stormy November night, our mystery lady must have the luck of the devil.'

Weir gave a shudder. 'Don't say such things!'

Guy laughed.

'It's not funny,' said Weir with indignation. 'Not when the storm was on All Hallow's Eve. I cannot rid myself of the notion that she's a portend of bad things to come. Her very presence in the house leaves me with an uneasy feeling in the pit of my stomach. I wish you had not brought her here.'

'I think you may have been reading too many gothic novels, my friend,' teased Guy. 'Would you rather I'd left her out on the sand to die?'

'No, of course not!' retorted his friend. 'I could not, in truth, sentence anyone to such a death. And I would be failing in my Christian duty to do other than I've done. Yet even so…' An uncomfortable expression beset Weir's face. 'I do have Annabel and the girls' safety to think about.'

'What do you think she is? A thief? A murderess?' Guy's eyes narrowed and he floated his fingers in the air and said in a sinister voice, 'Or a witch, perhaps? She does have red hair.'

Weir frowned. 'This is not some jest, Varington. Maybe she's innocent enough, but I can't shake this feeling that something has been unleashed, something that was held safe in check before she arrived.'

'Weir, the woman is in no fit state to set about any mischief. Even were she conscious, I doubt she would have the strength to walk to the other side of the room, let alone anything else.'

'Are you not concerned, even a little?'

'No,' replied Guy truthfully.

'Well, you damn well should be. It was you who brought her here. If she turns out to be a criminal, the blame shall be on your head.'

'Guilty as charged,' said Guy cheerfully.

'What are we going to do if she doesn't wake up soon?'

'We?' questioned Guy in a teasing tone. And then, witnessing the rising irritation in his friend's face, he repented, sighing and saying in a maddeningly non-chalant voice, 'Well, as on first impression she seemed tolerable to look upon, I suppose I might be persuaded to take an interest in her.'

'Varington! The devil only knows why I was so insistent on your coming to stay at Seamill.'

'Something to do with my charming company I believe.'

Weir could not help but laugh.

A knock at the door preceded the manservant who moved silently to Weir's side to whisper discreetly in his ear.

'Can't he come back later?'

More whisperings from the manservant.

Weir's face pinched with annoyance. 'Then I had better come and see him.' The servant departed and Weir turned to Guy. 'Trouble with one of the tenants. It seems it cannot wait for my attention. Please excuse me; I shall be back as soon as possible.'

Guy watched his friend leave before turning his attention back to the rifle in his hands.

* * *

Helena froze as she heard a door downstairs open and close again. Panic gripped her, so that she stood there unable to move, to speak, to breathe. Men's voices—none that she recognised—footsteps and the opening and closing of more doors. Then only silence. Her heart was thudding fast and hard enough to leap clear of her chest. She forced herself to breathe, to calm her frenzied pulse, to listen through the hissing silence. She knew she had to move, to escape, before whoever was down there came back. Her bare feet made no noise as she trod towards the stairs.

Guy ceased what he was doing and listened. All was quiet except for the soft creaking coming from the main staircase. It was a normal everyday sound, yet for some reason his ears pricked and he became alert. He remembered that Annabel and the children had gone out for the day, and his sense of unease stirred stronger. Guy knew better than to ignore his instincts. Quietly he set the rifle down upon the table and turned towards the door.

Helena reached the bottom of the staircase and, with a nervous darting glance around, moved towards the heavy oak front door. The doorknob was round and made of brass. Her fingers closed around it, feeling the metal cold beneath her skin. She gripped harder, twisted, turning the handle as quietly as she could. The door began to open. She shivered as the wind rushed around her ankles and toes. She pulled the door a little wider, letting the wind drive the raindrops against her face. Up above, the sky was grey and dismal. Out in front, the gravel driveway was waterlogged with rain that still pelted with a ferocity. Helena made to step down on to the stone stair.

'Not planning on leaving us so soon, are you?'

The voice made her jump. She let out a squeak, half-turned and saw a man in the shadows behind the staircase.

Helena reacted instinctively. She spun, wrenched the door open, and fled down across the two wide stone steps and up the driveway. The blanket was thrown aside in her haste. Gravel and something sharp cut into her feet; she barely noticed, just kept on running, towards the tall metal gate at the end of the driveway, unmindful of the rain that splashed up from puddles and poured down from the heavens. Running and running, ignoring the rawness in her throat from her gasping breath, ignoring the stitch of pain in her side, and the pounding in her head and the heavy slowness of her legs. She could feel her heart pumping fit to burst. And still, she ran and just ahead lay the road; she could see it through the iron railings of the gate. So close. And then she felt the grasp upon her shoulder, his hand slipping down to her arm, pulling her back. She fought against him, struggling to break his hold, lashing out at him.

He caught her flailing wrists. 'Calm down, I mean you no harm.'

'No!' she cried, and struggled all the harder.

'Ma'am, I beg of you!' She found herself pulled hard against him, his arms restraining hers. 'Look at me.'

She tried to wriggle away, but he was too strong.

'Look at me,' he said again. His voice was calm and not unkind. The panic that had seized her died away. She raised her eyes to his and saw that he was the pale-eyed angel from her dream. No angel, just a man, with hair as dark as ebony, and skin as white as snow and piercing ice-blue eyes filled with compassion.

'What the—' He caught the words back. 'You are not yet recovered. Come back to the house.'

'I will not.' She began to struggle against him, but could do nothing to release his grip.

'You have no shoes, no cloak, no money. How far do you think you will get in this weather?' The rain ran in rivulets down his face. Even his coat was rapidly darkening beneath the downpour of rain. She was standing so close that she could see each individual ebony lash that framed the paleness of his eyes, so close that she could see the faint blue shadow of stubbled growth over his jaw…and the rain that dripped from his hair to run down the pallor of his cheeks. 'Come back inside,' he said, and his voice was gentle. 'There is nothing to fear.'

She closed her eyes at that, almost laughed at it. Nothing to fear, indeed. He had no idea; none at all. 'Release me, sir.'

He did not release her, nor did his eyes leave hers for a second, and she could see what his answer would be before he even said the words. 'I cannot. You would not survive.'

'I will take my chance.' Better that than sit and wait for Stephen to find her.

'We can discuss this inside.'

'No!'

'Then let us discuss it here, if it is your preference.'

A carriage rolled by on the road outside, its wheels splashing through the puddles. She glanced towards the gate, nervous that Stephen might arrive even as she stood here in this man's arms. 'You are getting wet, sir.'

'As are you,' came the reply.

She could see by the determined light in his eyes that he would not release her. He thought he was being a gentleman; he would be no gentleman if he knew the truth. She shivered.

'And cold,' he said. 'Come on.' And gently he began to steer her back up the driveway to where the front door lay open.

Chapter Two

Guy did not release the woman until they were standing before the roaring fire in Weir's gunroom. He poured two glasses of whisky, pressed one into her hand and took the other himself. The amber liquid burned a path down through his chest and into his stomach. The woman stood there, the glass untouched in her hand.

'Drink it,' he instructed. 'God knows, you need it after that soaking.'

She hesitated, then took a sip, coughing as the heat of the whisky hit the back of her throat.

He could feel the glow from the flames warming his legs and see the steam starting to rise from the dampness of the woman's skirts. 'Why don't you tell me what this is about?' They stood facing each other before the fireplace. He could see the rain droplets still glistening on her cheeks. His eye travelled down, following the thick snaking tendrils of hair that lay against her breast, their colour deep and dark with rain. The smell of wet wool surrounded them.

She was not looking at him; her focus was fixed on

the whisky glass still in her hand, and he thought from her manner that she would give him no answer. A lump of coal cracked and hissed upon the fire. The clock ticked. The wind whistled against the windowpanes, causing the curtains at either side to sway. And then she spoke, quietly with a cautious tone for all that her face had become expressionless. 'Who are you, sir, and where is this place?'

'I forget my manners, ma'am.' He gave the slightest of bows. 'I am Viscount Varington and we are in Seamill Hall, the home of my good friend Mr Weir.'

He thought that she paled at his words. 'Seamill Hall?' Her eyes closed momentarily as if that revelation was in some way unwelcome news, and when they opened again she had wiped all emotion from them. 'It was you that rescued me from the shore,' she said.

He gave a small inclination of his head. 'You were washed up near Portincross.'

'Alone?' She could not quite disguise the anxiety in her voice.

And then he remembered the companions that she had cried out for upon the shore, and understood what it was that she was asking. 'Quite alone,' he said gently.

She lowered her gaze and stood in silence.

He reached out his hand, intending to offer some small solace, but she stared up at him and there was something in her eyes that stopped him. 'I'm sorry for your loss,' he offered instead.

'My loss? What do you mean, sir?' He saw the flash of wariness before she hid it.

'The death of your companions. You alluded to them upon the shore.'

'I cannot recall our conversing.' She set the whisky

glass down. Her hands slid together in a seemingly demure posture but he could see from the whiteness of her knuckles how tightly they gripped. 'What did I tell you?'

Guy could feel the tension emanating from her and he wondered what it was that she feared so very much to have told. He gave a lazy shrug of his shoulders. 'Very little.'

There was the hint of relaxation in her stance, nothing else.

'The boat's other occupants are likely to have been lost. Had there been anyone else come ashore, we would have heard of it by now.'

She stilled. It seemed to Guy that she was holding her breath. And all of the tension was back in an instant, for all that she stood there with her expression so guarded. 'But it is only an hour or two since you found me.'

'On the contrary...' he gave a rueful smile '...you have lain upstairs for three days.'

'Three days!' There was no doubting her incredulity. The colour drained from her face, leaving her so pale that he was convinced that she would faint.

Guy set out a hand to steady her arm.

'It cannot be,' she whispered, as if to herself, and again there was the flicker of fear in her eyes, there, then gone. And then she seemed to remember just where she was, and that he was present, standing so close, supporting her arm. She backed away, increasing the distance, breaking the link between them. 'Forgive me,' she said. 'I did not realise.'

'You have suffered a shock, ma'am. Sit down.'

'No.' She began to shake her head, then seemed to change her mind and stumbled back into the nearest chair.

'To where were you running?'

She did not look at him, just said in a flat voice, 'You have no right to keep me here against my will.'

'Indeed I do not.'

Her eyes widened. He saw surprise and hope flash in them and wondered why she was so hell-bent on escape.

'Then you will let me go?'

'Of course.'

'Then why…' she hesitated and bit at her bottom lip '…why did you stop me?'

'I didn't save your life to have you throw it away again. You are not dressed for this weather.' And what the hell kind of woman woke from her sickbed in a strange place and hightailed it down the driveway in a torrent of rain without so much as a by your leave to those who had cared for her? He looked at the woman sitting before him.

'I must leave here as soon as possible.'

'Why such haste?'

She shook her head. 'I cannot tell you.'

'Then I cannot help you.'

Her mouth twisted to an ironic smile, and he thought for a moment that she would either laugh or weep, but she did neither. 'No one can help me, Lord Varington. I am well aware of that. Besides, I am not asking for your help.' And there was such honesty in her answer that Guy felt a shiver touch to his spine.

'You have no money, no *adequate* clothing—' his eyes flicked down over the creamy swell of her bosom '—and you are unwell from your ordeal. How far do you think you will get without some measure of assistance?'

'That should not concern you, my lord.'

'It should concern any gentleman, ma'am.'

There was the quiet sound of a sigh and she looked away. 'If you have any real concern for my welfare, you will take me to the door and wave me on my way.'

'Why are you in such a hurry to leave? You have been in this house for three days—what difference will one more make?'

'More than you can know,' she said quietly.

'Come, ma'am, tell me what can be so very bad?'

She gave a small shake of her head and looked down.

Guy knew he needed something more to push her to speak. 'Or should I address that question to the constable? Shall we have him back to speak with you now that you have wakened?'

She stared up with widening eyes, her fear palpable. He saw the way that her hands wrung together and he felt wretched for her plight. Yet even so, he let the silence stretch between them.

'Please…please do not,' she said at last, as if she could bear the silence no more.

He stepped towards her, drew her up from the chair to stand before him and said very gently, 'Why not?'

There was just the tiniest shake of her head.

She was exhausted, not yet recovered from battling a stormy winter sea. She had been half-drowned, frozen, battered and cast up to die upon a shoreline. Her companions had died that night in the Firth of Clyde. That she had escaped death was a miracle. He eyed the bruise still livid against the pale skin of her forehead and stepped closer, so that barely a foot separated them. 'Tell me.' He stared into her eyes—a beautiful grey green, as soft-looking as velvet. The desperation there seemed to touch his soul. 'I promise I will help you.'

Her eyes searched his, as if she were trying to gauge the truth of his words. He could sense her wavering.

'I…' She inhaled deeply.

He held his breath in anticipation.

'I—'

The door of the gunroom swung open and Weir strode in.

The moment was lost. Guy's breath released in a rush.

'The strangest thing, Varington. Brown has just retrieved a blanket from the…' Weir's words trailed off at the sight before his eyes.

Guy watched the woman step away from him, and inwardly cursed his friend's timing. All of the emotion wiped from her face and she became remote and impassive and untouchable. The transformation was remarkable, like watching her change into a different woman, or more like watching a mask pulled into place to hide the woman behind, he thought.

'What the blazes…?' Weir's eyes swung from Guy to the woman and back again. 'You're soaked through to the skin.'

'The lady and I stepped outside for a spot of fresh air,' said Guy. 'It felt a trifle stuffy in here.'

Weir seemed to have lost the power of words. His mouth gaped. He stared.

'I was just about to escort your guest up to her bedchamber. She needs a change of clothing.' He began to guide her towards the door.

'Varington.' It seemed that Weir had found his voice.

Guy glanced back at his friend.

Weir gestured down towards the woman's feet.

Only then did Guy notice the trail of bloody foot-prints that she left in her wake and the crimson staining that crept around the edges of the skin on her feet.

But the woman continued walking steadily on towards the door.

'Your feet... I will carry you.' He caught her arm.

'There is no need, my lord, I assure you.' She appeared so calm that he wondered if it were he that was going mad. Hadn't she just tried to run away, leaving the warmth and protection of Weir's house, and for what? He was quite sure that she had nowhere else to go, why else had she taken the blanket? And when he had tried to stop her, she had fled from him, fought with him, pleaded with him to let her go. He had seen the terror in her eyes, the utter anguish. And now she stood there as if there was nothing wrong in the slightest. Guy stared all the harder.

Her face was white, the shadows beneath her eyes more pronounced. The bruise on her head told him that it undoubtedly throbbed, and the blood on her feet only hinted at the damage beneath. Yet she looked at him like she felt nothing of the pain; indeed, like she felt nothing at all. He wondered again who this woman was and what it was that she was hiding and why she so feared the constable. And he remembered Weir's allusions to her criminality.

He glanced at his friend.

Weir gave a nod, his face taut, unsmiling, worried.

Guy turned and accompanied the woman from the room.

It was all Helena could do to put one foot in front of the other. The soles of her feet were stinging red raw and her legs seemed unwieldy and heavy. Her head was throbbing so badly that she could barely think straight, and it seemed that her eyes could not keep up with the speed of the things moving around her. She swallowed down the nausea that threatened to rise. Yet through the pain and the discomfort she kept on going. One step and then another. Each one taking her closer to the bed-chamber. Keep going, she willed herself. Think of another way out. She wouldn't give up; she couldn't, not now, not while there was still breath in her lungs and blood in her veins. So she walked and focused her mind away from the pain. She thought of her plan; she always thought of her plan at such times.

The gunroom door closed behind them.

'Allow me…' Lord Varington held out his arm for her to take.

Her immediate reaction was to reject his offer, but in truth she felt so unwell that she was not confident that she could make the journey without stumbling. Better to take his arm than to fall. So she tucked her hand against his sleeve and slowly, without a further word between them, they made their way along the passage-way towards the stairs.

Helena was both resentful and glad of the support of Lord Varington. His arm was strong and steady, his presence simultaneously reassuring and disturbing. His sleeve was warm beneath her fingers and she could feel the hard strength in the muscle beneath. He smelled of cologne and soap, and nothing of that which she asso-ciated with Stephen. Everything of him suggested expense: his looks, his manner, his tailoring. Even his accent betrayed his upper-class roots. But Helena knew a rake when she saw one.

With his oh-so-charming manner and his handsome looks, she supposed Lord Varington was a man used to getting what he wanted when it came to women—and she felt a fool for so nearly trusting him and blurting out the truth. She wondered how much she would have revealed had the other man, Weir, not returned to the gunroom exactly when he did. The thought seemed to sap the last of her energy. She focused her attention on reaching her bedchamber.

Every step up the staircase drained her flagging strength. Her head was swimming with dizziness and her legs felt so weak that she scarcely could lift them to find the next stair. She leaned heavily, one hand on the worn wooden banister that ran parallel to the staircase, the other on Lord Varington. At the end of the first flight she paused, trying to hide the fact that her breathing was as heavy as if she had been running rather than tottering up the stairs.

'I think it might be easier if I were to carry you up the remainder of the distance,' he suggested in that deep melodic voice of his.

'No, thank you.' Even those few words seemed an effort. She did not look round at him, just concentrated all her effort on remaining upright, and tried to ignore the perspiration beading upon her brow and the slight blurring of her vision. She forced herself to focus upon the banister beneath her right hand. The wood was worn smooth and dark from years of use, and warm beneath the grip of her fingers.

The smile in his voice rendered it friendly and sensual and slightly teasing. 'That's a pity,' he said, 'after the last time, I was rather looking forward to it.'

She stayed as she was, unmoving, her gaze fixed upon the banister. 'I don't know what you mean, my lord.'

'Surely you cannot have forgotten your journey from Portincross to Seamill Hall—I carried you in my arms.'

The banister began to distort before her eyes. She squeezed them shut and gripped at it even harder.

'Ma'am?' The teasing tone had gone, replaced now with concern.

'I require only to catch my breath,' she managed to murmur.

'I see,' he said, and before she realised his intent, he had scooped her up into his arms and was walking up the staircase.

She struggled to show some sense of indignation. 'Sir!'

'You may catch your breath a mite easier this way.' He crooked a smile.

'Lord Varington…' she started to protest, but her head was giddy and her words trailed off and she let him carry her the rest of the way.

He laid her upon the bed.

She knew that she was wasting precious time, tried to push herself to sit up.

'Rest a while,' he said, and eased her back down. Only then did she notice the maid in the background setting down a pitcher and some linen. Lord Varington saw the girl, too, and beckoned her over. He took off his coat, casting it aside on one of the chairs by the fireplace. Helena watched him move to stand at the bottom of the bed and she knew she should get up and run. His intent was clear. Why else did a man take off his coat? But Helena did not move. She couldn't. It was as if she was made of lead. Her arms, her legs, her body were so heavy, all of them weighing her down. She stared as he rolled up his sleeves and she heard the sound of water being poured. And then, unbelievably, Lord Varington began to wash her feet. 'Sir!' she gasped, 'You must not!' The pale eyes flickered up to meet hers, and she saw in them a determination that mirrored her own.

'They must be cleansed if the cuts are not to suppurate,' he said.

She could see the maid's face staring in disbelief. But Lord Varington's hands were on her feet, wiping away the dirt and the blood and picking out the embedded gravel. His touch was gentle, caressing almost. One hand held her foot firmly, the other stroked the pad of linen against the sole. No man had ever touched Helena with such gentleness. His fingers were warm and strong and sensitive. Carefully working around each cut, each tear of skin, as if tending wounded feet was something that he did every day. The movement of his hands soothed her. And it seemed to Helena that something of her pain eased, and her head did not throb quite so angrily, nor her body ache so badly. So she just lay there and allowed him to tend her, and it seemed too intimate, as if something that would happen between lovers. She raised her eyes to his and looked at him and he looked right back, and in that moment she knew that she was as aware of him as a man as he was of her as a woman. And the realisation was shocking. She tore her gaze away, feeling the sudden skitter of her heart, and traitorous heat stain her cheeks. Lord Varington's hands did not falter. When he had finished with the cleansing he dabbed her soles with something that stung.

Helena bit her lip to smother her gasp.

'Whisky,' he said. 'To prevent infection.' Then he dried her feet and bound them up in linen strips.

He spoke to the maid. 'Bring some dry clothing for

the lady and help her change. And put some extra blankets upon the bed and more coal upon the fire.' Then he took up his coat and moved to stand by the side of the bed.

Helena pushed herself up to a sitting position, leaning back heavily against the pillows. 'Thank you.'

The expression on Lord Varington's face was unfathomable and yet strangely intense. 'Rest now, we will speak tomorrow.' And the door closed quietly behind him.

She looked over to where the maid was placing several large lumps of coal from the scuttle on to the fire. The room was quiet save for the wind that rattled at the window and the drip of water from the guttering. He would want to know everything tomorrow— who she was, how she had come to be washed up on the shore. Her heart sank at the prospect and she knew that she had to find a way out of this mess in which she now found herself.

'Well? What the hell just happened?' demanded Weir.

'Our mystery lady decided to leave in rather a hurry,' said Guy.

'What the blazes…? You mean, she tried to run away?'

'Unbelievable that it may be for any woman to flee from me, I know, yet…' he smiled mischievously '…in this case, true.'

'But what on earth can have possessed her?' Weir looked pointedly at his friend's damp clothing. 'I mean, she must have only just come to, and it isn't exactly walking weather, is it?'

'Hardly,' replied Guy.

'Then why?'

Guy shrugged. 'The lady is reticent to reveal her reasons. She does, however, appear unwilling to prolong her stay. Most probably she does not wish to inconvenience you further,' he lied. More likely she was fleeing the constable, but there was no need to make mention of that if he did not want Weir to eject her immediately.

'Damn and blast it! Can't be turfing her out when the woman is so clearly ill recovered. But...'

'But?' prompted Guy.

'You know that I do not like having her here.'

'Oh, come on, Weir, you cannot tell me that she is not a beauty.'

'She looks like a doxy.'

Guy smiled. 'Aye, but a damnably attractive doxy.' Indeed, she was quite the most beautiful woman Guy had seen, and Guy, Lord Varington, had seen a great many beautiful women.

'All that hair, and that dress, and bare feet and those ankles.'

Guy put his fingers to his lips and blew a kiss. 'Divine.' He smiled. 'But it is the sea we have to thank for her appearance. You judge her too soon, my friend. Perhaps she is the height of respectability.'

Weir snorted. 'That is profoundly unlikely.'

Guy laughed. 'I fear that her beauty has prejudiced you.'

'Nonsense! Did any of the neighbours see her outside?' He rubbed at his forehead with undisguised agitation. 'Hell, they're bound to draw only one conclusion.'

'Which is?' Guy raised an eyebrow.

Weir cleared his throat. 'I don't need to spell it out

to you, of all people, Varington. She'll have to be found some more suitable clothing.'

'More is the pity.'

'Will you not take this seriously?' Weir poured himself a glass of whisky and topped up the one that Guy had previously emptied. 'You must see my dilemma. I cannot have that sort of woman in this house, not with Annabel and the girls, nor can I ignore my Christian duty to help those in need. I cannot cast an unwell woman out into the street.' He broke off to take a gulp of whisky and said, 'Who is she anyway? Has she told you her name?'

Guy's hesitation was small and unnoticeable. 'We did not get to that.' He had no real way of knowing, other than his gut instinct, of whether the words she had spoken upon the shore were the truth or just the ramblings of a confused and barely conscious mind.

'One minute she's out for the count in my guest bedchamber and the next she's running down my blasted driveway dressed like a doxy!' Weir's mouth drew to a tight straight line. 'Lord help us, Varington, what am I to do?'

'Given her determination to leave Seamill Hall I do not think that you will have to do anything.'

'I don't like this one little bit. I think I should have the constable over to speak to her.'

Guy thought of the woman's fear at the mention of the constable. 'No need for that just yet.' This was one mystery that Guy intended on solving by himself.

Weir took another sip of whisky. 'And what the hell happened to her feet?'

'She ran barefoot across the driveway, must be some glass still out there from the broken lantern. Never had a woman running away from me—well, not one outwith a bedchamber and that didn't want chasing.'

Weir winced, but smiled all the same. 'Dear God, Varington.'

'Quite shocking,' agreed Guy good-humouredly. 'But there's a first for everything.'

Weir's eyes rolled. 'I was referring to the woman's feet.'

Guy laughed. 'The cuts are not deep. She'll recover quick enough.'

'Good,' said Weir. 'The sooner that she's gone, the better. It's as I said before. There's something about her that makes me uneasy and what with her trying to run off and our not even knowing who she is…' Weir stopped and looked at Guy. 'And she *was* trying to steal that blanket, was she not?'

'She was indeed,' said Guy, with a twinkle in his eye. 'Fortunately I managed to apprehend her before she could make off with the item.'

'You see…' Weir nodded sagely '…did I not say she could be a criminal?' And then caught a glimpse of Guy's face. 'Will you not be serious? Would you see Annabel and the girls suffer over this woman?'

Guy knew his friend's predisposition to worry and so he let something of the playful teasing drop away. 'I shall make it my duty to ensure that neither Annabel nor the girls suffer in the slightest. As you said, the woman is here because of me and she is therefore my responsibility.' His responsibility indeed, and for once Guy was being entirely serious.

Weir gave a nod. 'Amen to that.'

'Amen indeed,' said Guy, and drained the whisky from his glass in a single gulp.

* * *

Sunlight lit the sky as Helena sat by the window, looking out at the stretch of sea that was calm and clear and so pale a blue as to be almost white, water that mirrored the colour of Lord Varington's eyes. Seagulls called, circling in the sky and from the shore beyond came the rhythmic wash of waves against sand. She was dressed, as she had been since six o'clock that morning when she had given up watching the slow crawl of the hours on the clock.

She adjusted her legs, making herself more comfortable, and felt the press of the linen around her feet, bindings that Lord Varington had put in place. A wash of guilt swept over her, and yet she knew she could not allow guilt to stop her. Lord Varington would not understand. He did not know what it was to be so desperate that it was worth risking anything, even death, to escape. She thought of the words he had spoken yesterday, of his offer of help, of the kindness of his voice and the gentleness of his hands and the smile in his eyes, and Lord only knew how she wanted to believe him. Once upon a time she would have. Not now. Five years of Stephen had taught her better. And yet there was nothing of Stephen in Lord Varington.

She thought again of the tall dark-haired man, just as she had thought about him throughout the night. There was an attractiveness about him, both in his looks and his character. He was handsome and charming and flirtatious…and were it not for his interference she would not still be sitting here in Seamill Hall. Indeed, she reflected, she would never have been here in the first place; most likely she would have perished out upon the shore. It was a sobering thought.

She wondered why he was so concerned with her. The man Weir wasn't. Mr Weir would not have chased her the length of the driveway in the pouring rain; judging from the look upon his face he would have let her go and been glad of it. But then Mr Weir hadn't looked at her like he wanted her in his bed. Heaven help her, but she had troubles enough in her life without Lord Varington.

Helena sighed and let her gaze wander to the islands that lay beyond. St Vey was so clear that she could see the different shades of green and brown and purple grey, could see the glint of the sun picking out a brook that flowed over the rocks to the south, and in the north the dark outline of Dunleish Castle. It looked so close, close enough to swim the short stretch of sea that separated it from the mainland, as if she could reach across the water and touch it. St Vey lay only four miles off the coast, and that four miles had cost Agnes and Old Tam their lives. She felt the terrible stab of guilt and of grief. Helena stared for a long time at the island and the water and the sand, and mentally rehearsed her story.

She could go nowhere without owning an identity; that much was obvious. If she told the truth, her fate was sealed: a rapid return to Stephen and Dunleish Castle. She had thought long and hard about her problem, until, at last, in the wee small hours of the morning, came the seed of an idea. As a widow not from these parts, Helena could borrow some money, enough to finish what she had started, and leave Seamill Hall quite properly, without affecting anyone's gentlemanly sensibilities. Just enough money to finish what she had started: escape to a place where Stephen would not find her.

Helena would speak to Mr Weir's wife today, and

make the necessary arrangements. She would have to lie to them all—to Mr Weir and his wife and to Lord Varington. She ran a hand down her skirt, smoothing out the creases as she stood to go down to breakfast, and remembered a time when she had thought dishonesty to be the most reprehensible of sins. Such naïvety; Stephen had changed that. And yet she found the prospect of lying so blatantly, particularly to Lord Varington, did not sit comfortably with her. Part of her wanted to laugh at the absurdity of the situation. A few lies to a stranger were the least of her problems. But she heard the whisper of a little voice that this stranger had saved her life, and she remembered the touch of his hands upon her feet and the intensity in those pale eyes. She thrust the thoughts away, forced herself on. Survival was everything.

Chapter Three

The woman—Helena, as he suspected she was called—was already seated next to Weir's wife, Annabel, at the breakfast table when Guy entered the sunlit dining room. She was wearing a drab black dress, clearly something borrowed from one of the servants as Annabel was so much shorter. Pity, when her own sea-shrunken attire was so very much more becoming. Still, even in the servant's guise, there could be no mistaking that she bore herself with dignity. She was of average height and build. But Helena had a face that marked her out from other women, a face that any man would not easily forget: almond-shaped eyes, a small straight nose and lips that were ripe for kissing. Guy's eyes lingered over the deep flame of her hair, the cream velvet of her skin and the smoky green of her eyes.

She was exuding an air of calm watchfulness, as if all her actions, every answer, was considered most carefully before given, as if she desired to reveal nothing of the real woman. Yet beneath her composure he thought that he could detect an undercurrent of tension.

'Good morning, ladies.'

'Guy!' Annabel, all pretty and pink and blonde, gushed. 'We thought you had quite slept in, didn't we, Mary?' She glanced at Helena.

Mary? He allowed only the mildest surprise to register upon his face as he turned to look at her. The harsh black of the woollen dress served only to heighten the pale perfection of her skin and the vivid colour of her hair, which had been caught up neatly in a chignon. She did not meet his eyes.

'It seems that I have missed the introductions.' He sat down at the table, poured himself some coffee and looked expectantly at the woman who it now seemed was calling herself Mary.

'Oh, Guy,' said Annabel. 'Poor dear Mary has suffered so much—'

'Perhaps,' interrupted Weir, 'Mrs McLelland would be kind enough to recount her story again for Lord Varington? If it is not too much trouble, that is.'

Guy noticed how there was nothing of emotion upon her face, that she wore the same mask-like expression he had watched her don on Weir's entry to the gunroom yesterday.

'It would be no trouble at all,' she said.

Guy sat back, sipped his coffee and waited.

Helena took a deep breath and ignored the way her stomach was beginning to churn. It had not seemed so bad telling her lies to Mr and Mrs Weir alone. It was not something that she would have chosen to do, but needs must, and Helena's situation was desperate. But now that Lord Varington was sitting across the table, watching her with those pale eyes of his, her determination felt shaken. She forced herself to begin the story that she had spent the hours of the night rehearsing.

'My name is Mary McLelland and I am from Islay.' By choosing an island of the Inner Hebrides she was effectively ensuring that any trace that they might set upon her would be slow, so slow that by the time the results of any investigation arrived Mary McLelland would have long fled Scotland. She could see that Lord Varington was still watching her. She forced herself to stay focused, shifted her gaze to where the sunlight reflected upon the silver jug of cream set just beyond her plate. 'I am the widow of James McLelland, and I am travelling to London to stay with my aunt.'

'How came you to be washed upon the shore?' asked Lord Varington.

'A local boatman from the island agreed to take me on the first leg of my journey, for a fee, of course. When first we started out, the weather was cold and damp, but with little wind. Indeed, the sea was remarkably calm, but that soon changed during the sailing.' That bit at least was true, and so was the rest of what she had not yet told the Weirs. 'First the wind fetched up and then the rain began. I have never seen rain of its like. All around us the sea grew wilder and higher, tossing us from wave to wave as if we were a child's plaything, until the lanterns were lost, and we were clinging to the boat for dear life.'

Helena could no longer see the jug of cream, nor was she aware of the dining room or its inhabitants. Her nose was overwhelmed with the stench of the sea; her skin felt again the rawness of the battering waves. She heard nothing save the roar of the water. It seemed that she could see only the darkness, feel only the terrible fear that had overtaken her as she realised that they were going to die. Agnes was clinging to her, sobbing, wailing. Old Tam's shouts: *Hold fast, lassies. Hold as you've never held afore. And pray. Pray that the Lord will have mercy on our souls.* Struggling to stay within the boat as it bucked upon the water's surface. Soaked by the merciless lash of the waves. Gasping for breath. She sucked in the air, fast, urgent. The cry muffled in her throat by the invading sea. Felt the waves lift the boat, so high as to be clear of it, time was suspended. Agnes's hand in hers, clinging hard. And then they were falling. It was so dark. So cold. And silent…just for a while. The water filled her eyes, her ears, her nose, choked into her lungs, as the sea pulled her down. She could not fight it, just was there, aware of what was happening and strangely accepting of it. Just when she closed her eyes and began to give in to the bursting sensation in her lungs, the sea granted her one last chance, thrusting her back up to its surface, letting her hear Agnes's screams, Old Tam's shouts. Her skirts bound themselves around her legs and she could kick no more. And then there was only darkness.

'Ma'am.'

She opened her eyes to find Lord Varington by her side. She was alive. Agnes and Old Tam were dead… and it was her fault. The sob escaped her before she could bite it back.

His hand was on her arm, dragging her back from the nightmare.

She blinked her eyes, smoothed the raggedness of her breath.

'Drink this.' A glass was being pressed into her fingers.

'There is no need,' a voice said, and she was surprised to find that it was her own.

'There's every need,' he growled, and guided the glass to her mouth.

The drink was so strong as to burn a track down her throat. Whisky. She coughed and pushed the glass away.

'Take another sip.'

She shook her head, feeling revived by the whisky's fiery aromatic tang.

'She must go and lie down at once!' Helena became aware of Mrs Weir by her other side. 'The trauma of recounting the accident has quite overwhelmed her.'

The dreadful memory was receding. And Helena found herself back sitting at the breakfast table in the dining room of Seamill Hall. Only the rhythmic rush of sea upon sand sounded in the distance. She took a deep breath. 'Thank you, Mrs Weir, Lord Varington...' she turned to each in turn '...but I am recovered now. I did not expect to be so affected. Forgive my foolishness.'

'Dear Mary, you are not in the slightest bit foolish. Such a remembrance would overset the strongest of men,' said Mrs Weir stoutly.

Helena gave a stiff little smile.

'There is no need for you to continue with your story.' Mrs Weir looked up imploringly at her husband. 'Tell her it is so, John.'

Mr Weir looked from his wife to Helena. There was the slightest pause. 'You need not speak further of your shipwreck, Mrs McLelland.'

'There is not much more to tell,' she said, anchoring down all emotion. 'I do not know what happened other than I landed in the water. From there I remember nothing until I awakened to find myself here.'

'Mary, you are the bravest of women,' said Mrs Weir, and patted her arm.

Guilt turned tight in her stomach. 'No, ma'am.' She shook her head. 'I am not that. Not now, not ever.' There was a harsh misery in her voice that she could not disguise. Lord Varington had heard it, she could see it in the way that he looked at her.

'You should rest,' he said.

She turned to him with a slight shake of the head. 'I am fine, really, I am; besides, I must make myself ready to leave.'

'To leave, Mrs McLelland?' He raised an eyebrow.

'Mary means to catch the coach to Glasgow,' said Mrs Weir by way of explanation. 'She is intent on continuing her journey to London…by stage'

'Mr and Mrs Weir have been kind enough to agree to lend me what I need. I will, of course, return everything that I have borrowed as soon as I have found my aunt.'

'You must not worry, Mary. You need return nothing. The maid will be delighted to have a new dress, and John sees that I have more than enough money,' said Mrs Weir.

Weir said nothing, just sat with a look of undisguised relief upon his face.

Varington resumed his seat opposite Helena. 'Leaving so soon, Mrs McLelland?' She remembered that he had spoken similar words within the hallway when she had tried to flee, and that memory brought others that she did not wish to think about—Lord Varington carrying her up the staircase, Lord Varington tending her feet.

'I am quite recovered and can therefore no longer impose upon Mr and Mrs Weir's hospitality, and besides…' Helena folded one hand over the other, keeping a firm grip on her emotions '…my aunt is expecting me and shall be worried over my continued absence. I do not wish to add to her concern.'

Varington stretched out his legs and made himself comfortable within the chair. 'Write her a letter explaining all.'

'What a good idea,' said Mrs Weir.

Weir turned away, but not before Helena had seen the roll of his eyes.

'I would rather see her in person.'

'Have you no other relatives?'

'No,' said Helena, worrying just how far Lord Varington's questioning and her lies would lead them.

'And that is why you left Islay—to visit your aunt in London?'

'Yes.' Experience with Stephen had taught her it was better not to elaborate.

'I know London very well. It is my usual abode, apart from when I am coaxed away under extreme duress.' Varington smiled and glanced meaningfully towards Weir.

Helena swallowed, knowing instinctively that he was leading up to something.

'Where exactly does your aunt live?' he asked.

Helena had never visited London in the entirety of her life. She had not an inkling of its streets. *Be sure your lies will find you out.* The words whispered through her mind. 'It is not precisely in London,' she said, racking her brains for a village, any village in the vicinity of the capital.

All eyes were upon her, waiting expectantly.

Hendon was near London, wasn't it? For once Helena wished she had taken more interest in geography. Her mind went blank. 'Hendon,' she said, and hoped that she had not got it wrong.

'Your aunt lives in Hendon?' There was a definite interest in Guy's tone.

'Yes.'

'Do you know the place, Guy?' asked Annabel.

'Indeed,' he said with more confidence than Helena wanted to hear. 'I have a friend that lives there. What a coincidence.'

Helena's heart sank. He would ask her now her aunt's precise direction in Hendon, and what answer could she give? She dropped her gaze, staring down at her hands and waited for his question.

'And what travel arrangements have you made, Mrs McLelland?'

She glanced up at him, surprise widening her eyes, relief flooding her veins. 'I leave this afternoon on the one o'clock mail to Glasgow. From there I will take the stage and travel down the rest of the way.'

'May I be so bold as to suggest an alternative?'

Helena felt a stab of foreboding. 'Please do.'

'I will be returning to London myself at the end of the week. You are most welcome to travel with me.'

It seemed that her heart had ceased to beat. 'Thank you, my lord, you are generous to think of me, but I cannot wait so long to leave. I must find my aunt as soon as possible.'

Mrs Weir patted Helena's arm. 'But it shall be so much safer to travel with Guy than by stage, won't it, John?'

Lord Varington crooked a sensual smile in Helena's direction.

There was nothing remotely safe about Lord Varington, Helena thought.

Weir's eyes slid to meet his friend's.

'The stage is inconveniently slow,' said Lord Varington. 'You do know that it will take you practically four days to make the journey, don't you?'

In truth, Helena had no idea how long the journey would take. She had planned to travel by stage rather than mail for the majority of the journey because it was significantly cheaper and she had no wish to indebt herself to Mr and Mrs Weir for any more than was necessary. 'Of course,' she lied.

'I can do it in two,' he said.

'And so he can,' added Mrs Weir, 'it took him even less to reach us. But I imagine he would have some consideration for a lady passenger and drive a little more sedately than normal.'

Varington laughed. 'Indeed, I would.'

Helena could feel the noose tightening around her. 'There is no need to inconvenience yourself, Lord Varington. Besides, I really must reach my aunt before the end of the week. I will take the stage as I planned, and you—' she gave a kind of breathless forced laugh '—may travel every bit as fast as you wish without the encumbrance of a passenger slowing you down.'

'Mary!' Mrs Weir scolded.

'Then you really believe it a matter of urgency to arrive in London before Friday?' Varington turned the full force of his gaze upon her.

She could feel the guilty warmth in her cheeks. 'Yes, my lord. I thank you for your offer, but you can see why it is impossible for me to accept.'

'Very well.' He nodded.

Helena almost sighed her relief aloud…too soon.

'We will leave on Monday morning and I will have

you in London by Tuesday evening…a full day earlier than the stage's arrival. I cannot offer better than that.' A handsome smile spread across his mouth.

Mrs Weir clapped her hands together. 'Oh, Guy, you are too good!'

Helena froze.

'Isn't he, Mary?' Mrs Weir demanded of Helena.

'Indeed,' said Helena weakly, and cast wildly around for some excuse that might extricate her from the mess that her lies had just created. 'But I could not impose on you to change your plans in such a way. It would be most unfair.'

'It is no imposition, Mrs McLelland. I look forward to your company,' he replied, never taking his eyes from hers. 'Besides, I couldn't possibly allow a lady to travel alone and by stage.'

'Thank you,' said Helena, and forced a smile to her face, knowing that there really was no way out this time. Lord Varington had neatly outmanoeuvred her and there was not a thing that she could do about it.

Lord Varington rose and helped himself to some ham and eggs from the heated serving dishes on the sideboard.

'Please excuse me,' Helena said wanly, and escaped to the solitude of the yellow bedchamber, knowing full well that she must wait the rest of this day and all of tomorrow before travelling with Lord Varington to London. She could only hope that he would not insist on taking her directly to the home of her make-believe aunt.

Guy did not see the woman calling herself Mary McLelland again until the next afternoon. She descended the staircase at exactly two o'clock, just as he had known that she would. There was a hint of colour in her cheeks that contrasted prettily with her clear creamy complexion. Several strands of her hair had escaped her pins and she swept them back with nervous fingers. Guy cast an appreciative eye over the image she presented.

'Lord Varington,' she said rather breathlessly, 'I came as your note requested.' He noticed that she surreptitiously kept her hands folded neatly behind her back... out of sight...and out of reach.

'Mrs McLelland.' He moved from where he had been lounging against the heavy stone mantel in the hallway, and walked to meet her. 'I see you have had the foresight to have worn a cloak. You seem to be eminently practical; not a trait often observed in beautiful women.'

She ignored his comment completely. 'You said that a boat had been found, that it might be...' Her words trailed off. 'Where is it now?'

'The remains have been carried to Weir's boat shed, a mere five minutes' walk from here.' He waited for her protest at having to walk. None was forthcoming. She just gave a curt nod of her head and started to walk towards the back door. She had almost reached the door when he called softly, 'Helena.'

Her response was instinctive. She stopped and glanced back over her shoulder.

He smiled, and watched as the realisation of what she had just betrayed registered.

The blush bloomed in her cheeks, and something of fear and anger passed transiently across her features. 'My name is Mary McLelland,' she said quietly, but she did not meet his eye.

'If you say so...Mary McLelland,' he said, moving in a leisurely manner towards her.

He offered his arm. She took it because she could not

politely do otherwise. Together they walked down the back garden until they reached the start of the over-grown lane that led down to the shore and the boat-house.

Guy looked down at her thin leather shoes. 'Perhaps I should carry you,' he suggested. 'The grass is still wet from last night's rain and I would not want you to spoil your shoes or dress. And, of course—' he looked directly into her eyes '—there is the matter of your wounded feet.'

She threw him an outraged look. 'My feet are per-fectly recovered, thank you.' And she blushed again.

And Guy knew very well that she was remembering, just as he was, the intimacy of that moment in her bed-chamber. He smiled. 'Or if you prefer, we can turn back.' He waited with all the appearance of politeness, knowing full well what her answer would be.

'I am perfectly capable of negotiating the pathway, Lord Varington.'

'As you will, Mrs McLelland, but I must warn you that the surface is rather uneven.' Having successfully goaded her, he smiled again and waited for her to set off.

Wild bramble bushes seemed to have taken over on either side, their long thorny branches encroaching far into the path. Not only that, but the grass underfoot was wet, and peppered with jagged nettles, small rocks and shells and copious mounds of sheep droppings. Long riding boots protected Guy's feet and legs. He sauntered nonchalantly over every obstacle. The same could not be said for Helena. Despite picking her way with the greatest of care, it was not long before her shoes and bandaged feet were soaking. And to make matters worse, water was wicking from the grass up and over the edge of her skirt. Three times a bramble branch managed to snag her skirt most viciously, and twice upon the cloak borrowed from Annabel, the last of which to her chagrin necessitated Guy's assistance in freeing it. All around them was the smell of damp undergrowth, of earth and sea and fresh air.

The path eventually led them out to the shore and a rather dilapidated-looking large hut. The wood was a faded ash colour, bleached and beaten into submission by years of hostile weather. Guy slipped the key from his pocket. It turned stiffly in the lock. The door creaked open under the weight of his hand. And they were in.

It was a boathouse without a boat. The floor consisted of creaking wooden planks that were covered in a damp sugaring of sand. Over in one corner a pile of crates and lobster pots had been neatly stacked. In another was a sprawl of ropes and nets and in yet another a few barrels and casks. In the middle of the floor lay a small mound covered with a rumpled canvas sheet.

'But where is the rowing boat?' Helena peered around the hut.

Guy saw her pull the cloak more tightly around her body. He had made no mention of the type of boat in his note to her. And having viewed a map of the exact location of the island of Islay, Guy was quite willing to bet that no boatman worth his salt would have attempted to row the distance single handed in so small a boat as the remains of which lay in this boat shed. 'Here.' He indicated the canvas.

'But...' Her words trailed off as he moved forward and pulled the sheet back to reveal the pile of broken timbers.

He watched her face closely for any sign of reaction. 'I thought…'

'I should have warned you that it was badly shattered.' He crouched and began to separate the remnants of the boat, laying them out across the floor with care. 'Part of the bow is still intact.' He placed it close to her feet.

She dropped to her knees beside him, unmindful of the hardness of the wooden floor or the sand that now clung to the damp wool of her dress. She reached out a hand, caressed fingers against what had once been the bow of a small boat.

'I do not know. I cannot tell if it is the same boat.' She shook her head, a look of frustration crossing her brow.

'And there is this,' he said, uncovering a ripped piece of timber on which a string of bright letters had been painted.

He sensed the sudden stillness in the figure by his side. It seemed that she did not so much as breathe, just leaned forward, taking the torn planking from his hand to trace the remnants of the name.

'*Bonnie Lass.*' Her voice was just a whisper. She swallowed hard; without moving, without even laying down the wood, she closed her eyes. She looked as if she might be praying, kneeling as she was upon the floor with her eyes so tightly shut. Her face appeared bloodless and even her lips had paled.

'Mrs McLelland,' he said, and gently removed the wood from between her fingers to place it on the ground. 'Do you recognise what remains of this boat?'

She made no sign of having heard him.

He heard the shallowness of her breathing, saw how tightly she pressed her lips together in an effort to control the strength of the emotion assailing her. 'Helena,' he said quietly, and touched a hand to her arm.

Even then she did not open her eyes, just stayed as she was, rigid and unwavering.

He pulled her kneeling form against him, his hands stroking what comfort he could offer against her back, his breath touching against her hair. Yet still, she did not yield.

His fingers moved to caress her hair, not caring that several of her hairpins scattered upon the floor in the process.

He heard the pain in her whispered words, 'They should not have died. It was my fault. They were only there to help me. And now they're dead.' For all her agony she did not weep.

Guy held her, awkward and stiff though she was, and looked down into her face. 'How can it be your fault?' he said. 'It was an accident, nothing more than a terrible accident. A small boat out in a big storm.'

'You don't understand.'

'Then explain it to me,' he said gently.

Her eyes slowly opened and looked up into his. And for a moment he thought she would do just that. Every vestige of defence had vanished from her face. Stripped of all pretence she looked young and vulnerable...and desperately afraid. 'I...'

He waited for what she would say.

'I...'

And then he saw the change in her eyes, the defensive shutters shift back into place.

'I must be getting back. Mrs Weir will be wondering where I am.' She began to gather up her hairpins.

'Annabel knows very well where you are,' he said with exasperation.

Helena carefully picked each pin from the sandy floor before rising and turning to leave.

'Wait,' he said, catching her back by her wrist. 'You are certain that this is the boat in which you travelled?'

A nod of the head sent a shimmer down the coils of hair dangling against her breast. 'Yes.'

'With whom did you sail?'

He saw the pain in her eyes, the slight wince before she recovered herself. 'The boatman who agreed to take me.'

'Who else?'

'No one,' she said, and averted her eyes.

'Not even your maid?'

Her gaze darted to his and then away. He heard her small fast intake of breath and released her. She folded her hands together, but they gripped so tightly that her knuckles shone white. 'I have told you my story.'

He reached one finger to tilt her chin, forcing her to look at him. 'And that is exactly what you've told me, isn't it, Helena? A story.'

He saw the involuntary swallow before she pulled her head away.

'When I found you upon the shore you told me that your maid, Agnes, had been with you in the boat. In your distress just now you spoke of *them*, rather than *he*. Why will you not tell me what happened?'

She shook her head, stumbling back to get away from him.

He snaked an arm around her waist, pulling her to him, until he could feel the wool of her dress pressing against his thighs, feel the softness of her breast against his chest. He lowered his face to hers, so close that their lips almost touched. He could see each fleck within her eyes, every long dark red lash that bordered them, the delicate red arc of her eyebrow. His lips tingled with the proximity of her mouth, so close that they shared the same breath. 'The truth has a strange way of making itself known sooner or later, sweetheart. Are you sure that you do not want to tell me yourself?' Much more of this and he would give in to every instinct and kiss her as thoroughly and as hard as he wanted to.

The tension stretched between them.

His eyes slid longingly to her mouth, to the soft ripeness of her lips. He was so close as to almost taste her.

'Please, Lord Varington,' she gasped.

It was enough to bring him to his senses. Slowly he released her. Watched while she began to coil her hair back into place.

He replaced the boat wreckage in an orderly pile and re-covered it with the canvas, and when he looked again she had tidied her hair.

'We should return to the house.' She spoke calmly, smoothing down the creases in her skirt, fixing the cloak around her body, as if she hadn't just discovered the boat that had claimed the life of her servants and very nearly her own, as if she was not grieving and afraid. There wasn't even the slightest hint that he had just pressed her the length of his body and almost ravaged her lips with his own. Yet he had felt the tremor ripple through her, the strength of her suppressed emotion. There was no doubting that the woman before him was a consummate actress when it came to hiding her feelings. But Guy had glimpsed behind her façade, and what he saw was temptation itself. What else was she hiding and why? Guy was growing steadfastly more de-termined to discover the mystery of the beautiful red-headed woman.

Chapter Four

Later that afternoon Guy was sharing a bottle of whisky with Weir in the comfort of Weir's gunroom.

'Do you think that she was lying about the boat?' Weir poured yet another tot of whisky into Guy's glass and added a splash of water. 'Could be she'd never set eyes on the blasted thing before. I'm beginning to wonder whether this whole thing of her being apparently washed up on the shore that morning isn't just some kind of farce.'

'Her reaction to the boat seemed genuine enough. She'd have to be a damned good actress to have feigned that.' Guy accepted the whisky with thanks.

'Well, maybe that's exactly what she is.'

'Maybe,' he conceded. 'Certainly her name is not Mary McLelland, nor did she travel alone with a boatman from Islay. But whoever she is, and whatever she's up to, I think she recognised the wreckage of the *Bonnie Lass*.'

Weir stood warming himself at the massive fire that roared in the chimney place. 'Doesn't mean she was in it when it went down.'

'Maybe not,' said Guy.

'Don't you think it rather incredible that anyone, let alone a woman, could have survived being shipwrecked in such conditions?'

'Incredible, yes, but not impossible.'

'She might have arranged herself on the shore like that for some passing soul to find.'

'Come on, Weir. You saw the state she was in when I brought her here. Had I not chanced upon her when I did she would have died. And no one could have known I'd decided to walk along the beach when I did. It's not exactly my usual habit.'

'That's true. But even had you not gone out walking that morning, someone would have found her. Storms wash up all manner of things. The villagers would have been down looking for firewood and Spanish treasure.'

'There was firewood aplenty, but nothing of treasure,' said Guy with a grin, 'unless one counts a half-drowned woman in that league.'

Weir rolled his eyes.

'Besides,' said Guy, 'if she contrived the whole thing to land herself a bed here, why has she been so determined to leave since regaining consciousness? It doesn't add up.'

'Whether she was shipwrecked or not, that woman is bad news.'

'Don't worry, old man. I'll have her off your hands and out of your house tomorrow morning.'

'You seem rather determined to have her travel down to London with you. I must confess that although I'll be relieved to see the back of her, I beg that you will exercise some level of caution where "Mrs McLelland" is concerned.'

Guy gave a laugh. 'What exactly do you think that she's going to do to me?'

'God only knows.' Weir sighed. 'Just have a care, that's all I'm asking. I don't want anything happening to you. Tregellas would kill me.'

'And there was me thinking you had some measure of friendship for me, when in truth your concern is because you're afraid of my brother.'

'Everyone's afraid of your brother!' Weir took a gulp of whisky.

Guy smiled and refilled the two glasses. 'Still got your feeling of impending doom?' he teased

'Don't laugh at me. The blasted thing's lodged in my gullet and showing no signs of shifting. I'm serious, Varington, take care where that woman's concerned.'

'No need to be so worried, Weir. I mean to pay very close attention to Mrs McLelland for the entirety of our journey together.'

Weir's eyes became small and beady with suspicion. 'I don't like the sound of that. Just what are you up to?'

One corner of Guy's mouth tugged upwards. 'We wish to know the truth of the woman who is at present your guest, and by the time we reach London I tell you I will have it.'

Weir leaned back in his chair and gave a weary sigh. 'And just how do you intend to do that? She'll just feed you more lies as she's done so far. I wish you'd let me send for the constable.'

'Not at all, my dear Weir. You see, it's really quite simple.' Guy smiled. 'I mean to seduce the truth from her.'

A groan sounded from Weir. 'I beg you will reconsider. You can have women aplenty once you're back in London. And if musts, then even in the coaching inns on your way down, though the Lord knows I must counsel you against it.'

'Alas, my friend, you know that I have a penchant for widows with red hair.' Guy was smiling as if not quite in earnest. 'And it will be an easy enough and rather pleasant distraction from the tedium of the journey. By the time I'm home I shall know the truth of her, just in time to kiss her goodbye and set her on her way.' He loosened his neckcloth and made himself more comfortable in the chair.

'I have a bad feeling over this.'

'Relax, Weir. I've had plenty of practice in the art of seduction. I'll have Mrs McLelland spilling her secrets before we're anywhere near the capital.'

'I only hope you know what you're doing, Varington.'

Guy raised his whisky glass and made a toast. 'To Mary McLelland.'

'Mary McLelland,' repeated Weir. 'And an end to the whole unsettling episode.'

At half past seven the next morning a murky grey light was dawning across the skyline. The noise of horses and wheels crunched upon gravel and gulls sounded overhead. Helena inhaled deeply, dragging in the scent of the place, trying to impress it upon her memory. Salt and seaweed and damp sand. It was a clean smell and one that she had known all her life. After today she did not know when, or indeed if, she would ever smell it again. Mercifully the weather seemed to have gentled. Only a breath of a sea breeze ruffled the ribbons of her borrowed bonnet and whispered its freshness against her cheeks. Despite the early hour Mrs Weir was up, wrapped in the largest, thickest shawl that Helena had seen.

'I simply could not let you go without saying goodbye, my dear Mary.' Mrs Weir linked an impulsive hand through Helena's arm. 'You will write to me, won't you?'

'Of course I will.' Helena smiled, hiding the sadness that tugged at her heart. Once Mrs Weir knew the truth she would not want letters. In short she would not want anything to do with 'Mary McLelland'.

Mrs Weir pulled her aside and lowered her voice in a conspiratorial fashion. 'Mary, there is something I must say to you before you leave.' She patted her hand. 'There is no need to look so worried. It is just that…' She bit at her lip. 'Promise me that you will not heed any rumours that you may come to hear concerning Lord Varington or his brother while you are in London.'

'Rumours?' Helena stared at her, puzzled.

'Promise me,' said Mrs Weir determinedly. 'Guy is a good man.' Mrs Weir smiled and let her voice return to its normal volume.

'I do not let gossip influence my opinion of people,' said Helena.

'You must come back and visit me soon. London is such a long way and John is most reticent to leave his lands, else I would visit you myself.'

John Weir could not quite manage to force a smile to his face. 'Come now, Annabel, we must let Lord Varington and Mrs McLelland be on their way. They have a considerable distance to travel today.' So saying, he moved forward and drew his wife's hand into his own. The message was very clear.

Helena made her curtsy, thanked Mr and Mrs Weir

again for all their kindness and finally allowed herself
to look round at Lord Varington.

He was watching her while fondling the muzzle of
one of the four grey horses that stood ready to pull the
carriage. 'Mrs McLelland, allow me to assist you,
ma'am.' He moved towards her, took her hand in his and
helped her up the steps into the carriage.

Helena gave a polite little inclination of the head,
ignored the awareness that his proximity brought and
quelled quite admirably the fear of being enclosed
within a carriage for two days with the man by her side.
'Thank you, my lord,' she said stiffly.

Only once she was comfortably seated with a travelling rug wrapped most firmly around her knees and a
hot brick beneath her feet, all fussed over personally by
Lord Varington himself, did the carriage make ready to
depart. The door slammed shut. Lord Varington flashed
her a most handsome smile.

Helena experienced a moment of panic and struggled
out from beneath the blanket, which in her haste seemed
to be practically binding her to the carriage seat. But
Lord Varington had already thumped the roof with his
cane.

She heard Mrs Weir's voice through the open
window. 'Goodbye, Mary. Take care.'

The carriage moved off with a lurch, the horses'
hooves crunching against the gravel.

'No, wait!' she gasped.

Varington smiled again. 'Have you changed your
mind about visiting your aunt, Mrs McLelland?
Perhaps you wish to remain here at Seamill Hall. Shall
I stop the carriage?'

She looked into those ice blue eyes, and wondered

if he would do it. Leave her here, to wait for the next mail, to travel half the country by stage, all the while looking over her shoulder for Stephen. She was being foolish, letting her fears get the better of her. Lord Varington might well know that she was not being honest, but he could know nothing of the truth. Quite simply, she would not be sitting here now with him if he did. He might be flirtatious. He might be a little too curious for comfort, asking too many questions, tricking her into revealing things that she did not want to reveal, but Helena McGregor was no innocent when it came to the devices that men used for their own ends. At seven-and-twenty she had seen more of the dark side of life than most women could bear. But Helena had survived, because Helena was strong.

Lord Varington might well ask the questions. It did not mean that he would receive the answers that he wanted. Quite deliberately she closed herself off to her emotions, resuming the mantle of calm poise that she knew from years of experience would protect her…and deflect any attempt to come close to the real Helena. Her only aim in life was to escape Stephen. Nothing else mattered. She would do whatever she had to, just as she had always done. She hardened her heart and her resolve. She could weather whatever Lord Varington would throw at her.

'Mrs McLelland?' he prompted, recalling her from her thoughts.

'Thank you, my lord,' she said calmly, 'but that will not be necessary.' She turned her face away to the open window and raised her hand in response to Mrs Weir's waving. She waved until the carriage reached the bottom of the driveway and turned out on to the road, and the couple standing before the front door of the big house were no longer visible. Then the horses got into their rhythm, their hooves clipping against the stones and mud of the road surface.

Helena was sitting bolt upright, facing the direction of travel, her hands neatly folded together upon her lap. Across from her, Lord Varington seemed to be taking up the whole seat. His head was against the squabs, his legs stretched out so that the ankles of his long riding boots were crossed rather too close to Helena's skirts. She made an infinitesimal motion to shift her feet away from him.

Varington saw it and smiled. 'You might as well make yourself comfortable, Mrs McLelland. It's going to be a very long day. Long enough for us to dispense with formalities.'

In Dunleish Castle on the island of St Vey, Sir Stephen Tayburn was standing at the top of the north-east tower, leaning on the crenellations looking out at the sea. The sky was a pale muted grey streaked with brush marks of deep charcoal and a wash of delicate pink. The sea was calm—for now. The calm would not last. Sir Stephen knew that. What more could be expected? They were already into November and slipping closer towards winter, to the time when days grew shorter and nights grew longer and darkness prevailed—just the way he liked it. The wind caught at his cape, swirling it up and out as if it were the wings of some great dark bird. Everything of Sir Stephen was black—his clothing, his eyes, his heart, everything excepting his hair, which was a stark white. He sipped from the goblet in his hand, relishing the slightly sour taste of the wine. The door behind him creaked open. A figure emerged, hesitated, cap in hand.

'Sir.'

Stephen Tayburn did not look round, just continued surveying the scene before him.

There was the quiet shuffling of feet and a nervous cough.

'You have news for me, Crauford?' It was an imperious tone, a tone that barely concealed an underlying contempt. Still, he kept his face seaward, not deigning to look at the man.

'Aye, sir. I made the enquires, discreet like you instructed. Nosed around in the taverns and howfs o' the villages on the mainland.'

'And?' He moved at last, turning his dark terrifying gaze to the hook-nosed man standing so patiently by.

'There was talk o' a woman found washed up on the shore near Portincross. They tain her to Mr Weir's house and had the doctor look at her.'

Nothing of emotion showed upon Tayburn's face. 'So she was still alive?'

'Aye, sir, she was alive, all right. They've kept her there in the big house, on account of her bein' in a swoon.'

'How very convenient,' he mused. 'Has the woman a description? Was she seen by any of your…sources?'

'Oh, aye, sir.' Rab Crauford crept a little closer towards his master. 'Ma source has a pal whose lassie works at Seamill Hall.' His grin spread wider. 'The woman frae the shore has red hair.'

Tayburn's eyes narrowed and the set around his mouth hardened. 'Has she indeed.' His gaze raked the tall thin man before him. 'Have McKenzie ready the boat. I've a mind to visit the mainland this morning, Kilbride, perhaps…'

'Very good, sir,' said Crauford. 'I'll see to it right away.'

Sir Stephen Tayburn did not wait for his servant to leave before presenting his back and turning once more to look out across the rolling waves below. He drained the rest of his wine and belched loudly. The door closed behind him, and he heard the sound of Crauford's footsteps running down the winding stone stairs. Only then did he say beneath his breath, as if the words were a thought murmured aloud, 'I have found you at last, my darling Helena. What a homecoming you shall have, my dear.' A cruel smile spread across his mouth and over the sound of the waves and the wind was the dull crack of crystal as the grip of his fingers shattered the fine goblet within.

Helena's back was beginning to ache and her right hand was growing numb from clinging so hard and so long to the securing strap. The bouncing and rocking of the carriage was threatening nausea and she had long since closed her eyes to block out the view of the countryside racing by in a blur of green and brown. And still, they had not made their first stop, aside from the rapid change of the horses. She was just gritting her teeth and wondering how much longer she could endure it when she heard a thump upon the roof and the carriage began to slow. Her eyes opened and as the carriage ground mercifully to a halt she could do nothing to contain the sigh of relief that escaped her. The door was open and Lord Varington was leaning out, shouting something up to his driver. He withdrew back inside, shutting first the door, then the window and sat back in his seat.

'Is something wrong, my lord?' she managed to say

with what she hoped was a tone of polite enquiry, whilst disentangling her hand from the strap.

'Wrong, Mrs McLelland?' he replied.

'The carriage seems to have stopped. Have we reached the coaching inn?' she said, trying not to sound too wishful. Just as the words had left her mouth the coach began to move off, albeit at a much more sedate pace. Her fingers grabbed for the strap.

'Not yet.' One corner of his mouth turned up, as if he knew very well the measure of her desperation to reach their stop. 'I thought perhaps you might prefer that we travelled at a more comfortable pace for a while.' His eyes slid from her face to her fingers that wound themselves so tightly around the strap, and back again to her face.

Helena felt a flush of self-consciousness and released the strap in an instant. 'There is no need to alter your plans on my account. If you wish to travel faster, please do so. In fact, I would prefer that you did.'

He just looked at her in that knowing way. 'I am content to travel slower, for now.'

'Very well, my lord.' Surreptitiously she massaged her fingers, coaxing the blood to flow to the tips she could not feel, grateful for the break, but anxious also not to lose any time.

Lord Varington stripped off his gloves and then without pausing in the slightest, reaching smoothly across to take her right hand into both of his. 'My name is Guy,' he said in a slow delicious drawl.

'Lord Varington!' exclaimed Helena in as frosty a tone as she could summon, and tried to withdraw her hand.

Lord Varington's hands were firm but gentle in their imprisonment of her fingers. He showed not the slightest inclination to release them. Instead, he carefully peeled the borrowed glove away from her until her hand was bare. 'I fear that the strap has left its mark upon you,' he said, and traced a finger over the impression on her skin.

Helena shivered and gave another tug of her hand.

Lord Varington's fingers tightened by the slightest degree. 'Such a dainty little hand,' he said, and slid his thumbs across the back of her hand. 'Such slender little fingers.' His thumb caressed the length of her index finger, from knuckle to the tip of her nail.

'My lord, please be so kind as to release my hand immediately,' said Helena with the utmost of politeness.

In response, Lord Varington turned her hand over and began to stroke a sensuous massage across her palm, his thumb pressing first lightly, then leaning a little more strongly, sweeping small slow circles over her skin. His hands were warm, their movement against hers blatantly erotic. She shuddered beneath the pleasure that it ignited, tried to quell the inappropriate response that it engendered.

'Lord Varington,' she said again, with just the slightest of emotion in her voice. 'Release my hand.'

The Viscount did not oblige. Instead he ran both thumbs slowly down the full length of either side of her forefinger, moving then to do the same to each adjacent finger in turn. Skin slid against skin in a slow sensual slide until Helena's hand burned beneath his touch. A flame sparked low and deep in her belly and the breath shook in her throat.

'My lord, I must protest!' she said in a breathy whisper.

Lord Varington raised his gaze to hers, and in his eyes seemed to burn a pale blue fire of passion. Helena had never seen such a look in any man's eyes. He raised her hand until it was just short of his mouth, and then slowly, carefully, never taking his eyes from hers, he touched his lips to the centre of her palm. It was as if he had touched the very core of her being. A spontaneous gasp escaped her, and she found she could not take her eyes from his, could not move, could barely breathe.

'You are beautiful,' he said, and she could feel the tickle of his lips against her skin with his every word. 'Beautiful,' he said again, and lowered her hand back down to cradle it within his own.

She sat as if mesmerised, watching his head bending towards hers until he was so close that she could see the dark eyelashes that framed his magnificent eyes, could examine every detail of his face: the pallor of his skin, the way that his eyebrows were smooth and dark, the strong line of his jaw that led down to the cleft in the square of his chin. A lock of hair dangled dangerously close to his eye so that she longed to just reach across and smooth it away. But she could not, for Helena knew that he was going to kiss her and, despite the knowledge, she did nothing. Everything seemed to be in slow motion. He filled her vision. His cologne filled her nostrils. Her lips parted as if of their own will. She seemed drugged, powerless to stop the move of his mouth towards hers.

'Helena,' he whispered, and her name rolled off his tongue as if it had been made to do so. There was a richness to his voice, a sensual ripeness.

She felt her eyelids flutter shut. Tilted her mouth to accept his.

The carriage suddenly swerved to the side, throwing Lord Varington off balance and bringing Helena to her senses in an instant.

'What the he—?' He caught the curse back before it left his mouth and resumed his seat just as the coach came to a halt. A thud of feet sounded and the door swung open to reveal a rather red-faced coachman.

'Beggin' your pardon, m'lord,' he said. 'But a sheep ran out before us and it was all I could do not to hit the animal. It was a good thing that we weren't goin' at no speed else we would have like come off the road.' He clutched his hat between his hands. 'I hope that you and the lady were not harmed by the abruptness of my change of direction.'

'No harm at all, Smith,' said Lord Varington with an ironic twist of one corner of his mouth.

An exceedingly apologetic coachman retreated, and soon the coach set off at what seemed an even slower pace.

'Forgive my man's driving, ma'am. He is usually most proficient at handling the ribbons. Indeed, this is the first incident of its kind in all the years he has worked for me. But then I do not usually expect him to drive through the wilds of the country. I trust you are not too overcome by the shock?' Lord Varington's voice was filled with concern.

Helena gripped firmly on to the leather of the seat on either side of her. Lord Varington had unknowingly hit the nail on the head with his question. Helena was completely shocked and aghast, but not at anything the unfortunate coachman had done. Rather she was in a state of horrified disbelief at her actions immediately preceeding the swerving of the carriage. She had been on the verge of allowing Lord Varington to kiss her! And would have done so had not a sheep happened to stroll out into the path of his carriage. Lord, oh, lord!

He leaned forward towards her. 'Mrs McLelland? You seem to have gone rather pale. Are you feeling unwell?'

'I am quite well, thank you, my lord.' Helena flattened herself against the leather seat back, trying to make the space between her and Lord Varington as large as possible. Her emotions were in turmoil. She felt thoroughly undone. In all of five years with Stephen, Helena had not experienced anything that prepared her for the effect that Lord Varington seemed to exact upon her person. It was utterly ridiculous!

'It would seem that something has rendered you a trifle overwrought, ma'am.' There was that knowing half-smile playing about his lips. 'You appear to be a little breathless. It becomes you very well.'

Helena had never felt so vulnerable and the knowledge made her angry, not only with herself but also with Lord Varington. 'I assure you that you are mistaken, my lord,' she said curtly.

'Am I, Helena?'

'My name is Mary McLelland,' she snapped, 'and I would trust you, sir, to remember that you are a gentleman, and to behave accordingly.'

Lord Varington's head bowed in mock humility. 'Forgive me, dear lady, if I have done anything to…' those stark eyes lingered over her face '…offend you.'

There was nothing of sincerity in his attitude, Helena noted with more than a touch of asperity.

'Allow me to make reparation for my blunder.' He extended a hand in her direction.

Helena shrank back further, if that were at all possible given that she was practically plastered against the back of the carriage seat. 'That will not be necessary, my lord,' she said rather more quickly than was polite.

'But I insist.'

'No!'

Lord Varington leaned back against his seat with a bemused expression.

'What I mean to say, my lord, is that it would be better if we just put the incident from our minds, and forget that it occurred. We do, after all, have some considerable distance to travel together, and…and…' She ran out of words and glanced up at him, her cheeks stained a peachy pink.

His eyes held more than a hint of amusement. 'And it is better that there are no misunderstandings between us,' he finished.

She nodded.

'Very well, Mrs McLelland.' He smiled and extended his hand once more towards her.

She stared at it in dismay.

'Let us shake hands on our now newly defined friendship.'

Much as she had no wish to touch him, she could not very well refuse his suggestion. With a great deal of reticence she reached her fingers to touch his. It was a mistake. In her flustered state Helena had not yet fitted her glove back on, and neither, it became apparent, had Lord Varington fitted his. Bare skin met and touched. On the surface it was nothing more than a handshake. But Helena's skin tingled beneath the touch of his warm strong hand, and she felt the sudden stampede of her pulse. He did nothing improper, neither holding her hand for too long nor overly personal. He did not have to, not when he looked at her with that smoulder in his eyes.

'To new friendships,' he said, and smiled a most charming smile.

She said nothing, but Helena had the feeling that the journey with Lord Varington was going to be a great deal more challenging than she had anticipated.

Chapter Five

Lord Varington's carriage finally rumbled into the yard of the Graham Arms in Longtown, situated between Gretna and Carlisle. It was not where he had planned to stay, but Helena did not argue when Lord Varington said that they would go no further that night. The sky was now shrouded in black and dark grey clouds conspired to hide the light of the moon. Rain had been pattering against the carriage roof for the past two hours and the howl of the wind could be heard even over the racket of the wheels and the clatter of the horses' hooves upon the road. The coach stopped and the door swung open to reveal a sodden coachman struggling to fetch the steps into position.

'Leave those. See to the horses. The sooner we're all out of this weather, the better.'

The coachman did not argue, just hurried away to do his lordship's bidding.

Lord Varington jumped down, mud splashing up from where the soles of his leather boots impacted on the rain-soaked ground. Rain pelted against his coat, sitting upon the dark blue wool as sparkling droplets against the burst of lights from the building in the background. He turned to Helena, holding out his hand towards her. 'Come quickly, Mrs McLelland, if you do not wish to receive a thorough soaking.'

Helena pulled the hood of her cloak over her head and hesitated for just the slightest moment before placing her hand in his. The journey had been the longest of her life. She was exhausted, cold, and sore, and the thought of entering into yet another disagreement with Lord Varington was just too much to bear. A strong arm curled around her waist, and before she knew it, Lord Varington had lifted her out of the carriage and placed her feet upon the ground. At least her feet were well recovered, she thought ruefully. A loud bang as the door swung shut, and then his arm was around her shoulder, shielding her from the worst of the weather as they ran together across the yard.

Helena blinked at the sudden blaze of light. Heat rushed up to meet them as they entered through the heavy wooden door. The taproom was crowded with bodies. There was laughter and the buzz of chatter, the deep burr of male voices interspersed with the occasional high-pitched laughter of a female. Men in thick coats that were still steaming and damp, and two women, both of whom wore dresses cut indecently low to reveal their ample cleavage. Over on the opposite wall was a massive fire set in an old-fashioned stone hearth. Men were crowded round its heat, sitting where they could, some even upon the pile of logs that had been neatly stacked ready for the burning. All around was the smell of wet wool, beer and tobacco.

Several curious male stares were focused upon her

person. Helena drew her cloak more tightly around herself, and for the first time since setting off that morning was profoundly glad that she was with Lord Varington. Had she been travelling by stage, she would be in the position of having to negotiate her own room at the overnight stops. Entering places like this on her own, conscious of how precious little money she had in her purse.

The landlord was a small man with a large girth. He wiped his hands upon the apron stretched across his waist when he saw Lord Varington and made his way across to the bar, knowing an aristocrat when he saw one. 'My lord.' He nodded. ''Fraid all our rooms have been taken for the night.'

Varington pulled a purse from his pocket and sat it upon the bar. 'Are you quite sure about that?'

The landlord's small eye dropped to the purse, which Varington obligingly unlaced until the glint of gold could be seen within.

Helena had no idea how many gold coins the purse held, but there seemed to be a great many.

'Let me see what can be done,' said the landlord.

'We require two rooms,' said Lord Varington.

The landlord hurried off, leaving Helena standing at Varington's side. Five minutes elapsed before he returned with an oily smile. 'It's your lucky night, m'lord. Two rooms have just become available.'

'How fortuitous.' Lord Varington smiled.

The landlord grinned and in a single swipe the purse had gone, stuffed beneath his apron.

Helena saw the landlord's gaze switch to her, saw too the presumption in it.

'Directly across the landing from each other the rooms are, m'lord.'

'It just gets better and better,' said Varington, and smiled at Helena.

She did not need to see the crudity that crept into the landlord's expression at Lord Varington's words to know what conclusion the man had drawn. She felt the warmth rise in her cheeks, and all of her gratitude to Lord Varington vanished in an instant.

'And a private parlour?' Lord Varington looked expectantly at the landlord.

The landlord sucked in his breath and grimaced. 'Packed to the gunnels we are, m'lord, packed to the gunnels.'

Varington raised an eyebrow.

'It'll be ready in twenty minutes.'

'Most obliged.' Lord Varington flicked another coin into the landlord's hand. Then, turning to Helena, he positioned his arm for her to take. 'Shall we?'

The landlord bellowed for his daughter to show the lord and lady to their rooms. A pretty plump girl appeared, made her curtsy, glanced first at Varington, and then at Helena, gave a very knowing smile for one so young, and then led off towards a low wooden door.

Helena drew Lord Varington a look of pure ice, held her head erect, and touched only the barest tips of her fingers to his sleeve. Even with such minimal contact she could feel that the wool was damp. Causing a scene within the crowded taproom would only draw more attention to herself and, although there was a most definite irony in her taking umbrage at being thought Lord Varington's mistress, she found herself unwilling to be the focus of such attention.

As if knowing her every thought, Lord Varington threw her his most charming smile and then guided her in the serving wench's wake out of the taproom and up the narrow staircase, only pausing once he reached the door to her chamber.

There was a jangle of coins and the girl disappeared with an even bigger smile upon her face.

Helena disengaged her fingers immediately.

'Shall twenty minutes suffice?' he asked.

'Twenty minutes?' she parroted without the least idea to what he was referring.

'To dine. In our private parlour. Regardless of the quality of this place, we need to eat.'

Exhaustion was buzzing in Helena's head, and she was still damnably angry that Lord Varington had done nothing to repudiate the conclusion reached by the landlord, and indeed had seemed positively to foster the impression. 'I am tired, my lord. I think I would rather just go to bed.'

'You have scarcely eaten a bite all day, Mrs McLelland. Can I not tempt you to my table?'

'No,' she said, too weary to be polite.

'You wound me, madam,' he said, and touched a hand to his heart.

'For that I am sorry, my lord.'

There was a cynical flicker of his mouth. 'Much as I fear to incur your displeasure, I feel, speaking purely in the capacity of a concerned gentleman and friend, you understand,' he said as if in an aside to her, 'that I cannot enjoy the pleasure of a meal if I allow you to retire on an empty stomach.' The pale eyes twinkled.

Helena gave a sigh. She had the feeling that Lord Varington would not give up his persuasions anytime soon. The ache in her back intensified. She longed for nothing other than to shut the bedchamber door against the world and curl up safely and alone in the bed. 'Very well, my lord. I shall partake of a little food.'

'Excellent decision, Mrs McLelland,' he said, and before she knew what he was going to do, he raised her hand to his mouth, brushed his lips against her knuckles and released her. 'Twenty minutes,' he said with a bow, and stood back against the door frame that led into his own room, watching her.

Helena did not linger. She entered the room designated as her bedchamber, aware that, even as she closed the door, Lord Varington's eyes were still upon her.

Exactly twenty minutes later Guy knocked on the door leading to the room in which Helena was housed. He had washed and changed into fresh clothing. Now he waited to see Helena again—to work a little harder at learning the secrets that she was so desperate to keep hidden. The task was not onerous. If truth be told, he was enjoying flirting with the woman who called herself Mary McLelland immensely. She was beautiful; he had not lied to her of his opinion. All creamy velvet skin, flowing red hair and a figure that most men would appreciate. Nor had he lied in his words to Weir of his liking for fast widows and redheads. Helena most definitely came into the second category, and perhaps even the first. Dinner with a green-eyed vixen. He smiled at the thought. It had proved easier to persuade her to join him than he had anticipated, but then again she was clearly tired and Guy had been prepared to stand there all night if need be. He flicked a speck of invisible dust from the lapel of his coat and smiled as the door opened.

Helena was still wearing the same dark travelling

dress that she had been wearing all day. She had tidied her hair and, judging from the smell of her, had applied some lavender water.

'Mrs McLelland,' he said, and presented his arm.

She said nothing, just took his arm and together they made their way down to the private parlour.

The light from the candelabra in the centre of the dinner table showed the fatigue around her eyes. Her cheeks seemed to have taken on a slight ashen hue and there was a tightness around her mouth. Something of the rigidity had gone from her deportment and she was leaning every so slightly into the support of the chair at her back. She looked exhausted and extremely vulnerable. Guy felt a twinge of conscience.

The maid had left a newly opened bottle of claret and two clean glasses on the table beside the place settings of china and cutlery. He filled her glass and then his own, and still, she said nothing.

'It seems that the journey has exhausted you, ma'am.'

'I am a little tired, my lord.'

'Then that must be remedied. We shall travel more slowly tomorrow. I would not want you arriving at your aunt's in a state of fatigue.'

'I shall be refreshed after a night's sleep, sir. You have already reduced your pace on my account. I beg you will slow it no further.'

'You are too thoughtful of me, Mrs McLelland,' he said silkily.

'Not at all, my lord, I am but impatient to reach my aunt,' came the retort.

Guy smiled. Helena was trying hard to appear unperturbed, but he had not missed the nervous flutter of her fingers against the stem of her glass. 'Then have I no hope of winning your favour, ma'am?'

He saw the movement of her breast, the rise and fall of her shoulders as if she had taken in a deep breath of air and then released it. 'My lord, I thought that I had made my position clear earlier today.' There was no censure in her tone, only the unmistakable sound of bone weariness.

'You are a very attractive woman, and a man can but hope.' He stared across the table at her, willing her to meet his gaze, but she determinedly kept her eyes averted.

A knock at the door and the landlord and a small posse of servants hurried in, bearing numerous serving plates and dishes. Only when they had exited did he speak again. 'Shall I serve you?' he asked with deliberate *double entendre*.

She glanced momentarily up at that, and he could see from her expression that she had understood his meaning only too well. 'No, thank you, my lord.'

'As you wish,' he said, and inclined his head.

He sampled a little of every dish.

She sipped at her wine and took nothing.

'Can I not tempt you even a little?' he said, and looked meaningfully at her lips. 'The chicken is more than edible.'

Her face remained impassive. 'Thank you, my lord, but I am not hungry.' She took another taste from her glass before setting it carefully down upon the tablecloth.

Guy continued to eat his dinner. 'The cabbage is not soggy, Mrs McLelland, and the pork is nicely crisped.'

A faint tummy rumbling sounded across the table. A hint of colour touched Helena's cheeks. 'Please do excuse me,' she mumbled.

The corners of Guy's mouth curved. 'I think you

have not been honest with me, ma'am.' And reaching across, he took up her plate and placed a little from every dish upon it.

The colour in Helena's cheeks intensified at his words, but she began to eat the food he had set before her.

'Honesty is such an important attribute. What is your opinion on the matter, Mrs McLelland?'

'I have little opinion, my lord.'

'Come now, you do not seem to me to be a simpleton. You must have your own thoughts on the matter,' he said, refilling her glass.

'Very well, I am sure that you are right, sir.'

'So you agree that dishonesty is a sin?' he asked with an exaggerated expression of surprise.

She set down her knife and fork upon her plate, and looked up at him. 'I believe there are some cases where the sin may be excusable.'

'Such as?'

She took a gulp of wine and glanced away to the left, to where the flickering flames of the fire danced against the wall. 'Such as when a person is in fear for their life,' she said in a voice so quiet he had to strain to catch her words.

Something kicked in Guy's gut. And he had the sudden thought that he might have grossly misjudged the woman sitting opposite him.

There was silence between them.

'If that were to be the case, then that person need only appeal for help, and help would be forthcoming. That is something I could guarantee, ma'am.'

'In some situations there is nothing that can be done to help.'

'Perhaps it might appear that way to the individual within that circumstance, but there is always something that may be done to assist them.'

She looked at him then, and in that moment he knew that he was seeing the real woman behind the façade, the real Helena. And Guy thought he had never seen a more hauntingly beautiful woman.

'There are some cases that are beyond all hope.'

'Helena.' He reached across and took her hand in his, and this time there was nothing of his sensual teasing. 'Nothing is beyond hope.' He paused, then said, 'Let me help you.'

He saw the longing in her eyes, the need to unburden the terrible truth that she carried with her. Her fingers lay still and quiet against his, trusting, open. She parted her lips to speak…

A knock at the door.

The serving wench breezed in. 'Anything else I can get for you, m'lord?'

Helena quickly withdrew her fingers from his.

'There is nothing, thank you,' he said in a cooler tone than normal, and dismissed the girl.

But it was too late. The moment had gone, and so, too, had Helena's trust, for when he looked at her, there was that familiar wary caution in her eyes and her mouth was closed firm. He raked a hand through his hair with ill-disguised frustration. 'Helena—' he began.

But she cut him off. 'My name is Mrs McLelland. Forgive me, my lord. I am tired and would like to retire to bed now. We have an early start in the morning.'

Helena had gone, and in her place sat Mary McLelland.

'Of course,' he said, rising from his chair.

They did not speak again until he watched her slip

through the door to her chamber. 'Good night, Mrs McLelland,' he said softly.

'Good night, Lord Varington,' came the quiet reply.

He lingered a moment longer in the passageway, staring at the door through which she had vanished. Then slowly he turned around and walked alone into his room.

The evening had not gone quite according to Guy's plan.

It was a long time before Helena finally found sleep, despite her body aching with fatigue, despite her mind being so tired that she could not think straight. She wriggled out of her borrowed dress, and into her borrowed nightgown. She removed the borrowed hairpins and combed through her long tresses with the borrowed comb. And all the while she could think of nothing save that she had nearly revealed all to Lord Varington. Quite how it had happened she did not know. One minute she was deflecting his flirtatious behaviour quite well, the next, she was on the verge of pouring out her heart to him. Something about him had changed. It had happened while they had been talking in double meanings about the subject of dishonesty. The rake had vanished, replaced instead with a man whose eyes were filled with compassion and concern, whose hand was strong and reassuring, a man who said he would help her...and she had believed him. A moment's weakness. And had not the serving maid come into the parlour when she did, Helena would have told him all of it. She shuddered at the thought, lying there in the bed in the darkness of the inn room.

Through the wall came the muffled sound of snoring. Outside an owl hooted in the darkness. The tips of naked branches tapped a rhythm lightly against the glass panes of the window. How easy it would have been to have told, and how dangerous. If he knew who she was, what she was, his kindness would have vanished. In this one thing she had spoken the truth to him: there was nothing and no one who could help her. And Stephen would ensure that anyone who tried would regret it most bitterly.

Helena rolled over on to her other side, trying to find comfort, trying to find sleep. Both proved equally elusive. Stephen would be playing his own game for certain. She did not allow herself the luxury of imagining that he believed her drowned in the sinking of the *Bonnie Lass*. She could only be thankful that she had lied about her identity at Seamill Hall, especially given that Mr Weir might well speak to the constable again and Stephen was not unknown to that official. She prayed for the protection of Mrs Weir and her husband. She hoped that Stephen would not find them—for all their sakes.

She thought of Lord Varington's handsome face; thought, too, of the sincerity in his offer of help. But he did not know who she was. And she would warrant that his offer would change to something else altogether were he to discover that truth. The thought did not shock her. For the first time she considered exactly what being under the protection of Lord Varington might be like. It did not seem such a bad prospect. Her face grew hot at the idea. She thrust it away, ashamed of where her thoughts had led, mortified by what Stephen had made her. Even if by some slim chance she managed to escape him, she could never escape that… Stephen had ruined her for ever. And he had said that he would keep her for ever. She knew what he would do to anyone who tried to help her.

For the first time she realised that by accepting Lord Varington's offer of transport to London she might have actually endangered him. It was one thing to risk herself, quite another to involve the lives of others. The wrecking of the *Bonnie Lass* had taught her well. Agnes and Old Tam were dead. It was Helena's fault. And that was something she would have to live with for the rest of her life. She would not risk having another's life on her conscience. The sooner they reached London, the better. London: a big place, a busy place, somewhere into which she could disappear unnoticed. Helena's eyes stung raw in the darkness, but she did not allow herself the indulgence of tears. Such weakness would not help her, not when safety was still so far away. She closed her eyes and willed sleep to come. Sleep refused her call. Thoughts of Guy, Lord Varington came in its stead.

The journey the next day began slowly. Guy had instructed his coachman well. Instead of flying at breakneck speed, the coach was moving at an almost leisurely pace.

'My lord, we seem to be travelling a great deal more slowly than yesterday.' There was just the faintest hint of worry about her eyes. Yes, indeed. Helena hid her feelings well...but not quite well enough.

A smile played about his lips. 'A more considerate pace for a lady, I think you will agree.'

'You did not think so yesterday,' she pointed out.

'Yesterday I was attempting to reach Catterick.'

'But we did not make it.'

'No, we did not,' he agreed. One corner of his mouth curled up in a most suggestive manner.

'And where must we reach tonight, my lord?'

He turned the full weight of his gaze upon her and allowed a small pause before saying softly. 'That remains to be seen, Mrs McLelland.' He saw her comprehension before she abruptly turned her face to stare out of the window.

There was nothing save the rhythmic thud of hooves and the noisy rumble of the carriage wheels.

'I would prefer that we travel faster, my lord.' The words were spoken quietly and she did not take her eyes from the passing scene to look at him.

'You enjoy being shaken around a speeding carriage?' He gave a little laugh of disbelief.

'No.' She was no longer looking at the passing countryside. Rather her eyes moved round to find his. 'But I am eager to reach London.'

'To minimise the time you must spend in my company?'

'No.' Surprise washed over her face, then was gone as quickly as it had come. 'I wish to see my aunt, that is all.'

'In Hendon?'

'Yes, in Hendon,' she agreed, and dropped her gaze to examine the carriage floor.

Guy smiled. 'Tell me about this aunt of yours. Hendon is a small place and perhaps your aunt is not unknown to my friend.'

There was nothing in Helena's expression that gave her away. She made no telling movement, no sign that his request was not perfectly reasonable. Indeed, it was by her very stillness that Guy knew that he had caught her on the back foot. Like a swan, Helena was all tranquil and serene; underneath the surface told quite a different tale. Quite deliberately he sat back and waited, interested to hear what story she would tell. One lie would beget another, and each of those would spawn another two. Before she knew it, the lies would overtake her...unless she was a very accomplished liar. And for all his cynicism there was a part of Guy that hoped it was not so.

Eventually, after too long a silence, she found her voice. 'My aunt is an elderly spinster, quiet and unassuming, with little financial wealth. It is most unlikely that she would have come to your friend's attention. You are very polite, my lord, but I'm sure that my relatives are of no real interest to you.' She gave a small stiff smile that did not touch her eyes. 'Shall we not speak of London instead? I have never been there. Indeed, I have never left Scotland before yesterday.' Another forced smile before she continued with her chatter. 'Mrs Weir told me that you live in London all year round. You must know it very well, sir. Perhaps you could tell me something of the place. I would be delighted to hear it.'

'As I would be delighted to tell it. But you do me a disservice by doubting my sincerity. I assure you that I am almost as interested in your aunt as I am in you.' His eyes never left her for a minute. 'Pray tell me of your aunt.'

The green eyes met his. He could sense the tension in her.

'There is very little to tell,' she said.

'You could start with her name.'

Another pause.

'Miss Morgan...Miss Jane Morgan.' The knuckle of her forefinger touched against her lips.

'Miss Jane Morgan—an elderly spinster, quiet and unassuming, with little financial wealth,' he said in a parody of what she had already told him.

'Yes.' Her hand dropped from her mouth and she no longer looked at him.

'Then I look forward to meeting her.'

Her startled gaze swung round to his. 'What do you mean, my lord?'

'The next time I am in Hendon I will visit both you and your aunt.' He adopted an expression of bland innocence. 'What else did you think that I meant, Mrs McLelland?' he asked in feigned puzzlement.

'Why, nothing at all, sir.' But her cheeks were tinted peach, and he could see the uneasy air that hung about her.

'I must remember to take a note of your aunt's precise direction once we reach London.' Then he looked at her. 'You would not forbid my visit, ma'am?'

'No,' she uttered weakly, 'I would not forbid your visit.'

'Glad to hear it, Mrs McLelland.' He settled back against the squabs, stretched out his legs and smiled. 'Don't mind if I catch up on a bit of shut-eye, do you?'

She gave a faint shake of her head. 'Please go ahead, my lord.'

Another smile before he closed his eyes, confident that he had just launched a successful assault on the façade that was Mary McLelland.

'Will you take some refreshments, Sir Stephen?' enquired Annabel of the man sitting within their drawing room as if he owned the place.

Sir Stephen Tayburn turned to look at her, and it was all Annabel could do not to quail. 'No, thank you, Mrs Weir. I have not the time for such frivolities.' He spoke slowly, enunciating each word with meticulous care. His gaze lingered on her a moment longer before he turned his attentions to her husband, who was sitting closest to him. 'I understand you have a lady staying here at Seamill Hall.'

The look upon John Weir's face was not one of friendship. He knew of Tayburn and did not care for him. 'May I enquire of your interest in our house guests, sir?'

Tayburn's dark gaze met the younger man's. 'I believe that the lady may be a friend of mine.'

'Your friend?' Annabel's face flushed crimson. 'Oh, no, sir, I fear you are mistaken. The lady we found upon the shore was a poor widow by the name of Mary McLelland.'

'Indeed?' queried Tayburn and arched a black eyebrow. 'Pray be so kind, Mrs Weir, as to furnish me with a description of this poor widow.'

'Oh, she is of average height, with long red hair, and…green eyes, yes, I do believe that Mary's eyes are green.'

'Annabel, let me deal with this,' said her husband with a frown.

Annabel's mouth trembled into a moue.

Tayburn smiled and it was a terrible sight to behold. 'And you said that you found this *poor widow* washed upon the shore?' He stressed the words *poor widow* with particular malice.

'Well, not *us* precisely,' said Annabel in defiance of her husband. 'It was Guy.'

'Annabel!' said Weir with irritation.

'Guy?' The name sounded sinister upon Tayburn's lips.

'I contacted the constable directly that the woman was found and there have been no reports of a missing female in the past days,' said Mr Weir.

'My friend left to visit her cousin last week, on the night of the storm. I had no reason to think that she had not arrived safely until a letter arrived from her cousin this morning enquiring as to her whereabouts.' Tayburn held Weir's gaze directly. 'Upon hearing the news I acted immediately and made the appropriate investigations. They, sir, have led me here. I need not tell you that the description of the woman that you found matches that of my friend.'

'Except that the lady goes by the name of Mrs McLelland, and is a respectable widow,' said Weir.

Tayburn's upper lip curled with undisguised contempt. 'Perhaps. But then again my poor friend may have been rendered unconscious by her accident; such a state in women may result in subsequent confusion of the mind. Was this "Mrs McLelland" perhaps unconscious when she was found?' he asked nonchalantly.

Weir could say nothing other than the truth, even though it was dragged quite grudgingly from his lips. 'She was, sir.'

'Ah,' said Tayburn with a degree of satisfaction. 'Then you will not object to my meeting the "lady" in question.' It was a statement rather than an enquiry.

'I'm afraid that is not possible, my lord.' Weir took his place before the fireplace, standing with legs astride, hands behind his back, every inch the master of Seamill Hall.

Tayburn got slowly to his feet and walked over to stand directly before Weir, closing the distance between them until he was too close. 'And why might that be, Mr Weir?' he said in a deathly quiet voice.

Tension crackled between the two men.

Weir swallowed convulsively, but stood his ground. 'Because, sir, Mrs McLelland is no longer here.'

Tayburn's eyes narrowed until they were nothing more than black slits in the sallowness of his face.

'She has gone to stay with her aunt.'

'Indeed? And where is Mrs McLelland's aunt to be found, sir?' The *sir* was a hiss at the end of his sentence.

'I do not know.'

Tayburn stepped closer, forcing Weir to step back towards the fire. 'Come now, Mr Weir, put your mind to the task.'

'I think you should leave my house, Sir Stephen.'

'And I think you should damn well tell me the truth. I'm going nowhere until I know where the hell she's gone.' Another step closer to John Weir.

Weir was looking straight into the empty blackness of Tayburn's eyes and he knew that the stories he had heard concerning this man had all been true. And yet if he told the truth then he knew that Tayburn would go after Guy. 'I believe she said that her aunt lives in Northumberland,' he said.

Tayburn laughed and Weir paled at the sound of it. 'Try again, Mr Weir. The truth this time, if you please.' One more step and Weir was backed against the mantel, and there was the smell of scorched wool. Weir formed a fist and made to punch Tayburn, but not fast enough. Tayburn had the muzzle of a pistol pressed to the coat lapel that covered Weir's heart.

'No!' cried Annabel from the other side of the room. 'Leave him alone!'

'Tell me what I wish to know if you do not want your wife to become a widow by the end of this day,' said Tayburn. 'I'm very good at comforting widows and orphaned children...' he cocked the trigger '...especially pretty little blond ones.'

'Mary McLelland left here yesterday, travelling to Hendon near London,' said Weir from between gritted teeth.

'Better.' Tayburn smiled. 'Now, tell me the rest.'

'There's nothing more to tell.'

Tayburn gave a sigh and tightened his finger on the trigger.

Annabel shouted, 'He's telling the truth. Mary left for London with Guy. We can tell you nothing else.'

Tayburn relaxed the gun and moved back.

Weir heaved a sigh of relief.

It did not last long, for Tayburn moved swiftly towards Annabel. 'And who exactly is this "Guy"?'

Annabel's blue eyes opened wide with fear. 'L-Lord Varington,' she said, shrinking away from him.

'Varington offered to take Mrs McLelland in his carriage as he was travelling back down to London.' Weir manoeuvred himself to stand between his wife and Tayburn.

Tayburn's lips pressed narrow and hard. 'Varington... Varington...' he whispered softly, as if to himself, then suddenly snapped the question, 'Tregellas's brother?'

'Tregellas's brother,' confirmed Weir, hoping that association would be enough to deter Tayburn.

One side of Tayburn's lips snarled back, revealing rather discoloured teeth. 'So she's with Varington, is she, eh? Then I had best fetch my dear Helena back.'

Tayburn threw Annabel a chilling smile. 'Goodbye, Mrs Weir,' then swiveled his gaze to her husband. 'Mr Weir. If I find you have withheld anything of the truth, I shall be sure to call upon you both again.' His eyes bored into those of John Weir. 'Such a charming little creature, your wife. Evil days are upon us, Mr Weir. Have a care that nothing of misfortune befalls her.' And with that he was gone, as quickly as he had arrived, leaving Annabel and Weir alone in the drawing room of Seamill Hall.

Chapter Six

Lord Varington was sleeping peacefully.

Helena was sitting rigidly staring out of the window.

His face was relaxed in repose, with nothing of the usual rakish sophistication and everything of a boyish innocence.

Her eyes were focused on the passing countryside, the huge rolling hills and deep carved valleys of northern England, majestic, awe inspiring, but Helena saw none of it.

The Viscount moved in his sleep, instinctively adjusting his weight on the seat, shifting his legs closer to Helena. His movement distracted her from the dismal route down which her thoughts were racing. She unwound her hands that were clinging so firmly together, placed them on the seat on either side of her, and looked at him, really looked at him. She examined every plane, every angle of his face, the fall of the dark hair across the pale forehead, the straight dark brows that swept low across his eyes, the strength of his nose, the sensual lips that, even in sleep, had just the faintest suggestion of a smile about them. It was a most appealing face, Helena decided, a face upon which the character of the man that bore it was indelibly stamped. Strong and sensual, but with a vulnerability that was hidden in his waking.

She found that she was staring at his lips. His was a mouth made for kissing, and Helena did not doubt that it would not want for practice. Just his touch upon her fingers had been enough to stroke a quiver of desire within her. She wondered what it would be like to feel his mouth on her own. Despite the coldness of the carriage, she felt a heat rise in her cheeks and jerked her gaze away. She was fleeing Stephen, for goodness' sake, not looking for some other man who would call himself her protector and give her nothing of protection! Taking a deep breath, she resolved to push such thoughts from her mind.

She was just concentrating on not looking at Lord Varington when it happened.

There was a noise like the splitting of wood, followed fast by an almighty thud forceful enough to shake Helena to the bone. The carriage collapsed violently on one side, but did not stop. She grabbed for the securing strap, held tight, felt the scrape of the carriage's body against the road. It happened so fast there was no time to scream, no time to cry out, or protest; so fast and yet in that moment time seemed to slow. The carriage was still moving, not forwards but somewhere to the side. Horses whinnied, the coachman bellowed and Helena could hear the terror in both the cries of man and beast. And then there was a scream and the world turned upside down and she had the sensation that the whole carriage was falling, dropping weightlessly through the air. *Lord Varington*! She tried to speak, to shout, to cry, but she could not find her voice. And amidst all of the chaos her mind was calm and quiet, thinking in such an everyday way, *We're going to die*. She knew it in that small flash of time that encompassed her lifetime, knew it with an absolute certainty. It was as if she was standing outside all of the frenzy, watching dispassionately, uninvolved, accepting. And she wanted to laugh at the absurdity of it.

Her arm felt as if it was being wrenched from its socket and she knew that she could not hold on much longer, and even as she thought it she felt the leather of the securing strap begin to slip through her fingers. She hung there, like a haunch of meat suspended from its hook, the securing strap and her failing arm above her head, the other arm useless by her side. Her back was against what had been the roof of the carriage. She could see the fine needlework on the leather of the carriage seat, the intricate even little stitches, the pile of the dark brown cushions. She tried to grab the strap with her other hand, but it was no use. Time stretched and elongated: the man's shouts, the horse's screams, the carriage falling, the slide of the leather within her fingers…and then all noise ceased and she was holding her breath, waiting. The almighty thud when it came sounded as if a whole woodland had been shattered into tiny twigs. It was a roar, an explosion. The carriage hit solid ground and came to a halt. Helena's body flicked like a whip from the force of it and she was flung downwards. A silent scream. An involuntary closing of her eyes. Arms flailing wide.

'Mrs McLelland!' Helena heard someone shout a name before she landed hard, her legs buckling beneath her, her body collapsing. She lay there stunned and still at last amidst the quietness of the wind and creaking timber. A tiny window of peace, in which there was no movement, no sound, just the silence of the moment. And then the horses were shrieking again, and the man was yelling again, and she felt the slight shift of the carriage body beneath her.

'Mrs McLelland,' he said more loudly, and this time she realised that it was Lord Varington, and that she was the Mrs McLelland to whom he was speaking.

She opened her eyes to find most of her view obscured by the remnants of the grey bonnet that had bent and twisted around her face during her fall. For all that she could not see, she could feel that she was lying curled on her side, her legs drawn up, her weight lying on top of her left arm. Beneath the fingers of her right hand she could feel the jagged timber carcass of the carriage, the dampness of soil and the coarse spring of grass. There was a pressure on her left shoulder and her head was resting on top of something solid and warm and alive. Lord Varington. She struggled to move, to sit up.

Lord Varington's voice sounded close by. 'Do not move, Mrs McLelland. Stay exactly as you are. Any sudden movement may risk tipping the carriage more.' His fingers touched firm against hers. 'Are you hurt?'

In truth Helena did not know. 'I do not think so.' Nothing throbbed in pain. In fact, she felt numb all over, numb and shocked and relieved all at the same time.

'Thank God,' he said, and there was a definite relief in his voice.

'We're alive,' she said, scarcely believing it. 'What happened?'

'Sounded like we lost a wheel and have come off the road.'

The horses began to shriek and the carriage creaked and began to move again.

'Lord help us,' she whispered, and she felt Lord Varington's hand close around hers. The shrieks turned to screams, terrifying, gut-wrenching screams that made the hairs on her head stand on end, and then the screams faded into the distance and there was only silence. There was no more movement of the carriage.

'M'lord, m'lord! Are you alive in there?' the coachman shouted from outside.

'I believe that we are, Smith.'

'Don't move, m'lord. Please, dear God, don't you or the lady move.'

Helena could hear the fear in the coachman's voice.

'Where are we, Smith?'

'Gone over the edge of the road, down a sheer drop towards a valley, m'lord, couldn't stop the team, I could see it was going to happen and I still couldn't stop them. Horses just went mad with fear. Panicked. I thought we were gonners.'

'Where has the carriage come to rest?'

The coachman's voice was hoarse. 'On a ledge, a ruddy great ledge, about ten feet down from the road. Horses damn near pulled us off it again. Had to cut them free, m'lord, all of them are lost.'

'You did what you had to, Smith, and for that I'm grateful. Can you open the uppermost door?'

There was a pause before the coachman replied. 'M'lord, the carriage is balanced right on the edge. I fear my weight upon her will send her over.'

Helena felt the sinking in her stomach. There was

no way out. They were trapped on the edge of a pre-cipice and the only direction that the carriage would be taking was down.

She felt the slight squeeze of Lord Varington's fingers around hers, and still, she could see nothing because of the crush of her bonnet over her eyes.

'Is there anything around us that could be used as an anchor, Smith?' Lord Varington spoke loudly, but did not shout.

A silence that seemed too long, while the coachman looked around.

'Aye, m'lord, there's a tree growing where the ledge meets the hillside. Only a small tree, mind, not strong enough to take the weight of the carriage.'

'It doesn't need to,' replied Lord Varington. 'Fetch a rope, Smith, and secure one end around the tree. Tell me when you've done that.'

'Aye, m'lord.'

There was the sound of Smith moving about outside.

'Lord Varington.' She could feel the strong steady beat of his heart against her cheek and knew that her head must be lying against his chest. And then his fingers were beneath her chin, unfastening the ribbons of her bonnet, one hand carefully prising the remain-der of the bonnet from her head, until at last Helena could see the true nature of their predicament. The carriage was on its side with Helena lying curled across the remnants of the door. Her head was on Lord Varington's chest, his left arm was pinned in place by her left shoulder. Lord Varington lay where he had landed, his head positioned close to the edge of the carriage's shattered window. But Helena was not looking at Lord Varington. Instead she stared at the view through the hole that had housed the glass of the window.

'Mrs McLelland,' he said, drawing her focus to himself.

She turned her gaze up to his.

His face was so pale as to be powder white, which seemed only to exaggerate the darkness of his hair and the deep crimson of the blood splattered and smeared upon his forehead, cheek and chin, and the stark pale clarity of his eyes.

'You're hurt,' she whispered, feeling the fear grip tight in her stomach.

'A scratch,' he said. 'Do not let the blood fool you.'

But Helena knew that what marked Lord Varington's face came from no scratch. 'What are we going to do?'

'Hire another carriage. This one seems to have seen better days.' He smiled a mischievous sort of smile.

How could he joke at a time like this? Perhaps he didn't realise. She let her gaze drift once more to what lay beyond Lord Varington's head, to the view from the gap where the window had been. The bottom section of it, the section closest to where Helena and Lord Varington lay, was filled with the firm solidness of ground, scrubby grass on damp brown soil. But halfway up the ground stopped, and beyond was only the sheer drop into the valley below. The grass way down there looked very green, lush almost for the time of year. And she could see the small white dabs of sheep and the rich chestnut of the broken horses mixed with the red of their blood. She knew then what the screaming had been, she knew too why it was now so silent. And she felt sick.

'Do not look at it.'

At the edges of her vision the cold draught of the wind fluttered Lord Varington's hair. 'We're going to die, aren't we?'

'Look at me,' he said.

But it seemed that she could not draw her eyes away from the view below.

'Helena.'

She looked at him then.

'I will get us out of here. Trust me.'

Trust, the one thing Helena could not give.

'Trust me,' he said again.

Their eyes locked together and it seemed that she could look into his very soul and see his honesty. Her ears were filled with the steady reassuring beat of his heart. And Helena trusted him.

She gave the smallest of nods, feeling the brush of the superfine of his coat against her cheek.

'My lord, it is done,' Smith shouted.

'Very well.' Lord Varington did not take his gaze from Helena's face. Then spoke for Helena's ears only. 'We can escape this.'

Escape—everything came back down to that. 'Or die in the trying,' she said, and heard the huskiness in her own voice.

'My lord?' shouted Smith again.

'Stay back, Smith, until the door opens, then throw the rope as quick as you can. Mrs McLelland shall climb out first. See to her safety.'

'Yes, m'lord,' said the coachman.

His hand released hers, moved to touch gently against her cheek. 'Stand up as slowly and as easily as you can, keeping your weight back towards the side furthest from the drop. No sudden movements. Just slow and easy.'

'If I climb out first, will not that cause the carriage to tip?'

'Not necessarily.'

'But it is a possibility, is it not?'

'Yes…' he smiled '…it is a possibility.'

Helena was not fooled by the lightness of his manner. She knew that Lord Varington was offering her her life at the expense of his own. Her flight from Stephen had already cost two innocent lives. Helena could not let there be another. 'I think it would be better if you were to climb out first, my lord.'

He smiled again. 'I have escaped from worse situations than this. Much as I am touched by your concern,' he said in a teasing tone, 'you need not worry about me.' His thumb touched gently to her cheek. 'Climb out of the carriage and I will follow you.'

A small silence.

'I will not leave you to die,' she said with determination in her words. 'You must climb out first.'

'Really?' he drawled, and she saw the sudden smoulder in his eyes and the sensual tilt of his mouth. 'I did not know you had such a care for my welfare, ma'am.'

She just looked at him.

His smile deepened. 'I understand perfectly, dear lady. You are too shy to admit the truth of your feelings towards me. Come, now, there is none to witness our speech or our actions, Mrs McLelland, or may I call you Helena?'

She stared at him in disbelief. 'No, you may not,' she snapped. 'Have you forgotten our circumstance? That we are within a carriage in imminent danger of tipping over a precipice?'

'Why let a little thing like that stop us, Helena?' And his voice was mellow and teasing with sensuality.

'My name is not Helena,' she said.

'Is it not?' came the reply. 'That's a pity, for it's a name that suits you well.' His thumb slowly traced the contours of her face—'It's from the Greek, *helenos* meaning bright'—so lightly as to scarce be a touch— 'and you would brighten any of my days'—and then was gone.

'Have you run mad, Lord Varington?' Her heart was thumping in her chest. 'You cannot seriously be seeking to take advantage of our situation?'

She heard the smile in his voice. 'As if I would do such a thing.' He winked, and blew her a kiss.

It was the final straw. 'You wish me to climb out first. Very well, I shall do so, sir.' And before she could change her mind, she looked away from him and got slowly to her feet.

Varington said nothing.

She turned and reached up to the door handle, twisting it with infinitesimal care. The handle did not budge. She tried again, applying a little more pressure, but the handle remained unyielding. 'The door is stuck,' she said. 'The handle cannot be moved.' She glanced back down at him then. 'My lord...'

'Try the handle again.'

She gave a nod and turned away to work at the handle until her fingers grew red and sore, and still, the handle did not shift. A noise sounded behind her, the creaking of wood, and then Lord Varington was at her back with his hand upon the carriage handle. His exertion brought a grunt to his lips and a fresh drip of blood down his face. Helena heard the click of the lock move and the door began to open. Lord Varington stood behind her, leaning over her. He took the full weight of the door on to his hands, pushing it up first, then edging it back gently to rest upon the carriage body. He was so close she could feel his warmth, his strength, smell the now familiar scent of him. The carriage creaked again as the door rested back against it.

'The rope, Smith!'

And in response a length of rope partially still coiled appeared at the open doorway, raining down towards them. Varington caught it in his hands and fastened part of it around Helena's waist.

She felt his breath by her ear. 'I shall lift you up through the doorway. Climb down the carriage body and jump clear of it as soon as you are able. Smith will help you.' Not one trace remained of his teasing flirtation. His voice was steady and serious. Realisation slipped into place. 'Lord Varington.' She turned her face to the side so that she might at least see him as he stood behind her. 'You were not intent on seducing me at all, only on making me leave the carriage first.' She saw his smile.

'Are you disappointed?'

Helena gave a half smile, half laugh, knowing full well the brink on which they stood. She twisted her head further round that she might look the better at him. 'Thank you for all that you have done for me...for all you are doing. Thank you,' she said again softly.

Only the soft hush of their breath sounded. Blue eyes held green. He lowered his face towards hers, and laid his lips against the edge of her eyebrow. It was a chaste kiss, a gentle kiss, a kiss that acknowledged her gratitude and more. And then his lips were gone, and she knew it was time. She felt the press of his hands just above her hips and then he was lifting her up and through the doorway. She half-fell on to the carriage body, hearing it grunt and creak beneath her weight, slid down it, jumped away from the wheels. Then the coachman was there, grabbing her arms, pulling her to safety, untying the rope and throwing it back down to the carriage. And behind her sounded the scrape of wood, the rip of leather and the crunch of glass.

'No!' The cry tore from her throat and she struggled to her feet, pushing away the coachman's arms, turning back towards the wreckage of the carriage. But where the carriage had stood there was nothing save for the crushed, torn grass and the rope that stretched across it.

'No!' she shouted, and stared at where the carriage had been. From far below came the crash and splintering of wood, the carriage being torn apart on impact. She had seen the horses. She did not want to see the carriage…or what remained of Lord Varington. She stood there, frozen in her disbelief. The horror was too enormous to comprehend. 'Varington!' and her whisper was stolen by the wind and carried away.

'Mrs McLelland.' She barely heard the coachman's words. 'Look, ma'am, look!' Smith was running towards the scarred edge from where the coach had slipped. And she did not know why… until she saw a hand appear, a bloody hand gripping at the rope, and she saw what she had not seen before—that the rope was taut and moving in tiny jerks, as if it supported a man's weight, as if someone were climbing up it. And then Smith was pulling him up, grabbing hold of him to heave him back up on to the ledge.

Lord Varington sat for a minute catching his breath in the grey drizzle of rain. Mud caked his riding boots and smeared the front of his clothing. The pale buff of his pantaloons was unrecognisable beneath the blood and filth, and his coat was torn and stained. His head was bent low and his dark hair fluttered in the wind.

She walked towards him, hardly knowing that she moved. 'Lord Varington.' She heard the relief in her own voice. 'I thought...' Her eyes flickered to the edge of the ledge, then back to his face. She dropped to her knees, unmindful of the mud and broken glass. She did not know how she came to be in his arms, his hands warm around her, pulling her into him, holding her close.

'We're safe now, Helena.'

And she clung to him.

The tremble started in her ankles and spread up through her legs, into her stomach, her chest and even her throat, until everything was quivering. Helena strove to hide the signs of weakness, yet the tremble grew. She made to pull away so that he would not know that she was shaking, but the strong arms just held her tighter. Her mouth opened to forge an excuse. The excuse did not come. There were no calm words of politeness, no ladylike poise. The façade that Helena had carefully sculpted during the years with Stephen crumbled. A sob sounded. Just a single sob. But that one sob led to another, and another, until, to her extreme mortification, Helena realised that she was crying. Crying for how close Lord Varington had come to death. Crying for Agnes and for Old Tam. Crying for everything she had lost through the years. And all the while the rain drizzled down around them.

'Hush,' he soothed. 'I have you. You're safe.' He cradled her against him and there was nothing of the rakish sensuality in the softness of his voice or the gentleness of his hands. 'You're safe,' he whispered again and again, until at last the tears and the trembling had stopped, and all that was left was the shudder in her throat.

She laid her cheek against his chest and let herself feel what it was like to be held by a good man. For the first time in many years Helena was truly safe. She relaxed against him, feeling the hardness of his body, smelling the clean scent of his cologne, absorbing his warmth. Something in her heart blossomed. For all of his flirtatious behaviour, this was a man who had saved her life upon the shore, a man who had changed his plans to take her to London rather than see her travel alone by stage, a man who had almost died to free her from the wreckage of a carriage. And what had she given him in return? Dishonesty. Distrust. Suspicion. She crooked her neck, looked up into his face, seeing again the bloody gash down the side of his face. 'You're hurt. We must seek help.'

'It is a scratch. But you are right, we must seek help. We have the climb back up to the road to negotiate.' He glanced up. The rain was falling in earnest now and, although it was still early in the day, the skies were dark and foreboding.

Lord Varington coiled the rope around his waist and made the climb up to the road. The grass was slippery from being wet and there was little purchase for his feet. Helena watched, the breath catching in her throat with every slip of his foot, until he disappeared over the top and on to the road. From there he secured the rope and threw the end down to Smith. The coachman fastened a length around Helena's waist and she half clambered, was half hoisted up to the road, where she untied the rope and cast it back down to Smith. The coachman was just scrabbling clear of the valley when the distant rumble of a coach sounded. It rounded the corner, its pace somewhat cautious in view of the weather, and slowed even before Lord Varington flagged it down.

Helena and Lord Varington stood side by side waiting for the carriage to halt.

'There is something I need to tell you, my lord,' she said. Her heart was beating too fast. *Truthfulness comes at a price*, the little voice inside her head was whispering. It was madness to tell him, and yet she knew that she had to. It was the least that he deserved.

'I know,' he said.

'I do not think that you do,' she said quietly, knowing full well that once he knew the truth everything would be changed. 'I've lied to you from the start.'

One corner of his mouth curved up in a wry smile. 'Not quite from the start,' he said. The coach came to a stop and the window dropped open, and Lord Varington stepped forward to speak to the man whose face appeared there. Then the door was opening and the steps being put into place.

Helena sat beside Lord Varington opposite the gentleman traveller. Outside, Smith climbed up to sit beside the coachman. And the coach trundled off down the road towards Appleby, through the mud and the heavy teeming rain. The truth would have to wait...for now.

Chapter Seven

Helena stood in the small bedchamber of the inn, naked save for the sheet wrapped around her. Her shift and stays were draped over both the chair and the fireguard that she had positioned a little way from the fire that burned in the grate. The flames leapt high and golden, throwing out a heat that was too hot against the linen wrapped around her, yet still she made no move to shift away. She was sitting too close to the hearth, trying to dry the wetness of her hair. It hung heavy and damp over her bare shoulders, drying slowly into wild curls and waves. The fire scalded her skin pink, yet it did nothing to chase the chill that she had felt since the carriage crash. She closed her eyes, leaned her head back the better to dry the top of her hair and tried not to think at all.

A soft knock sounded at the door. 'Mrs McLelland.'

She jumped at the sound of Lord Varington's voice, scrambling to her feet, heart suddenly pounding.

'I am not dressed, sir,' she said with what she hoped sounded to be a reasonable and calm voice.

'You tempt me to abandon what I am here for.' She could hear his smile. 'The landlady has sent some spare clothing for you to wear while she dries that which you have given her. I have it here for you.'

She had not thought that he would bring her the clothing in person. She walked over to stand by the door, speaking through the thick wooden panels. 'Thank you, my lord. If you would be so kind as to leave the clothing there, I will collect it.'

'Very well,' he said. 'When you are ready, come downstairs. There is a private parlour for our use and I have requested some hot food.'

And once they were alone in the parlour, there would be no more hiding. She would have to tell him the truth. Dread squirmed in her stomach and it seemed she could not face a confrontation with Lord Varington, not tonight. She would be stronger in the morning. Then she could tell him, not now. 'I am not hungry, just tired. I would rather retire early, my lord, if you do not mind.'

Nothing sounded through the wood. She moved closer, straining to listen. Still nothing. 'My lord?'

Finally he spoke. 'As you wish, Mrs McLelland.' His voice sounded tired. There was none of the persuasions he had used the previous night. Indeed, he did not even wait for a reply before she heard the tread of his footsteps recede along the corridor.

Part of her was relieved, part disappointed. She sighed, ensured that the sheet was tucked securely around her bosom and turned the key in the door. The door opened a few inches. The bag of clothing lay where Lord Varington had left it immediately outside the door. Her line of vision showed the corridor to be empty. Stooping, she extended an arm cautiously through the aperture. Her fingers closed tight around the handle of the bag and she pulled it towards her. Just as she opened the door wider to admit the bag, a booted foot appeared between the door and the door frame. Helena gave a gasp, released her grip on the bag and tried to slam the door.

'Allow me,' said Lord Varington, and carried the bag into the room.

'Lord Varington!' Helena exclaimed. 'What on earth do you think you're doing?'

'Carrying a lady's baggage,' came the smooth reply.

Her mouth gaped and her eyes flashed wide with shock. One hand clutched defensively across her breast, ensuring the sheeting was tucked securely, the other moved to grip the door edge. 'Please leave at once.'

He walked across the room and set the bag down on the floor by the window, giving no sign that he had heard her.

'Lord Varington.' There was anger and indignation in her voice.

'Close the door, Helena. The draught from the passageway will give you a chill.'

She stared at him as if she could not believe what he was saying.

'We have much to discuss tonight, and if you do not intend coming down to the parlour, then we had best speak of it here and now.'

'I am not dressed, my lord!'

He let his eyes rove from the perfection of her face to the glorious curtain of hair that hung heavy and still damp over the creamy white of her bare shoulders. Above the winding of the sheet he could see the rise of her breasts, and could imagine exactly what lay beneath.

The imagining caused certain obvious reactions within his body, even though it was cold and fatigued. He clamped his jaw tight and let his gaze sweep lower. The sheet ended just past her knees. Her legs were pale and shapely; her feet bare and free from linen bindings. 'I had noticed,' he murmured, and forced himself to look away. He made a show of walking over to the fireplace, stirring at the coals with the poker.

Voices sounded from the direction of the staircase: women's laughter, the thud of feet.

Helena quickly closed the door and hurried over to where he was crouched. Her voice dropped low. 'What can you be thinking of, my lord? This behaviour goes beyond the pale.'

His head ached like Hades and there was a distinct pain in his leg. Fatigue sat like lead in his muscles. Hunger gnawed at his belly. He straightened and turned to look at her. 'Now will you come down to the parlour?' he said softly. 'It has been a long day and I did not wish to waste time hovering in the passageway coaxing you to do so.'

She blinked and stared up at him with those bewitching green eyes. She looked very much as if he had just snatched the wind from her sails. 'Can we not wait until morning?'

'No.' He twitched his eyebrows and gave a rueful smile. 'You'll have changed your mind come morning, and I would like to know the real identity of the woman that I'm accompanying to London.' He moved past her, heading towards the door.

'But the carriage… We are still for London?' It was Mrs McLelland that spoke, not Helena, yet Guy could hear the subtle undertones of hope and of desperation.

He stopped and looked round at her. 'We must wait

for a hire carriage to become available, which may take a day or two. Our arrival in the city will be delayed, but, yes, we are still for London.'

It seemed that her skin paled. 'Is there nowhere else from which we can hire a carriage more immediately?'

'Unfortunately not. I tried all of the surrounding villages. There are none to be had.'

Something akin to panic passed over her face, and then it was gone. 'There must be something?'

He gave a subtle shake of his head.

Helena looked away, thought furrowing her brow. 'Then I must catch the stage…or the mail.' As if remembering he was still there, she glanced back at him. 'Are we on the mail route? If so, I could be on the next coach coming through. The landlord would know. I must ask him at once.' He could see the sudden tension that racked her body, hear the higher pitch of her voice. She knelt down by the bag of clothes, and was struggling with small frenzied actions to unfasten it with one hand, while the other still clutched the sheet to her breast.

He did not move. He did not need to. 'Would you abandon me so readily, Helena?' he asked quietly.

The question seemed to pull her up short. Her hand ceased its motion. The green eyes shot up to his. And to his surprise he could see the pain in them. 'I must,' she whispered. 'I have no choice.'

'We both know that is not true,' he said.

Her teeth caught at her lower lip, and as she bowed her head, her hand resumed its work upon the bag. 'You know nothing of my situation.' He heard the struggle within her voice. 'I thank you for everything that you've done for me, my lord, but I cannot stay here. I have to get away.'

'From whom are you running?'

A sudden sharp intake of air, and when she looked at him there was a look of terror upon her face. 'No one!' The denial was too swift, too easy.

'You said that you would tell me the truth.'

She looked away in anguish. 'Please do not ask me, not now…'

'I offered you my help, Helena, and I meant it.' He moved to stand beside her.

She stilled.

'Let me help you,' he whispered.

Slowly she rose so that they stood facing one another, with barely two feet separating them. 'You would not offer your help, sir, if you knew the truth.'

He searched her eyes, trying to fathom something of her, finding only hurt and fear and betrayed innocence. Whatever this woman had done, Guy could not imagine that it would change his offer. 'Let me be the judge of that.'

The tiniest flicker of hope. 'To help me would be to place yourself in grave danger. I cannot allow you to do that.'

'It's too late,' he said. 'I've already helped you.' He paused just long enough to let the implication sink in.

There was a hiss from the fireplace. The noise from the crowded taproom below was a faint buzz in the background. She gave a nod. 'You are right.' Her eyes closed as if gathering strength, and when they opened again he knew that she would tell him what he wanted to know.

Her voice was quiet but clear as she began. 'I beg your forgiveness, my lord, for my dishonesty. I never meant for anyone else to become involved in any of this.'

He did not speak, just let her continue in her soft lilt.

'My name is Helena McGregor. I am the eldest daughter of James McGregor of Ayr, and…' she hesitated, took in a deep breath and could not meet his eyes '…and I am the mistress of Sir Stephen Tayburn.'

Tayburn! God in heaven! A shiver rippled down Guy's spine.

'I tried to escape him. Fled with the help of my maid and my father's old servant that came with me to Dunleish. I did not dare to leave them behind for Stephen to punish for my crime. The story I told you of the boat and the storm was true, except that we sailed from the island of St Vey, not Islay.'

'That would explain why you were washed up near Portincross.'

She gave a small nod.

'Have you heard of Sir Stephen? Do you know what manner of man he is?' She looked at him then, not a shred of the mask left in place to cover her emotions. There, in place of the calm polished poise, was naked vulnerability.

'I doubt there is anyone who does not,' he said, and then wished that he had not, at the look that crossed her face. 'He keeps you at his castle? What of his wife? I thought he was married to Harris's daughter.'

'He is.' Her voice was very small. 'She lives at Dunleish too.' And again she would not meet his gaze.

'You all live together?' Guy felt his eyebrow rise of its own accord. Something turned in his stomach.

Another small nod. 'I did not want it to be that way. I did not understand the arrangement when I agreed to…'

'When you agreed to be his mistress,' he finished for

her, and could not keep the distaste from his voice. How in Hades could any woman, particularly the woman standing so defencelessly before him, agree to such a thing? Hell, the man was evil incarnate.

No reply.

'My God, what must he have offered you to tempt you to his bed? I cannot imagine that Tayburn would be a considerate lover.'

She winced at that.

And still, he could not stop himself. Knowing that she had willingly given herself to such a beast. Knowing what he knew about Tayburn. 'How long have you been with him?'

'Five years.'

'You've stayed with him for five years! Hell's teeth, Helena, are you out of your mind? Is your need for money so very great that you must sell yourself to the likes of him?'

She edged back, her face frozen and pale.

'Why?' he snapped. 'Do *you* not know the manner of the man? Do you not know of what he is capable? Or don't you care, is that it?'

She shook her head, continuing to expand the distance between them.

His hand shot out, closed around the soft flesh of her upper arm and pulled her back to him. Her skin was cool and smooth beneath his fingers. The smoky green of her eyes had darkened. The top of her head reached only to his chin. Her bare feet stood toe to toe with his riding boots. He was gripping her tightly, too tightly. It was the shock of hearing Tayburn's name. He loosened his fingers.

She made to pull away.

'No.' His voice was firm even if his grip was not. 'I'll hear the rest of it first, if you please.'

Helena gave up her resistance. He felt the resignation in the arm beneath his fingers. The scent of her tickled beneath his nose. She was so close he could have lowered his mouth to hers and taken it. She was looking at him as if he had just struck her, a look so wounded that he had to remind himself of what she had just told him. She was Tayburn's whore, for heaven's sake!

'You know the rest. You saw the wreckage of the boat. I can only assume that Agnes and Old Tam drowned.' She blinked several times and looked down to hide the moisture in her eyes. 'When I awoke to find myself in a place I did not recognise, my first thought was to run before I could be found. But then you fetched me back and…' her words faltered '…and I realised that you were not going to let me slip away unnoticed. I could not tell anyone who I really was; Mr Weir would have had me shipped back to Stephen in the blink of an eye, as would the constable. And so I became the widowed Mary McLelland. Under her guise I thought there was still a chance I could escape him.' She cast him a look that begged for understanding. 'I had to get away from Seamill Hall. If he knew where I was, then Mr and Mrs Weir would have been in danger.'

'They *are* in danger, thanks to you.' And him. It was Guy that had brought her into their home, and Guy that had laughed at Weir's feelings regarding Helena.

'I never meant for that to happen. What else could I do? I couldn't tell Mr and Mrs Weir the truth!'

'But you could let them clothe you and take their money.'

'I intend to pay them back, every penny of it.'

He shook his head, his mouth adopting a sneer. 'With what? Money from your non-existent aunt in Hendon?'

She was so pale he thought she would faint, but she didn't, she just looked up at him with those beautiful eyes. No wonder she had snared Tayburn, looking like she did. She could have snared any man in the country. Guy doubted that he had ever looked upon a more physically attractive woman. Superficial perfection. But beneath it Helena McGregor could have no heart to be mistress to such a man. That she could have given herself to that monster. Something crawled in his stomach and his blood ran cold as memories of a man not so very different from Tayburn resurfaced. The horror of those memories served only to heighten his outrage.

'No, I—'

He cut her off. 'Or maybe you were planning on selling yourself to raise the money. What is your price, Helena?'

'It wasn't like that! You don't understand!'

Guy Tregellas was a man not often moved to anger, but when the devil was unleashed in him the anger splurged hot and hard. 'You haven't answered my question. How much? Come, don't be coy. If the price is right, I may well be your next customer.'

Anger flashed in her eyes. The hand that had been clutched to her chest raised and moved to slap his face.

He caught the wrist, before her palm made contact, dragged it back down, imprisoned it with the other behind her back.

'Or maybe you find me not to your taste. After all, how can I compare to Tayburn?'

Her breath came in short sharp pants, her breasts rising and falling in fast rhythm.

'I know of men like him, Helena, of what they like to do.'

'No!' she cried out, and struggled against him.

Their bodies collided as she sought to escape.

He held her with a firm determination, ignoring the feel of her softness bumping against him, ignoring the sweet womanly smell of her.

And then the sheet moved. She must have felt the end of it loosen from where she had safely tucked it beneath her arm, for she suddenly ceased her struggle and froze. The sheet slipped lower, revealing the swell of her breasts, bathed golden in the glow from the fire.

He stared down at the tops of the pale mounds. The only thing holding the sheet in place was the fact that she was pressed so hard against him. He felt a familiar tightening in his groin, felt the burning of desire. Fatigue and hunger were forgotten. He licked his lips and let his gaze meander back up to her face.

She was staring up at him like a rabbit caught in a trap, all stunned fear and panic. 'Please, my lord...' The sob caught in her throat.

How many times had she uttered that word to Tayburn? Hell, he'd be damned if he'd take her against her will. Slowly he loosened his grip over her wrists and stepped back from her. She clutched at the sheet but not before a fleeting glimpse of the body that lay beneath it had been revealed.

There was no hiding his blatant arousal. He turned and walked from the room while he still had the self-control to do so, cursing the woman left standing within for being Tayburn's whore. Cursing himself all the worse because even that knowledge did not stop him wanting her.

The door closed with a firm click and still Helena did not move. She stood staring at the oaken panels through which Lord Varington had stridden. What other reaction had she expected? Understanding? Kindness? Compassion? She was a fool a thousand times over. She disgusted him. He loathed her. He would not help her, not now that he knew the truth. Just as she knew that no one would help her.

Silence rang in her ears. The imprint of Lord Varington's fingers burned around her wrists. At least there would be no more lies. The sheet clutched between her fingers was warm where it had been pressed against him. She remembered again the revulsion that had crossed his face on learning the truth. Her eyes shuttered as if that could dispel the image. No more pretending to be what she was not. For all the awfulness of the situation Helena found comfort in that. She was a fallen woman, a soiled woman. Nothing could change that. But she had survived all that Stephen had done to her. And she would survive the future.

When Helena's eyes opened again she knew that she would keep going, because she had to. Her travelling bag had been lost with the carriage, but at least she still had the purse that Mrs Weir had given her. The inn was on the main road to London. All she need do was wait for the next mail-coach to arrive, then take a seat to London. It was her only hope of safety. Slowly, Helena moved towards the bag of clothes sent by the landlady. Piece by piece she began to reassemble her defences around her. She had told the truth and the truth had cost dearly. The bag opened. With fumbling fingers she pulled out the clothing that she needed.

She was fully dressed and her almost-dry hair combed and pinned up into a neat chignon when the knock at the door sounded. Helena jumped and eyed the door with suspicion. 'Who is it?' She was half-expecting the deep tones of Lord Varington's voice, but a girl answered.

'It's Rose, ma'am. I work here, and I've brought your dinner.'

The smell of food wafted under the door. 'I didn't order any food.' She couldn't afford to. Helena thought of the precious money within Mrs Weir's purse and how long it would have to last.

'His lordship said as to bring you up a tray.'

There was a slight pause before Helena asked, 'Is Lord Varington there?'

'No, ma'am,' the voice said. She sounded young, little more than a girl. 'He's down in one of the parlours. It's just me.'

The key turned silently beneath Helena's fingers. Her hand hovered ready to engage the lock in an instant. Slowly she opened the door by the smallest crack and peered out.

A girl stood there, wearing a brown dress and an apron that had once been white. Her hair matched the wool of her dress and had been bundled up into the huge cap that was pinned upon her head. She looked fifteen at the most. Helena breathed a sigh of relief and opened the door wider to receive the tray.

The girl looked at her strangely, as if she wasn't sure of what to make of her. 'Shall I just set it down on the table for you, ma'am?'

Helena gave a nod. 'Thank you.'

The tray was placed on the small table close by the bed. 'Mind your fingers, ma'am. Plates are just out of the oven. Right hot they are.'

'Thank you,' Helena said again. The girl was almost through the door before she added, 'Did his lordship say anything else?'

The girl stared round at her. 'No, ma'am. Nothin.' Do you want me to take him a message?'

'No, thank you,' Helena said quickly. 'But there is something that you could find out for me, if you would be so kind. I need to know if the mail-coach stops here.'

The girl's feet padded back down the passageway. The key turned easily in the lock. The tray of food and wine beckoned. Her stomach growled. She moved the tray to her lap and sat down upon the bed.

It was only two hours later, when Helena lay down, still clothed in the landlady's dress, beneath the covers of the bed. The fire had burned low, leaving just a pile of glowing coals. The discarded emptied tray sat where she had left it, on the same small table on which it had arrived fully laden. Downstairs the carousing had diminished, but not died. Outside the night was miserable. Rain smattered against the windowpanes and wind howled. She nestled below the blankets and was glad of the shelter. Tomorrow night would see her in London. But she did not want to think about that. Not now. Not until she had to. She needed to rest, for the mail-coach passed early and it waited for no one. She sought the black comfort of sleep, but did not find it. The image of his face would give her no peace. Even with her eyes closed she could see it as if it was etched for ever upon her mind. But it was not the face of the man who had forced her into becoming his mistress that haunted her. It was another man altogether. A man that looked at her with both desire and distaste. A man whose smile had vanished with her revelation. Varington.

A slight noise sounded from her door. Helena stilled her restless turning and listened. There was a clatter as the key that she had left sitting within the lock fell suddenly to the floor. Something scraped in the lock. Helena sat bolt upright, staring at the door, alarm ringing in her head. Her throat was suddenly dry, her heart hammering in her chest. Dear God! She glanced about, eyes strained through the gloom to find something she might use as a weapon. There was nothing save the candlestick and the stub of her candle. Her fingers closed around the coldness of the metal, and she lifted it quietly to her. A creak. Then a chink of light showed as the door slowly, steadily began to open.

Stephen! The word stuck in her throat so that it seemed she could not breathe. Her hand tightened around the candlestick. Waited to see the dark promise she knew that his face would hold. The door widened. She readied herself. Tried to suppress the sudden churn of her stomach. A figure shielding a lit candle walked silently forward into her room. She shrank back, opened her mouth to scream, but none came. Stephen! The word formed upon her lips. 'Stephen!' This time his name escaped as a whisper. And it seemed that in that single word was all of her terror, all of her dread.

'Helena.' He uncovered the candle and moved towards her.

She stared all the harder, her pulse throbbing all the more. For the light of the candle had shown that his hair was not white like snow. The man who had just broken into her bedchamber was dark like a raven, and even through the sombre light of the single candle she could see that his eyes were pale.

'I'm not Tayburn. You needn't be afraid.'

'Lord Varington?' The candlestick slackened as relief coursed through her veins. 'I thought…I thought that he had found me.'

He stopped where he was, just short of the bottom of the bed. 'I didn't mean for you to think such a thing.' There was no smile on his face, but neither did it hold the distaste she had earlier witnessed. 'I would have knocked, but after what I said to you this evening I did not think that you would admit me. I apologise both for my uninvited entry now and for my earlier behaviour. I was a trifle…surprised…to hear mention of Tayburn's name.'

Her relief was rapidly evaporating. 'How did you get in? I locked the door.'

He pulled a key from his pocket and held it up to the candlelight. 'For the right price the landlord was willing to part with his spare key.'

She shivered. 'What do you want, my lord?' As if she needed to ask. What did any man want that came to a woman's bedchamber at night?

Just the slightest hesitation before he answered, 'To talk to you.'

'I would have thought you had heard enough of me to last you a lifetime.'

He ignored that. 'I hear you are planning to be away on the six o'clock mail.'

She looked at him, comprehension dawning. 'The serving girl told you.'

No reply.

'You need not concern yourself with me any more, my lord.' She spoke with quiet dignity.

'You cannot outrun him, Helena.' There was a weariness in his voice.

'I can try.' She swung her legs over the side of the bed and set the candlestick back down in its place.

'He will find Weir and Annabel eventually. It's just a matter of time before he discovers where you went and with whom.'

'Oh, God!' Her teeth found her bottom lip and bit down. 'I'm so sorry. I never meant for them or you to be involved.'

He gave a nod of his head. 'I know.'

She looked round at him at that. 'If he finds you, tell him the truth about the carriage accident and that I travelled on to London alone. Maybe then he'll just come after me.'

'You don't really believe that, do you?' He walked to the bottom of the bed and sat down on its edge. The candlelight cast shadows on his face. Beneath his eyes were smudges of fatigue.

'I pray that he will find neither of us.'

A little grunt of disbelief sounded in the room and he gave a cynical smile.

'You need not go back to London. Perhaps you could go abroad for a short while, just until things blow over.'

'I have no intention of hiding from Tayburn,' he said.

'Please,' she whispered. 'You asked me if I knew what he was capable of…' She tasted the blood from her lip. 'And I tell you I *know* him. So please, Lord Varington, if you value your life, do not let him find you. My conscience is already laden. Don't seek to weigh it any heavier.'

'Do not worry, Helena. Tayburn does not frighten me.'

'Then you're a fool or you do not know him!'

Something in his expression shifted and a cold distant look came into his eyes. 'I'm no fool, and I do not underestimate him, for I once knew a man very like him.' He spoke softly but she could hear the deadly intent in his voice. 'I'll change nothing of my life for Tayburn.'

There was no point in pursuing the matter. She could see that he would not change his mind.

As suddenly as it had come, the darkness of his mood seemed to disappear. He glanced at her. 'What were you going to do when we reached London? I take it there is no aunt in Hendon.'

She gave a little shake of her head, and felt the long plait into which she had woven her hair sway against her back. 'It would be safer if you did not know, my lord.'

He gave a noise that was half disbelief and half laugh. 'For whom?'

'Both of us.'

'You're mistaken, Helena. If you run, Tayburn will pursue until he catches you.'

'I have to at least try,' she said. 'I've come this far.'

'Have you in the least idea what it will be like for you as a woman alone and penniless in London?'

'I will find myself employment. I'm not afraid of hard work.'

'Employment?' The word dripped with cynicism. 'And the nature of this employment will be…?'

'A governess, a seamstress, a maid…I do not know precisely. Whatever position I am able to secure.'

'Even the lowliest maid of all requires a reference from her previous employers.'

She was aware of the sinking feeling in her chest. He was right, of course. She realised that she had been naïve in her expectations; that her thinking had been too concerned with escaping Stephen and not enough with what she would do if she ever found that freedom. Lord Varington's words rendered her dreams of renting a clean and pretty sunlit room, of finding genteel employment, of saving her money to buy a small dressmaking shop, seem ridiculous. She raised her chin defiantly. 'I will find a way.'

'Except that the way might not be quite what you are expecting. You wouldn't last five minutes before some scoundrel had you in his grasp, forcing his attentions upon you. London is not a nice place for an unprotected woman, Helena. There are other men like Tayburn out there, some even worse than him.' And he could not keep the bitterness from his voice at the dark memories those words triggered.

She shivered at his words, but she could not let him dissuade her. She had to keep going if she wanted to survive. 'What do you suggest that I do? Go back to him? I'd rather take my chances in London.'

'There is another way,' he said quietly.

Another way? Could there be? She looked at him.

'A way that I believe would be beneficial to us both.'

She saw the look in his eyes, knew what he was going to say even before he said it.

'A certain proposition...'

She felt the blood drain from her face, felt the tightening twist within her stomach. 'No.' The denial was so faint that she was not sure that she had uttered it aloud.

But he did not stop. 'You're a beautiful woman, Helena. You cannot be unaware of the fact that I'm attracted to you. And I do not think that you're entirely indifferent to me.'

She knew what he thought her, what the whole world thought her. She just did not want to hear it confirmed from his own lips. 'Please, do not, Lord Varington.'

'A mistress may choose her protector. If you were to come under my protection…' He raised a suggestive brow. 'I assure you it would be preferable to what awaits you in London.'

'No. I cannot. It's—'

He held up his hand. 'Just hear what I've got to say before you give me your answer. As my woman, Tayburn could not touch you. You would be safe.'

'I could never be safe. He will not just let me go, especially to another man.'

'He would have no choice in the matter. You would have whatever you wanted, *carte blanche*.'

She turned her face away, stared down at the floor. He was offering to buy her, just as Tayburn had done, only then she'd had no choice, and now…

'I will set you up in your own establishment in London and give you money to do as you wish.'

Her eyes squeezed tightly shut. He was bidding for her services.

'I would protect you from him, Helena.'

Emotion cracked raw in her breast. Her hand balled in a fist and touched firm against her mouth. She did not speak.

'You need not decide right now. Think over what I have said. At best you'll end up in a hell-hole in London under some cove. At worst, you'll run for a little while longer, giving Tayburn the thrill of the chase, before he catches you. If that's what you want, Helena, then get on that mail-coach tomorrow morning. If you decide otherwise, then we will make our arrangements accordingly.' She could feel the force of his focus even though she was not looking at him. It seemed that there was something wrapped tight around her chest that was making it difficult to breathe. Slowly, almost against her will, she turned to meet his gaze.

Her eyes traced the line of the cut that ran down the side of his face. The paleness of his eyes seemed darker within the shadows of the room, his face menacingly handsome. Their gaze held for what seemed an eternity and then he rose, causing the small flame above his hand to flicker wildly. 'Sleep well, Helena.' And with that the tall dark figure walked towards the door and was gone. The key turned in the lock and then there was silence.

Chapter Eight

The morning was as dark and cold as the night. Helena shivered as she trod quietly down the inn staircase at a quarter to six the next morning. She had not slept at all. Lord Varington's words had made sure of that. She knew that he had only spoken the truth. Knew too that Varington was everything a woman could want in a lover; that there had always been some measure of attraction between them since he had found her upon the shore near Portincross. A small voice within told her she should grab his offer with grateful hands. Was it not the solution to all her problems? But her heart balked at what that would mean: that Stephen was right—that she was nothing better than a whore. Accepting his offer would confirm it to Lord Varington, and that thought hurt more than it should have.

She asked the landlord for a cup of coffee. Counted a few of her precious coins on to the table. Sat alone in the little parlour sipping on the hot bitter brew while she contemplated what he had offered her. She did not need to weigh the pros and cons. There had only ever been one answer to his offer and she could have given him that last night. Lord Varington's view of her and her thoughts of him did not influence the matter at all. Another sip of coffee and she roused herself.

'How much do I owe you for the bedchamber and the food last night?'

The small gruff man looked at her with confusion in his eyes. 'Lord Varington will settle the account.'

'I will settle my own, sir,' she said in a quiet determined voice. 'If you would be so kind as to tell me the sum owing.'

He named a price that seemed rather exorbitant to Helena. She showed nothing of her thoughts and pressed a pile of her rapidly diminishing coins into the landlord's hand. They disappeared from sight with surprising speed, as did the landlord himself when he spotted who had just come into the room.

The cup shook between Helena's fingers.

Lord Varington did not so much as look in the landlord's direction. He moved silently towards her, gave a small bow and sat down. 'Good morning, Helena.' And not once did his eyes leave her face. He was dressed in yesterday's clothes that had been cleaned and dried and repaired.

'My lord.' She quickly placed the cup down on the table so that he would not see the tremble of her fingers.

His eyes swivelled to the landlady's bag sitting on the floor by her side, then swung back to her face.

'You've made your decision, then.'

She said nothing, knowing that there had never been any decision to make.

The silence stretched between them.

'Before you go, will you tell me what it was that Tayburn offered for you to become his mistress?'

She looked him directly in the eye. 'My father's life,' she said.

The rumble of the approaching mail-coach sounded outside.

Shock registered across his face.

A knocking at the door and the landlord's face appeared. 'Mail will be in the yard in two minutes, ma'am.'

'Thank you.' She nodded her dismissal to the man and stood, gathering the bag into her hand.

'You should have told me,' he ground out from between gritted teeth.

'You didn't ask,' she replied softly, and walked towards the door.

'Wait!' There was an urgency in his voice.

She halted in her tracks.

'Is that not all the more reason to come to me?'

She turned and looked at him. 'And confirm what Stephen has made me?' She shook her head. 'I do not think so. I am not fleeing him to run to another man.' Then her chin raised a notch. 'I will make my way in life through honest and respectable means.'

'And you believe Tayburn will sit back and let you go? Your impatience to reach London is not so that you may see the sights! You know what manner of man he is, Helena.'

'Then I must ensure that he does not find me,' she said with a great deal more confidence than she felt.

'We both know that is an impossibility.' He stood up and walked slowly towards her. 'Men like Tayburn never give up. If it takes him one week or ten years, he will find you.'

She swallowed hard and looked away.

'And what of your family? Can you be so sure that Tayburn shall not mete his revenge at your flight upon them?'

Her breath shook. She clasped fiercely at the bag. 'That is why I go to London and not Ayr. I have made no visit to them, sent no note, no message while I was at Seamill Hall. Do you not think that I long to see them? I tell you it is infinitely so, but I would not risk bringing Stephen's attention to them. My family knows nothing of my escape; indeed, there has been no contact between us since he took me away. They kept their agreement with Stephen. It is I, not they, who have angered him.'

'Do you think that matters to a man like Tayburn?'

'All of Stephen's attention will be focused upon finding me. He will not think of my family.'

'If that's what you want to think, I shall not dissuade you from the comfort that you find in that delusion.'

A whisper of dread rippled down her spine. 'There's nothing I can do to help them…save go back to him.'

'It's too late for that, Helena.'

Her eyes rose to his. 'Should I then have stayed with him for ever? Am I wrong to have sought my freedom?' The bag hung awkwardly in her hand.

His gaze was intense. 'No.'

A clatter of horses' hooves sounded coming into the yard. Men's voices shouted.

'I must go,' she said, but it seemed that she could not tear her eyes from his. She wrenched her gaze away and, before her courage deserted her, walked briskly through the inn door. His voice sounded behind her.

'Helena, I can help your family. They can be protected. I give you my word that I will not let him harm them.'

The words echoed in her head as she ran across the inn's yard towards the waiting coach. And she thought—what if Lord Varington was right, what if Stephen took his revenge on her family? There was nothing she could do to protect them, even if she returned to St Vey right now. The damage had been done, and Stephen was a vindictive man. God help them. She could not protect them, but Lord Varington could. She was halfway across the yard when she stopped.

'Make haste, miss. We can't wait!' the guard shouted, reaching his hands down for her bag. 'Throw your baggage up to me!' The coach door swung open.

Over her shoulder she saw Lord Varington standing in the door frame that led into the inn. Beneath the light of the lanterns and with the dark coat moulded around his body he looked tall and muscular. He was watching her with a peculiar expression upon his face. One that she had not seen before. And in the line of his jaw and the press of those lips, in the sculpted straight nose and the stark pale eyes with their dark dark lashes, there was not one sign of weakness. The barely healed scar running down the side of his face emphasised his ruggedness. A strong man, in every sense of the word. Strong enough to stand up to the devil himself. Strong enough to save those she loved. The guard shouted again. Inside the coach a disgruntled woman shrieked, 'It's bleedin' freezin' in here. Take your time, won't you, love!'

She addressed herself to the guard. 'My apologies, sir. I fear I have made a mistake. I cannot travel today after all.'

'Bloody women!' the guard snorted, and slammed the door. Then the horses were clattering back out of the yard and the coach had gone, and with it any chance Helena had of leaving.

She did not look round, Just stood staring after the mail-coach with its lanterns and its luggage and the two men perched atop driving, until it merged into the inky blue of the morning. Until she was standing alone in the middle of the yard of the Crown Inn at three minutes past six on a November morning. And then she felt a warm presence at her shoulder and knew that it was Lord Varington. He took the bag from her frozen fingers, then gently tucked her hand into the crook of his arm.

'Come, Helena. It's cold out here. Let's go inside.'

Sir Stephen Tayburn lolled back against the bolsters and watched the grey gloom of the countryside pass by his window. His carriage rolled down the Kilmarnock road heading for Dumfries, from where he could travel to Gretna and the border that would take him into England. The team were fresh and pulling him at a brisk speed. Tayburn showed no sign of agitation; indeed, he showed no sign of any emotion at all. His face was one of calm indifference, a mask that hid the monster within. Only those that knew him would have seen the darkness in those narrow black eyes and realised the depths of his anger. He sat motionless, voiceless, expressionless, and yet within the confines of that carriage the atmosphere was heavy with suppressed rage. The woman sitting opposite him felt it, just as surely as she recognised when to hold her tongue; not that Lady Tayburn had any reason to fear her husband's wrath, not when it was so steadfastly directed against Helena. She adjusted the blanket that was draped around her legs. The movement drew Tayburn's notice.

He turned his dark gaze upon her, and even though she knew that it was not her that he would hurt, she could not help but feel afraid.

'Feeling cold, my dear?' he enquired in a voice that smacked of something other than sincerity.

'No, Stephen. I am fine, thank you.' She hid her hands beneath the blanket so that he would not see them gripping together.

The black eyes focused harder. 'Fine,' he repeated softly, and even though the words were innocent enough, slipping from Tayburn's mouth they seemed downright threatening.

Caroline Tayburn shifted uneasily in her seat.

Another silence erupted, but Tayburn kept his gaze fixed firmly on his wife, knowing full well that it made her nervous. Seconds became minutes. Minutes ticked by. He waited, and watched.

Eventually she could stand it no longer. 'Do you think that we shall catch up with them soon?'

He smiled, and even after ten years of marriage it was enough to make Caroline Tayburn blanch and look away.

'I'm not trying to catch up with them,' he said carefully, and his smile broadened.

Lady Tayburn made a show of fixing her blanket.

He struck quickly, like a serpent, snatching, then retreating. By the time he sat back, the blanket was in his hand. 'Do concentrate, Caroline. You know how much I dislike inattention.'

'Of course. Please forgive me,' she muttered and, winding her hands tightly together, stared at the carriage floor.

'I do not mean to waste my time stopping at every

damn coaching inn on the road. Why should I, when I know full well where he is taking her.'

Lady Tayburn said nothing.

'London.' He leaned forward, pronouncing the word as if she was a simpleton that would not understand it. 'I will call upon Varington when we reach London. And where Varington is, we shall find Helena. I am sure that she will be interested to hear my news of how matters in Ayrshire have developed.'

'I thought…' She let the words trail off unsaid.

'You thought what?' he sneered. 'That she was going to visit her aunt?' A short sharp laugh barked in the carriage. 'She has no aunt in London!' he spat. 'Don't you think I'd know about it if she did?'

Lady Tayburn nodded submissively. 'Of course you would.'

'Of course I would,' he repeated softly. 'Now what is her plan, I wonder?' he said as if asking the question of himself. 'Are you sure she did not speak of her intention to you?'

'S-she said nothing, nothing at all. Just as I told you before we left.' She shrank back against her seat.

'What *did* she tell you? Hmm?' He examined the nails of his left hand.

Lady Tayburn shook her head.

'I can't hear you,' he snapped.

'N-nothing.'

'Where would she go?'

'I do not know.'

'Where would you?'

It was a dangerous question, and Caroline Tayburn knew it. 'I would not leave in the first place.'

'Good. Helena would do well to learn from you, my

dear. But then again, she is so much younger and more foolish. I thought she had learned something in the years she has been with us. Evidently I overestimated her.' He smiled and it was the smile of the devil himself. 'Do you think that she will like what we have waiting for her at Dunleish?'

Lady Tayburn gave a slight shake of her ringlets.

'And if Varington has touched her...' His eyes darkened with the promise of murder. 'She belongs to me. She is mine. Mine,' he said again with conviction. 'And nobody takes what is mine, not even if he is Tregellas's brother.'

It was a full day before the hired carriage clattered into the yard of the Crown in Appleby, and only fifteen minutes later that it departed again with Lord Varington and Helena on board. Lord Varington's pace was reck-lessly hurried, especially for a carriage that had neither the quality of springs nor plush comfort of his own. Nevertheless Helena made no complaint. Indeed she was glad that she was forced to think of something else other than the presence of the man sitting opposite and what he now was to her. Protector, in name if not yet aught else. Last night he had kept to his own room and she to hers. Helena was torn between relief and disap-pointment.

'You are sure that returning to Ayrshire is the best thing to do?' Helena clung to the securing strap as she asked the question.

'Positive.'

'If you are mistaken, my lord...'

'I am not mistaken, Helena.' The corner of his mouth flickered up in that self-assured teasing manner so familiar of him. 'And you need not keep calling me "my lord". My given name is Guy.'

She blushed like some schoolroom miss. 'Guy.' His name sounded too familiar upon her tongue, reminding her of what she had promised this man in return for his protection.

His smile deepened.

As did the peachy hue upon her cheeks. 'I did not expect that we would turn around directly and head back to Scotland.'

'Neither will Tayburn.'

She hoped that he was right. 'What is your plan?'

'To ensure the transfer of your family to a place of safety.'

She watched him across the small space that divided them, confident that this man would do all that he had promised, knowing that she had made the right decision. 'Thank you, my lor…' She caught herself and then said, 'Thank you, Guy.'

'You're welcome, but it's no more than I agreed to do,' he said.

Her gaze dropped, all the more aware of exactly what her side of the agreement was.

'And we shall both rest a deal easier knowing that Tayburn cannot manipulate you through them.'

'Yes.' Such a little word to convey such a depth of emotion. Hope. Relief, A wedge of disbelief that in one fell swoop Sir Stephen Tayburn's power could be destroyed. 'It has been five long years since the nightmare started. I can scarcely believe that it will soon be over.'

'How has he held you to him all this time?'

'You evidently do not know St Vey. There is nothing on the island save Stephen's stronghold—Dunleish

Castle. It was my prison. He kept me locked in my bed-chamber for the first year. Thereafter, I was permitted access to various other specified rooms, such as the drawing room, and the dining room. Only in the last few years have I seen something of the outside, but always with a guard, never alone. There was little chance of escape, Stephen was careful of that.' She glanced away out of the window before adding, 'And I had seen only too well what befell those that crossed him.'

'Then how came you to escape at all?'

Some strong emotion flitted across her eyes before she closed them. And when she looked at him again she was quite composed. 'My father had little choice but to give me to Sir Stephen, but he sent his old servant Tam with me to Dunleish so that I might at least know one friendly face. Old Tam came to know of a man who could cut a key from a mere impression. Using the key to my bedchamber, he made just such an impression in a small slab of soap. The next I knew was a copy of the key being slipped beneath my chamber door. I stitched it into the hem of my dress and waited for an opportunity to make use of it.'

Guy slid his hand into his pocket and, producing the small silver key, held it out to her. 'It was found when your dress was being cleaned and repaired.'

'Thank you,' she said, and, taking it from him, she slipped it into the pocket of her dress.

'I take it the night of the storm was just such an opportunity.'

She nodded. 'Stephen was taken up with his guests and his celebrations for All Hallows Eve. It seemed the perfect time. We thought we would make it to the mainland before the storm started.' A pause. 'But we were wrong.'

Guy was sitting back as if the carriage seat was an easy chair in his club. He did not seem to feel the vibration from the road or the swing of the carriage as it rounded a corner.

She saw him reach across, let him take her hand. Warm fingers enclosed around hers. 'You're safe now, Helena. Tayburn will never hurt you again.'

'I can only pray that you are right.'

They stayed overnight in Gretna Hall coaching inn in Gretna Green. And Helena slept comfortably, soundly...and alone. She wondered when he would claim what she had agreed to give. The fact that he had not, only confirmed how different he was to Stephen, as if there could ever be a similarity between the two. Through the journey, rushed though it was, there was ample time for conversation, which was an art that Lord Varington conducted with ease. Helena, so used to guarding her words and suppressing any facial expression that might reveal her true feelings, found it wonderfully liberating. Just as matters had been before Stephen came into her life. She listened while Lord Varington told her of London, smiled at his stories of the intrigues of the grand ladies and gentlemen of the *haut ton*, and even gave a chuckle when he progressed on to the Prince Regent and the poor man's strange foibles. It seemed that Lord Varington did not take life too seriously. At no point did he make mention of their arrangement. If anything, he was less flirtatious in his behaviour than he had been prior to her revelation. Rather, he wanted to know her views on fashion, hunting, gardening, everything and anything—even politics. For the first time in years Helena voiced an opinion. Hesitantly at first, but then gaining in confidence with each hour that passed.

On the afternoon of the second day, she found herself telling him a silly tale from her childhood and could only wonder that the man sitting opposite her could so easily make her forget all that had passed in the last five years. Daylight was fading fast, but that made no difference to Helena. She could still see him. Indeed she did not need to look at him at all to be able to see every detail, for his image was etched upon her memory. That lazy sensual smile was never far from his face and his eyes crinkled when he laughed, which if the past two days' journey was anything to go by, was often. She had to conclude that Guy, Lord Varington, was indeed an extremely handsome man.

Chapter Nine

Sir Stephen Tayburn watched while the small plump serving woman placed the plate of roast beef next to the dish of potatoes on the table in the parlour. Sounds of the inn's other customers filtered through the half-open door from the public room. He picked up his knife and prodded at the meat. 'It's burnt. Take it away, and bring me another.'

The woman looked at the moist tenderness of the joint of beef and opened her mouth to disagree. One look at Tayburn's face was enough to have her hastily close it again and remove the plate with speed back to the George's kitchens.

Lady Tayburn sat at the opposite side of the table. She made the mistake of glancing in her husband's direction.

'What the hell do you think you're looking at?' he said softly.

Caroline Tayburn averted her face and murmured, 'Forgive me, Stephen, I had forgotten how overset you are by Helena's disappearance.'

'Overset?' The word almost spat from his tongue. 'I do not think so, dear wife. That would imply I have some kind of care for the woman. She is a possession, nothing more. She is pretty to look at and pleasant to use. But perhaps you are glad that she has gone. Perhaps you are jealous of the time I spend with her.'

Lady Tayburn gave no response.

It did not stop her husband from continuing. 'I had forgotten the pleasures of sharing your bed, Caroline. Last night was...' he paused '...almost enjoyable.'

Unable to help herself, Lady Tayburn shivered.

It was enough to bring a malevolent smile to her husband's face. 'Is that the real reason you tried to dissuade me from our trip? All your talk of bad weather and poor roads was nothing more than an excuse. You do not wish me to fetch Helena back to Dunleish because you wish me to lavish my attentions solely upon you.'

'No!' the lady gasped, then recovered some semblance of control over her emotions. 'No, indeed, you are mistaken. I hold Helena's company in high esteem.'

This time he barked a laugh. 'Do you, indeed?' And the smile on his face could have stripped rust from a paling.

'How magnanimous of you to say so, my sweet.' The acidic curve to his mouth intensified. 'Especially when you know full well that her presence stops me from visiting your bed every night.'

Lady Tayburn kept her focus firmly fixed upon the tablecloth.

'Take consolation in the fact that the longer it takes to retrieve Helena, the more time we may spend together.' He reached across the table and, with one finger beneath her chin, tilted her face up so that she had no choice but to look at him. 'Indeed, I begin to wonder if we should take the journey a trifle more leisurely so that we may better enjoy each other's company.'

The woman's face washed white.

'Perhaps I should leave the trollop to Varington and content myself with you…dear Caroline.'

Caroline Tayburn looked positively ill.

Tayburn cocked his head to the side and watched his wife. 'But then again, it would be remiss of me to abandon her, would you not say? In the meantime I shall not allow myself to fret. Until Helena is safely back within my fold, I'll take solace in *your* company, Caroline, every day…and every night.'

He let his hand drop and the sly smile upon his face revealed two yellowed incisors.

Where his finger had touched against Caroline Tayburn's delicate skin beneath her chin was the beginnings of a bruise.

It had been late afternoon by the time Helena and Guy arrived at the Star Inn in Ayr. It was a large stylish place, used to receiving the best of visitors. The staff were efficient and well trained. Guy was reminded of the quiet comfort of his club in London. No one commented upon the presence of a lady who, by the manner in which she was garbed and her lack of a maid, was quite clearly not Lady Varington. The Star appeared to be the height of discretion, even placing his lordship and the lady in adjoining rooms, much to Helena's embarrassment.

As they had neared the burgh of Ayr she had become quieter, more withdrawn. Although nothing of her demeanour betrayed her, from her modestly folded hands to the serene expression upon her face, Guy had sensed an underlying anxiety that was growing by the minute. Their arrival at the inn had not banished the worry from her eyes. He moved the curtain and peered down on to the street outside. Despite the dying light Ayr was still busy. The rumble of cart and carriage wheels, clatter of horses' hooves and buzz of voices carried through the paned-glass window. Guy twitched the curtain back into place and, moving silently towards the door that connected his bedchamber with the one in which Helena had been placed, stopped. He lifted his head and stayed very still, listening for any sounds that might reveal what she was doing. There were none.

Then out of the silence came a soft knocking at the connecting door. Guy caught his breath and stilled the sudden thrumming of his heart. He hesitated only for a moment before grasping the handle and opening the door.

'Helena.' He smiled. 'Please come in,' and stepped back to let her enter.

She made no move. Only stood there as if made of stone. 'Forgive me, Guy.' Her utterance of his name gave it a peculiarly intimate tone.

Her face was pale with fatigue, but the whisper of a blush touched to her cheeks. For one brief moment he wondered if she had come to him in the sense of a woman to a man. Excitement flickered at the idea, even as he knew it was not so. Helena might have been a mistress for five years, but she had a propriety about her that belied such a sullied past.

'I did not mean to disturb you.'

'Then rest assured I am not disturbed,' he said. 'You may come in,' he coaxed, and opened the door wider.

Still, she did not move. She stood in the same dark dress that she had worn for the past days, even though he had sent ahead to have a few new clothes awaiting them. The hem showed the dust and dirt of their travels. Her cloak had been discarded and her hair had been combed and pinned again. He could only be glad that her bonnet had been crushed in the carriage accident for Helena's hair was glorious to look upon.

'I know you planned to visit my family tomorrow morning, but I wondered if it were possible that we might go there this evening instead.' He saw the gentle rise and fall of her breast, knew how concerned she must be to come to knock upon the door to his bed-chamber to ask such a thing.

'If it is your desire, we may visit them immediately.'

The smoky green eyes widened slightly and the carefully composed expression fell from her face. 'I would like that very much, Guy,' she said.

One corner of his mouth crooked up. 'Then fetch your cloak, Helena, and I shall organise a fresh team of horses.'

'There is no need. My father's house is in Strawthorn Street, barely a mile from here. We would be quicker walking.'

'Very well.' He gathered up his new silver-topped walking stick, hat and gloves.

It had been a dry and frosty day and the cold snap seemed set to continue into the night. The sky was all pale blues and lavenders and pinks as the iciness of evening closed in. Throughout the air the smell of smoke tumbled with the scent of fresh air as the couple made their way down the main street in Ayr.

'It has been so long since I was last here,' Helena said, and the warmth of her breath clouded in the cold air. 'I thought never to see it again.'

Guy patted the small hand that was tucked through the crook in his arm. 'Then I am sorry to disappoint you.'

'No, never that,' she said softly, and gave him a shy smile.

Something warm expanded in Guy's chest. It was a most peculiar feeling and one that he had not experienced before. Before he could contemplate it further two small ragged boys ran up by his side.

'Please, sir, can you spare a farthing for the guy.' The thin-faced urchin's hand stretched out. His small friend did not look hopeful.

Guy dropped some coins into the child's hand. Judging from the exclamations that followed and the rather speedy departure of the two small boys, it was a much greater sum than they were used to. He looked up to find Helena watching him with a smile.

They continued on their way with Helena pointing out this building and that, and telling him something of the town. Yet all the while he could feel her impatience to reach their destination. If it had been at all acceptable, Guy did not doubt that Helena would be running full tilt. Then they turned off and she led him down a maze of narrower streets. The houses grew smaller, less expensive. With every step Helena's feet grew faster.

'It's just round this corner,' she said breathlessly. Her nose was nipped pink by the cold air and her eyes sparkled with anticipation and excitement and fear. She clutched his arm all the tighter.

They were barely into Strawthorn Street when he felt her suddenly grow rigid. She stopped. It was as if she ceased to breathe. She stared ahead down the street, her eyes wide and disbelieving, her cheeks suddenly blanched. Her lips opened as if to cry out, yet no sound was forthcoming. Guy followed the line of her vision to what it was that she stared at with such horror. Halfway down the road on the right-hand side between two houses that stood prim and quiet were the blackened remains of a building. Her hand slipped from his arm and then she was off and running, uncaring of the fact that she presented a most unladylike sight. The dark swirl of skirts was hitched up, exposing her ankles, and her hair, so neatly pinned and tucked, loosened and began to escape. Helena ran as if the flames were still licking round the door, as if she could hear the shouts of the occupants within. By the time Guy reached her she was standing before all that remained of her family home—a pile of charred timber and stone.

'Helena.' He touched a hand gently to her shoulder.

She pulled back, dislodging his fingers.

Guy had never seen such shock or pain as flashed in her eyes.

'We're too late,' she whispered. 'Too damn late.'

'We must not leap to conclusions, Helena. Perhaps one of the neighbours can tell us what happened here and the fate of your family.'

'You were right. He has killed them.' And her voice held a quiet despair worse than a thousand shed tears. 'It's all been for nothing.'

'We do not know that,' he countered, but even as he said it he acknowledged the thought that she was most probably right. The stench of burning and smoke still clung to the place.

'Stephen is nothing but thorough. This is the work of his hand. I know now why he has not yet found me. He has been busy…with this.' She indicated the blackened mess that surrounded her. Then her focus fixed and she stooped and picked up something that lay close to her shoe: a large half-burned book. With tender care she eased it open. The outer edge of the pages crumbled to a sooty dust beneath her fingers. On the frontispiece through the scorching the printed letters were still legible—Family Bible. On the page opposite were the faded scripts of her great-grandfather, and her grandfather and her father. Each birth, marriage and death in the McGregor family had been recorded in neatly flowing ink. She said nothing, just traced one finger over each of the smoke-damaged words, locked in a world of pain and remembrance.

The light was fading fast, the sky glowing a deep crimson red amidst the blue and lavender hues. 'Helena.' He gently wrested the book from her fingers, tucked it beneath his arm and steered her back out on to the street. Her face was as pale as the day he had found her so still and lifeless upon the shore. Yet she did not cry, not as she had done after the carriage accident. Her eyes were dry, her face impassive. Guy had seen such reactions in the Peninsula, in men that had watched the atrocities of war. He also had more personal experience of such shock. Helena could not yet believe the terrible scene she had just witnessed. It would not take long before the truth permeated her mind, and when it did he did not want her to be standing here on a cold and darkening street. Where his fingers pressed against her arm, he could feel the beginnings of a tremor. She was so cold that it brought a chill to his hand. Whatever had to be done here, it was clear that Helena was in no fit state to undertake it.

'We must get you back to the inn.'

A shake of her head and the last of her pins dislodged, so that her hair flowed long and wanton over her shoulders. 'No. I must find the truth of this. Mr Robertson will know. I'll ask him how it happened…when it happened.'

'Come back to the inn,' he said. 'I'll return and discover all there is to know.'

'Mr Robertson…' she began, then stopped. Then tried again. 'He will not know the truth of where I went, of what I have been these last years.'

'Rest assured, Helena, he shall learn nothing from me.' He made no mention of the fact that the curtains the length of the street had been twitching since their arrival.

'Come,' he said again, and, leaning forward, pulled the hood up over her head, tucking the soft silkiness of her hair in behind the black wool. 'It's a cold night, and I would not want you to catch a chill.'

And with that he guided her back down the streets through which they had previously walked with such hopes.

Guy did not leave until he had watched Helena finish the whisky that he had ordered, and tucked her up in bed. He quelled the desire to climb in beside her, take her in his arms and offer her what little comfort he could. Instead, he pulled on a great caped coat and walked back out into the darkness of the night. Helena needed to know what had happened at the house in Strawthorn Street. She needed to know whether her family were alive or dead. And, more to the point, so did he, given that he had promised their safety. He set his face against the cold and strode out, wondering quite what he had taken on with the beautiful redheaded woman that lay upstairs in the inn.

'It was a terrible night, sir.' The old man nodded knowingly. He had been tall in his time, but the years had shrunk and bent him. He was thin to the point of being gaunt and his hair was a wiry grizzled grey. His cheeks were of wrinkled leather, his eyes stared fierce and blue and he wore clothes that were in fashion twenty years ago. The house was small and silent and cold. The maidservant had refused Guy entry when he first approached, but Mr Robertson had eventually been persuaded to relent—with the promise of a five-pound note.

Guy made all the right noises that he knew would prompt the man to tell him what he wanted to know. And it seemed that once the McGregors' neighbour started to talk, he had much to say.

'Happened nigh on a week ago. Smelled the smoke mysel' I did, but it was Bonfire Night and I thought it was just weans and another o' their fires.' He pulled a sour face. 'This time o' year it's aye the same. Fires and fireworks everywhere. I get nae peace for them. Bloody Bonfire Night.' He held on to the arms of the shabby chair. 'By the time I saw the flames it was too late. McGregor's house was well alight.'

'What of Mr and Mrs McGregor?'

The old eyes darted a look of surprise at him. 'I thought Miss Helena would have told you. It was her that you were outside wi' earlier, wasn't it?' He paused and waited expectantly.

Guy inclined his head. 'Indeed it was, Mr Robertson.'

'I thought as much.' He gave a knowing nod.

'You were about to tell me of Helena's parents,' Guy prompted.

Mr Robertson took a moment to think about this and then, as if making up his mind, continued with his words. 'Mrs McGregor, Miss Helena's mother, died giving birth to the youngest daughter, Miss Emma. It was McGregor himsel' that raised the family.'

'Forgive me, but I did not know,' said Guy.

'Four of them,' continued the old man, 'all lassies, more's the shame; no' a son amongst them.'

Guy suppressed the twitch of his jaw.

'The middle two were married off last year and the year afore, and no' afore time, I say. McGregor was too slow in gettin' them off his hands. He was still lumbered wi' Miss Emma.' He suddenly leaned forward in a conspiratorial manner. 'I aye knew that it wasnae true, you know.'

'What is that?' Varington asked.

He dropped his voice, as if someone would hear them within the confines of the house walls. 'The story o' Miss Helena's death,' he said smugly.

Guy waited for Mr Robertson to expand.

'They put it about that she had died o' scarlet fever, but I knew it wasnae true. I saw those men that took her. Alive and well she was when she climbed into Sir Stephen Tayburn's carriage.'

Guy raised an eyebrow, but only marginally. 'Perhaps you are mistaken, Mr Robertson.'

'No' me,' replied the old man robustly. 'His crest was clear as day on the door: a black deil on a red background. But I kept the knowledge to mysel'. I'm no' some gossipin' fishwife. Besides, I knew somethin' of what was going on afore. I had seen the way Tayburn looked at her. And when a man looks at a woman like that, it means only one thing. The lassie didnae stand a chance. Especially no' when Tayburn had McGregor set upon.' His thin lips tightened. 'What a beatin' that man suffered. Nigh on died, and that's no jest. He was never the same afterwards. Could barely run his business.'

'What was the nature of Mr McGregor's business?' asked Varington.

'He ran a company of weavers. Owned a factory down by the river. Tayburn invested in McGregor's business, that's how they came to know one another. Then the business hit a slow spot, and Tayburn demanded his money back—all o' it.'

'And McGregor couldn't pay.'

'No, indeed, he couldnae. Hardly a bean to his name by that stage. He didnae always live here. At one time the family had a house o'er in Wellington Square.'

Guy looked none the wiser.

'The mansion houses,' he said by way of explanation. 'Where all the rich folk live.'

'But with Mr McGregor's failing business they were forced to move.'

'Precisely,' said Mr Robertson. 'This is a fine street, is it no'?'

'Undoubtedly.'

'But no' when you're used to what they were. Bit of a comedown for them. Anyway…' he sniffed and dabbed a handkerchief to his nose '…Tayburn came round this way no' long after McGregor's attack. By that time, what wi' the doctor's bills and the like, they couldnae afford a single servant. It was Helena that kept house for her father, and Helena that Tayburn saw on his arrival. It doesnae take a genius to work out the rest. A pretty young lassie like that suddenly disappears and the next thing McGregor's business has an upturn in fortune. A new investor steps in to save him from ruin. Rumour has it that it was Tayburn, same rumour that says it was Tayburn behind the attack on McGregor in the first place, though it's no' for me to comment upon.'

'I see,' said Guy.

'So she's wi' you now, is she?'

Guy took out a five-pound note and sat it on the table in between them. 'About the fire,' he said, 'what became of Mr McGregor and his daughter?'

'They found the charred remains o' McGregor's body the next day.'

'And the daughter that lived with him?'

Mr Robertson sniffed again, and rubbed his nose.

Guy placed a second banknote on top of the first.

'McGregor had some visitors just afore the fire. Miss Emma, she went off wi' them.'

'Do you know who these visitors were?'

'Same ones as took Miss Helena, all them years ago. Tayburn's men. Robertson never forgets a face,' said the old man, and tapped a thickened nail against the side of his nose. 'You'd best watch your back, son. Tayburn's no' a man to be crossed. You mark ma words. Best stay clear o' the Deil o' St Vey, son, if you value your life.'

Chapter Ten

Helena heard the light knock at the connecting door. She was not asleep. The image of what her family home had become was lodged firmly in her mind. Nothing would shift the picture of that blackened shell of a house. She saw it when her eyes were closed. It haunted her when her eyes were open. Everywhere she looked she saw only those charred remains. She knew, of course, that her father and sisters were dead. Knew inside her head. That was the only logical conclusion that could be drawn. She had run, and Stephen had taken his revenge in the way he knew would hurt her most. She had underestimated him—again. But what she knew and what she felt were two different things. In her heart she could not believe they were dead...not after everything she had endured to save them. No matter how she tried to rationalise things, the knot in her stomach would not unwind. She lay rigid and un-yielding on the plush soft comfort of the bed. Alone. Disbelieving. Afraid.

The knock came again. He did not wait for an

answer. The handle turned and he walked into the room. She could smell the coldness of the night air on his clothes, feel the slight chill that emanated from him. She sat up, scrambled from the bed to stand before him, braced herself for what he would say.

'I spoke with Mr Robertson, your father's neighbour.'

'Yes?' She made no effort to quell the impatience in her voice. She wanted to shout out, 'Just tell me and be done with it!' but the look in his eye prevented her. She feared the worst and hoped for the best.

'The news is not good. Your father perished in the fire.' No doubt McGregor had been beaten and left for dead before the fire took hold, but Helena need not know of that. It was bad enough without embellishing the gory details.

A gasp sounded before her hand clutched to her mouth as if she would catch back the emotions ready to spill forth.

'I'm sorry, Helena.'

Her eyes closed momentarily and when they opened again all trace of the threatened hysteria had vanished. In its place was an unnatural calm composure. 'What of my sisters?'

He paused.

The façade did not last. He saw the shuttering of her eyes and the terrible shock that washed her face so pale that he thought she would swoon from the spot on which she stood.

'No, it's not as you think.' He moved forward, pressing his hands to the outer edges of her upper arms as if he would stop her from falling. 'Two of your sisters are married and no longer reside in Strawthorn Street. I cannot say for sure, but I believe them to be safe. But your youngest sister…'

She stilled in his arms. 'Emma,' she said, and it seemed that she held her breath, waiting for what he would say.

He guided her gently back and sat her down on the barely rumpled sheets of the bed. 'Helena, it seems that Tayburn has taken her.'

A silence followed his words. And it was pregnant with the most dreadful of imaginings.

'Stephen,' she whispered, and just the sound of his name brought a sinister feeling to the bedchamber. The candles guttered in the draught and the air seemed to chill. 'What have I done?' she cried. 'Dear Lord, what have I done?'

The mattress dipped as he sat down on the bed beside her. Very gently he took her hand in his. 'You have done nothing wrong, Helena. The fault is not yours.'

A sob escaped her before she could bite it back. 'I escaped, and so he has killed my father and taken Emma in my stead.'

'No.' Varington uttered the word with a conviction that carried to Helena.

'She shall not endure him,' she said. 'He will kill her.'

Again that single strong determined word. 'No.' Guy pulled her to face him. 'He plans to use her as leverage, to force your return. And as such, she is safe for now.'

She stared at him, wanting to believe him, but not quite doing so. Her eyes were awash with fear and guilt and shock and horror.

'Helena.'

But she had already turned her head away and was looking towards the fireplace with her usual air of fake composure. 'Then I shall go back to him,' she said in a quiet voice.

The thought of Helena returning to that villain

wrenched at Guy's gut. He understood only a little of what Tayburn had done to her: blackmailing her into being his mistress, subjecting her to a life that Guy could not bear to think about. God help him, but hell would freeze over before he let Tayburn harm one hair on Helena's head ever again. He knew what Tayburn would do, and so did Helena; he just had to make her face the truth, no matter how hard that might be. 'So that Tayburn may have you both?'

She shook her head. 'He will let Emma go.'

Guy took her hand within his, hearing both her longing and her guilt, knowing it was the echo of his own nightmares. 'Helena, you know that he will not.'

'Then all is lost,' she said. Her voice was filled with an aching desolation and it seemed that beneath Guy's fingers her pulse slowed and weakened, and he felt the extent of her pain.

Guy's face was grim. 'No,' he said, knowing that his strength must carry them both.

Her eyes swung to his. He saw the sudden flicker of hope.

He smiled and with gentle fingers stroked away a curl of hair that dangled close to her eyes. 'I will call him out.'

Helena gave a small incredulous laugh. 'You surely do not speak in earnest?'

One corner of Guy's mouth lifted higher, crooking his smile. 'I tell you I am deadly serious,' he said as if challenging Tayburn to a duel were nothing at all out of the ordinary. She needed to hear confidence, strength, arrogance even. He smiled lazily, betraying nothing of the emotions that raged beneath the surface.

'It is Sir Stephen Tayburn of whom we speak. He will kill you before you ever make it to a duelling field.'

He raised an eyebrow. 'I appreciate your confidence in my abilities.'

'It has nothing to do with that. Stephen has no honour. He cares nothing for the rules of engagement. If he wishes you dead, then that is what you will be, no matter how skilful you are with a pistol.'

'I'll call him out all the same.' And he knew that he wasn't only doing this for Helena.

'It's utter madness! You cannot hope for success.'

'Oh, but I can and I do, Helena,' he said with brutal honesty.

She stared at him as if she could not fathom him, puzzlement marring her brow.

'Why?' she asked.

He gave a casual shrug of his shoulders, playing it down, unwilling to betray the truth of the feelings that Tayburn stirred up. Memories from across the years of a man too like Tayburn. Memories of the darkness Guy could not forget. All the old pain that Guy had locked away was in danger of seeping back out.

'Why would you call him out over his abduction of my sister? You do not know her; she is nothing to you.'

'But you are,' he said. 'And had your father and sister been safe, I would call him out just the same.' It was the truth, he realised. He knew the damage that a man like Tayburn could do and, looking down into Helena's eyes, seeing the extent of her hurt, he knew that he had to stop him.

There was nothing but the softness of their breaths as their eyes clung together. It was Helena that was first to look away.

'Do you wish to be forever looking over your shoulder, never knowing when he might snatch you back? You are with me now and I will ensure that Tayburn knows it. If he has any grievances over his loss, he may settle them in the duel.' A steely determination settled in his eyes. He would not be swayed from his course.

'You would risk your life for my sister and for me. Yet you owe us nothing.'

'Have you forgotten my offer so swiftly, Helena? I offered protection for both you and your family.'

Beneath the flicker of the candle on the bedside table her eyes appeared to darken and soften. 'I know.' She bit her lip. 'I just did not think…' Her words trailed away unfinished.

They watched each other through the silence before she leaned in closer towards him, a wash of colour staining her cheeks.

'Helena.' There was a slight hoarseness to the word. The borrowed white nightdress gaped at the neck, exposing too much of the creamy white skin below. Guy could smell her sweetness, the clean pleasant scent he knew was her own. He wanted her now more than he had wanted her all along. Wanted to offer her the refuge that he had so often sought in coupling, a respite from the pain. And yet he knew that such a base reaction went against all decency. He reined in the urge, raked a hand through his hair. Hell, what was he thinking of? She might well be his mistress, but Helena had been brutalised by a monster, and she'd only just learned of the death of her father and abduction of her sister. Only a barbarian would bed her under such circumstances. Guy wrenched his gaze from hers and got to his feet.

'Guy.' She reached a hand towards him, resting her

fingers against the sleeve of his coat. In her eyes was gratitude.

His gaze sharpened. His hand moved to cup her face, and his thumb moved in a gentle stroking action. And in that moment he was tempted to kiss her, to touch her, to show her the way it should be between a man and a woman. But now was not the time. He wanted her, but not like this, not a coupling out of gratitude and pain. He dropped his hand before temptation could get the better of him.

His eyes were watching her with a hunger. She knew it was desire, but there was something else there too. There was nothing of Stephen's foul lust in him; Guy's eyes were as pale and clear as Stephen's were dark and murky. But for all that he wanted her, and Helena was in no doubt as to that, he made no move to take her. Indeed, he looked as if he were about to retire to his own chamber for the night. As if she were still respectable. As if he might have some care for her. This man who would risk his life to save both her and her sister. A fierce tenderness enveloped her heart. She rose without knowing that she did so and moved to stand before him.

'Good night, Helena.' And the smile he threw her made her heart skip a beat.

He was so tall that her head only came to his chin. She could look many men level in the eye, but not Varington. He was tall and strong, and instilled with a sense of decency. It had been a long time since any man had shown her such kindness.

'Thank you,' she whispered and, lifting her face to his, touched her lips to the edge of his jaw line. It was intended as a kiss of gratitude, a kiss in acknowledgement of all that he had done for her, a kiss between friends. But neither Helena nor Guy were prepared for the effect. Her lips fluttered like a baby's breath over his skin, resting with the briefest lightest touch upon his skin, but in the transience of that single moment awareness surged so strong as to obliterate everything. Blood coursed wildly through her body. Excitement spiralled deep in her stomach, spilling out in tingling surges that threatened to engulf her. She saw her own shock mirrored in his eyes, the blackness of his pupils expanding to fill the pale surround. She heard a gasp of breath and did not know that it was her own.

His head bowed and she felt the soft brush of his eyelashes against her cheek as his breath skimmed the column of her neck. Someone groaned, but she knew not whether it was Guy or herself who made the sound. Her head pulled back, exposing the vulnerability of her throat beneath. Her skin danced hot and dizzy with anticipation so that, when at last his lips closed upon its softness, she gave a sigh of relief. His mouth nuzzled hungrily against her throat, sliding slowly, steadily, up towards her mouth.

'Guy,' she whispered his name breathlessly into the room.

But he silenced her when his mouth at last found hers and their lips danced together in mounting passion. The smell of him, the heat of him, his proximity took her to a place she had never known. Her fingers entwined themselves in the black ruffle of his hair. He kissed her as she had never been kissed before, so that something of himself reached down into her and imprinted itself there. Her fingers traced the contours of his face, revelling in the roughness of the dark stubble that peppered his skin. It was as if he were the air and she were a woman suffocating for need of it.

He stroked her hair, caressed her spine beneath, pulling her in tight so that her breasts crushed against him. And all the while their mouths were locked in a hunger that she had never before known. His hands swept down to cradle the roundness of her buttocks. And then he lifted her up and into him so that, even through the layers of their clothing, she knew his arousal. Her arms clung to him, merging their two bodies as one.

From outside came a sudden flurry of bangs and explosions as if a volley of shots had been released from muskets. Guy stilled, stopped. Instinct and training kicked in. He set her down and moved quickly to the window, stealing a glance through the edge of the curtain so that his actions within the dimly lit room would not be visible to those on the street. In the distance of the night sky a spectacle of colour was exploding against the black.

'Fireworks.' An infinitesimal ripple of the curtain material and he was back by her side.

Fireworks outside, and fireworks of a different sort entirely within the bedchamber of the inn. Her lips were swollen from what they had shared. Helena stood awkwardly, unsure of what to say, what even to think. She wanted to feel his arms warm and strong around her, needed his lips to sear away all memory of the burnt-out house, all imaginings of her father and her sister, but something held her back. Stephen had called her a whore, and she had done nothing save endure his touch. But this man was different. With one kiss Guy had awakened a part of herself that she did not know had existed. And with its wakening she feared that Stephen had been right—for she wanted Guy never to stop. She wanted him to tumble her on the bed and make love to her.

Passion clouded by fear and guilt. Guy all too easily read the changes in Helena's emotions before the mask of impassivity slipped back upon her face. She made no move to reject him—indeed, she made no move at all, just stood there and waited. His blood raced hot and hard and he wanted nothing more than to strip the tent of a nightdress from her body, lay her back upon the bed and make love to her. He wanted it more than he ever could have imagined that a man might lust for a woman. He wanted her so much that it hurt. He moved his hand and caught the ends of her hair, rubbing the silken waves between his fingers. He caught the hank up, wrapping it round and round, the back of his fingers sliding up the cotton of the nightdress until they brushed against the hard pebbles of her nipples. Their gazes locked. He knew she would not deny him. They had an arrangement, after all. She was his mistress, and he, her protector. He had every right to take her body. He wanted her. She stood stock-still and let his knuckles stroke her, until he saw the darkening of her eyes. He moved forward. Her lips parted. Her eyes shuttered as he leaned closer to her face. With great self-control he placed a single chaste kiss upon her forehead.

'Good night, Helena.'

Her eyes flashed open in surprise. But Guy was off and walking towards the connecting door.

'Guy?' The word echoed with both relief and disappointment.

He turned and smiled his most devastating smile. 'Sleep well.' And then he disappeared into the chamber where his own bed awaited, before his resolve could weaken. Helena McGregor might be his mistress, but he had seen the fear and gratitude in her eyes. He would teach her that he was not like Tayburn, even if it meant forgoing his own pleasure.

Early the next morning Helena and Guy departed the inn in Ayr and headed north on the coastal road. The day was clear and bright with a glistening frost that had not yet vanished. Bare earth that had been sodden now stood frozen as if it had been churned in great chunks, the imprints of feet and hooves and wheels captured in some kind of sculpture that would last only until the thaw. Sheep, their coats long and unkempt and stained with mud, grazed seemingly oblivious to the freezing temperatures, jaws moving in rhythmic grinding as they chewed the cud and stared with suspicious pale Pan-like eyes. What had been deep muddied puddles across the surface of the road had frozen solid, the perfection of their opaque icy surfaces smashed by passing traffic. The carriage passed several burnt-out bonfires in fields. The blackened heaps were a constant reminder to Helena of the house she had witnessed yesterday and all that went with it. And something hard and heavy weighed upon her.

She sat very still. Beneath her feet was a brick and around her knees was tucked a blanket, both provided by Guy. Yet Helena felt neither the cold of the day nor the heat of the brick or blanket. All she was aware of was the terrible ache in her heart and of all that had been lost.

'Penny for them.' The deep melodic tilt of Guy's voice interrupted her thoughts.

She drew her gaze from the window and looked at

him, unsure of what he had said, afraid to admit that she had not been listening.

'A penny for your thoughts,' he said. 'You seem lost in contemplation.'

She didn't know what to say, couldn't tell him the truth of what she was thinking: that three people were dead and her sister imprisoned, and all because she had decided to flee Stephen. That all of it was her damn fault. That the pain of that knowledge was almost unbearable. She schooled her face to show nothing. 'I was thinking how fine the weather is today.'

It seemed that his eyes looked directly into hers and she knew that he did not believe the trite, silly answer she had given. She glanced away, afraid of how much was exposed, feeling awkward and foolish and confused. Almost desperately, she stared from the window at the passing winter landscape.

'Helena,' he said softly

She could feel the heat of his gaze upon her and, although he had not moved in the slightest, it was as if he was reaching out to her. At last she could bear it no longer and turned her eyes to meet his. The sun bleached his skin a marble white and added a blue lustre to the short dark hair that fanned feathers around his face so that there was something of an unearthly appearance about him. In the white winter sunlight his eyes were a clear icy blue, and his lashes a dark sooty black, and he beheld Helena with a scrutiny that seemed to reach into her very soul.

She felt two patches of heat warm her cheeks. 'I am fine.' Anything to stop him looking at her like that.

'It does not seem so.'

Her teeth nipped at her bottom lip, hard.

'We will get your sister back, and soon.'

She nodded, not trusting herself to speak.

'And Tayburn will pay with his life.'

More like Stephen would destroy Guy too. And all of her worry and all of her fear welled up so that she could contain it no longer and the tears spilled over to roll silently down her cheeks.

'Helena.' He sighed, and moved across the carriage to take her in his arms. He cradled her against him, murmuring quiet words of comfort in her ear. 'Do not cry. I promise you that he will never hurt you again.'

'He will kill you,' she said, and the breath was ragged in her throat. She felt the caress of his hand against her hair.

'No, Helena, he will not.' And in his eyes was such supreme confidence that, in spite of all she knew about Stephen, she almost believed him.

'It is all my fault, you know,' she whispered. 'My father, Emma, Agnes, Old Tam…' She refused to look away, forced herself to hold his gaze. 'Had I not run, then they would all still be safe.'

'You must not blame yourself, Helena.'

'Even if that is where the blame rests?'

'No!' he growled, and his fingers touched to her chin so that she could not look away. 'You are as much Tayburn's victim in all of this as the rest of them. Hell, you stayed with the villain for five years to protect your family. You have no reason to feel guilty.'

The pain was so bad that she thought her soul was being torn apart. 'And it was all for nothing, wasn't it? Five years with Stephen and now my father is murdered and my sister in his power!' And she began to sob.

He pulled her on to his lap, holding her tight against

him, rocking her, stroking her as if she were some small child.

'Sweetheart,' he whispered, and he held her until there were no more tears to be cried, and her eyes were dry and tender. The terrible tension inside of Helena had gone and in its place was a strange kind of exhaustion. There was only the rumble of the carriage wheels and the rhythmic clip of horses' hooves. She found she was clinging to him, and made to extricate herself from the intimate position. But Guy's arm only tightened around her. She looked up into his eyes, and she knew that he was going to kiss her, and, God help her, she wanted him to.

Guy lowered his face to hers. When their lips touched it was everything and more than Helena remembered from the previous evening. He kissed her with a warm gentleness that drew the breath from her body, and with it every last thought of Stephen and her father and Emma. His mouth massaged with a gentle insistent pressure until she melted against him, forgetting all else except the man whose lips were so giving to hers. Her palms lay flat against his chest, open, yielding, feeling the strong steady beat of his heart. The dark blue superfine of his coat was soft beneath the caress of her fingers. Cold heated to warm. Warm flamed to hot. Their lips were made to be together, their kiss to last a lifetime. In that moment there was only Guy.

When at last Guy drew away and looked down into her eyes with such tenderness, Helena knew that she was lost.

He lifted the travelling rug that had fallen to the floor and tucked it over her knees. His left arm draped around her shoulders with the lightest touch, but one that imparted his warmth and comfort and protection. Helena felt a strange kind of peace settle upon her and something of her pain diminished and she knew that it was because of the tall dark-haired man sitting by her side.

They arrived at the Eglinton Arms Hotel in the small town of Ardrossan, some five miles from the village of Kilbride. The hotel was large and more than ready to accommodate a member of the aristocracy. Indeed, it had been established for just such a purpose by its owner, the Earl of Eglinton. The Eglinton Arms was luxurious and boasted a discreet and well-trained staff; nevertheless, Helena could not help feeling uncomfortable when the manager was apprised of the fact that she was not Lady Varington, nor was she travelling with a maid. Guy's declaration that his valet and Mrs McLelland's maid had been delayed did not so much as raise an eyebrow. She also knew very well why Guy had chosen to stay in the hotel when not a week since he had been a most welcome guest at Seamill Hall. Indeed, he would undoubtedly still be welcome, but he could not very well arrive there with his mistress in tow.

It was Guy's preference that they took a tray in their room. He had not failed to notice that many of the male patrons were finding it difficult to loosen their gazes from Helena. It was hardly surprising given her uncommon beauty. In the new expensive green travelling dress and fur-lined cloak and muff that Guy had purchased for her in Ayr, Helena stood out from the crowd. And Guy had reason enough to desire that their presence in the area was not remarked upon.

The Scotch broth warmed them from the inside out.

In truth, Helena had no appetite for food, but she knew that she must keep her strength up for what lay ahead. For all of Guy's confidence she could not relax her fear. Helena knew Stephen. Guy did not. She, more than most, knew of what the man was capable. She worried if Guy understood what he had taken on by helping her.

'Finish your soup, Helena, and then I must visit Weir and Annabel.'

She glanced away, rosy embarrassment flooding her face.

'Helena,' he said, and, reaching across the table, laid one of his hands over hers. 'You know why I do not take you with me, don't you?'

She forced her chin up, and looked him in the eye. 'You need offer me no explanations.'

He raised an eyebrow.

'I do not expect to be made welcome in any respectable household,' she said. 'That is perfectly understandable…'

'Helena,' he growled, but she continued unabated.

'Besides, I would not wish to cause embarrassment to Mr and Mrs Weir.'

'I do not take you with me out of concern for your own safety,' he said.

'As I said, you need explain nothing.'

'Helena,' he said with a touch of exasperation, and his hand closed around hers. 'Tayburn, or his men, may be in Kilbride or the immediate area. For all we know, he may have discovered something of your visit to Seamill Hall. Until I know the lie of the land, it is safer that you stay here.'

Her face turned pale. She wetted her lips and looked away. 'Forgive me, I thought…'

'I'm not ashamed of you, Helena. Never think that.' He gave her fingers a gentle squeeze of reassurance. 'Perhaps I should take you with me to Seamill Hall just to prove my point.'

She smiled.

'Well?' he said. 'Shall you come with me?'

She laughed. 'No.'

'Why ever not?'

'You know why not,' she replied. 'You are teasing me.'

He smiled in all innocence. 'Am I?'

'Guy!'

His smile became suddenly roguish. 'You have not answered my question?'

She gave a huff of exasperation. 'Guy, I am your mistress.'

His eyes narrowed and darkened into a smoulder and one corner of his mouth quirked in a most suggestive manner. 'Aren't I the lucky fellow.' He looked pointedly at her lips and murmured, 'Lucky indeed.' The dishes were set hastily on the tray and the tray removed to the floor by the door.

He crossed the room back towards her at a faster pace than she had seen him travel before. It was practically a stride.

But before he could reach her, Helena was out of her chair and backing away towards the window. Her heart was hammering in her chest and there was a liquid warmth deep in her belly at just the anticipation of his touch. 'Guy, we have much to discuss.'

His smile was positively wicked. 'Indeed we do, but it can wait a little longer.'

She knew she should not refuse him. He was, after all, her protector in every sense of the word.

He stepped towards her.

Helena dodged to her left and, swinging round by the fireplace, inverted their positions. Now Guy stood with his back to the window, and Helena was facing him with her back to the bed and the door. He swept a brazen gaze over her body and began to move with a slow, determined stealth in her direction.

There could be no mistaking his intent. Helena gave a squeak, and, seeing that her path for escape was blocked in one way by Guy's advancing frame and in the other by the large double bed, made her split-second decision and made a bid for escape across the breadth of the bed. It was the wrong choice. The long skirts of her new dress impeded her progress across the mattress so that it amounted to an unladylike scramble. She had almost made it to the other side when something closed around one of her ankles and hoisted her backwards.

Helena gave a yelp of surprise and found herself being rolled on to her back with Guy leaning the length of his body over hers.

'Almost, but not quite fast enough,' he said, and there was a definite amusement in his voice.

She noticed that he did not lay his weight upon her, but took it on his own knees and elbows. Helena was not a fragile woman, but Guy was all lean hard muscle that would have crushed her had he not acted with such consideration. His eyes narrowed and darkened with desire. Helena knew that if he kissed her any semblance of resistance would be lost and there were things that must be said. 'Guy...' She tried to attract his attention from the road she knew his thoughts were taking. 'Guy, listen to me.'

'I'm listening,' he said, and lowered his face towards hers.

'You will have a care when you go to Kilbride, won't you?'

The dark sweep of Guy's lashes lowered as his gaze scanned down to her mouth.

'If he learns that I was at Seamill Hall…'

Something of the smile vanished. The pale eyes sent a spiralling of excitement down deep in her belly. 'Do not worry. I will warn Weir and Annabel of Tayburn.'

She shivered just at the mention of Stephen's name. 'Then you concede that he is a very dangerous man?'

'I never denied it,' he said in a lazy tone.

Helena's blood ran cold.

'But not as dangerous as me.' He smiled again and leaned down lower until their faces were almost touching, so close that when he spoke she could feel the warm moisture of his breath against her cheek and the tickle of his lips against her skin.

His fingers traced a light, teasing path from the hollow in her throat down to the edge of her bodice, his fingers caressing the creamy swell of her bosom. There was a tremor running through him as he unfastened her dress and pulled down the fine wool and the layers of flimsy materials that lay beneath it—a tremor such that he had not experienced since he'd been a green lad— until at last the fullness of her breasts lay exposed. He stared in awe.

'You're beautiful,' he whispered, and cupped his hands around her. She was smoother than satin, softer than silk, and he revelled in the feel of her. Beneath his caress her nipples beaded and he felt their gentle thrust against his hand. 'Sweetheart,' he murmured, and replaced his hand with his mouth to suckle her. Lord, but she was sweet, and he wanted her, wanted her with a desperation that he had never thought to feel. He lapped harder at the rosy bud and heard her soft gasps.

'Helena…' he raised his head to look at her, saw the passion darken her eyes '…I want to make love to you.'

She nodded.

His fingers brushed her nipples as his mouth made to claim hers.

'It is your right.'

Guy froze. 'My right?' And the thought that she was doing this out of duty, as she had done for Tayburn, curbed his desire. He touched the gentlest caress with one finger to the delicate skin beneath her ear.

'Do you wish me to continue?'

Helena was very conscious of the press of her naked breasts against the hardness of his chest, and of every other place that their bodies touched even by the slightest degree. She said nothing.

The finger stopped its motion, and everything about him was still. 'Was your flight across this bed from me in earnest, Helena?'

Her heart slid up her chest to thud in the base of her throat. Her chest was so tight that every breath seemed to come as a short sharp pant. She knew what any respectable lady should say. But then again she was not in the least respectable. 'We have an agreement. I will not renege on my side of the bargain.'

'That is not what I asked you,' he said.

The words teetered on the tip of her tongue, words that would tell him that she wanted him never to stop, words that would confirm her as a harlot. Pride would not let her say them.

Silence roared loud in her ears. Guy touched his lips against hers with a featherlight touch and then the mattress dipped and he was gone. Cold air filled the space where he had been.

'I must speak with the manager,' he said. 'I'll be back soon.' The lazy carefree smile was still on his face, but Helena thought that she saw the hint of something else beneath it. She closed her eyes against the sense of loss and lay where she was until she heard the door close.

Chapter Eleven

Helena did not go with Guy that afternoon to Seamill Hall. He left the carriage at the hotel, opting to travel on horseback. Half the distance to Kilbride he covered by road before turning down on to the beach and continuing along the firm caramel sand. Only when he was close to Weir's boathouse did he slow the beast, trotting him past the large faded shed and up the bramble-lined lane through which he had walked with Helena. Thus, Guy arrived at the stables at the back of Seamill Hall, left the horse with a surprised-looking stable-boy and gave the scullery maid a fright by appearing at the back door. Eventually he reached the drawing room and waited only a small time before Weir joined him.

'Varington!' Weir strode forwards and grasped Guy's hand in his own. 'Is everything well? You're back so soon, and Brown said that you came to the back door.'

'I took the horse for a canter along the beach. It was easier to cut up the back way.' Guy smiled and deliberately evaded the question.

'Sit down. Whisky?'

'That would be most welcome. What of Annabel and yourself? Are you both well?'

'Yes, yes,' Weir said with a touch of impatience. 'Perfectly well. But what has happened? Surely you cannot have returned from London already?' Pale golden liquid sloshed into two glasses, one of which was thrust unceremoniously towards the Viscount.

Guy accepted the proffered glass and downed the measure in one gulp. A satisfied blow of breath sounded and he relaxed back into the armchair. 'That stuff is damned good! You Scots have named it well *uisage bthea*—water of life.'

Weir knew better than to press Guy further. Past experience had taught him that Guy's stubborn streak meant he would offer an explanation only when he was good and ready.

'Had any interesting visitors in the past days?' The question was asked with a nonchalance that belied what Guy was really feeling.

The penny dropped with Weir. 'Hell! Tayburn didn't catch you, did he?'

'He's been here, then?' Guy said, passing his empty glass to Weir for a refill.

'Oh, he was here, all right. Arrived the day after you left... looking for his lady friend.'

'How very interesting,' drawled Guy, but there was a slight sharpening of his focus.

'Didn't I say that woman was bad news? To think I had her staying here in my house, chatting with my wife and children. She's the devil's mistress!'

'Not any more.'

'God in heaven! You didn't... You haven't... Tell me it is not so, Guy. Even you could not be that audacious.'

Guy sat back with what he hoped was an unfathomable expression. He had no intention of telling Weir the truth of matters between himself and Helena. It was better to let his friend draw his own conclusions.

'I know you said that you meant to seduce her, but that was when we did not know who she was. Perhaps you've not heard of Sir Stephen Tayburn, but I can assure you he's infamous in these parts.'

'I've heard of him.' The revulsion rolled within him just at the thought of the villain.

'Then you'll have also heard that he's not a man to be crossed. My God, the man's a fiend. I do not jest when I say that you've signed your own death warrant if you've taken his woman.'

Guy raised an eyebrow. 'You're being a tad presumptive. I did not say that my seduction of Helena was successful.' He thought of Helena weeping in his arms on that ledge with the carriage smashed far beneath them. He thought of her face, ashen with shock, as she stood before the burnt pile of rubble that had been her family's home. Hardly a seduction.

'But it was, wasn't it?'

He forced a laugh. 'It would be ungentlemanly of me to say.'

'You said that she's no longer Tayburn's mistress. Is she yours?'

'I will admit that she's under my protection.'

'Oh, hell, you'd better tell me all of it,' said Weir, rubbing his fingers against his forehead in nervous anticipation. 'You would not be back here sitting in my drawing room if there was not a very good reason. Nor,' he said with a snort, 'would you have descended to using the back door.'

'I could not be sure if Tayburn was having the house watched.'

'I take it by the fact you're still alive that Tayburn did not catch you?' Weir peered closer at Guy's face, noticing the newly healed cut running down the side of his face. 'Or did he?'

'He came after us, then?'

Weir gave a brief nod.

'When?'

'The morning after he was here. He owns a house near Brigurd Point. Keeps a four in hand there. Apparently he had his wife brought over from St Vey and was seen heading out on to the road like a bat out of hell. There's been no sight of him since. Hunter has the estate at Hunterston. There's nothing that gets past him; he knows everything that's going on. I spoke to him only yesterday: apparently Tayburn's boat is still moored at Brigurd Point, which means he's still on the mainland somewhere. If he were on the island, the boat would be on the other side. Tayburn knew the identity of the woman travelling with you, no matter what I said to the contrary.'

'I'll deal with Tayburn.'

Weir topped up the whisky glasses and pressed one into his friend's hand. 'Pray God that you do, Varington, pray God that you do.'

'The matter is already in hand.' The softness of Guy's tone belied the hardness in his eyes.

Weir glanced up, suspicion and the first inkling of fear upon his face. 'I do not like the sound of that.'

'Then you need not hear it,' said Guy simply.

'Damnation, Varington, I'll not just stand by and let you go up against Tayburn for the sake of a woman to warm your bed.'

Guy's eyes met Weir's and held. 'He has taken Helena's youngest sister out of revenge.'

'Good God!'

'I have no intention of allowing him to pursue Helena and neither will I leave her sister to his mercy.'

Weir rolled his eyes. 'Dare I ask you to tell me what you are planning?'

Guy smiled. 'Of course, old man. I was going to call him out—'

Weir waited.

'But now that I know Tayburn is on his way to London and not in his lair at all, a rather inviting opportunity makes itself known.'

Weir screwed his eyes shut in a cringing expression. 'I have a horrible suspicion where this is going. Please tell me that I'm wrong.'

Guy's smile deepened. 'How far is it between here and Tayburn's island?'

'Varington, you do not want to do this.'

'Oh, but I do, old chap, and I will. So let us discuss the details of just such a journey.'

And they did. By the time they had finished Weir had drained the whisky from his glass and was looking decidedly pasty about the gills. 'I wish to God that you'd never found that wretched woman.'

Guy wished no such thing.

'Let me come with you.'

'No. I've involved you and Annabel in this too much already and for that I'm sorry. I need not tell you to have a care over both your welfares when Tayburn returns.'

Weir gave a grim shake of his head.

'Besides, there's something else that I need you to do for me. And you aren't going to like it.'

'Then you had best tell me what it is.'

'I want to leave Helena here while I'm gone to St Vey. I know you'll see that she's kept safe.'

'You're right, I do not like it one little bit.'

'But you'll do it for me all the same?' Guy prompted. A nod. 'You owe me, Varington. Hugely.'

'I won't forget,' said Guy grimly, and finished his whisky.

Helena stood by the window of the bedchamber in the Eglinton Arms Hotel and watched Guy ride into the yard. He was as strong a horseman as he was everything else. The sunshine and blue skies had faded to a cold white grey, against which Guy cut a severe swathe with the dark perfection of his tailoring. In his elegant dark blue jacket, hat and stylishly tied neckcloth, he looked rather out of place riding through the small Scottish town. She drew back as he passed through the stone gateposts, but not fast enough. The handsome face looked up, saw her, smiled and inclined in acknowledgement. Just the sight of him pushed her pulse up a notch and made her remember the heat of his breath against her breast. She whirled around and clutched at the back of the chair positioned close to the fireplace, so tightly that her knuckles shone white. Footsteps sounded coming up the stairs. Helena's stomach tightened. She tried to tell herself it was because he brought word of Stephen. In part she was right; but only in part. Helena knew full well the other reason that caused such sensations throughout her body; she just didn't want to admit it right now.

A polite knocking, accompanied by his voice. 'Helena.'

She moved towards the door, turned the key. A deep

breath, and then the doorknob twisted within her fingers and the door swung open. He stood there with just the faintest hint of a smile upon his face. He had looked handsome down in the driveway; he was even more handsome at close range, devastatingly so, and Helena was struck anew at how much his presence affected her. Lord, she barely knew the man! She lowered her eyes that he might not see the truth in them, and stepped back into the room for him to enter. That he locked the door after him was a testament to his caution. Stephen's shadow lingered around the periphery of both their minds.

'I trust that your visit went well?'

'Well enough,' said Guy. 'Weir and Annabel are both in good health.'

Helena retreated to stand behind the chair once more, resting her hands loosely on top of its back, taking refuge in the illusion of it as a barrier between them. 'Of that I am glad.'

'Annabel asked for you.'

She glanced up in surprise. 'She does not know? Stephen has not found them? Perhaps he believes me dead in the wreckage of the *Bonnie Lass*, after all.'

Guy did not move from his position in front of the fire, but she saw the compassion that entered his expression, and she knew that her hopes were in vain. 'No, I'm afraid that Tayburn knows both that you were at Seamill Hall and that you left with me.'

Helena's fingers stole towards her mouth before she checked the gesture. But she could not deny the sudden nausea that rolled in her stomach or the aridity of her mouth. Words escaped her. And in that moment she could do nothing other than cling to the back of the chair harder than ever. She was glad of its presence, for she did not know whether she would have been able to maintain her poise without it. She took a deep breath and her words, when they came, were calm and quiet. 'Then you are in very grave danger.'

'Oh, dear, what a worrisome discovery,' he said with irony.

'It's not too late to extricate yourself from this mess. If you go now, Stephen need never know anything more than you transported me to London. It was the gallant act of a gentleman, nothing more.'

'Have you forgotten that I came here to call him out?'

'How could I?' She stared at the handsome profile. 'But I can no longer let you do that.' And then, as if speaking to herself, she said, 'I shall throw myself on his mercy. Tell him that I came to my senses as soon as I arrived in London and returned to him as quickly as I could. He need know nothing further about you.'

'Tayburn has no mercy, and besides…' he turned away from the fire and came towards her '…we have an agreement.' He stopped directly in front of her. 'Unless you wish to change that, Helena? Perhaps you find my company disagreeable.'

She shook her head, unwittingly freeing a tendril of hair to dangle at the side of her cheek. 'You know that I do not,' she said softly, 'but he has Emma. And now he knows not only that Mr Weir and his wife gave me shelter, but that you and I travelled together.' She touched her fingers to the tight band of pain that was forming across her forehead. 'My father and Agnes and Old Tam are dead. And if I do nothing, then more will follow. Seven lives for my freedom. The cost is too high.' She let her hand drop and looked him directly in the eye. 'Had I known the price, I never would have left.'

'We've been through all of this, Helena. You did nothing wrong. And besides, you cannot go back—the die is already cast.'

Her brow creased. 'What do you mean? If I go back to him, it should temper his revenge against Mr and Mrs Weir…and you.'

'You know it will make not the slightest difference. Sacrificing yourself on Tayburn's alter shall not change what he has planned.'

She gripped the chair back so tightly that she thought it would snap beneath the pressure of her fingers. The terrible coldness was spreading through her again, bringing back with it all of the pain that she could not forget. 'Then God forgive me for what I have unleashed upon you all.'

He came to her then, stood behind her, covered her cold tense fingers with the relaxed warmth of his hands.

'What shall I do?' And for the first time in her five long years Helena was truly at a loss. It was one thing to endure the pain herself, quite another to stand by and watch it inflicted on others, knowing herself to be the cause. 'What shall I do?' she whispered again.

Guy gave no answer, just turned her slowly around in his arms, and tilted her face up to his, scanning her eyes as if he could see the torment in her soul, as if he understood exactly what it was that she felt.

'I know what he will do to her and I cannot bear it.' Her voice cracked.

'Helena,' he breathed, and the sound of her name upon his lips was as soothing as a caress. 'You need not bear it, for we shall stop Tayburn very neatly in his tracks.'

She stared up into his eyes, seeing the absolute confidence in them. 'There's nothing we can do while he has Emma.'

'Then we had better fetch her back.' And the smile that spread across his mouth was filled with deadly promise.

'How can we?' She stared at him as if he had run mad. 'He has her at Dunleish.'

The smile stretched deeper. 'Tayburn is not presently at home. I understand that he expressed an interest in travelling to London.' One eyebrow raised in a suggestive manner.

'London?' Her eyes widened. 'He is pursuing me!'

'He thinks he is pursuing us,' Guy corrected. 'Just as we knew he would…eventually.' He smiled a lazy smile. 'Thus leaving your sister alone in Dunleish. How very convenient…for us.'

'You cannot mean to…' Incredulity made her stare all the harder. 'You would not dare…'

'It is a simple enough solution, sweetheart. I shall be back tomorrow, hopefully accompanied by your sister.'

'No!' She gripped his arms. 'It is too dangerous.'

'I'm touched by your concern,' he said, and dropping his gaze to her lips, his smile became flirtatious.

'Do you think just to walk in there, take Emma and walk back out again?'

'Something like that,' he murmured, and slipped his arms around her.

She shivered, but whether it was from his touch or from the thought of what he planned to do she did not know. 'It is madness.'

His breath tickled against the side of her neck as he lowered his mouth to her ear. 'Madness that Tayburn shall not expect.'

She had to admit he had a point. No sane-minded man would venture willingly into Dunleish Castle. She chewed at her lip, feeling her skin tingle where his breath caressed.

'It is a good opportunity to rescue your sister.'

He was right, of course, if Emma was indeed still alive. She gave a little nod. 'It does not mean that I like it, but I suppose it is better than you calling him out.'

Guy did not correct her mistaken assumption. Instead he allowed the tip of his tongue to tease against her neck.

Helena released an involuntary gasp of pleasure and strove to keep her mind focused on their conversation. 'When…?'

His tongue traced a dance up to her jaw.

She tried again. 'When do you think to go there?'

He touched his tongue to the centre of her mouth, and as her lips parted and softened in response, he whispered, 'First light.'

She shivered at his words, but then his mouth closed upon hers, deliciously demanding, and his kisses silenced her questions.

Those that knew Sir Stephen were often heard to say that the devil looked after his own, and indeed Tayburn had an inordinate ability to come up trumps in the most tricky of situations. His flight to London in pursuit of Helena was no exception. For as luck would have it Tayburn happened to choose the very same coaching inn to rest overnight as Guy and Helena had used not so many nights previously.

Tayburn dispatched his wife to bed and spent the rest of the evening in the taproom, occupying a whole table to himself that not even the roughest of navvies dared to comment upon. Indeed, despite the crowd of bodies within the public room, it was as if there was a small exclusion zone around Tayburn. Men sensed something of the white-haired man's nature and were wise enough to give him a wide berth. It was a raw primeval power and Tayburn revelled in the fear that he saw in the faces around him. He drank his brandy and bided his time, letting the bodies become accustomed to his presence, like a wolf that sat within the heart of a flock of sheep, lulling them into a false sense of security by his inactivity and apparent inattention. It was not long before the buzz of conversation resumed around him. Tayburn sipped his brandy and listened to words of inconsequence spoken in accents that made the following difficult, but Tayburn had nothing else to do—for now. And so he continued to listen for an hour, and then another, until the drink had unguarded both tongues and suspicions. It was then that he heard it.

'That redhead he had with him was a tasty piece and no mistake.' The young man wiped the dribble of ale from his chin and continued to regale his friends with his thoughts on the woman. 'Well, it was that he had them sup in a private parlour. He was like the bloody cat that got the cream. No wonder he didn't want the likes of us to have a good old gander at her. Hell, but I'd sell my soul for a night with his missus.'

'She wasn't his wife,' said another. 'Harry there…' he indicated towards the landlord waiting behind the bar '…said she weren't lady to that lord.'

'Like that, was it?' leered the first man. 'Wish that I'd have known at the time. I gave her a friendly look and those green eyes looked right through me as if I were nothing. Right snooty she was. If I'd known she was his fancy piece, I'd have taken her down a peg or two.'

'And cross that aristo she was with? I don't think so, Frankie. You're all talk, you are. You'd have been scared shitless if he'd pulled a pistol on you.'

'Happen I've a pistol or two of my own. I'm no chicken-heart.'

A serving wench came over and dumped another pitcher of ale down on the bar beside them. 'Courtesy of the gentleman in black over there.'

Three pairs of eyes stared over at Tayburn.

Tayburn gave a nod of his head and raised his glass in their direction.

The man, Frankie, lifted his own in return.

'Who the hell is he?' his mate whispered.

'Cursed if I know,' came the reply. 'But free ale is free ale. Let the fool pay for our drink if he wants to. I'm not complaining.'

They laughed and worked their way quite merrily through the contents of the pitcher.

Tayburn bought them three further pitchers before two of the men decided they had best find their own ways home to their wives and their beds. Frankie was not wise enough to follow suit. He had no wife and he knew that his rented room would be cold. A glass of brandy appeared in his hand—courtesy of the same gentleman. The liquid was strong and seared a warmth in his throat. It was not often that Frankie had the chance to taste real French brandy. He decided to stay a while longer. And when Tayburn beckoned him, Frankie made his way somewhat unsteadily over to his table.

Another few glasses of brandy secured Tayburn all that he needed to know about the beautiful redheaded woman and the lord that had accompanied her. He had no further need of Frankie. Tayburn smiled at him and even in his drunken stupor the younger man quailed.

'No one calls me *fool*,' said Tayburn, and his smile was small and deadly.

Tayburn and his wife departed early the next day. The ostlers commented that it was strange that he headed back north when that was the direction from which he had arrived the previous evening, and in such a hurry. An hour later they found Frankie's body. His throat had been cut.

Chapter Twelve

That night Helena lay next to Guy in their bed within the Eglinton Arm's Hotel. Outside a patter of rain had set up, thrumming steadily against the glass of the large bow window in their bedchamber. A fire still burned in the grate, lighting the darkness with its orange glow. The smell of the candle that Guy had just extinguished drifted through the air. There was silence save for the pelting of raindrops and the run of water in the guttering outside.

Helena lay on her back, eyes open against the darkness, and waited to see what Guy would do. The expectation was obvious, but the previous nights had shown a different side to the man. She knew that he desired her, had known it almost from the moment they met. And yet he had not taken her, not fully as was a man's right to take of his mistress—not yet. She thought again of the way that his mouth had covered her breast, of the heat of his kisses and the aching wantonness with which her body had responded. And the way he had stopped so suddenly, even though his arousal was still firm and unsated. *Was your flight across this bed from me in earnest?* he had asked, as if her answer was so very important to him. She had wanted him, wanted him to touch her, to make love to her. The blush rose over her body at the memory and her thighs grew warm. The mattress moved and she felt Guy roll on to his side and lay his hand upon her stomach. She shivered beneath his fingers before lying completely still.

'Helena.' His voice was a husky murmur through the darkness and it seemed that he could feel the soft warm skin through the fine silk of the ivory nightdress he had bought for her. He heard the soft catch of her breath in her throat as he slid his hand slowly up to rest against her ribcage, close to her breasts. 'Are you cold?' he whispered, feeling the tension that surrounded her.

'I'm quite warm, thank you,' she said as if they were chatting politely over tea in a drawing room, instead of lying next to one another half-naked in bed.

He wanted to make love to her, to heal all the hurts that Tayburn had dealt her, but he did not know the depth of Helena's wounds. She had been forced to Tayburn's bed against her will and he'd be damned if he'd do anything similar. Despite his glib words to Weir, Guy knew that he would not attempt a seduction of any kind. He desired her with a force that gnawed at him night and day, but seduction smacked of bending her to his will, albeit in a more sophisticated fashion than the brutality Tayburn had used, and he could not do that to Helena, not after everything that she had endured.

'You are shivering.'

'No.' The denial was swift and adamant. 'You're mistaken.'

His fingers stroked against the base of her breasts,

feeling that which she could not hide—the harried thumping of her heart.

'You need not be afraid, Helena. I'm not Tayburn. I will not hurt you.'

'I'm not afraid.' The denial was uttered in a small tight voice as if her lips were as rigid as the rest of her body.

He gave a soft sigh of a laugh and dropped a kiss against her eyebrow. 'My poor sweetheart, you don't have to pretend any longer. I have no intention of letting Tayburn reclaim you. You're quite safe, and it's perfectly acceptable to show some measure of emotion. Indeed, ladies are positively expected to be having attacks of the megrims one minute and the vapours the next.' He smiled, feeling the soft silkiness of her hair against his mouth.

'You forget, Guy, that I am no lady.' She had not moved; she still stared up straight ahead towards the ceiling.

His hand moved from her body to her neck and then, gently cupping her cheek, he turned her face to his. He could see only the shadow of her features in the light cast from the glowing embers, and knew that she would see nothing more of him. Yet he lowered his face until their noses almost touched and stared into her eyes. 'You were a lady when Tayburn took you, were you not?'

She gave no answer.

'Were you not, Helena?' he said again, more forcefully.

'Yes,' came the whisper back.

'Then you are a lady still. No matter what happens, remember that.'

He felt the brush of her eyelashes against his as she closed her eyes. He ceased to think. As a matter of instinct his mouth lowered to hers and delivered a kiss that was both gentle yet firm, a kiss that both reassured and aroused.

She melted against him and returned the kiss in full.

It was almost his undoing. He groaned, as his tongue danced against hers, lapping and stroking and kissing in an ecstasy of delight. His arousal throbbed, seeking release as it pressed against her sweet softness. He felt her body answer his call, felt her heat, her invitation. His body clung to hers, striving for the coupling that his mind would not allow. Heaven help him, if he did not stop now he did not think that he would be capable of doing so until he had made her his own. And so, slowly, he forced his retreat, pulling gently back from lips that were everything that he wanted, easing his manhood away from such torturous temptation. He looked down into her eyes, seeing there a heavy-lidded desire that mirrored his own, and it was all he could do not to cover her mouth with his own once more and slide his length into her.

'Sweet Helena.' He gently stroked her cheek. 'Have you any idea of what you do to me?' There was silence save for the soft hush of her breath. He gave a sigh. 'When we free your sister, Tayburn will have no further hold over you.' He stared down into her face. 'Now we had best go to sleep. Tomorrow shall be a long day.' And with that he finally released her and turned over.

Helena looked at the strong broad back that Guy presented to her with mixed emotions. He was right, tomorrow would be a long day, a long and dangerous day. No matter what Guy said, Helena knew that there was a very real chance that he might not return from Dunleish. Many men had entered the castle; few ever left it alive. He was risking his life for her, to free her sister—a girl he did not even know. And all because he had taken her as his mistress—in name only. He had given her his protection and taken very little in return. Yet Helena knew that he wanted her; she felt his need as powerfully as if it were her own. None of it made any sense. He could have taken her at any time of his choosing, knowing that she would give no resistance.

And being bedded by Guy would be nothing of pain and everything of pleasure…the sweep of his hands, the ardour of his kiss… She still trembled from his touch…still ached for him. But for all that she longed for him, there was a part of her that dreaded to play the harlot, to confirm that that was all she was—a harlot, a whore. He was keeping his side of the bargain. Surely it was only honourable that she kept hers? And then she caught her line of thought—honourable! When could there ever be honour in that role? She raised herself up on her elbows and looked across the small distance that separated them. Warmth emanated from the dark shape facing the wall. His breaths came slow and even, as if he was already asleep. Helena knew that he was not.

'Guy?' she whispered his name through the darkness before she could think better of it.

She could see the change in his shape as he lifted his head and peered over his shoulder at her. 'What is it?'

A pause.

'You know that you risk your life in going to Dunleish?' Her voice sounded slightly breathless.

'Sweetheart,' he murmured over his shoulder, 'you have told me all I need to know. I have the map and all is prepared. Now, empty your head of such thoughts and go to sleep. Everything will be well tomorrow.'

'Do not underestimate him, Guy. I'm afraid that you do not know what you have taken on with Stephen.'

He rolled over and, gathering her into his arms, kissed the skin of her cheek beside her mouth. 'I know a lot better than you realise.'

'You do not know him.'

His fingers rubbed against the top of her arm. 'Men like Tayburn are all the same. Know one and you know them all,' and there was some emotion in his voice that she did not understand.

Her skin grew warm beneath his hand. 'No man is like Stephen. He is the very devil.' And she could not suppress the shiver that rippled down her spine. 'I fear for your life.'

Guy pulled her closer. 'Then do not. I have no intention of losing it and every intention of delivering Emma to you tomorrow.' He kissed her again; a small chaste kiss on her forehead. 'Now, go to sleep,' and started to move away.

Helena stayed him, resting her hand on his lean hard flank. 'Guy.'

He stopped. Beneath her fingers she felt him tense. 'Yes?'

Helena licked her suddenly dry lips. 'I am not tired,' she said, and felt a warmth flood her cheeks at her boldness.

'Are you saying that you want me?' His surprise was blatant.

She gave a little clear of her throat. 'Perhaps.'

'Perhaps?'

She felt his body come up against hers. Felt his breath upon her cheek. The pulse in her neck was throbbing so hard she thought she would not be able to speak.

'I know that you want to…that you want…' Her words trailed off. 'I will not resist.'

'It's not about what I want,' he growled.

She swallowed hard, not understanding, not knowing what to say. There was silence…and silence…and more silence.

His chest rose and fell in a slow steady movement. All else about him seemed frozen to immobility.

'You've given me your protection and taken nothing in return,' she said, unable to bear the silence any longer.

'What is it that you would have me take?' he asked, and she could hear the sadness in his tone.

'I…' Again the words escaped her.

'I told you, I'm not Tayburn, and I will *take* nothing from you,' he said, and there was an undercurrent that she did not understand through his words. This time there was no comforting caress, no kiss of affection. He turned on his side and went to sleep.

Helena lay where she was and thought over all that had happened. When she finally found sleep, it was not Stephen or Dunleish or even Emma that occupied her mind, but the enigma of the man that slept so soundly by her side.

It was still dark when Helena awoke to the sounds of splashing water. Over on the chest of drawers a single candle burned, casting a gloomy light throughout the bedchamber. Guy stood with his back to her, rinsing beneath his arms with water from the white china basin. Even within the dimness of the candlelight she could see the droplets of water glistening against the skin of his back. He had a sinewy musculature that belied his self-professed hedonistic lifestyle. Whatever he said to the contrary, Guy, Lord Varington, did some activity that kept his body lean and honed and fit. Helena found that she was staring. He leaned to the side, grabbed a towel and dried first his face and then his body. Helena knew that she should not have been watching him, but the knowledge did not move her eyes away, nor did she give him any indication that she was awake. She studied the broad line of his shoulders and the definition of each muscle until Guy turned round and glanced at her as if he sensed her attention.

''Morning, sweetheart.'

Helena had the grace to blush. 'Good morning,' she said, and rapidly averted her eyes.

He was smiling and she knew he knew that she had been staring. He rubbed a hand across his chin, testing the roughness of the skin, then, without even bothering to don his shirt, went to rummage in his bag.

'What time is it?' she asked

'A little after seven, I would guess,' came the reply from the vicinity of the foot of the bed.

'You do not need to look at your watch?'

'I always wake at seven. My watch is on the table. Check for yourself if you wish.' He rose and she saw that he held in his hand a razor and a small mirror. 'It's at times like these that I miss Collins.' So saying, he propped the mirror at the side of the candle and, wetting his shaving brush within the water, started to lather the soap on the brush's badger bristles.

'I can do that for you if it will make it easier.' The words were out before Helena realised that she was going to say them.

He stopped what he was doing and turned round to look at her. 'Have you ever shaved a man before?'

'Yes,' she said, then, seeing the dark expression that flitted across his eyes, added, 'After my father's attack he lost the use of his right arm. He did not trust anyone else to shave him save for me.'

He gave a soft laugh and held out his hand to the side in invitation. 'Then I put myself in your capable hands.'

She climbed out of the bed and came to stand by his side. 'I must tell you that it's been some time since my shaving practice. But I shall do my best.'

'I'm relieved to hear it.'

He manoeuvred the chair to the side of the chest of drawers close to the wash basin, and sat himself down. 'Here, take this.' He passed her the lathered shaving brush. Then he sat back and held his face up, ready for her ministrations.

Helena would rather have found a tie to catch back the curtain of her hair, but it was too late for that; her hands were already covered in soap from the brush. She moved to stand at his side, feeling the carpet rub against the bareness of her feet. Rather than meet his gaze, she started straight away, gently stroking the lather across the dark stubbled skin of his cheeks, lathering the soap up further to also cover his chin and throat. Beneath her fingers she felt the upward tilt of his mouth. She reached across, rinsed the brush and her hands in the water, dried them on the towel and picked up the razor. It opened to reveal a wicked-looking blade that glinted in the candlelight. A weapon by another name— one slip and a man's life could be severed.

'Are you ready?' she asked.

He raised his chin, exposing his throat. 'I trust that you shall keep a steady hand, Helena.' A corner of his mouth tugged up. 'I am completely at your mercy.'

Her eyes flickered from the blade in her hand to the soap-smeared skin of his throat and back again, realising the extent of his vulnerability and exactly what that meant. 'You trust me.'

The smile flickered again. 'Of course.'

Helena felt the response of her own mouth. Then she put all such thoughts from her mind and, with the blade in hand, bent lower over his throat.

Helena's touch was gentle. She shaved him with an efficiency that rivalled his valet's, but with a tenderness with which Collins could never have hoped to compete. The blade within her hand contacted his skin in short strokes, razing all trace of the beard's beginnings. She covered his throat, his cheeks, his upper lip, and even the contours of his chin without so much as a nick, leaning close so that she might see what she was doing within the dimness of the room, so close that he could smell her scent and feel the brush of her long tresses against the bare skin of his chest and arms. Having her so near was a taste of both heaven and hell. He wanted to cast the blade aside, take her into his arms and kiss her thoroughly before laying her back on the bed and making love to her. But he could not. He strove not to give rein to such thoughts and contented himself with watching her face.

Between her brows there was a tiny crease of concentration. The flicker of the candle flame caused golden lights to dance in her eyes. Her focus followed the blade across his skin, a soft scrape, left or right, up or down, following the direction of the hair growth, wiping the blade clean after each scrape. The small repetitive movements relaxed him, chased away all tension. And by the time Helena had rinsed his face, patted it dry and pronounced that he was all done, Guy was feeling strangely contented for a man about to embark on a hazardous mission.

He stood and rubbed his knuckles against her arm. 'I could get used to that.'

They shared a smile.

'Now you had best get dressed and quickly.'

She looked at him with a start of surprise. 'You wish me to come with you?'

He looked right back at her with a twinkle in his eye. 'Only as far as Seamill Hall.'

'What do you mean?'

He bent, retrieved his shirt, and pulled it on over his head. 'I have arranged with Weir that you will stay there today.'

'I cannot.'

'Make haste, Helena. We do not have much time.'

'I am…' She hesitated, blushed and forced the words out. 'I am your mistress, for pity's sake, Guy!'

He stopped fastening the buttons and cocked an eyebrow. 'And don't I know it.' He smiled a warm seductive smile and looked meaningfully into her eyes.

'I cannot embarrass Mrs Weir so by arriving on her doorstep.'

'Helena, I shall feel better for knowing that you are with Weir and not here alone while I am gone for such a time.'

'But if you are certain that Stephen has departed for London…'

'And left behind men who are loyal to him.'

There was a small silence between them, and then Guy resumed his buttoning once more. 'Will you go to Seamill Hall as I ask?'

'Very well,' she said, confused by what she saw in his eyes.

'Good.' He seemed relieved.

'You have the map that I drew?' she asked.

'Safe in my pocket. If Emma is not in the chamber you marked, is there anywhere else he might have hidden her?'

She looked at him. And he saw the flit of fear in her eyes. 'The dungeon. But pray God he has not resorted to that. There are sights there that would turn Emma's mind.'

'Never fear, I will bring her back to you.'

She mustered a small brave smile at that and rushed to make ready for the journey. They completed their *toilettes* in a comfortable silence. She did not speak again until the cloak was wrapped around her shoulders and they were ready to leave. The baggage was already packed upon the coach. It was now or never. She did not think that she would have a chance to speak to him at Seamill Hall.

'You will have a care, won't you, Guy?'

The lopsided cheeky smile was back on his face. 'No, I intend to be completely reckless.'

She shook her head and gave a sob of a laugh.

And then his arms touched to her shoulders. One hand moved up and his thumb touched lightly against her cheek. It seemed that he was about to say something, something that Helena instinctively knew was of the greatest importance. With great tenderness he brushed her hair from her cheek. 'Helena, there is a purse and a letter tucked down the side of my small travelling valise. If things go awry and I do not come back from Dunleish by tomorrow night, then I want you to take the money from the purse—'

She interrupted him with a gasp. 'No, please do not—'

But his arms wrapped themselves around her and he

captured her to him. 'Hear me out, Helena. There is not much time left and it is important that I say this.'

A nod and she caught back what words she would have said.

'Take the money from the purse,' he repeated, 'use it to travel post-chaise to Cornwall and seek out my brother. Hand the letter to him in person, no one else. His name and direction are penned upon the paper. Lucien will ensure your safety. Give me your word that you will do this.'

'I would not just abandon you in Dunleish!' she exclaimed.

'Promise me, Helena.' And his eyes stared down into hers with a determination that she had not seen before.

She nodded.

'Say the words,' he insisted.

She sighed, and looked at him with a great weight around her heart.

'Helena?' he prompted.

'Very well,' she said at last. 'I promise.'

He seemed to relax at her words. Then his face lowered to hers and she saw the closing of his eyes before his mouth slid against hers.

Too soon he moved back.

'We had best be gone before Tayburn realises the error of his call and decides to head for home.' Guy laughed. One last kiss from her mouth and they moved towards the door.

The knob was turning beneath his hand as she said his name, 'Guy.'

He paused, looked down at her.

'Thank you,' she said, and meant it with every fibre of her being.

The smile that he gave her showed that he understood. Sensuous and caring and reassuring all at once. Helena's heart squeezed tight. And then they were off and walking along the thick pile of the carpet and down the broad expanse of the staircase. Outside the early morning was still thick and dark.

When he left her at Seamill Hall the sky had lightened to a charcoal grey with the first hint of dawn. By the time that daylight surfaced in full, she knew that the rowing boat would be well on its way across the Firth of Clyde to the island of St Vey, carrying Guy towards Dunleish. No matter how hard she tried to stop, she could not help but hear Guy's words play again and again in her mind: *before Tayburn realises the error of his call and decides to head for home.* And the chill made the blood in Helena's veins run cold with foreboding.

Pine creaked against oak as the oars swept their rhythmic circle, pulling them through the cold grey seawater. The small wooden boat slid forwards as easily as a warmed knife through butter and Guy supposed that the current must be in his favour, aiding his progress towards the island. He scanned the distance ahead. It seemed close enough to swim. One look at the chilly water was enough to banish any such notions and he was glad that he had worn the caped overcoat and gloves. The sky was lighting from the east, washing out the darkness, turning night to day. Wind ruffled his hair and nipped at his cheeks. Not for the first time he wondered if Helena's sister was still alive. He set his jaw firm and turned his mind from such speculation. He did not want to think what it might mean for Helena were she not.

Helena. A vision of her face swam into his mind. Fixed in concentration as she shaved him, the perfectly shaped brows, the beautiful smoky green eyes, the slope of her small straight nose and the ripe fullness of her lips. Within the candlelight her skin had glowed a smooth golden cream and her hair was as red and long and riotous as any beauty from a Pre-Raphaelite painting.

She had wielded the razor with such gentle competent strokes, such steady hands. No woman had ever done such a thing for him before. She had smiled at him, with no sign of the mask that hid her emotions from the world. And Guy had never seen a more beautiful sight than Helena's smile, nor heard a better sound than her laughter. Just the memory gladdened his heart and turned his own mouth up into an arc. Thank you, she had said, and Guy had known that those two small words covered a multitude of emotion. It was as if all barriers between them had fallen away and he had seen the real Helena, the woman she had hidden from Tayburn. In the sharing of that moment something had bound them together. Guy felt it still, and he knew that it could not be undone. He knew too that he would do whatever he had to, to free her from Tayburn. A gull appeared overhead, gliding on a current of air, precarious in the wind's buffeting. He pulled harder at the oars and the boat moved silently on towards St Vey.

Helena had dreaded it but her reception at Seamill Hall had not been as bad as she had imagined. Mr Weir had been polite and stiff; his dislike and disapproval no worse than before. Of his wife there had been no sign, and that hurt more than all of Mr Weir's censure ever could.

The morning wore on with a creeping slowness; every passing hour only adding to Helena's anxiety. The book that Mrs Weir had sent for her to read lay opened upon her lap. She read the same page again, the black print of words meaningless again. A sigh, and she gave up the pretence, snapping the book shut with agitated fingers. She tried to reason with herself. Stephen was not at Dunleish. Guy knew what he was doing. He had her map. She had told him everything she knew of the place: where Stephen's men would stand guard, the day's routine, who was who in Stephen's little empire, right down to descriptions and names. So why could she not rid herself of this feeling of dread?

The book tumbled on to the bedcovers and she rose from where she was seated on the comfort of the mattress to wander to the window. It was not the cosy yellow chamber in which she had stayed before. This room was larger, colder and decorated in a range of chilly blue hues. The view from the window was not of the sea, but of the front garden and the main road that passed before the big house. Dove-grey clouds drifted over a cold pale sky. Rain drizzled, adding steadily to the puddles that remained from last night's deluge. The road was quiet. No passing traffic. Helen's fingers tapped impatiently upon the window ledge. She chewed at her lip, then nibbled at her thumbnail. A group of sparrows hopped near a crab-apple tree. Nothing else moved. Another sigh, and she gave up her place at the window and wandered over towards the fire.

The fingers of her right hand slipped into the pocket of her dress and touched absently the silver key that she had placed there on impulse before leaving the Eglinton Arms Hotel that morning. She wondered where Guy was precisely. He must surely have reached the castle by now. Had he found Emma? She placed another log from the box on to the fire and moved the guard back into place. Please, God, let them be safe, both Emma and Guy. She turned away and caught sight of the portmanteaux and bags tucked neatly in the corner of the room. Her eyes were drawn to Guy's small valise at the top of his pile; just one part of the matching set that he had bought in Ayr during their recent stay in the town.

The wrecking of the *Bonnie Lass* and Helena's subsequent journey south was a lifetime ago. Days had stretched to years. Had she really only known him for little under a fortnight? It seemed to Helena that they had always been together. Her life with Stephen was like some horrible nightmare that had faded in the daylight. Five years of nothing. Only now was she alive again. 'Guy,' she whispered the word aloud and the soft catch of his name seemed to resonate in the room around her. *If I do not come back from Dunleish…* The hairs on the back of her neck prickled. Pray God bring him back safe. *There is a purse and a letter tucked down the side of my small travelling valise.* She did not want his money, she wanted him.

Helena walked slowly forwards until the pile of dark brown leather baggage lay at her feet. A purse and a letter. The straps of Guy's valise were not buckled. The valise opened easily. Her hand swept lightly over his neatly folded clothes. She lifted the uppermost shirt and raised it to her face, until it met with her nose. Her eyes closed as she inhaled the clean scent of him, feeling the cotton soft against her cheek, softer still against her lips and the kiss that she pressed to it. She remembered the feel of his hands upon her, the magical touch of his mouth, and when she laid the shirt carefully back in its place there was an ache in her heart. It was a small pain that was both joyful and sorrowful. Helena had felt it before during these past days. Only now did she understand what it was. And the knowledge made Guy's trip to Dunleish all the more worrying.

She stopped where she was, letting the revelation sweep over her, letting it fill every pore. It was a glorious feeling, and one that made her heart sing. She smiled, and let her hand wander down the side of Guy's valise, until it found the purse and letter. The purse contained a pile of gold coins and a roll of white banknotes. She tucked it back down out of sight. The letter... The smile was wiped from her face. Her eyes opened wide and the breath rushed from between her parted lips. Happiness cracked in a sudden explosion of shock and splintered into shards around her. In the ensuing silence everything stopped: Helena's heart, Helena's breath.

The hurriedly penned script upon the letter's front was bold before her eyes. It taunted her with her own foolish trust. For Helena recognised the name written upon the paper, the name of the man Guy had said was his brother: The Earl of Tregellas—the so-called Wicked Earl, a man of whom Stephen had spoken, a man whom Stephen admired. Her eyes pressed shut and then opened again as if by doing so the name would have changed to something more palatable. Tregellas. It lay there, written in Guy's own hand. *Lucien will ensure your safety*, he had said. Helena set the letter down on top of Guy's folded shirt and backed away towards the bed. *I have known a man like Tayburn.* His words played again in her mind. Helena shivered and suspicion hung heavy upon her, smothering all else that had gone in its path.

* * *

The trek from his landing point upon St Vey to
Dunleish was much as Guy had expected. The small
sandy bay where he had moored the boat was located
on the south side of the island; Tayburn's castle was on
the northernmost coast. The rocky terrain near the
landing bay forced him to keep to a coastal route ini-
tially. None of that had been unknown to him. So far
Helena's words had proved accurate. Sand clung to his
boots as he walked steadily on across the firmness of the
shore. She had told to him to follow the line of the beach
for the first part, and so he had. It increased the distance
greatly, but the ground underfoot was easier and safer
than scrabbling over the huge rocks.

He cut up on to the hills as soon as he was able. Everything of the place was coarse and sparse and tough.
Even the grass beneath his feet was short and scrubby.
The few trees that clustered here and there were bare and
bent, lichen patterning their grey spindles of branches.
There were great clumps of gorse that looked as if they
had been ravaged by the worst of the weather, their small
spiny leaves as hostile as everything else on the island.
With great loping strides he paced himself to cover the
ground. The compass in his pocket confirmed his direction, Helena's carefully drawn map told him the rest. He
headed on, oblivious to the smir of rain that wetted his
skin and clothes and hair, his eyes watchful, ever alert
for the presence of danger. He knew that there was little
else on the island except the castle, but caution cost little
and saved much. The past had taught him that much.

In less than an hour he had reached the ledge hidden
above the shore. He dropped to his haunches, lay flat

on his stomach and crawled out towards the edge of the rocky platform. Leaning out over the precipice, he peered round past the sheets of sheer rock…to the castle that lay beyond.

Cut from the red sandstone that filled the hills beneath his feet, Dunleish Castle was more of a large fortified keep. It was tall in design, with such small narrow windows that Guy knew it would be dark within the thickness of those walls. The tops of the walls were crenellated in the fashion of castles of old and in each of the four corners, adjoined to the main body, were tall thin towers. It was from one of these that a flag hung at half-mast—proclaiming that the castle's master was not presently in residence. He scanned the other towers, saw a figure leaning against the wall in one—the lookout. Tayburn must have a lot of enemies to keep a man permanently in such a post. Guy looked for only a moment longer. Then, still on his stomach, he wriggled back from danger, retreating to the safety of the ledge. One last glance around, then he turned and disappeared into the rocks behind him.

The cave was dark, but Guy had come prepared with a candle lantern and tinderbox. With the tiny lantern held before him, he moved towards the back of the cave and stepped through the narrow gap into the tunnel. The small flickering light revealed only a few steps ahead, but Guy knew where the tunnel would take him. The leather of his soles sounded loud upon the gritty stone beneath. The air grew stale. Water dripped down the dark hewn red walls. He followed on, until at last the passageway ended and before him lay the two wooden crates used by Helena and her servants in their escape. He took what he needed from his pockets before shrugging off his greatcoat on to the floor. At last he looked up to the small wooden hatch overhead. And the smile on his face was grim and determined. Guy stood up on the first crate and prepared to enter the south-west tower of Dunleish Castle.

Helena paced the blue bedchamber in Seamill Hall for the hundredth time. The book lay abandoned on the bed. She could not stop thinking about Guy and Emma and Dunleish. And neither could she banish the name that she had seen written upon that letter. Tregellas, the Wicked Earl, a man like Stephen by all accounts, a man to whom Guy would send her, a man who was his brother. It didn't make sense. Intrinsically she trusted Guy, could not believe there was anything sinister about him. He had treated her well, with respect, with kindness. He wanted her, yet he did not take her. Had said he would *take* nothing of her.

She closed her eyes and could see the strong lines of his face, the piercing paleness of his eyes, the playfulness of his smile. Even now he was on his way to a monster's lair to save her sister. She did not doubt that he would give his all to do it too. Could he rescue Emma from Stephen, just as he had rescued her?

There had to be some other explanation about his brother. Maybe Stephen had been wrong. She doubted that: Stephen was never wrong. She sat down by the window, mulling the matter, barely seeing what was before her. A small red-breasted robin hopped along the garden wall to perch upon the gate. Black birds scurried beneath the russet-leaved bushes. Three women walked past up on the road with baskets hung over their arms. A horse trotted by. Helena decided she could do nothing other than ask Guy of the matter when he returned…if he returned. She tried to push the fear from her mind, to stay positive.

Guy was right. It was a risky venture, but the odds were stacked in his favour. Stephen was not there and that alone meant there was a good chance of Guy's success. And it was better surely than Guy calling Stephen out. Or so she tried to convince herself. But her hands grew as cold as ice and a ripple of foreboding snaked down her spine. She glanced uneasily around the bedroom. Nothing was out of place. A clock ticked upon the mantel. Flames licked lively in the fireplace. But the air was growing colder. Helena knew she was not a woman given to fancies. She had spent the last five years deliberately deadening all feeling. And yet now… She scolded herself for being foolish. Daylight dimmed. She glanced out of the window, looked up to the sky. The clouds had darkened, rendering the day sinister and gloomy. Helena shivered. She was becoming like those women Guy had spoken of—fanciful, hysterical. She would sit by the fire, quietly read Mrs Weir's book and wait for Guy to return.

But Helena made no move. Indeed, she found that she could not draw her eyes from the road at the top of the garden. She stared as if transfixed by the sight. Her scalp began to prickle. The hairs on the back of her neck stood on end. Her stomach clenched tightly. Still, Helena could not take her eyes from the empty road. Then she heard it: the distant gallop of horses, the far-off rumble of carriage wheels. The noise grew louder, and louder still, until a carriage appeared, its dark body swaying with the recklessness of its speed. The mouths of the four black horses that pulled it were foam-flecked and bloodied, their coats gleaming with sweat, but Helena was not looking at the horses. Her mouth gaped open. The blood drained from her face. Her heart plummeted into her stomach. She whirled and ran for the bedroom door, the wood hitting hard against the wall as she threw it open, the sound of her running footsteps echoing along the corridor. The coach sped off into the distance, its crest still visible upon its mud-splattered doors—a black devil on a red background.

Chapter Thirteen

'Mr Weir!' Helena burst into the drawing room to find only his wife sitting by the window, stitching her embroidery.

'Helena?' Annabel Weir's face contorted with shocked puzzlement. 'What on earth are you doing up? John said you had some sort of contagion and that I mustn't go near.'

Helena would have laughed at the crudity of John Weir's lie had she not been so desperate and determined to save Guy. Every second was critical. 'Where is your husband, ma'am?'

'Where he usually is—in the gunroom. But what is—?'

'Sorry,' shouted Helena over her shoulder as she sprinted to the door. 'No time to explain.' She threw open the door and almost collided with Mr Weir, who had heard the running footsteps and Helena's shouting.

'What in heaven's name!' His face scowled his anger. 'You were to stay within the bedchamber. That was the agreement. Guy shall hear of this.'

She was breathing hard from exertion and anxiety. 'Guy is in danger,' she panted. 'Stephen is back. His coach has just passed along the main road, travelling at speed.'

'Don't be absurd,' snapped Weir. 'Tayburn's in London.'

'He has returned.'

'It's not possible. He couldn't be back so soon, there's not enough time—'

'Mr Weir, we must warn Guy.' Her voice raised in frustration.

'Calm down, madam. You cannot even be sure that the coach was Tayburn's.'

It was all Helena could do to keep from yelling at him. 'Do you doubt that I know Sir Stephen's crest?' she demanded. 'Need I tell you what it stands for? You may stand here all day speculating on whether I have the right or wrong of it, and let Stephen catch Guy at Dunleish, but I, sir, will not.' She saw the subtle shift in his expression.

'We cannot stop Tayburn,' he said.

'We can try,' she countered. 'Will you help me or not, Mr Weir?' An idea was forming in her head. 'Guy took your rowing boat, but you have another, do you not?'

'I have a small sailing boat moored at the jetty.'

Then there was hope. 'Send one of your men on horseback to Brigurd Point. Have him hole the bottom of all boats there. We can sail from here, cutting up and landing at Dunleish.'

'They will see us. The waters all around the castle are exposed; that's why Guy took the route he did.'

'It does not matter,' she said. 'There is no time to do aught else. We can concoct a story to satisfy the guard.'

'He leaves a guard?' Weir's eyes squinted.

'Oh, yes,' she said grimly. A calm determination overrode her panic. Helena knew what she must do. 'There is always a guard.'

And then the pair of them whirled into action. Mr Weir barked orders to have a horse saddled with speed, then ran to the gunroom. Helena raced back upstairs, grabbed the dark fur-lined cloak and was back downstairs outlining a semblance of an explanation to his wide-eyed wife by the time Weir returned.

'Annabel, take the girls and the carriage to your parents' house. You must leave here immediately. Stay there until I come for you.' Mr Weir dropped a kiss to his wife's cheek.

'But, John…'

'Do as I say, Annabel. I do not want you here for Tayburn or his men to find.'

Mrs Weir's face was white and petrified, but she nodded at her husband's words.

There was no more time. Helena and Weir turned and began to run, leaving the back door to slam in their wake. The groom had already left, a small wood axe tucked neatly in his pocket. One horse stood ready, a boy holding the reins. Mr Weir stepped up in the stirrup, pulled Helena up before him. The beast sensed the tension, whinnied, reared up. Mr Weir steered him down the narrow briar-clad lane to the shore and then they were off, galloping across the ripple-marked sands, taking the short cut to the jetty. And with every drum of the hooves, every thrust of the saddle, Helena silently shouted his name: *Guy!* Again and again, *Guy! Guy! He is coming,* until it formed a mantra that obscured all else from her mind. Willing him to hear the silent message across the miles.

* * *

Guy ceased his tread upon the stone spiralling stairwell and listened. The distant hum of noises. The faint bang of a door. Nothing close. Yet he felt the sense of danger all around him, stronger now than ever before. He carried on up the stairs, tried to shrug it off, ignore it. The feeling persisted, growing in strength. For some reason he thought of Helena, Helena with her red hair flowing long in wild wanton waves. Helena reaching out to him. Lord, but he was growing soft. But he smiled all the same. He found the top of the stairs, stole quickly and quietly along the corridor. And then he was at the chamber marked with an X on the map. There was no key within the lock. No guard at the door. Guy's eyes narrowed. The doorknob twisted beneath his hand and the door swung open. He pushed it right back in case anyone was standing behind it, then stepped across the threshold and no further. The room was dim, lit by neither candle nor firelight. The tiny narrow window looked out at a sky that had darkened to a charcoal grey. He scanned the space, eyes moving quickly, taking in the small bed in the corner beside the blackened hearth and the pile of thin blankets. There was not another stick of furniture within the room. He sensed the movement rather than saw it.

The girl was standing in the corner along from the door and furthest from the window.

He stepped quickly forwards and whispered her name. 'Emma?'

She stared at him in defiant silence, fear blatant in her eyes.

'Helena has sent me to rescue you.'

Still, she gave no response and he wondered if Tayburn's treatment had rendered her senseless.

'Emma,' he said again, reaching a hand slowly towards her. 'We have not much time. Quickly. Come, I will help you.'

'Helena sent you?' she whispered at last.

'Yes.' His fingers beckoned her forward.

'Then she really is alive?'

'Very much so when I left her on the mainland.' Guy flashed the girl a reassuring smile.

She made a funny little noise, half sigh, half sob, and then her hand found his.

'My name is Varington.'

She nodded.

Keeping the girl behind him he turned to leave the room.

'Wait!' she whispered.

He turned with impatience.

'We cannot leave Agnes and Old Tam. I heard him say what he was going to do to them. He is saving them to make her watch.'

'Helena's servants? The ones she believed had drowned the night of her escape?'

Emma nodded. 'They helped her get away.'

'Where are they?'

'In the dungeon. He said he would send me to join them if I tried to leave this room.'

'So you stayed.'

Another nod. 'You don't know what he's like. I don't know how she could have stood it all those years. He hasn't even touched me and I cannot bear it.'

Guy's voice was grim. 'Then we had best make our way to the dungeon.'

* * *

The black carriage bypassed Kilbride village before drawing up at the house near Brigurd Point. Tayburn barely waited for the carriage to stop before he leapt down. The front door of the house was already open, the manservant waiting in the hallway, silver tray in hand with a crystal glass of his master's brandy upon it. Tayburn snatched the glass, drained its contents and clattered the empty glass back down on the tray. Then, without so much as a word in the direction of his wife who stood silent and unsure in the hallway, he turned and was gone, back out of the house, on to the fresh horse standing ready for him, galloping towards Seamill Hall.

Caroline Tayburn's respite was short, for her husband returned less than half an hour later, slamming the door in his wake, his face ruddy with rage.

'Ready my sailing boat this instant!'

The house sprang into action. Bodies ran this way and that, voices murmuring quietly.

'Caroline!' he roared. 'Caroline, where the hell are you?'

She appeared in the doorway to the drawing room.

'About bloody time! We leave for Dunleish—now.' His eyes were dark and devilish, the snarl on his lips promised violence.

Lady Tayburn's gaze slid to the girl whose arms were imprisoned in her husband's grip. She saw the maid's clothing and guessed that Stephen had brought the girl back with him from Seamill Hall. 'What...what has happened?' asked Caroline, and then regretted it.

Tayburn turned the full force of his gaze upon her and

she shrank back. 'While I have been chasing the length and breadth of the country, Varington has slipped across the water to Dunleish. I'm sure that Weir's maid here will be only too happy to relay the details of the matter to you once we are aboard the boat.' He threw the girl at his wife. 'Keep her safe. If she escapes, I'll kill you both.'

The maid, Senga, stumbled and fell her length along the floor.

Tayburn turned at the approach of his manservant.

'Well?' Tayburn moved towards him.

The man retreated. 'Sir.' His voice shook and his face was white.

Senga started to scramble to her feet.

'Stay down!' barked Tayburn at her, then turned his attention back to his man. 'What have you to tell me?' he demanded in a quiet, deadly voice.

His servant swallowed hard and in a hushed whisper told the news that Sir Stephen would not want to hear. 'The boats have been holed.'

Not one muscle on Tayburn's face shifted. There was silence. Three faces with horrified anticipation stared at him. Nobody moved.

'Take the large sailing boat from the boathouse. If it is not ready to sail in ten minutes, you will find that your head is no longer attached to your body.' He hunkered down on his haunches and looked directly into Senga's eyes as she lay on the floor. His fingers moved to grip her face. 'You did not tell me of that little detail, my dear.'

'I didnae know,' the girl sobbed, 'honest, I didnae.'

'That's what they all say.' The pressure of his fingers increased against her cheek. 'You'll be pleased to know that both the wind and tide are in our favour.' The fingers pressed harder still. 'And *Cerberus* can outrun any boat in these parts. You had better utter a prayer for your master.' And then he released her, and, stepping over her prostrate body, disappeared up the staircase of Brigurd House.

Helena's eyes were still closed when she heard the thud of the heavy studded door swing shut behind them, and she knew that she had returned to Dunleish. The ruse had worked: Weir's pretence of dragging her back here against her will, returning Sir Stephen's woman in hope of currying favour. The familiar smell of the place filled her nostrils and she feared for one horrible moment that she would not be able to go through with their plan. And then she thought of Guy...and of Emma, and knew what she must do.

Weir was talking with them again. She even heard a laugh, the chink of glasses, the pouring of liquid, the smell of brandy. And then she felt herself passed to another and willed herself to stay limp and fluid-like as she was. Her head lolled against the man's arm and she stoppered her nose against the unwashed smell of him. The opening and closing of doors, and then they were climbing, his feet heavy, almost slovenly against the stone below, hers brushing lightly against the walls as the stairwell wound round to the right. Up to the first floor. Her eyes were still closed as he laid her clumsily down on the bed. She did not need to open them to know where she was.

A jangle of keys sounded, then the mumble of Rab's voice, as he spoke almost beneath his breath, 'No escapin' for you this time, hen. Just wait till his lordship sees what we have for him.'

Footsteps and the thump of the door. Scrape of key in the lock, shutting her in securely; there was, after all, no way out of the room except through the door. The footsteps receded and the jangle of the keys grew faint. She opened her eyes and saw the damp plaster-moulded ceiling above. Helena smiled and knew she was exactly where she wanted to be—locked alone in the room that Stephen had given over to be her bedchamber.

She sat up quickly, swung her legs over the side of the bed and stood up. From the wooden chest in the corner she retrieved a pile of clothes, which she positioned to loosely resemble the sleeping form of a body beneath the blanket on the bed. Then she slipped her fingers into the pocket of her dress and produced the silver key. She stared at it for a moment, praying that Weir would be able to keep the men distracted. She pulled her fur-lined cloak more tightly around her and, forcing herself to stay calm, she stepped towards the door. The click of her shoes sounded loud against the floor. She stopped, listened, heard nothing. The shoes slipped easily from her feet and were quickly hidden beneath the bed. And when she stood again she knew that she was ready. The stone floor was chilled against her bare feet. Noiselessly she padded across to the door, inserted the key into the lock and turned it.

The corridor outside was empty; there was no moulded plaster out here, no painted or papered walls or furniture. The walls were the bare red sandstone blocks laid by men three hundred years ago. The floor comprised great slabs of stone. The whole passageway was lit by a single old-fashioned flambeau positioned at a midway point, its unsteady flicker of flames casting deep shadows. Helena knew where she was going. Quickly and quietly she hurried further along the corridor towards the room over which she had marked an X on the map, knowing that, if Emma and Guy were not there, she would have to go down to the dungeon.

Having freed Old Tam and the maidservant Agnes from the dungeon, Guy led their exit from that dismal place. The little group hurried along the flambeaux-lit damp corridor, heading towards the south-west tower and its secret escape.

From up above came the almighty slam of the front door, the echo of the thud reverberating throughout the castle. Everyone halted.

'What was that?' The words were Emma's, although everyone thought them.

Foreboding prickled across Guy's scalp. And the answer that whispered through his mind was not what he wanted to hear. It was not possible. Tayburn was in London. He could not be here. Yet the sensation of danger persisted through the blanket of logic. 'It's nothing. Keep moving and keep quiet.' His voice was steady and confident. He gestured them to keep walking. The light of the flambeau high on their left-hand side glittered and danced upon the blade of Guy's knife. No one in the little group noticed that his grip around the handle had tightened.

A scream sounded. A haunting shrill cry that carried down from the floors above. A cry that pierced their ears and was no more. The ensuing silence seemed only to heighten the horror of what they had heard.

'It's him. He's back.' Fear made the words shake as they slipped from Emma's mouth.

The maid gave a whimper and clutched at the wall. 'May God have mercy on our souls.'

'Keep going,' Guy said grimly, and forced them onwards.

* * *

Helena was in the dungeon when she heard the scream and her stomach turned upside down. She had heard such screams before and knew very well what it was and who had caused it. The retch forced its way up to her mouth. First one and then another, until she thought she would vomit the contents of her stomach upon the floor. Her legs began to shake and the over-whelming rush of fear paralysed her so that she could not move or speak or even breathe. She stood there in the dank dismal room with its ripe stench of death; no matter how much she willed her feet to move, they remained frozen. And then, in the dark horror of what surrounded her, she thought of Guy. Guy, with his all-too-perceptive gaze. Guy, with his smile that moved so readily to his mouth. Guy, who had risked every-thing…for her. And as the warmth in her heart thawed the fear, Helena's eyes fastened upon the glint of the small metal tool that lay amidst the filth of the floor close by the opened manacles. She moved forward, stooped, and as her fingers closed around it the courage rose within her, for she knew that Guy had been here and that he had not left alone. Over in the corner the rats were squeaking, but Helena did not hear. Nor did she notice the damp stinking straw beneath her feet as she ran towards the door. For Helena knew Guy's plan. There was only one way he would leave the castle. She began to make her way towards the south-west tower.

They were treading down the stairs of the south-west tower, only yards from the room with the secret tunnel. Guy stepped off the last of the stone stairs, rounded to the right. And stopped. The smile wiped from his face. His grip upon the knife handle tightened instinctively.

'Get back!' he yelled behind him. But it was too late. He looked ahead into the blackness of the man's eyes. Saw the white hair drawn back and tied with the black ribbon and he knew the name of the man he looked upon without any need for an introduction: Tayburn.

Chapter Fourteen

'Varington,' Tayburn said with a slight sneer. 'Come to steal more of what is mine?' His eyes looked from Agnes, to Emma and back to Guy. 'It seems that we share the same taste in women.' Tayburn stood, relaxed in his manner, almost leisurely. His gaze flickered momentarily over the old man in the background. 'But then again, maybe you have quite a different reason for stealing this particular choice of…possessions.'

A ripple of fresh air fanned across the still dankness of the passageway as Guy looked into the darkness of the man's eyes and knew he was in the presence of evil. There was something about Tayburn that did not need the man to speak or move or even make so much as an expression upon his face. Just his presence seemed to foul the air.

'What, nothing to say to me in return, Varington? Cat got your tongue?' His black eyes glanced away. 'It soon will have,' he said in a much quieter tone, but still loud enough for Guy to hear.

Guy retreated, one step and then another, until the

women and old man were backed further up the stairs, then he jumped back down to the lowest stone-carved step so that his body blocked Tayburn's route to Emma and Agnes and Old Tam. 'Your argument is with me. Let the others go.'

Tayburn laughed and the sound sent a shiver to the depths of Guy's soul. 'I find myself attached to these particular possessions. I am loath to let them go.'

'They are no man's possessions.'

The laugh diminished to a smile, and it was a truly horrific sight to behold. Guy heard Emma's gasp from behind him. 'They are what I deem them to be. Besides, you have nothing with which to bargain.'

'Really?'

'You're in my castle. And now that you're here you shall never leave, not even when the flesh has been stripped from your bones. As I said, you have nothing with which to bargain.'

'He has Helena!' Emma shouted with false bravado from her perch up on the stairs behind Guy. 'If you kill us, you shall never get her back.'

Tayburn raised one dark slanting eyebrow so that it touched against a lock of his colourless hair. 'Really, my dear, you are misinformed. He has not even that. Helena is back here where she belongs…with me.'

'No!' Emma shouted.

Guy could hear the vehemence in her denial. 'It makes no difference. I will not bargain with Helena's life,' he said.

'Then we will all lose ours,' sobbed Emma.

Tayburn smoothed back a strand of hair that had freed itself from his ribbon. 'She saw my carriage pass, you see.' He turned his attention to his middle finger of his right hand and picked at a nail. 'And had some foolish notion to warn you of my return.' He glanced up at Guy. 'Weir brought her here.'

Guy betrayed nothing by his face. Helena would not come back to this place, a place she had risked all to leave. And he had her promise that she would seek out his brother if the plan went awry. But then he heard again the words she had uttered during their conversation that morning. *I would not just abandon you in Dunleish!* And he knew that Tayburn was telling the truth. In that moment he saw again the sweetness of her smile, and heard again the softness of her voice, and something contracted in Guy's chest. Helena. He had seen her hurt and her sadness, her fear and her fury, her passion…and her love. And Guy knew what it was that he felt as he stood there in the depths of Tayburn's lair. He recognised the emotion even though he had never felt it before. And he almost laughed that he could suffer such a revelation right here, right now, with Tayburn and his men armed and before him and with those he had tried to help frightened and cowed behind him.

'And in return I have brought him one of his maidservants. She proved most co-operative after a little persuasion.'

Still, Guy did not speak. Outnumbered. Out-armed. Unwilling to abandon those he had come here to rescue. Guy's army training kicked in. Emotions shut down. Eyes scanned relative positions, distances, potential exits. Brain measured strengths and weaknesses. Mouth played for time.

'He's lying, isn't he?' Emma's voice wobbled with uncertainty. 'Isn't he?' and there was a helplessness in her pleading.

'I never lie,' Tayburn said in a good-natured tone. 'I have no need to.' His eyes gleamed black and deadly.

'I find that hard to believe,' muttered Guy.

'Which? My unparalleled honesty or the fact that the trollop is back here under lock and key, returned to me?'

Guy gave a disparaging laugh. 'Both.'

'You'll see for yourself, Varington, soon enough.'

The corner of Guy's mouth flickered. 'Really?' He raised his eyebrows in mock surprise. 'Somehow I don't think so.' From his vantage point he had clear views down each of the passageways that led to the stairwell, but Guy had seen enough. He kept his eyes fixed upon Tayburn.

Tayburn's upper lip curled by just the slightest degree, exposing eye teeth that were too long and pointed to have been fashioned by nature. 'What can you mean, Varington? I hold all of the cards, I believe: Helena, the poxy servants that aided her escape, her sister, Weir…and, of course, you. And you, you hold, let me see…' He pretended to think, scratching a finger against his chin. 'Mmm, that's right, you, Lord Varington—' the finger spun off his chin to point condemningly at Guy '—hold precisely nothing.'

Guy shrugged, as if it were of no consequence. 'Perhaps,' he admitted. 'But then again, it may be that your vision has been somewhat obscured.'

'What the hell are you talking of?' Tayburn scowled.

'Merely a matter of the wool being pulled over your eyes. You did not think I would come here to Dunleish without a card or two of my own up my sleeve, so to speak.'

The black eyes narrowed to a slit and Tayburn stepped forward, revealing for the first time the long sword in his left hand. 'Nothing remains hidden from me,' he said. 'I know everything.' And each word was enunciated with meticulous care. He touched his right index finger slowly, meaningfully, to the centre of his forehead—the third eye. Guy felt the fear that rippled through both Tayburn's men and the little group that huddled on the stairwell. And he understood something of the villain's power.

Tayburn raised the sword and pointed it directly at Guy.

The smile that broke across Guy's face infuriated Tayburn just as Guy had intended it to. 'Do it now,' he said, and never for a moment did the pale gaze waver from the dark one of Tayburn. Tempting death. Facing evil. The smile did not falter. 'Now,' he repeated, 'if you dare.'

And it seemed that Sir Stephen Tayburn was only too happy to oblige.

Helena's bare feet made no sound upon the stone floor of the passageway. The voices ahead told her precisely where she must go. She heard the short panicked scream of a woman and knew it was Emma. Quickly and quietly she made her way on, following down the passageway, just another shadow that moved beneath the flickering of the flambeaux, the long fur-lined cloak pulled around her. A slight dark shape.

She was close enough to discern the words. The voices were no longer just a hum or babble. Her feet carried her closer and closer still, until she reached the small dark alcove in the wall and slunk into it. Twenty paces at most to where Stephen and his men stood by the recess of the stairwell. Guy was there, backed up against the stairs, the knife in his hand holding off Stephen—for now. She could not see Emma and guessed that her sister must be somewhere up on the stairs.

The voices carried clear enough: Stephen's taunting, crowing, making her blood run cold, telling Guy that she was here, ensuring that he knew she was lost. Her stomach churned and the thought of Stephen raised the nausea to the back of her throat until she feared it would betray her presence. She pressed herself against the wall, clinging to the damp rough stone, fearful to let go, knowing that he was round there, knowing what he would do to her. And across her mind the thought flashed that she could just run away while Stephen and his men were distracted.

Then she heard Guy. 'I will not bargain with Helena's life,' he said, and his voice was firm and resolute. She felt ashamed of her fear and of its selfishness and most of all of the tempting little thought that had beckoned her and which, albeit for the tiniest second, she had contemplated. *I will not bargain with Helena's life*. Somewhere deep inside the small flame of determination within her roared to a fire. And she would not risk his life. Not against Stephen. Not Guy. Not the man she loved. She had no weapon. She had no one other than herself. Neither fact mattered. Stephen meant to kill Guy. And Helena meant to stop him. She stepped silently into the passageway and began to walk, step by noiseless step, towards Sir Stephen Tayburn.

Even as she walked she did not know truly what she meant to do. But she could see Guy quite clearly now and her soul was filled with a fiery determination to save him. He spoke with Stephen as if the two were seated across a gaming table and not facing one another across the dim passage deep in the monster's castle. Without fear. Holding off Stephen and his men. The knife blade glinted within Guy's hand and Helena knew that Stephen would have his sword. She wondered that none of them heard her. Expected with every footstep, with every breath, that they would look round and discover her. But they did not.

Curiously, now that she was out here and moving to face him, her fear was less than it had been skulking behind the corner. Step by step, closer and closer, creeping ever forward. Her hands were open and by her side. The cloak hung useless across her shoulders. Still, she walked on, her sole purpose to give the others one last chance, to save them from Stephen. Not once did Guy look at her, not once did he see her. She wondered, within the madness of the moment, if she had faded to invisibility. Until she heard Guy's words…

'But then again, it may be that your vision has been somewhat obscured.'

'What the hell are you talking of?' She heard the scowl in Stephen's voice.

'Merely a matter of the wool being pulled over your eyes.'

And she knew then what to do, for she understood Guy's message.

Her feet stepped and her fingers were at her collarbone, unfastening the heavy weight of the cloak. Step. The cloak unfurled, a silent sail upon the mast of her body. Step.

'Do it now,' he said, and never for a moment did Guy's gaze waver from Stephen. 'Now, if you dare.'

Too late Stephen sensed her presence. Too late he turned. Helena threw the cloak over his head and all hell broke loose. With an almighty roar he fumbled with the material that blinded him, struggling to pull the cloak clear. But the sword was heavy and unwieldy in his hand and the material thick and copious. A string of curses and obscenities flowed from beneath the cloak. Stephen's minions stood as if frozen, shock etched upon their faces at the unexpected drama unfolding before them. Stephen roared for their assistance, but his sword was flailing around him, desperate to prevent Guy from getting near, and no man there was foolish enough to brave it. One of them shouted, 'Drop your sword, sir. We cannae get near!'

Tayburn's sword stayed firmly in his hand.

It took a woman to face it. Helena did not hesitate. One small window of time, and then it would be gone. All that separated her from Guy was the long whirling blade in Stephen's hand. She ran, dodging Stephen's violent movements as best she could across the small space of flagstones.

'Guy!'

Then she was in his arms and pushed behind him in one swift flowing move. And even though the cloak was being ripped from Stephen's eyes as she watched, she was filled with relief.

Guy moved fast, striking just as the fur-lined material landed in a pile on the floor. One hand yanked at the snow-white hair, pulling the head back, exposing Tayburn's throat. The knife in his other hand was small but exceedingly sharp. Its blade touched against the stretched skin of Tayburn's throat.

'Tell your men to drop their weapons or you're dead.' Guy stood tall behind Tayburn.

'I'll see you in hell first,' Tayburn sneered.

The smile upon Guy's face was tight and grim. The

pressure of his right hand increased. A thin red edging appeared along the length of the knife blade where it contacted Tayburn's skin. 'God knows how much I've dreamed of this moment. Go on, give me an excuse to slit your throat open and watch the lifeblood ebb from your veins. It would not atone for all you have inflicted upon Helena, but it would be a start.'

Tayburn's eyes, as black and hard as polished jet pebbles, stared at his men, and still, the words did not come from his mouth.

Guy's right hand moved infinitesimally and a tiny rivulet of blood dribbled down Tayburn's neck.

Tayburn's men stared with unease at what was unfolding before their very eyes, trapped in a dilemma to which there was no right outcome.

'Do as he says. Drop your weapons,' Tayburn ground out.

'Pity,' said Guy with sarcasm. 'I was looking forward to dispatching you.'

Tayburn said nothing, but his malice was palpable, a living breathing thing.

Three knives, two pistols and a cudgel clattered to the floor.

Helena made to move forward to collect them.

Guy stayed her with a word. 'No.' He would not have her stray too close to any of Tayburn's rabble. He shouted the instruction over his shoulder, 'Tam, take their weapons and distribute them amongst the women. Keep the cudgel for yourself. And take the rope from my left pocket and bind each man's hands.'

Helena's eyes widened as the old man came out of the darkness of the stairwell. 'Tam?' The word was filled with disbelief.

'Miss Helena...' the old man sighed '...I was so feart for you. We both were.'

'Tam.' Guy gestured towards the pile of weapons. 'It would be better to save the reunion until we are elsewhere.'

Tam nodded and did as he was bid.

Guy spoke to Tayburn's men. 'You lot, get in front of me where I can see you, and take us to the front door. Do as I say and no one gets hurt.' Only when they were in front of him and facing away up the corridor did he speak to Helena. 'Helena, you know the way out of here. Stay at my shoulder and let me know if they are playing me false.' Guy kept his voice curt and to the point. He allowed his eyes to meet momentarily with hers, willing her to stay strong, and then it was back to the task in hand. The situation was precarious and it would take only one slip for the advantage to fall to Tayburn. One sign of weakness and all would be lost. And Guy had no intention of losing Helena, not to Tayburn, not to anyone.

A soft murmur of assent.

'If you think that you can just walk out of here, then you are grossly mistaken, Varington.' Tayburn's voice was strained against the blade. 'Escape is impossible. Just ask Helena, she'll tell you, won't you, my love?'

Guy felt Helena stiffen by his side and when she spoke her words were low and filled with loathing. 'I am not your love,' she said. 'I was never your love.'

'But you are mine all the same, Helena McGregor. And you'll never escape me.'

'Quiet!' Guy jerked Tayburn's head back harder. 'We'll all escape you, Tayburn, because you're going to take us to the front door. Now, start walking before I change my mind and slit your throat.'

'Very amusing, Varington; I've men everywhere. Kill me and you'd not make it two paces out of here before they'd cut you down.'

'Really?' Guy raised an eyebrow. 'Loyalty bought through fear and brutality is a shallow thing. Do you honestly think that your men would act to stop me once you are dead? Why would they risk their lives once the threat you hold over them is gone? Face it, Tayburn, with you dead there's not a man present that will lift so much as a finger to stop us walking out of here.'

Tayburn's mouth tightened. 'Liar!' But the word had a hollow ring to it.

Slowly the motley group moved off towards the north-west tower, making their way beneath the flickering flambeaux that lit the way along the corridor.

Helena could scarcely believe that they would make it. It seemed an audacious plan. And yet they edged their way, step by step, inch by inch along one damp red-stone passageway after another, ever closer towards the great blackened front door. The tension within the group was almost unbearable. They moved in silence, only Guy's voice sounding every so often in caution. Tayburn's men led on, unarmed, hands bound behind their backs. Next came Tayburn, hands tied, knife held to his back, an unwilling hostage, being frog-marched by Guy. Helena walked by his side, the pistol heavy in her hand. Behind her, Old Tam, Emma and Agnes provided a rearguard.

They were on the stairwell, heading up towards the front door via the north-west tower. She was under no illusion to the danger. She didn't need the warning that flashed in Guy's eyes to know. The stairs were narrow, too narrow to let Guy keep his hold upon Tayburn. He shifted the knife to prod against Tayburn's back, kept a grip of the rope that bound the villain's hands in his own. The stairwell was dimly lit, making it all too easy to stumble, to fall. It was here that Tayburn's chance of escape was greatest. One slip. One mistake. That's all that Tayburn needed. Helena prayed that he would not get it.

Her left hand leaned against the dampness of the wall, following the curve of the stairwell, ensuring that she did not miss her footing. They moved onwards, upwards, stair by stair, and gradually the staleness of the air that had hung around the dungeons faded. They passed a window, nothing more than a slit in the wall, and fresh sea air filled their nostrils. Even though the whole place was damp and cold, Helena could feel the sweat prickle against her back. And still, they kept going. The pistol pulled heavy at her wrist, yet she kept it levelled, ever ready to meet the challenge she was convinced would come. Tayburn moved without resistance, hands tied, Guy's knife pressed against his back. So why did Helena have the overwhelming conviction that something would go wrong? It was as Tayburn had said—they could not simply walk out of Dunleish. Could they? Helena's feet moved ever up, and not once did her eyes cease their scanning, not once did her fingers slacken their grip against the pistol's handle. The paltry light dimmed. The flambeau that should have burned to light the stairs stood black and cold. And in the air hung the scent of its dowsing.

Helena felt the hairs on the back of her neck stand on end. The entirety of her scalp prickled. Tension stretched the air until it was tight and thin. Guy could feel it too. She watched him slow, pull Tayburn back in closer against his body. Tayburn emitted a small breathy groan. She couldn't see Guy's knife, but she suspected it prodded all the harder at Tayburn's flesh. And she was glad. *Be careful*! she wanted to shout to Guy. *There is something amiss*! But that would only distract him and she could not risk such a thing. Besides, she had no basis, other than her own instinct, for the sudden resurfacing of her fears.

Beneath the blackened stump of the expired flame the air seemed to chill. There was only the sound of their feet treading upon worn stone. Anxiety wound Helena's body so tight that she could almost feel the constriction around her chest and throat. She tried to shake it off. Willed herself not to think upon it. If they could just make it out of the stairwell, then it was a straight passage to the door... and escape. So close. A shaft of light beckoned ahead. Nearly there. They were going to make it. Lord above, but they were going to make it.

It was the last thought that passed through Helena's head before Tayburn suddenly twisted around and levelled a hard kick at Guy, the force of which propelled him against Helena. Her hand grasped at the wall, but there was nothing to grip on the bare curve of stone. She felt her feet stumble beneath her, could not catch her balance, shouted a warning to those below as she began to topple backwards towards the long spiral of the stairs.

The fall did not come. Helena found herself jerked back up. Someone was pulling hard against her outstretched arm, hoisting her back to safety.

'Helena!' She heard his voice beside her ear, felt herself pressed momentarily against the warmth of his body. Only when he was sure that she was safe did he release her. But it was too late. Tayburn was gone. They could hear the clatter of his boots up the last of the stairs out on to the passageway above; could hear too the roar of command to his men. In that single moment of decision Guy had chosen to loose his grip upon Tayburn's rope in order to save Helena. And Helena knew it. She knew too the price that his sacrifice would cost. She could hear it in the gleeful urgency that filled Tayburn's voice.

'No!' she whispered. 'Oh, God, no,' and the gaze that she raised to Guy's was full of anguish. 'We must head back down!' She grabbed his hand and whirled.

'No.' Guy touched her shoulder.

She turned, plucked at Guy's coat, trying to pull him forward. 'Quickly, come on!'

'Helena, we cannot reach the tunnel before him.'

Tam and the two women stopped where they were. Emma and Agnes's eyes bulged with fear.

'You might without me. Go on without me, ma lord.' It was Tam that spoke.

'It is a fine thing you offer, Tam,' said Guy, acknowledging the old man's bravery, 'but I need you to look after the women. Find the tunnel, get them to safety. I'll delay Tayburn as best I can.'

Tam gave a nod.

And then Guy's hand found Helena's and pulled her up the stair that separated them, so that she was close to him. His fingers brushed against her cheek, his touch so light she was not sure that he touched her at all. His head lowered to hers and his mouth found hers. The kiss was swift and fierce and concentrated, as if he had condensed a multitude of feelings into that one sliver of contact. He moved away, but not before the whisper of his words had found her ear. She stared at him in disbelief and felt the tears prick against her eyes. It did not matter that Stephen was above. It did not matter that she would die. She had heard his words and in comparison all else seemed small and inconsequential. *I love you, Helena McGregor*. Then he crept stealthily up the stairs, knife in hand, ready to face Stephen.

Guy heard their footsteps recede as Tam led the women down the stairwell. He did not look back, just kept his gaze focused ahead, ready, waiting for the attack that he knew would come. Helena's scent filled his nose, blocking out the damp smell of Dunleish. The heat of her lips still lingered on his, warming him from the cold. The imprint of her soft body was a barrier to all hurts. And he was glad that he had told her the truth before it was too late to do so. He prayed that she would reach the tunnel, but he suspected the worst. Tayburn's men would no doubt be scuttling towards the bottom of the south-west tower, intent on blocking Helena's route to freedom. Even so, Tayburn would never have her. Guy swore it on all that was holy. Death was in the air. Tayburn had been right about one thing—Guy would never leave Dunleish alive, but then again, neither would Tayburn. Tayburn would never touch Helena ever again; Guy would make sure of that.

Helena followed the others only as far as the next floor down.

'Emma.' She pressed a kiss to her sister's cheek. 'Forgive me for bringing all of this upon you. Did Tayburn…?' She could barely bring herself to ask the question. 'Did he hurt you very badly?'

Emma gave a sigh. 'He kept me locked in a room, but that is all,' she reassured her sister. 'He did not touch me. You are all he thinks of, no one else. Not even that poor creature who is his wife. She sent me food and blankets. She knew I was here and yet she spoke not one word against him.'

'Poor Caroline. Her fear and pride are too great to do anything else. Do not judge her so harshly, Emma.' She pulled Emma into a hug. 'Thank God, you are safe.'

Emma drew her a wry smile. 'I do not think any of us are very safe at this minute.'

'Come on, Miss Helena, Miss Emma, this is no time to be bletherin'.' Old Tam waved them on with gnarled old hands.

Helena released her sister and caught hold of Agnes's hand. 'Dear Agnes, you are as a ghost come back from the dead to me. I thought that you and Tam had perished in the wrecking of the *Bonnie Lass*.'

'No' us, miss. We had the misfortune to be washed up at Brigurd Point. They soon had us sent back here.'

'I'm so sorry.' Helena squeezed the maid's hand.

'Lassies!' Old Tam admonished.

Helena dropped her voice to a whisper. 'Go on ahead. Get Tam out of here. There's a rowing boat beached down near Gull Point; keep to the shoreline and head for that. I'll meet you there.'

'But we can't leave without you. Where are you going?' It was Emma that raised the protest.

'Don't worry, I'll be there,' lied Helena. 'There's something I have to do first. Now, get going or none of us will make it out. I'm counting on you to ready the boat.' And then she slipped away along the passageway before anyone could protest further.

* * *

Guy's back hugged the wall close to the top of the stairs. He shifted the knife into his left hand and slipped the right into his coat pocket.

'You might as well come out, Varington. Or would you rather I had my men fetch you like a rabbit from its hole?' Tayburn made no effort to disguise the excitement in his voice.

'Afraid to face me yourself, Tayburn, that you must have your minions do your dirty work?'

'I'm afraid of nothing,' came back Tayburn's voice.

There was a pause, a silence. 'We both know that is not true,' said Guy.

Tayburn laughed, and the sound was grating and cruel.

'Which of us do you think Helena will choose? You or me, Tayburn?'

Tayburn's laughter stopped. 'She's mine, whether she wills it or not.'

'She was never yours.'

Tayburn grabbed a pistol from the man nearest him. 'You think to just steal her from me? Nobody takes what is mine and lives. And know this, Varington, I'll make her sorry for running to you, more sorry than she could ever have imagined.'

Guy gritted his teeth and blocked out the image that Tayburn sought to sow.

'Shall I let you watch? Watch while she writhes beneath me in my bed? Watch while I touch that creamy soft skin?' Tayburn's voice was creeping closer.

Guy's jaw clamped tighter. His right hand slipped from his coat pocket and in it was a pistol.

'Come on, Varington, you know that you want to.'

Guy listened to the voice rather than its baiting words, pinpointing that Tayburn was almost centrally located perhaps fifteen feet from the top of the stairs. Close enough. Guy's feet pushed hard against stone and he rounded the last few stairs to the top two at a time, propelling round the corner and out of the stairwell at full force. The pistol aimed at the spot from which Tayburn's voice had sounded. His finger moved over the trigger, tensed to squeeze the metal lever that would send the lead ball into Tayburn's heart. Something knocked Guy's legs from beneath him, sending him sprawling face first in the filth of the floor. The pistol clattered to the ground, its bullet knocking a shard of stone from the wall, before landing misshapen and useless. He felt the weight of a man drop on to his back and then his arms were wrenched behind until they were almost clear of their sockets. A hand ripped at his hair, forcing him up to his knees while his wrists were bound so tight that the blood ceased to flow there. Someone pulled his head back hard, jerking his face up until his eyes focused upon Tayburn.

'Didn't hear Wylie coming up behind you, did you, Varington? You're not as good as you think.' Tayburn smiled. 'You should have killed me while you had the chance; I won't be so obliging with you.' He drew back his arm and landed his fist against Guy's jaw.

'Stop!' The voice rang out from the other end of the passageway.

Tayburn stopped. Looked around. And his eyes glittered with greed and lust and disbelief at the sight that met his eyes. 'Helena,' he said, 'how good of you to join us.'

'Let him go, Stephen.' Helena walked slowly forward.

Tayburn's men started to move towards her, but he

gestured them back. 'Why would I want to do that? He's had you, tasted you, *my* woman. There's a choice of options, but release is not one of them.' His eyes swept over the contours of her hips, following up to where the fine wool of her bodice curved around her breasts.

The sway of her hips ceased. She paused. 'Then you are not prepared to negotiate?' she asked.

'As I told *him* a little while ago—' Tayburn's foot dug against Guy's thigh '—one can only bargain when one has something worth bargaining with. Enlighten me as to what you have, Helena.'

She stood, her back very straight, her shoulders squared, her head held proud. 'I have myself,' she said.

He gave a grunt of amusement. 'You stand there as if you're some fine lady. Let me remind you that you're my whore, Helena,' he said, and enjoyed the cruelty of his words. 'You are mine to have when I wish. So I ask you again, with what do you bargain?'

Several tendrils of hair had escaped their pins to snake down her cheeks. She stepped closer until she was level with the window just beyond the great studded front door of Dunleish. His men's eyes swivelled between their master and herself. 'There is a difference between what is taken and that which is given.' Her gaze flickered fleetingly to Guy's, held for a second and swung back to Tayburn. She understood now why Guy had not bedded the woman he had made his mistress.

'No, Helena!' The words spilled from Guy's mouth.

Helena forced her face to remain impassive. 'Set Lord Varington free and I shall give you what you have only ever taken.'

'Do not do it, Helena!'

She could hear the anguish in Guy's plea, and, for all that her strength held, a single tear spilled from the corner of her eye and traced a solitary track down her cheek.

Tayburn looked from the pain and anger on Guy's face to the pale fragility of Helena's. And it was everything he could have wanted. 'You will wait until he's free, then you will refuse me.'

But she heard the desire in his voice. Tayburn was tempted. 'No,' she said. 'I give you my word.'

'Your word!' he spat. 'What does that mean? Nothing!'

'Helena, no. This is madness. He will kill me regardless. Do not do this thing. I am not worth it.'

But Guy's words only strengthened her determination. The price was small to save the life of the man she loved. Her hand slipped to her head, plucked out the pins one by one, and the deep red waves uncoiled to fall as a long heavy cloak over her shoulders. And as she did so a shaft of sunlight pierced the thick wall of sandstone, passing through the high slit of a window to bathe Helena in its spotlight. The light was soft and bright, its timing magically illuminating Helena's ethereal beauty, so that she seemed an illusion against the darkness surrounding her. Every man there turned to stare, entrapped in the spell woven by the simple action of the sun slipping from behind a cloud. And at its centre Helena remained oblivious to the effect that the sunbeam had wrought.

The rope bit into his skin as Guy strained his wrists against the binding. Blood trickled down from the wound to wet his fingers, but he did not slacken his effort. Helena might think that Tayburn could be held to a bargain, but Guy knew better. His life was forfeit;

Tayburn would never let him leave the island alive despite Helena's bargain. The fiend would take what she offered and give nothing in return. And Guy had no intention of letting Tayburn take anything from Helena ever again.

The sunlight flooded the single spot where she stood, streaming through the narrow hole in the wall as a beam straight from heaven, and everywhere else stayed dim and dank and shaded. Within the light her hair glowed a long burnished red, her skin was a soft velvet of cream and her smoky green eyes seemed to smoulder. A vision of Venus. A sight to enchant any man's gaze. But Guy saw that she had hidden every emotion from her face and he knew that she wore her mask, as he called it. Beneath it was a different woman altogether, a woman only Guy had seen, and she was more beautiful than the physical perfection that showed on the surface. And, despite the desperation of his situation, he felt his spirit soar with love. Love filled every pore of his being, until at last his gaze fell away into the darkness. Guy bided his time, waiting and watchful. His chance would come. Death was inevitable, but he'd damn well take out Tayburn in the process…and Helena would be safe.

She saw the men's faces and the way that they stared. She saw the lust and greed that Stephen could not hide. And she looked into the pale blue eyes of the man that knelt upon the floor and saw love and torment and guilt and anger. They did not need words. They did not need touch. Their love reached out and bound them together. Helena deliberately turned her face away and did not look again at Guy. She focused on Stephen. 'When Lord Varington's boat is clear of the shore, then I will go with you.'

'You ask a lot,' said Stephen.

She said nothing, just waited, the expression of sensual serenity upon her face belying the fear that welled within her. Guy's life hung in the balance, to be decided by the perverse whim of a tyrant's lust.

There was silence. Time stretched out long and languorously, until Helena thought the mask would slip from her face.

But she need not have worried. Stephen wanted that which he could not have. 'Get him to his feet. Take him down to the bay.'

Helena watched Stephen's men manhandle Guy along the passageway and out of the front door. Her feet carried her step by step in Guy's wake, and at her side stalked the dark figure of Stephen. She could smell him and, even though he did not touch her, her skin crawled with his proximity. Not once did she let herself think of what she had promised Stephen. Not once did her mind stray to the horror of what lay ahead. She thought only that Guy was being set free. The waves rumbled upon the shore. Overhead gulls circled and swooped. The speckled gravel of sea-crushed shells crunched as the bottom of the boat was pushed over them to slide into the cold winter water. She watched as Guy began to unfurl the sails. Noted that he was no sailor, for he appeared to be having a problem with the inside of the boat.

Guy let the men march him outside. The light white sky was a contrast to the gloom within the castle. His eyes squinted instinctively against the brightness. He would have to act soon. Time was running out. He started to dig in his heels, to struggle against the arms that held him, but the men only dragged him harder and faster across the uneven grass and rocks, down towards the sand, down towards the water. Guy saw where it was they were taking him. Across the small distance, beached just out of reach of the water was a small sailing boat—Weir's sailing boat to be precise. It was all Guy could do not to smile.

He gave up resisting, save for a small token effort and let the men propel him over the sand and haul him into the wooden belly of the boat, before a knife blade snatched at his wrists to free their binding. He did not try to escape as four pairs of arms loosened the boat from its bed of sand and gravel. The boat bobbed upon the water and the men walked with sodden feet and legs back on to the beach. Guy was on his knees, but he was not praying. He pulled haphazardly at the furl of the sail, knowing it would partially shield him from Tayburn's view. Then his hands moved swift and sure to the stern of the boat and rested upon the long oilskin-wrapped object that he knew Weir always kept there. He remembered Weir's words: *Seagulls make for good target practice.* This time he did smile and the smile was harsh and resolute and determined.

Stephen's voice sounded beside her. 'So, Helena, Varington is free, just as you wanted.'

Her gaze clung to Guy's figure in the small boat for a moment longer, then she wrenched her eyes away. 'Yes.' The single word dropped between them. The bright clear light dulled to grey as the clouds moved to hide the sun. Helena turned away. She did not look back. She did not notice that Stephen's own large sailing boat was not beached upon the shore where he had left it. Stephen took her arm. She did not pull away, just let him lead her back towards Dunleish and everything that awaited her there.

As Stephen turned to look back at Guy, an almighty bang sounded. And when he looked round at Helena again, there was an expression of shock upon his face. Her gaze tore round to where Guy had been. Wisps of smoke billowed around the half-furled sail. She saw Guy draw back the rifle in his hand. Stephen's arm tightened around hers, and she watched as he clasped his chest as if he was suffering an attack of conscience. And when he took his hand away his skin was dripping with the deep crimson of blood. The red stain spilled out from his shirt so that even against the black of his coat Helena could see the soaking spread of blood. More shots ripped through the air. Helena gave a yelp and tried to withdraw her hand, but Stephen had trapped it tight under his right arm. He gave a grunt and slumped to his knees, pulling her down with him.

'No!'

But even weakened as he was, Stephen refused to release her. He did not speak, but his black embittered gaze held hers and she felt the resurgence of all of her fear.

Men shouted and she looked up to see Stephen's sailing boat bearing down upon Guy.

Stephen could not have seen it. The boats were to his back. But he knew all the same. For all the pistol shot that had lodged in his chest, Stephen's strength did not seem to have diminished. He pulled Helena closer, until her face was near to his. 'My love,' he whispered.

Helena's eyes opened wide in shock and fear.

'You would have given yourself to me?' he said.

A nod and the wind whipped her hair across Stephen's face.

He sighed and smelled its sweetness before Helena moved it away. He beckoned her closer, and despite all that he had done, she could not deny a dying man, so she lowered her head that she might hear the weak whisper that was his voice. 'And then, afterwards, I would have given you...' He coughed and the breath laboured upon his lips. 'I would have given you...' he said again, 'Varington's head on a platter. He would not have made it halfway across the water before my men had him.'

Helena did not hear the crack of rifle shots on the shore. Silence echoed Stephen's words.

Stephen smiled and the black eyes shuttered, and she was left staring in disbelief and horror.

'Helena!' Guy's voice pulled her from the nightmare. She looked up, saw him down on the sand, running towards her. There seemed to be none of Stephen's men left to follow him. 'Helena!' Guy shouted again.

She was shaking as she pulled herself clear of Stephen, and her breath came in ragged gasps. 'Guy!'

And then he was there, pulling her into his arms, stroking her hair, her cheek, holding her against him as if he would never let her go.

'Guy,' she said again, and she thought her heart would break for love of him.

His arm stayed around her waist as they walked back to the castle to free Weir and Senga and Caroline. She did not speak, just let herself feel safe in his presence. Behind them the bodies of Stephen's men lay still and lifeless upon the shore, like the master they had served.

She felt suddenly so tired that it was an effort to raise each foot, to keep on taking one step after another. *It's over,* she whispered to herself again and again, barely able to believe it. She glanced behind her as if to make sure that it really was. Stephen lay where he had fallen. A great dark patch staining his coat and shirt. Dead.

Guy held Helena as they sailed the boat down the island's coastline. Even when Emma, Agnes and Old Tam were discovered and aboard, and Weir was steering them back to the mainland, Guy kept his arm around her. No one commented. Propriety was long forgotten. They had survived, all of them. Tayburn was dead. They were safe and they were going home. And nothing else mattered. The boat skimmed over the water and, although the hour was still early, barely three o'clock, the day began to fade. Night and Seamill Hall beckoned, and the nightmare that was Tayburn lay behind them.

Chapter Fifteen

The fire in the bedchamber was a warm golden flicker of flames. Helena stood alone, thawing the chill from her hands with its heat, staring into the magical array of flames. Stephen was dead. Dead. She was free at last. But no matter how much she knew the truth of it, she still felt an underlying unease. Every creak upon the stair, every howl of the wind, sent her eyes to the door and a shiver of apprehension straight to her core. A knock at the door sounded and she jumped, staring at it, heart beating wildly. The knock came again, this time accompanied by a maid's voice.

'I've brought warm water for you if you want to wash and Mrs Weir said to tell you that dinner will be served at half past five.'

Silence followed the maid's words.

'Do you wish me to come back later, ma'am?'

Helena roused herself from her stupor and, moving swiftly across the room, opened the door to where the maid stood. 'No, thank you, Martha,' said Helena and, rather than admit the maid to the room, she took the filled pitcher from her hands. 'It's kind of you to bring me the water. Thank you,' she said again, and forced a smile.

But the maid was not looking at Helena's face. Indeed, the maid did not meet her eyes at all. Martha's gaze remained fixed on Helena's shoulder.

No doubt the girl knew the truth of Helena McGregor. Kilbride was a small village. It was just a matter of time before they knew the rest.

So much had changed in the space of a single day, that it hardly seemed possible. A lifetime of changes in those few hours. Stephen was dead and, even had it not been so, what had happened in Dunleish meant that Helena would never be the same again. Emma was safe, and Agnes and Old Tam too. And Guy… She could not let herself think of him, not with the maid standing there so intently. The girl's face held an expression of horrified fascination and she was staring at Helena with distaste. 'Thank you, Martha,' Helena said a little more forcefully, and made to close the door.

The maid showed no sign of moving. Her gaze remained riveted upon the top of the green dress.

'Martha?'

At last the maid's eyes moved slowly to meet her own. 'Is that…?' She stopped and her hand came up hesitantly between them. 'Is that…?' She hesitated again. 'Blood, ma'am?' And her finger pointed at Helena's shoulder.

Helena twisted her head to follow where Martha's finger directed. The soft green material surrounding the shoulder and upper sleeve of her left arm was smeared with a dark stain. Stephen's blood! Helena felt her gorge rising. 'It's nothing,' Helena managed before shutting the door. She walked briskly across the room and sat the pitcher down upon the table beside the blue-and-white patterned china basin.

She tried not to think at all, just reached round to where the line of tiny bead buttons fastened at the back of her dress. Her arms contorted, her fingers prised. One button unfastened, then another two, but despite the stretch of Helena's arms she could not release any more. The lower line of buttons remained steadfastly resistant. Helena doubled her efforts. The buttons slid beneath her fumbling fingers, but would not be persuaded through the buttonholes. Perspiration prickled and her arms began to ache. With every passing second she became increasingly aware of just what was soaked upon her dress. She knew she was being foolish, that she had been happy enough when she had been unaware of the markings on her clothes, but the thought of Stephen's blood repulsed her. She tried again, working her fingers harder, faster. It made no difference. Her skin crawled beneath the darkness of the stain. Helena cursed and, as the beginnings of panic took hold, contemplated wrenching the material apart, regardless of what that would do to the buttons. She would never wear the dress again.

Knuckles rapped against the door.

She stilled.

'Martha?'

The door opened and closed again.

Helena glanced back.

It was not the maid that stood in her bedchamber, but Guy. His eyes burned with something she did not understand. 'The doctor has left. He said that Caroline is suffering from nervous exhaustion. Weir will write to her father to take her home to his country estate.'

She nodded, her hands dropping to her sides.

'Helena?' He moved towards her. 'What is—?'

She turned away. She did not look down at her dress. She did not want to see Stephen's blood. It was bad enough feeling the press of it against her skin, knowing it was there. 'I must change. It's his blood, you see,' she said, as if that explained everything.

Guy saw the colourless cheeks and the deliberate aversion of her face from the dark stain upon the material of her dress. 'Helena.' He reached out and took her limp hands within his.

'His blood is upon me,' she said, and swallowed hard, 'and I am having some difficulty with the buttons of this dress.' He could see her struggle to hold herself together. 'I…'

He looked down into her face and saw her need and felt her pain. Helena's emotions were raw and exposed. No mask, no pretence, not from him. His smile was small and gentle and understanding. 'I know,' he said, and released her hands.

She did not move, just stared up at him and waited, so trusting that it quite smote his heart.

His hands touched to her shoulders and he gently rotated her until her back faced him. Then slowly his fingers moved to the line of small emerald buttons and, one by one, he began to unfasten them. There was silence in the room save for the quiet flutter of the flames. He could feel her warmth through the layers of material that separated their skin. His fingers worked with a steady rhythm until at last the soft green wool gaped to reveal the white of her undergarments beneath. With all the buttons unfastened, he peeled the dress from her body, letting it pool upon the floor. Guy moved round until he faced her, took her hand and helped her step free. He paused, holding her gaze with his. 'The blood has soaked through.'

'Yes,' she said, and the single word resonated between them.

The red stains were bright against the pale petticoats and shift. He said nothing more until he had removed the layers of material and she stood naked before him. He did not look at the rich creamy velvet of her skin or the curve of her breast or hip. Instead he took her hand in his and guided her across to the table. He poured the water from the pitcher into the basin, took out his handkerchief and immersed it. 'The water is warm.'

'Martha brought it just before you arrived.'

He could hear the slight breathlessness, the tremor beneath her words. He longed to pull her into his arms, to envelop her, to kiss her and make love to her, but he could not, not when she had been through so much, not when she was so vulnerable. He squeezed most of the water from the square of white cotton, the drops splashing back down into the basin. And then gently, with the most infinite care, he pressed the wet material to her skin and began to wipe away Tayburn's blood.

He worked slowly, methodically, rinsing the handkerchief as required, until every last trace had been removed and her skin gleamed damp and pale and unblemished, and the water in the basin was a translucent red. He shrugged off his coat and wrapped it around the nakedness of her body. 'The blood is gone,' he said simply, although he wanted to say so much more, and dropped a kiss to the top of her head. He walked across the room and gathered up the abandoned and bloodied clothing, knowing how important this was to Helena, and moved to kneel by the fire.

Helena had felt Guy's patience and gentleness in every caress of the wet handkerchief against her skin. She gave herself up, letting each stroke wash away a little more of Stephen's marks, seeing in Guy's eyes a tenderness beyond anything she had ever known. His coat was warm and snug. They knelt side by side before the hearth, like a couple before an altar. There was no need for words. She knew what he was going to do. She wanted it. She needed it.

He placed the first item upon the fire. The flames embraced the dress, thrusting golden fingers around and through the green wool until it burst into a ball of golden light and then fell away to nothing. Piece by piece Guy burned each item of bloodstained clothing until, at last, there was nothing left, and they knelt together in silence and watched the remnants of what had been. Helena knew that the act had drawn them together like no other, for he had demonstrated that he understood. He had removed every last trace of the blood and Stephen was no more. He had saved her and cleansed her and freed her. He was looking at her now, and the ice blue of his eyes reached in and touched her soul, sending splintering sensations to shimmer deep in her belly.

'It is done.' He smiled and kissed the tip of her nose. 'Now you need to put on some clothes before you catch a chill.' He rose to his feet, but not before she had scrambled to hers.

'No.'

The word seemed to echo between them. He stopped and stared down at her.

She felt a wave of warmth heat her cheeks. 'That is…there is so much for us to speak of.'

'Yes, there is…' his smile was gentle '…but you have been through a lot today, Helena, and you need to rest. I shall send a maid up to you.' He allowed himself to stroke her cheek but only once, and then he moved away before temptation got the better of him.

She watched him walk across the room, watched his hand reach towards the door, his fingers wrap around the doorknob. 'Don't leave.'

He stilled and, even though he was not facing her, she saw the sudden tightening of the shirt across his shoulders. He turned. 'You want me to stay?' he said slowly, as if he could not quite believe her words.

'Yes.' The blood was rushing loudly in Helena's ears.

The distance across the room seemed to shrink so that she could hear the slight catch of his breath and see the surprise and hope dart across his features.

'Why?'

His question was so unexpected that she just stared at him for a moment. The answer was so simple that she wondered that he needed to ask the question. She loved him and she would love him for ever. She would be his mistress, she would bear the knowing looks of other men. She would suffer the exclusion from the decent world, and gladly so if it meant she would be with Guy. She loved him and she wanted him. She wanted to feel his body move over hers, to shiver beneath the gentle touch of his hands. She wanted to kiss him, and taste him and touch him. She wanted to give what he had refused to take. She wanted Guy, all of him and every last bit.

'Helena,' he prompted, 'you have not answered me.'

'Does it matter?' she said softly.

'Yes.' His answer was stark and uncompromising. 'It matters very much.'

'I thought I had lost you,' she said. 'When I saw Stephen's sword at your breast...' A sob sounded from her throat.

'Helena.' Her name was a sigh in the silence of the bed-chamber. He moved quickly, closing the space between them, taking her into his arms. 'Hush,' he said, and pressed his lips to her forehead. 'The nightmare is over.'

'Oh, Guy!' She stood against him, resting her palms flat against the breadth of his chest, feeling the hard planes of muscle through the soft cotton of his shirt. Her face tilted up to his and she looked directly into his eyes. They were standing so close she could see every minute detail, from the variations in the arctic blue of his iris to the stark black ring that surrounded it and each and every dark eyelash. 'He would have killed you.'

His gaze dropped to her lips before rising again to her eyes. 'Yes,' he said, 'but, thanks to you, he did not.'

She felt the stroke of his hand against her hair, swayed instinctively towards him as his mouth closed gently upon hers. It was a kiss of gentleness and reassurance. His lips were soft and undemanding, giving, never taking. And in the intimacy of their touch was a message of love and of longing. It was a kiss to last a lifetime. Even when he drew away and just held her against him, she could still taste him, his essence like a honeyed balm soothing her soul. 'Guy?'

'Yes?' He tilted her chin up so that he could look into her eyes.

And she knew that she would tell him the truth. 'I will answer your question.'

He waited. His chest rose and fell against hers. His breath was soft and light. Flames whispered in the background. Outside a robin whistled.

'I want you to stay, Guy, because I love you.' She drew back, opening up a small gap between them. 'I love you,' she said again, 'and I want to be your mistress.' There, she had said it. Silence rang after her words.

A smile curled at his mouth, and there was something warm and possessive and teasing in his gaze. 'Foolish love,' he whispered, and, wrapping an arm around her back, he pulled her close until the full length of their bodies were pressed together. 'You cannot be my mistress.'

She stilled, unsure of his meaning, his words and actions in blatant contradiction of each other. 'I do not understand.' A sudden fear tugged at her. 'Are you saying that you do not want me?'

'Helena…' his smile deepened with sensuality and suggestion '…surely you know better than that. I have wanted you since I first saw you, and for every minute of every day since.'

A blush flooded her face. 'Then why—?'

'Sweetheart, you cannot be my mistress…' he paused and rested his thumb upon the soft cushion of her lips '…if you are to be my wife.'

The world tilted on its axis. Helena stared at him and thought she must have misheard.

'If you will have me for your husband, that is,' he added with a grin.

'You want to marry me?' She felt her mouth gape open.

'I admit it is not the most romantic of proposals.' One dark eyebrow arched. 'So *will* you have me?' he asked.

'You are in earnest!' she gasped, and the room spun around her.

'Entirely,' he replied.

And it seemed that she had floated to a dream world of perfection and happy endings. 'Yes,' the word slipped quietly from between her lips.

The curve of his mouth deepened, showing the white of his teeth. 'You do not sound too certain, beloved,' he said.

'Yes!' she shouted, and a fountain of happiness welled up within her, and she thought that, in all the years that she had lived, she had never experienced such joy. 'Of course I will have you!' she said as he lifted her up and whirled her about the room. Their laughter entwined as their bodies pressed closer and their eyes sparkled with joy and excitement and happiness.

Guy's coat slipped from Helena's shoulders to lie abandoned on the floor. 'My love,' he breathed, and delivered her still laughing on to the mattress.

She lay naked beneath him, her eyes warm with love and desire, her skin soft and begging for his touch. He reached down and began to pluck the pins from her hair, uncoiling the long shimmering tendrils until it spiralled a deep spangled red over her breasts, reaching down to brush against her hips. He tangled his fingers through its length, immersing his hands in its silken texture, touching it to his lips, inhaling its scent. 'You don't know how much I've longed to do this,' he whispered. His eyes met with hers before he moved his gaze to wander down the contours of her body. 'You're so beautiful.' And then his fingers trailed lightly, seductively, along the path his eyes had taken.

He heard her gasp, felt the shiver beneath his fingers.

'You are cold, my love,' he said, and made to tug the bedcovers aside to cover her.

'No.' Her hand stayed his, then progressed up his arm with a slide until she reached his neckcloth. 'I am not cold.' And her fingers fumbled with the knot until at last he felt the linen strip loosen and unwind, and saw it flutter down to land beside them on the bed. She rubbed her hands across his chest, feeling the smattering of dark hair beneath his shirt. 'In fact, I believe it is you who are overdressed, sir.'

'Minx!' He growled a laugh. 'That is something that can soon be remedied.' Guy ripped the shirt from his body with uncommon haste, revealing his broad naked shoulders and the hard musculature of his chest. Her eyes widened at the sight of him. He smiled as he followed her gaze, then left the bed only long enough to divest himself of his boots, his pantaloons and underclothing.

Her eyes feasted upon his nakedness. Never had a man looked so glorious. He was strong and lean and hard with muscle. The dark hair covered lightly across his chest, narrowing to a line that led down across his abdomen to lower regions. His skin was pale, but of a different tone from her own. She had never seen a man like him, and the sight of him stirred anticipation deep in her belly.

When he came to her again, she opened her arms, pulled him down upon her so that flesh touched full against flesh and their bodies quivered with need.

'Helena,' he said with deep and guttural longing, and claimed her mouth with his own. Lips slid together, hard and urgent, hot and moist. The tip of his tongue brushed a tantalising tease, licking her lips, entwining with her own in motions set down at the start of time. Sucking. Gasping. Needful.

Helena's body was aflame. Desire burned her thighs; need clouded her mind; love overwhelmed her heart. Time ceased to be. Nothing existed outside this one single moment with the man that she loved. They feasted upon the intimacies of each other's mouth, sharing their breaths.

He stroked her hair, slid his hands down to capture the fullness of her breasts, feeling the hard budding of her nipples beneath.

'Oh, Guy,' she moaned, and arched her back to press herself all the harder into the exploration of his hands.

His fingers outlined magical patterns around the soft ripe globes, carefully avoiding their delicate pink centres, even though she wriggled in an effort to force them to his touch.

'Such impatience,' he said, but Helena could hear that his breath was short and uneven and his voice somewhat unsteady.

'Guy!' she pleaded, and drew her fingers down the length of his back to clasp the strong firmness of his buttocks.

A jolt of desperate need shuddered through him, but he reined himself back in, determined to take things slowly, intent on pleasuring Helena, not himself. His fingers moved at last to her nipples, rolling the firm buds between the thumb and forefinger of each hand.

She quivered and arched all the harder, thrusting her pelvis up towards his.

The groan escaped from Guy's throat before he could catch it back.

The erect nipples tightened and pushed against his fingers.

Where his manhood throbbed against her leg little shivers of pleasure and desperation vied for release.

His mouth left hers, his breath searing a pathway down her neck, down further still to replace his fingers over the rosy bead of one breast. He suckled, relishing the taste of her, hearing her small gasps of pleasure. He felt her need as strong and purposeful as his own, and his fingers crept between her thighs as his mouth moved to service her other breast.

'Guy!' She melted against his hand. 'I need you!' Helena could feel the tight urgency escalating within her. Something was happening that she did not recognise. She was reaching for something she did not understand, striving with all her being for that one thing. And all she knew was that she loved the man stretched over the length of her, and that she needed him inside her, to fill her completely and utterly with his love. He moved down her, rubbing the taut tip of his arousal against her. Her hands pulled his hips down on to her, but he resisted, manoeuvring her out to the side so that she lay almost at a right angle to him.

'Guy?'

But he just smiled and pulled her closer so that her legs wound round and through his, and she opened to him. And then, just when she thought she could bear it no more, he drove into her, filling her with himself, as his fingers touched her pearl of pleasure. Long sliding movements, in and out, and all the while his hand unlocked a world of hidden pleasure for Helena, until the tightening escalation exploded in an overwhelming flood of sparkling bliss that made her cry out his name and pull him to her, and kiss him and stroke him and bask in the heat of his love, until it cooled to a delectable throb. Only then, when he knew her own need sated, when he had stroked her cheek and kissed her lips, did he move again, thrusting faster, harder, and all the while holding her eyes with the blue fire of his gaze, until she felt him shudder, spilling his seed within her, and he collapsed down on the mattress by her side.

'My love,' he said, and touched his lips to her forehead, her eyelids, her cheeks, in a myriad of whispered kisses. His hand moved slowly to stroke her hair, to slide down against her neck. 'My brave love.'

The last traces of Stephen's influence had been obliterated by Guy's loving. All the hurt of the previous years rolled away. Helena's spirit soared. There was no need for words. She nestled in closer to the warm curve of Guy's body as he pulled the bedcovers over them. A union of bodies; a union of souls. She would be his wife. And on that last delightful heady thought, Helena drifted to sleep.

The week had passed quickly since that dreadful day upon St Vey, so quickly that Helena could scarcely believe that tomorrow would be her wedding day. Outside the sky was grey and an incessant patter of rain drizzled against the window. She stole a glance at the tall dark-haired man sitting by her side on the small sofa in his room in Seamill Hall. He was so devastatingly handsome, so wonderful and…he loved her. Her heart swelled at that, so that it seemed to expand to fill her whole chest. He loved her just as she was, knowing all that he did of her. He loved her and he meant to marry her. It was a dream come true. Love, happiness, a husband, a family. Yet there was a shadow of unease that lurked at the edge of Helena's mind, and she could not sleep for the worry of it.

'You're very quiet, sweetheart. Is something wrong?'

Guy looked down into her face. 'Indeed, you've been growing quieter with each passing day. Not changed your mind about marrying me, have you?' He smiled a cheeky smile and her heart turned over.

She tried to hide the anxiety, tried to say the words of denial, but with Guy there could no longer be any pretence. With him she could only ever be herself. And she knew that she was going to have to ask him about the one last thing that lay between them.

There was a small pause before she asked, 'Have you told your brother that we are to be married?'

'You know that I have.' A line of puzzlement creased between his brows and he laughed.

'But he is not coming to the wedding, is he?'

A glimmer of understanding showed on Guy's face. 'The baby really is about to be born any day, otherwise both Lucien and Madeline would be here.' He stroked a finger against her cheek. 'It isn't some excuse he's concocted, my little worrypot.'

Another pause.

'Did you also tell him…' She hesitated and did not meet his gaze. 'Did you also tell him of my background?'

Guy reached over and took her hand in his. 'I told him all he needs to know, Helena, nothing more, and nothing less.'

Helena closed her eyes as her composure threatened to slip.

'Helena,' said Guy softly, 'you need not worry. Lucien will welcome you to the family. Ironic though it sounds, he has been trying to get me to reform my ways and take a wife.'

'I'll warrant that I'm not what he had in mind…well, not for your wife anyway.'

His hand tightened over hers. 'What manner of talk is this?'

'People will say that our marriage is a *mésalliance*. You are a viscount. Your brother is an earl. You know what I am,' she whispered.

'Yes, I know what you are,' he said, and there was strange expression upon his face. 'You are my life, my love, and tomorrow you will be my wife.'

Her eyes clung to his. 'Oh, Guy.' His hand was warm and strong over hers.

'Then what does it matter what others might think?'

'It matters what your brother thinks, does it not?'

Guy shrugged his shoulders in a dismissive gesture.

'What if he turns against you?'

'Why should he do such a thing?'

'You know very well why.' She chewed at her lip and looked at him. 'You cannot deny there will be a scandal over our marriage.'

'My family is not exactly scandal-free.'

'Will…will you be safe?'

'Safe?' Guy was looking at her as if she had run mad.

'From your brother?'

'From Lucien? Of course.'

'He will not seek to harm you over this?'

'Helena, why should Lucien seek to injure me over anything? He's my brother.' He quirked an eyebrow, and smiled a bemused smile.

'He is Earl Tregellas, is he not?'

'Yes.'

She hesitated before adding, 'The one that they call the Wicked Earl?'

There was a silence.

Guy sat very still. 'Where did you hear such a thing?'

'Stephen spoke of him…with admiration. He said Tregellas was a man after his own heart.'

The words hung in the air between them.

'Tayburn was mistaken,' said Guy. 'My brother is nothing like that fiend.'

'But they do call him the Wicked Earl,' she said softly.

He stared at her. 'I would not have thought you to judge a man by gossip and hearsay, Helena.'

She felt the warmth staining her cheeks. Too late she recalled Annabel Weir's words from what seemed a lifetime ago: *Promise me you will not heed any rumours that you may come to hear concerning Lord Varington or his brother…* And her own reply, *I do not let gossip influence my opinion of people.* 'Forgive me,' she uttered. 'You are right. I should not have spoken so.'

Guy gave a sigh and pressed her fingers once before releasing her hand. 'And I should have told you the truth of it all before now.'

'Guy—'

But he cut her off. 'You have a right to know, Helena. Maybe then you will see that there is nothing to fear from Lucien. He just wants me to be happy. Besides, there shouldn't be any secrets between us.' His stomach clenched just at the thought of talking about it. All that pain belonged in the past, not here, not now. He did not want her to see how much it affected him, to show this woman who needed him to be strong how weak he really was. And then he felt her hand slip around his fingers, felt the small squeeze of support.

'You don't have to tell me anything, Guy.'

'I want to,' he said. 'I need to.' And knew it was true.

She gave a small nod.

'It all started such a long time ago—more than six years. The woman to whom my brother was betrothed was murdered in the most horrific way imaginable. The shock of it killed my mother, and, as if that were not enough, the *Ton* believed my brother guilty of the crime. They called Lucien the Wicked Earl while the real villain, Farquharson, walked free.'

He saw the shock and compassion on her face.

'It was just a matter of time before Farquharson struck again, and this time his intended victim was Madeline. Lucien married her to save her from that devil.'

Helena's teeth bit into her lip. 'This Farquharson was the man you spoke of when you said that you had known a man like Stephen?'

'He was more like Tayburn than you can know,' he said.

'What happened to him?' He could hear the slight tremor of fear in her voice and was sorry that he had put it there, but, for all of its horror, Helena needed to know the truth, all of it.

'He's dead.'

'And your brother's wife is safe?'

He nodded and let the silence grow between them, unable to look round, unwilling to meet her eye.

'What is it that you're not telling me, Guy?'

Silence had never seemed so loud.

'I…' The words seemed to dry from his mouth. 'Farquharson captured my valet and me. He made me watch while he tortured my man. And there was not a damned thing I could do to stop him. Stupid, really.' He threw her a grim ragged smile. 'Spent years in the Peninsula surrounded by bloodshed and death, yet nothing prepared me for that. Collins, my man, survived. He's happily married and living in Dublin. But I can never forget…no matter what I do.'

'He tortured you too, didn't he?'

Guy felt her fingers stroke against his. He had never spoken of the details of that terrible night, not even to his brother. He nodded.

'Oh, Guy.'

He felt her arms wrapping around him, pulling him against her.

'My love, my sweet love,' she murmured again and again, and only when she wiped away the tears from his cheeks did he realise that he was crying. And even that did not seem to matter because he had told Helena the worst of it, and there was no more to tell.

She kissed him and took her hand in his and led him over to the bed. And she loved him with such tenderness, until there was nothing left of that terrible nightmare, until there was only Helena and her love.

They were married the next day in a quiet ceremony in the drawing room of Seamill Hall. Old Tam gave the bride away. Annabel, Emma and Agnes cried the whole way through. The last of the shadows in both their lives had gone, and as if to reflect that, the day was bright and clear and lit by sunshine. After the wedding breakfast they left their guests to their merriment and escaped down to the shoreline.

The sand was firm and golden beneath their feet as they stood on Kilbride's beach, looking out at the water beyond. The sea breeze caught at Helena's neatly pinned hair, freeing the curls to whip and dance free, and moulding her wedding skirts to her legs. She drew the fresh air into her lungs, smelling the tang of the sea in it, and knew that her happiness was complete. The sun warmed the chill from the air, and Guy's arm was warm and strong beneath her fingers.

Guy reached down and plucked a kiss from her lips.

'Guy!' she protested and with a rosy blush pushed his hand away. 'We are in a public place.'

He smiled a sensual smile and raised one wicked eyebrow. 'But there is no one about to see,' he teased.

He was right—there was not a soul to be seen. She smiled, tracing her fingers against the fine roughness of his cheek, remembering the dream from what seemed like so long ago, in which she had looked up into Guy's face and thought him an angel sent to save her. And Guy *had* saved her. He really was her dark angel of salvation. Their eyes locked and she revelled in the intensity of his love. For Helena there was, and had only ever been, Guy. It was as if they had been made to be together, as if each brought life to the other. In that moment was a lifetime of love. It flowed between them. Both knew it would flow for ever. No need for words. No need to say what the soul already knew.

His mouth moved to briefly nuzzle her fingers, never breaking the look that they shared. 'We could live here in Scotland. We would not have to uproot your sister and I know that you love the countryside.'

'And I know that you do not!' She laughed. 'You hate its wildness as much as I love it. My home is with you, even if that does happen to be in the pell-mell of London. And as for Emma, I fancy she will prefer London as much as you do.'

'I find I have developed a liking for this particular Scottish coastline. All the bracing sea air and plethora of precipitation.'

'You mean all the wind and rain!'

He smiled a teasing smile and dropped a small kiss first to one cheek and then the other. 'But what I like most of all is beachcombing. It's amazing what a man may find here upon the shore.'

'Lord Varington!' she huffed.

'Seaweed.'

She swiped at his arm in mock indignation.

'Shells.'

She placed her hands on her hips and raised her brows.

'And…' the teasing light vanished from his eyes '…his one true love.'

'Oh, Guy!'

She closed the space between them. Their lips met, and moved in passionate affirmation of their love.

Then he swung her up into his arms and began to tread the path back to Seamill Hall. And out beyond the sand, beneath the weak winter sun, the sea was a peaceful polished glass of pale ice blue.

* * * * *

Special Offers
Regency Ballroom Collection

Classic tales of scandal and seduction in the Regency Ballroom

Scandal in the Regency Ballroom
On sale 4th April

Innocent in the Regency Ballroom
On sale 3rd May

Wicked in the Regency Ballroom
On sale 7th June

Cinderella in the Regency Ballroom
On sale 5th July

Rogue in the Regency Ballroom
On sale 2nd August

Debutante in the Regency Ballroom
On sale 6th September

Rumours in the Regency Ballroom
On sale 4th October

Scoundrel in the Regency Ballroom
On sale 1st November

Mistress in the Regency Ballroom
On sale 6th December

Courtship in the Regency Ballroom
On sale 3rd January

Rake in the Regency Ballroom
On sale 7th February

Secrets in the Regency Ballroom
On sale 7th March

A FABULOUS TWELVE-BOOK COLLECTION

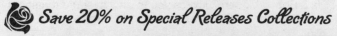

Save 20% on Special Releases Collections

Find the collection at
www.millsandboon.co.uk/specialreleases

Visit us Online

0513/MB416

The Correttis

Introducing the Correttis, Sicily's most scandalous family!

On sale 3rd May

On sale 7th June

On sale 5th July

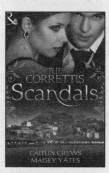

On sale 2nd August

Mills & Boon® Modern™ invites you to step over the threshold
and enter the Correttis' dark and dazzling world...

Find the collection at
www.millsandboon.co.uk/specialreleases

*Visit us
Online*

0513/MB415

The World of Mills & Boon®

There's a Mills & Boon® series that's perfect for you. We publish ten series and, with new titles every month, you never have to wait long for your favourite to come along.

Blaze.
Scorching hot, sexy reads
4 new stories every month

By Request
Relive the romance with the best of the best
9 new stories every month

Cherish™
Romance to melt the heart every time
12 new stories every month

Desire™
Passionate and dramatic love stories
8 new stories every month

Visit us Online

Try something new with our Book Club offer
www.millsandboon.co.uk/freebookoffer

M&B/WORLD2

What will you treat yourself to next?

*Ignite your imagination,
step into the past...*
6 new stories every month

INTRIGUE...

Breathtaking romantic suspense
Up to 8 new stories every month

*Captivating medical drama –
with heart*
6 new stories every month

MODERN™

*International affairs,
seduction & passion guaranteed*
9 new stories every month

n o c t u r n e™

*Deliciously wicked
paranormal romance*
Up to 4 new stories every month

RIVA™

*Live life to the full –
give in to temptation*
3 new stories every month available
exclusively via our Book Club

You can also buy Mills & Boon eBooks at
www.millsandboon.co.uk

*Visit us
Online*

M&B/WORLD2

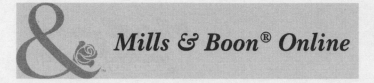

Mills & Boon® Online

Discover more romance at
www.millsandboon.co.uk

- 🌹 **FREE** online reads
- 🌹 **Books** up to one month before shops
- 🌹 **Browse our books** before you buy

...and much more!

For exclusive competitions and instant updates:

 Like us on **facebook.com/millsandboon**

 Follow us on **twitter.com/millsandboon**

 Join us on **community.millsandboon.co.uk**

 Visit us Online   Sign up for our FREE eNewsletter at
www.millsandboon.co.uk

WEB/M&B/RTL5